Mythophidia

A Collection of Stories

Mythophidia
A Collection of Stories

Storm Constantine

IMMANION PRESS
Stafford, England

Mythophidia
Storm Constantine
© 2008

Cover Art: Peter Hollinghurst
Cover Design: Storm Constantine/Simon Beal
Interior Design and Layout: Storm Constantine

Set in Souvenir

IP0022

An Immanion Press Edition
http://www.immanion-press.com
info@immanion-press.com

ISBN 978-1-904853-57-2

Immanion Press
8 Rowley Grove
Stafford ST17 9BJ
UK

Books by Storm Constantine

The Wraeththu Chronicles
*The Enchantments of Flesh and Spirit
*The Bewitchments of Love and Hate
*The Fulfilments of Fate and Desire

*The Wraeththu Chronicles (omnibus of trilogy)
The Artemis Cycle
The Monstrous Regiment
Aleph

*Hermetech
Burying the Shadow
Sign for the Sacred
Calenture
Thin Air

The Grigori Books
*Stalking Tender Prey
*Scenting Hallowed Blood
*Stealing Sacred Fire

Silverheart (with Michael Moorcock)

The Magravandias Chronicles:
Sea Dragon Heir
Crown of Silence
The Way of Light

The Wraeththu Histories:
*The Wraiths of Will and Pleasure
*The Shades of Time and Memory
*The Ghosts of Blood and Innocence

Wraeththu Mythos
*The Hienama
*Student of Kyme

Short Story Collections:
The Thorn Boy and Other Dreams of Dark Desire
*Mythanima
*available as Immanion Press editions

Contents

Introduction

One of four volumes collecting my shorter works, Mythophidia's theme is the serpentine and the exotic. The snakes in these pages are seducers and deceivers, whose pretty jewelled coats might attract the eye, yet ultimately poison the heart.

Kiss Booties Night Night

The inspiration for this piece came from the anecdotes of friends of mine, who were in a band and who had played at a fetish night club in London in the early 90s, when such things – in the mainstream at least – were pretty new. The title actually comes from something that was said to one of the women by a man who'd crawled up to her, interested in her pointy spiky boots! Well, once I'd heard the stories, my imagination kicked into gear and I had my own story to tell.

An Old Passion

I wrote this story fairly soon after getting to know Andy Collins, from whom I found out all about psychic questing. I didn't really know much about this phenomenon, but of course it pricked the interest of my muse who immediately smelled the opportunity for a story. The questers in this piece are not based on the characters of Andy or any of his group, I hasten to add. These are completely made up questers! The story appeared in a limited edition convention booklet in Australia.

Just His Type

This tale appeared in 'The Mammoth Book of Vampires Stories by Women'. As with the previous story, the idea of psychic questing lies behind this little tale. After various conversations, in which I'd discussed with friends some of the dangers of this type of work, I wanted to explore the darker side of it. People with a fragile state of mind can be at risk, and also the fearless obsessive. It's best to have your feet firmly on the ground. As before, the characters are not based exactly on any real people – even though there are undeniable similarities between Andy Collins and Noah, the writer in this story, simply because Noah is an author who runs an earth mysteries group. That's where the similarities end though. Andy has not, to my knowledge, ever got himself into a sticky situation like this! Or if he has, he's not telling...

Remedy of the Bane

This piece first appeared in Realms of Fantasy in 1996, and it was based on an allegedly true story. A long time ago, someone told me about a royal princess, who taunted the guards of her parents' palace. The guards weren't allowed even to raise an eyebrow while they were on sentry duty, which created great sport for the princess. If she could induce one of them to react to her, she'd report them and they'd be punished. Whether this tale is true or not is really irrelevant. The fact is it provided a great idea for a short story.

I wanted the princess to be an ambivalent character. While there is no doubt she has a streak of callous cruelty, she is also a victim of her circumstances. She is driven to behave in the way she does because of frustration and bitterness. The story is also about ethics, and whether an immoral act is justified if its end is for the greater good. The protagonist of the story wrestles with this dilemma. He has the means to destroy the princess and save his colleagues from unfair punishment, but in so doing he will become no better than she is. He is also perversely attracted to the princess' capricious and wanton behaviour. The ending of this story has a bittersweet overtone. When I wrote it, it made me realise that no story ever really has an end.

Sweet Bruising Skin

Ellen Datlow and Terri Windling have compiled a series of successful anthologies, based around traditional, or perhaps not so traditional, fairy tales. 'Sweet Bruising Skin' was written for the collection, 'Black Thorn, White Rose', the second in the series, which was published by AvoNova Morrow in 1994. The story was based on the fairy tale 'The Princess and the Pea'. I'd always thought there was something sinister about that story. Versions of it I'd come across were always very short, but I sensed a lurking weirdness behind them. What kind of skin must a princess have for it to be so easily marked? Surely such a sensitivity would make a normal existence impossible? Anyway, I had my own ideas about the prince's mother's involvement in the proceedings. And here they are.

Curse of the Snake

This is the earliest completed story I still possess. Although I wrote compulsively from childhood, my writing was meandering and lacked narrative structure. I never actually finished anything, or thought about the most important of story techniques: that everything has to have a beginning, a middle and an end. I wrote this particular piece in 1976, just before the Punk explosion, and it was the first story I ever completed properly. Back then, I never showed my work to anyone, and certainly didn't consider trying to sell it. A typescript of 'Curse of the Snake' lay hidden in an old folder in my filing cabinet for over twenty years, unread by anyone except me, until it made its first appearance in 'The Oracle Lips' collection, published by Stark House. It makes me feel a little odd to think that this can be seen as the original piece that inspired and gave birth to everything I've written since.

Nocturne: The Twilight Community

I can't remember exactly when I wrote this story, but it was somewhere between 1980 and 1981. It was inspired by the club scene of late Punk and the New Romantics, which at times seemed to me to be very shallow. People might dress up with all the makeup and cool clothes, but there was often little beneath the masks. Also, the bitchy gossip that went on was frequently quite cruel and destructive.

Night's Damozel

The idea for this story was born during a late night discussion on poisonous plants, and some of the imagery in it came from Eloise Coquio, although it was me who wrote the story. This piece is set in the fictional world of the Magravandias Chronicles, but whereas 'Sea Dragon Heir' and its sequels have a Medieval feel to them, this story is set in a modern-day world.

The Heart of Fairen De'ath

The following story properly belongs in 'The Thorn Boy and Other Dreams of Dark Desire' collection, since it's part of the cycle of stories included in that book. But when Stark House republished 'Thorn Boy' in a new, expanded format, 'The Heart of Fairen De'ath' had already been accepted for another collection of my work – a collection that never happened and which Immanion Press has now brought to fruition. As with several of my other stories, when I decided to try and sell it, I changed the male protagonist to a female in order to make it more acceptable to editors. It eventually appeared in 'Weird Tales' in America. Here, as with the other stories, is a re-edited version of the original, restoring Filerion's gender to its original state.

Poisoning the Sea

This story was inspired by the Waterhouse painting of the same name, which is sometimes known as 'Circe Invidiosa.' I have a print of this painting in my living room and have always loved its dark mood and smouldering Circe.

Such a Nice Girl

This story is a sequel to 'Candle Magic', which appeared in 'The Oracle Lips' collection. It remained unsold for a long time, until I reworked it for a magazine. The version that appears here is the uncut one, since I had to trim it for the publication that bought it.

The Oracle Lips

Ideas for short stories strike me at odd times. The seed of 'The Oracle Lips' occurred in 1997, in the back of a friend's car, in an underground car park in Wolverhampton, a town in the Midlands. A group of us were there for a day's shopping, and before we left the car, I touched up my lipstick. I blotted my lips on a tissue and then the idea came. I said to my friend, 'Lip prints are as personal as marks on a palm. I wonder if you could tell someone's fortune from them.' I thought about this again throughout the day, and by the end of it, I had the beginning of a story. It was fortuitous, because I'd recently been contacted by Laurence Schimel to submit a piece for his 'Fortune Tellers' anthology. Clearly, the subject of prognostication was burning away at the back of my mind. I wanted to do something different with the theme, rather than resort to a tale about crystal balls or tarot cards.

Storm Constantine
August 2008

Kiss Booties Night-Night

The sun, a fevered blister, hung low in a pagan sky of ceremonial colours; purple, red, deepest orange. She stood among the rattling sticks of petrified reeds, on the edge of the slow-moving slick they called the river. Behind her, the manse was dark, but for the winking violet lights of the security systems at eaves and porch. The garden was so beautiful. She never grew tired of it: the rank weeds; the blackened ivy over the walls of the ice-house; last year's lilies not cleared away, fainting at the feet of this year's forced growth that had been brought in from the hothouses of the city centre, soon to die out here in the air.

She put a tarless cigarette between her ink-lacquered lips and drew in a stream of chemical fume. Her boots caught the light of a security beam far across the river. Otherwise she was non-reflecting, her skin pale and flat like bleached ashes, her dark clothes a void against the descending night.

Maradissa Ferone, heiress. She played at having a career - buying and selling the more intriguing artefacts from the past that had escaped destruction into the present. She loved the past. Sometimes, she designed parties, which she sold to the sons and daughters of her dead parents' friends; Creatures of the Contemporary - as they styled themselves - who lived further up-river, where the ugly old factories had been turned into apartments and the river strained and treated to become something sterile, which it was safe to touch, if not to drink.

Maradissa lived alone, although she was not reclusive. She was often sighted in the more expensive night-haunts of the Industrial Park, west of the river. Several times a year, she would throw a themed party at the manse. Many people thought the decay was contrived, but it was not. Maradissa took pleasure in watching the slow dissolution of all that her mother had worked to achieve; the manse, a rotting heritage. This was not a rebellion against her mother, or her mother's success, but simply a statement that everything was running *her* way, now. Unlike her peers, Maradissa shunned cosmetic surgery, but for the decorative scarring on her breasts and stomach. She was always the same sex.

Tonight, a hurrying air, a sense of imminence, volted through her as she stood beside the river. Her skin prickled as she watched the roiling surface of the water. When this feeling came, she savoured it. It was fear. It was excitement. Life still held promise in the throes of apprehension. She was dressed, ready to drive to the Park, in period Gothic of the late twentieth century: tight, matte black, and spikes. Her hair was a frothing black halo, teased and stiff and lightless. Smoking the cigarette, she stoked her excitement. Sometimes she had to make it come like this; take in the chemicals, watch the poisonous sunset, psych herself up.

She threw the remains of her cigarette into the river, smoothed her taut black thighs, enjoying the feel of herself. There was power in the fume she had taken, power in the lowering night, the colours on the oily surface of the water. There were no seasons here and the smells of the land were confections. She turned away from the river.

Feeling watched.

She paused, knowing how the smoke could warp her senses. It could kindle a feeling of agitation, of being an actress for an invisible audience. It could bring with it a fleeting understanding of gods.

For a few sanctified moments, the silence of the garden was absolute, then the lilies rustled their thorns.

Maradissa walked purposefully towards them. She was not afraid, and still young enough to believe in her own immortality. As she approached, something scrambled away from her; the foliage of life and death rattled loudly. Maradissa did not challenge, made no sound, although it was clear to her that whatever hid among the lilies was too large to be animal. Instead, she plucked an ivy cane from the ice-house wall and struck the place where the rustling had started.

Silence. Something crouched, something feared.

For a moment, Maradissa considered entering into the gripping shadows of the hanging plants. She even put one pointed boot upon the soil, then retreated. She would speak to her butler about it; the sniffers could inspect the grounds. She had no time to deal with intruders, certainly not those that ran from her.

He did not think she was beautiful, for to him she was beyond beauty, a goddess. She was remote and perfect, apparently unaware that her grounds were full of unseen gardening graduates, working to maintain the grave-yard disarray that she loved. Michael had worked in her gardens now for nearly a month, and only during the last week had realised, or become aware of, the strong feelings she kindled within him. At first, he had seen her only briefly, whenever she left the house to climb into her car. He'd been fascinated by her appearance, the bizarre clothes. Other gardeners joked cruelly about her eccentricity. They were scornful, resentful, jealous of her wealth and luxuries. They liked to make lascivious comments, speculate about how well she'd perform in bed. Most were scathing. Their bitter envy made them want to debase her. Michael did not feel like that. His fantasies of her did not involve sex. He wanted to speak to her, worship at her feet. Those feet, clad in shiny black, forced into the pointed shape. It must

17

hurt her.

Every evening before sundown, a bus came to pick up the gardeners and take them back to their apartments in the Colonies, but for the last two days, Michael had lingered behind when his colleagues went off-duty. He'd worked out that as the mistress of the house never entered the gardens during the day, she must do so after dark. And he was right. Hidden among the ragged foliage, he could watch her undisturbed for a glorious half-hour or so, before the security systems were activated. She was regal, mistress of her domain as she stalked around its boundaries.

His trespassing had terrified him at first, for he knew the very least penalty for discovery would be dismissal, but he could not resist this private pleasure. If he was careful, she need never know. But then, he wanted her to know. One day, he might even dare to make his presence known to her, an abject slave to her power. In part, he wanted to invoke her outrage. He had never felt this way before.

Now, he knew that she had sensed him in his hiding place. He'd watched her lean body become tense: so much shiny gloss in the ragged crepe of the dried leaves around her. He'd scuttled backwards into the comfortless arms of an ancient rhododendron, and here he had crouched down, peering through the thick leaves. She had walked towards him. He had smelled her perfume, the scent of her cigarette and the reek of the lacquer with which she styled her hair. He had never been able to study her so closely: a black and white ghost in the twilight. Her mouth, he realised, was small, its lack of generosity further emphasised by the severe black lipstick. This slight fault only made her more alluring. She'd stood, poised, a lithe cat ready to pounce, and he'd been frozen before her; terrified and longing for her predator eyes to fix upon him. Then, relaxing her muscles, she appeared to dismiss whatever sound had alerted her and wandered back towards the house.

Michael fell to his knees upon the damp earth. His heart pounded madly. She had known he was there, but she had not chased him off. Neither had she shown fear, but he'd not expected that, in any case. She had become a conspirator in his fantasy.

In the hallway of the house, Maradissa drew on her long black gloves and spoke to her magic mirror. In it, no reflection, but an image of her butler Leony, who lived some distance away in an apartment that Maradissa owned.

'Something in the gardens tonight,' Maradissa said, admiring her long fingers in their velvet. 'Not invited. Check it for me?'

Already Leony was reaching for the pads that would activate the sniffers. Late. They should have come on before sundown, but Maradissa's loitering by the river had probably deferred them.

'Nothing unsanctified,' Leony said, looking at a display Maradissa could not see. 'Staff working late?'

Maradissa pulled a face at the mirror. 'They watched me.'

Leony laughed. She was allowed certain privileges. 'What do you expect?'

Maradissa smiled back, thinly. 'No one stays here after sundown unless I request it. See to it, Lee.' She made a pass across the mirror with her gloved hands.

'Your word, oh mistress, is my command,' said Leony, a diminishing genie in the mirror as it clouded and darkened and veiled its magic.

Before the sniffers were released to patrol the grounds, Michael had slipped like a shadow over the wall. It took a long time to walk back his apartment, and once there he felt too unnerved to eat his evening meal. As it lay cooling in its delivery slot, he lay on his bed, his stomach churning, and prayed to his goddess. She must hear him. He was her soul's servant.

Maradissa met her friends, Crickforth and Evalie, in the bar called The Bat Cavern on Eldritch Boulevard, at the edge of the park. It was a haunt favoured by all those whose espoused Maradissa's chosen fashion period; a lot of black was seen around. Crickforth and Evalie were drinking bright green cocktails from triangular glasses.

'Babba, you just have to see!' Evalie announced as Maradissa slid onto the fishnet-covered seat beside her.

'See what?' Maradissa peeled off one of her gloves and put it beside her drink, lifted her glass with the ungloved hand.

'The most divine freaks!'

Maradissa looked at Crickforth. He had suffered a mild stroke recently, which had frozen the left side of his face. His parents had cut his allowance, owing to the fact that a new fashion drug had been responsible for the stroke, and were punishing him further by making him wait for corrective surgery. Crickforth, always an optimist, was using his deformity as a fashion accessory at present. He limped a bit and wore one black leather glove, a patch over his drooping eyelid. 'She means the fetzers,' he explained with half his mouth. 'There's a Fetzer Nite on.'

Maradissa sipped her drink. 'Oh? So what?' She delivered an admonishing glance to Evalie.

Evalie poked Maradissa's arm. 'Oh, where's your sense of adventure? The fetzers represent *your* time, my bab, your time. Of course, you're interested.'

Maradissa shook her head. 'They most certainly *do not* represent my time, as you put it. What are you implying?'

Evalie would not be deterred. 'But it was all the thing back then. 'Eighties and 'nineties chic! Fetish nights, glamour-wear.'

'A little more than that,' Maradissa said, quietly.

Her remark was ignored. 'Mara, we *must* go and see them.'

'We wouldn't get in.'

'With your contacts?' Evalie chided. 'Don't be ridiculous.'

Maradissa shrugged. For outrageous sights, they could visit any number of bars in the Park; there was always something to look at. The fetzers were something else. They thrived on debasement; or on debasing. Nowadays, there were therapies to see to that. Sexual and social neuroses could be worked out in group VR; safely. Maradissa had studied thoroughly the periods that interested her, but she was selective in what she adopted, or adapted, from the past. It was only a matter of time before the fetzers were persuaded to abandon their obsessions. Already, complaints had appeared on the bulletin boards. Whatever the fetzers had chosen to drag into the present, they had embellished and exaggerated it. Maradissa was aware of the rumours. It was unhealthy, and no protest about how it was all a kind of harmless fancy dress could convince those who saw it as a crack in the social seam. 'I don't think we should risk corrupting Crickforth,' Maradissa said, with a smile.

Crickforth grimaced. 'It wasn't my idea!'

'Mara, don't be tiresome,' Evalie said. 'Have you no curiosity? It's bizarre the fetzers got a licence for tonight's meeting. Strings were tweaked, obviously!'

'Not really,' Crickforth argued, wiping spittle from the dead corner of his mouth. 'It's best to keep these things regulated.'

'Well, whatever,' Evalie said with a careless wave of her hand. 'We could at least watch them going into the club.'

Maradissa considered this suggestion. The mere

thought of the fetzers made her feel annoyed - or angry - she wasn't sure which. Her father had once said to her, "You risk becoming what you resist"; to have a strong aversion to a thing somehow gave it power. 'Where's it being held?'

'Key-mart's multi-storey,' Evalie answered lightly, sensing compliance.

The night club had once been a car park, in the days when there had been a plague of cars. Below it, the converted aisles of the supermarket housed counsellors' booths, the tables and machines of sex yogis, and the darkened cells of light-therapists. Sometimes Maradissa and her friends took enlightenment drugs there or discussed non-existent dilemmas with earnest thin people. Naturally, the therapists and counsellors and self-appointed gurus had taken exception to the fetzer meeting taking place above their shrines, and had staged a non-violent protest outside, which everyone was ignoring.

The sidewalk was packed with neo-goths, zippers, body art flappers and haute couture junkies of every stripe. Chemical spliffs were passed freely among the cheerful throng that watched the fetzers walk up the ramp to the doors of the club. Most of the fetzers were in normal dress, clutching carryalls with a change of costume inside. They hurried past the on-lookers with set expressions. Others, mainly middle-aged male transvestites, who were into it for laughs rather than illicit pleasure, paraded and minced and made lewd gestures at the crowd, which was catcalled appreciatively.

Maradissa despised them all. To her it was an embarrassing display.

'We *must* go in,' said Evalie.

Maradissa glanced at Crickforth, who shrugged. 'Could be fun.'

Maradissa shook her head, exhaled a tolerant sigh and then pushed through the crowd.

With her Ferone Corporation credit cards, Maradissa sailed past the door-keepers, Crickforth and Evalie in tow. People in the crowd, who knew them, shrieked out amused and gentle obscenities, at which Evalie, bringing up the rear, made dismissive signals.

Inside, it was cold, with localised areas of intense heat. Maradissa shivered. The air was red. 'Changing room?' asked a uniformed receptionist.

Maradissa afforded him a scornful glance. 'Bar.'

In the event, Maradissa found it hard to be disgusted. The fetzers were playing at it. The occasion was no worse than a Gothic Renaissance night at the Pit Vault, only the costumes were sillier, and the music rather more vapid. Two men crawled past her on all-fours, leashed to a tall woman in badly-applied makeup, who was possibly a man. One sniffed Maradissa's feet. 'Now puppies!' said the leash-woman, and tapped her charges affectionately with a whip that appeared to be made of embroidery silk. The puppies looked at one another and giggled; such a fun game. Maradissa eyed them condescendingly, while Evalie hooted in pleasurable distaste.

After a while, the plethora of exposed genitals, naked breasts framed in straps and metal, bare tattooed buttocks and costumes of extreme brevity lost their shock value. Maradissa sat at the bar and gossiped with Evalie about people they knew. Crickforth was discussing the benefits of a new amenities centre in the Tech Park up-river, with a man who was encased in black leather from crown to toe, but for an open zip which exposed his mouth, and a hole at groin from which a flaccid penis hung.

'We could be anywhere, in any bar,' Maradissa said, interrupting Evalie mid-sentence. 'This is just another theme club. Only the clothes, or lack of them, make it different.'

Evalie nodded. 'Still, I wanted to come. I wanted to *see.*'

Maradissa slid off her stool. 'Can't help wondering what I'll find in the wash-room, though!'

'Want me to come with you?'

Maradissa rolled her eyes. 'Ev, *please!*' She pushed her way into the crowd.

The fetzers were friendlier than members of other cult-groups Maradissa had met. Her own neo-Gothic culture tended towards cliquishness and aloofness. Here, everyone she passed smiled and greeted her as if she had known them for years. It seemed foolish to maintain a frosty attitude.

In the ladies' wash-room, both men and women clustered around the mirrors, squealing with laughter as they refreshed their face paint. A thin middle-aged man, clad only in leather straps and rather heavy make-up, grinned in Maradissa's face. 'Great night, isn't it!'

Maradissa adopted a quizzical expression. 'Mmm.'

'Voyeuse!' The response was good-natured, rather than critical.

'No,' Maradissa responded, and then restrained herself from explaining why she was there. 'It's interesting here, but rather tamer than I thought.'

The man gave her a sly look. 'There are levels of experience,' he said. 'You just have to look for them. Visit the Chamber, and then say tame.'

'There is more?'

The man laughed. 'There is always more. For those who want it.'

But I don't want it, she thought. Still, there was no point in visiting this place without examining every option on the menu. She might discover something worth reporting to Evalie and Crickforth.

It took her some time to find the Chamber, because no one seemed willing to give explicit instructions concerning its location, but eventually, deep in the centre of the club, she found the entrance to the shrine of forbidden pleasures. There were curtains of shiny PVC across the doorway. As she lifted them and passed through, she noticed with amusement the health scanner that monitored her heart, before a mechanised voice breathed out an approving welcome.

Beyond, the light was redder, the air steamy. Figures were just moving shadows within the crimson fog. Maradissa heard the sounds; retching, laughter, groans, the slap of something yielding on flesh, something brittle shattering. Tribal music throbbed beneath this symphony of indulgence. On the floor, there was blood.

She felt both revolted and dazed. The light drew her in: through the sounds, through the steam peopled with indistinct forms. Occasionally, a seeking hand might reach out to stroke her, but she avoided their anonymous touch.

Crossing a slick-floored chamber, Maradissa entered a corridor of flesh - dampened latex fabric looped across the walls and ceiling, hanging down in writhing tatters. Here, there were sighs in the air and soft squeals of pleasure. Purple-pink light pulsed at the corridor's end, and Maradissa advanced towards it - cautiously, slightly in fear, slightly in anticipation. The flesh tunnel opened out into a vast chamber, where ribbons of incense curled around the cupreous scent of blood and the sharper, chemical reek of leisure anaesthetics.

Fascination and horror surged through Maradissa where she stood at the threshold. The smoky air purled in upon itself like a veil drawing aside. *Come, sweet flesh. Enter in...*

The pleasure of machines. They were part biological,

like alien robots, towering, spreading and curious. Metal black. Manikins of subjection were mere bound scraps between the elegant pincers, the intestine coils of slinking alloy, the investigating probes, the scalpel-clawed prehensile digits. Their movement was hypnotic. Maradissa saw a swatch of hair hanging down from within an iron helmet. An arm shuddered pale within a tangle of dark cables. Above her, screens the size of hoardings advertised the forbidden sensuality. She understood that within the minds of these willing victims, the slow excoriation of flesh was twisted into dream-like virtual imagery that bloomed with mythic fantasy. Their pain was regulated to peaks they found acceptable. All was silent but for the slither of metal coils, the occasional mechanical hum. Every human mouth was plugged with rubber.

An undulating limb lifted up like the neck of a serpent from the tangled mass of flesh and machine. It turned an unwinking, glowing eye upon Maradissa, then snaked towards her slowly. A non-human voice breathed, 'Welcome...', and in its echoless cadence, Maradissa heard the secret message of pleasures exquisite and undreamed of.

For one brief moment, she almost fell, mesmerised and willing, into the embrace of the fleshless arm. Then her stomach roiled involuntarily, and she had to turn away quickly, a hand to her mouth.

A woman had come into the Chamber behind her, blocking an easy exit. She was tall and fairly attractive, naked to the waist, clad in rubber leggings. Her torso was laced with bloody scars, and she held a thin blade in one hand. 'Don't run, my pretty.' The woman held out her hands to Maradissa. 'You want to be here. I am the Priestess of Perversity. Come, I will lead you to a nest.' She gestured at the machines.

Maradissa shook her head and tried to push past the

woman, but the priestess grabbed hold of her arm. 'Don't be afraid. It's your first time, isn't it?' Her voice was soft with reassurance.

'Let me past,' Maradissa said, roughly pulling her arm from the priestess's hold. 'I'm not meant to be here.'

The priestess' expression changed slightly, hardened. She pulled back her lips into a sneering laugh and pressed the blade she held to her stomach. 'Open up!' The scalpel-thin knife sliced into her flesh.

'You're sick!' Maradissa hissed, and made to push past her. She averted her head, not wanting to look at the fresh wound, afraid there would be no blood.

The woman blocked her way again and laughed. 'Sick, huh? What are you doing here, little girl?'

Maradissa glanced up at her, could not help noticing the thin wet stream on the woman's upper belly. 'I just... got lost.'

The priestess shook her head. 'Oh, really? I don't think so. You came here to see, didn't you? You're curious. Want to see how the big girls and boys play. That's OK. If you want to look, I can show you around.'

Maradissa was momentarily paralysed by fear, unsure of whether the woman was right in her assumptions. Then, firmly, she shook her head. 'No. Thank you.'

'It's all right.' The priestess smiled warmly. 'Everyone has a first time.'

Maradissa swallowed, tasted bile. 'I'm not like you. Let me past.'

The priestess gestured at her. 'Oh, no? Look at you in your pretty, kinky gear, your little painted face! You're not that different from us.'

Maradissa recovered her composure, raised her hands like a barrier. 'You've got it wrong, she said. 'Excuse me, please. Or is assault part of your repertoire?'

The woman narrowed her eyes. 'Only if you want it.'

27

Maradissa uttered a short, dry laugh, rolled her eyes. 'No, thank you. I'm not into pain.'

The woman put her head on one side. 'Aren't you?' She reached out and slid her hand down Maradissa's side. 'I think everyone is, if they're honest. We're honest. This is reality. We are healthier because of it. Come on, loosen up. Enjoy yourself. Don't waste your visit. You wouldn't be here if you didn't really want to be.'

Maradissa backed away, affected her most haughty tone. 'I'm not interested, actually. Please, excuse me. I have friends waiting and they'll come looking for me soon.'

The woman folded her arms, the knife blade pointing into the air. She gave Maradissa's clothes and jewellery an assessing glance. 'Oh, I see. It's a little rich kid come to gawp at the freaks, is it?'

'Yes, I'm rich,' Maradissa agreed, unable to resist admitting it. 'So what? You're no healthier than I am. You must hate yourself to cut your body like that. I happen to like my body, and I respect other people's'

The woman sneered. 'Oh yeah? And that perfect nose is your own, is it? That faultless figure? You're into knives, girly, everyone's into knives!' She uttered a chilling screech of laughter, then pushed Maradissa back into the flesh tunnel, with the retort, 'Go home to Mummy and Daddy. Your kind isn't wanted here.'

Maradissa was burning with nausea and humiliated anger by the time she found Evalie at the bar. The injustice of being judged a surgery-junkie was almost as bad as what the Chamber had concealed in its bloody mists. She was not like them. It wasn't true. They were freaks. She was not. 'I'm going,' she snapped at Evalie. Crickforth had disappeared. 'Stay if you want!'

'You've been ages,' Evalie said, getting off her stool. 'What happened? Are you OK?'

'No,' Maradissa said. 'I want to go home.' For the first time in two years, she felt conscious of her age, and realised she was missing her mother.

On the way home, Evalie sympathised with Maradissa's revulsion, but was too eager for details, seemingly unaware that by describing what had happened, Maradissa felt she was somehow legitimising it. The words should not be spoken. She dropped Evalie off at her parent's estate. 'Stay here tonight,' Evalie offered. 'Don't go home alone.'

Maradissa shook her head. 'No. I'll be fine.'

'Then, I'll come and stay with you, if you like.'

'Ev, I'll be fine. Honestly. I was just taken by surprise back there, that's all. It'll soon be forgotten.' Maradissa didn't want anyone to know how upset she was. She smiled and waved and drove away.

At home, Maradissa sat in her salon and drank some brandy, which she rarely touched. She was aware of feeling soiled. The house seemed cold and empty. She played some music disks, but the lyrics seemed too pertinent. Images filled her mind; the laughing, painted faces, the exposed bodies, then the hidden pleasures of the inner chamber and the Priestess of Perversity's grin as she opened up her flesh with a blade. Disgusting! How could people be like that? What was there in human nature that made it manifest? Something primitive. And yet, when Maradissa dreamed that night, she was held in the embrace of a metal lover without a face, who invaded her hungering body with devices too large for her to accommodate. She felt her flesh tear, but the pain was translated into a different sensation, like smelling the most exquisite perfume, tonguing the most exotic liqueur. Then she was screaming against the invasion, gathering an occult strength. She transformed herself into the metal lover and what shivered pale beneath her precise force filled her with

29

an aching tenderness of feeling. She awoke disorientated, her body tensing to the receding pulse of erotic thrill.

Once she had dressed, Maradissa called Leony. 'I'm not feeling too good,' she said, keeping the mirror shadowed. 'Make sure I'm not bothered, will you?'

'Do you need anything?'

'No. Just privacy for a while. I'm tired'

'Overdoing it, huh?' Leony laughed. Sometimes Maradissa went into retreat after lengthy, non-stop parties. 'Listen, that intruder you spoke about last night. I've looked into it. A new staff member. Didn't understand the sundown regulation. It's all fixed now. I briefed his supervisor.'

'Fine, fine. I just don't want to be pestered.'

'Feed and medicate yourself properly.'

'I will.'

Michael had been horrified when his supervisor had confronted him about why he'd stayed behind at the manse the previous evening. Red-faced, he'd blurted an excuse about wanting to get a particular job finished. 'We have set work schedules,' the supervisor said, her eyes hard. 'You don't get paid for over-time.'

If she'd guessed Michael's true reason for lingering in the garden, she did not press the matter. Michael felt bereft, cheated. The supervisor didn't understand that Ms Ferone wanted him in her garden, and because their potential relationship had to be secret, the mistress could not reveal the truth.

All day, he worked near the house, peering through the windows at every opportunity. He saw his idol drifting from room to room, a glass in her hand. She seemed distracted - obviously agonising over her decision to report his presence to the supervisor. She had made a mistake and would have to rectify it herself. Michael was powerless, her pawn. Sometimes, it seemed as if she was aware of his eyes, hidden in foliage beyond the windows, for she would start as if at a sudden sound, and glance through the panes. He longed to stand up, show himself, but knew that was not part of the ritual. He knew he would have to engineer a way to remain in the gardens after sundown again, but not yet. There would be a sign when it was time.

That evening, Michael had to go home with all his colleagues. He found he was glad to get back to his apartment, because he could lie on his bed and think about Maradissa. He imagined the click of spike heels upon the hard floor beyond his door, the tap that might come upon the laminated wood from sharp, lacquered nails. He imagined her coming in across the threshold, standing over him, saying, 'You are mine.'

For three days later Maradissa refused to go the Park with any of her friends. She needed solitude, and spent a lot of time meditating, trying to face up to the demons spawned from the episode at the fetzer nite. She dressed herself in a loose purple robe, kept her hair clean and straight down her back, wore no make-up. She found she wanted to bathe frequently, as if there was something to wash away. It was as if she'd witnessed a terrible atrocity, and had to exorcise the trauma of it. Her mind was drawn to reinvent images of what the Chamber had contained, her thoughts colouring in more detail. Her meditations of calming scenes would mutate without her noticing it into hideous fantasies that left her feeling soiled and ashamed. Self-disgust prevented her from seeking outside therapy. The experiences exhausted her, numbed her with an unfamiliar weakness. She was used to feeling strong and in control.

Hiding in her manse, Maradissa ignored the calls piling up behind her mirror's surface. Let Leony deal with them, offer excuses for Maradissa's silence. She had more important things to attend to. She fought with her demons alone. The fetzers haunted her dreams, the secret fetzers of the inner Chamber. She dreamed that the Priestess of Perversity came looking for her. She scratched the windows of Maradissa's manse with sharp, metal claws, murmuring, 'You want me to come. You want what I can give, what I can teach you.'

There were dreams, too, of tying faceless bodies down upon weird contraptions of wood and leather, anticipating with dread and desire an unknown torture that soon she would possess the knowledge to inflict. And the priestess was there to tell her, 'You see. You *do* belong with us. You just didn't realise in what capacity.'

During the day, she battled constantly with a feeling of being watched, sure there was an invisible presence beyond her windows staring in at her, compelling her to become aware of it. She chided herself for thinking it might be the Priestess, or some psychic emanation of the woman. Fleetingly, she remembered the incident in the garden before the fetzer experience. That must be it. A gardener looking in at her. Perhaps she should call Leony, but she felt too lethargic to bother. There was no sense of threat from the scrutiny, only an air of intense interest. Then, the night would come again, and Maradissa could not convince herself that it wasn't the fetzers who were watching her, bodilessly observing some weird kind of transformation taking place within her mind. The Priestess had cast a spell over her in the Chamber and now waited for her magic to take full effect. In the dark, contorted fetzer spirits surrounded the house.

One morning, Maradissa woke up angry. She would not be driven mad by what she'd witnessed in the Chamber. All the nightmares since were no more than phantoms of the mind. She leapt up from her bed and threw out her arms at the wan morning light beyond the windows. Enough! With this inner shout, it felt as if something inside her shattered and came out of her in a wave of emotion. She felt light-headed, as if there was more space around her. There were parts of other people's realities that were ugly, but they were not part of hers. She had fought the spell of the Chamber and won, defeated the demons of dark desire.

She called Evalie on the magic mirror.

'How are you?' Evalie asked. 'I've tried to call for days, but all I got was the butler. Everyone's been worried about you.'

'A virus. I've beaten it!' Maradissa said cheerfully. 'Now, I need some entertainment. Out tonight?'

'Yes! Yes! Pick me up?'

'OK. Usual time.'

Michael knew that tonight had to be the night. It was impossible for him to linger behind after work, so at lunchtime, he'd pretended to be ill and took the rest of the day off. His goddess had seemed so miserable for days. His heart had ached to see her pale, forlorn face peering from the windows of the house. But that morning, he'd caught a glimpse of her and had seen that her spirits had lifted. She'd been smiling again, that cool, aloof smile, and had no doubt made a decision.

As the gardeners' bus rolled off towards the Colonies, Michael was hiding near the gates to the Ferone manse. He waited until the bus was out of sight round a corner and then slipped between the metal portals as they ground ponderously shut. He knew that security systems would soon be in operation, but trusted that Maradissa would be aware of his presence and delay their activation. As her devotee, he was ready. He'd been alert for signs and now would act.

In the garden, Maradissa was dressed for the night. Spike-heeled boots, a catsuit of glistening black. She smoked beside the river. In her heart, a new feeling. The familiar kindling of excitement, the potential of the future, but tempered by serenity, a sense of separateness. Nothing could touch her now. She'd been reborn, stronger and more aware.

Then, the feeling of being watched sneaked up on her senses. She froze for a moment, a brief image of the Priestess of Perversity padding across her mind. Ridiculous. It was the gardener again. Immediately, she realised that the first time she had sensed him had not been because he'd been unaware of the regulations. It was so clear. He had been watching her, and watched her still. Slowly, she turned around, and saw him, this time, hiding in the lilies. A pale face through the dead and living leaves. She felt irritated, a little flattered perhaps, but resented the intrusion into her private time. The fume had empowered her. She was not afraid, and could defend herself against anything.

'Come out here!'

The man did not move. She could see the round holes of his eyes; he looked transfixed. An unfamiliar sensation shivered through her. When she walked towards him, she saw he was young. She had expected an older man.

'What are you doing here?'

He cowered down among the dead lilies, his hands steepled, trembling, before his face, as if in some kind of religious obeisance.

Maradissa laughed. 'Why are you frightened? Don't be absurd. Explain yourself!'

He seemed to find his courage then, and made to scrabble backwards through the leafage. Maradissa grabbed his arm, and it was as if his flesh turned to fluid in her hold. He did not resist her, but hung there limply, leaning against her legs. Maradissa pushed him away. 'Get off my premises. You'll lose your job for this!' She expected him to give her an appealing glance, say something. Instead, he lay there in the crackling foliage, beautiful and vulnerable. She saw, in his eyes, his feelings. How long had he watched her before he'd gathered the courage to stay after hours? He'd been reprimanded, but now risked dismissal, if not prosecution. What was he waiting for? What did he want from her?

Maradissa paused. It seemed that time condensed into a single moment, of which she was queen. She was conscious of her long limbs clad in shiny fabric, the slavering, fanged maw of her sex.

She straddled his fallen body, the heels of her boots digging into the soft soil. He lay still, waiting, his hair spread out over the crackling leaves. She imagined tearing the thin fabric of his shirt away, exposing his breast, like an empty canvas awaiting the marks of her nails.

Maradissa laughed uneasily, took a step to the side, stood over him. She felt dizzy. Time to go. She must dismiss him, go back to the house, call Leony, report the trespass. Evalie was expecting her and life must go on - it must!

The boy curled onto his side, still looking up at her with strange beseechment. He made no sound.

Maradissa extended one foot, placed it upon his face, so that her heel pressed against his trembling mouth. He reached up with grimed fingers, and the scent of leaf-mould was released, primal, almost anaesthetic.

He took hold of her foot, licked the leather. 'Kiss booties night night,' he said. And her heel drove into the soft flesh of his mouth.

An Old Passion

Well, of course she threw a garden party as soon as the place was decent. She had to show it off, and who can blame her? I went with Cathy, because Ted wouldn't go with me. 'She was unbearable when she was only slightly rich,' he said. 'Now, we're talking about torture, an afternoon in Hell.'

'I'm sure it won't be that bad,' I said, but privately I agreed with him. I'm not sure what made me go, really. I knew my skin would be crawling with annoyance by the end of the afternoon, but I suppose I was just curious. My friend had acquired a stately home. She was living in it. I had to go and see.

Helen had gone to school with Cathy and I, and because we all still lived in the area around the village where we'd grown up, we'd kept in touch. Cathy and I had married the sons of farmers, as our parents had expected, while Helen had gone off to college and run wild for a while. She had come back to the village now and again throughout her teens and early twenties, adopting every city fad that was going, showing off to us, her provincial sisters, stuck out in the sticks. I don't think we ever really liked her. You can't actually *like* a person like Helen, so familiar yet so distant, but we were always curious, always entertained.

Something went wrong when she hit quarter century, although she never confided in us about it. She came home, skulked dramatically round the village for a few weeks in dark glasses, looked tragic and wore wide hats like a film star. Then it was forgotten, whatever *it* was, and she was her usual bragging self again. Still, she stuck around after that, wheedled her way in with the new money, who drank in the pubs on the edge of the village.

While Cathy and I met our husbands and duly began to produce families, Helen secured jobs from her new friends, drove around in a new car, bought a cottage, did it up (quite well, too), and kept on partying. Sometimes, she'd visit us and gently scorn what she called our 'giving in to tradition'. Of course I envied her, who wouldn't. She was graceful and wild and witty, and had *fun*.

'Where did we go wrong?' Cathy asked one day, after a morning get together, as we watched the dust of Helen's car disappearing down Cathy's driveway. 'God, I hate her, the bitch! Where *did* we go wrong?'

Then we laughed together, went back inside, and had another gin. Our lives weren't that bad, really.

Helen was thirty-two when she met Roland Marchant. He was the one she'd been waiting for, the son of an industrialist, busy being propelled up the ladder of affluence by Daddy, oozing wealth and smarm. Helen met him at some do or another she'd gone to with friends and, with an unerring huntress' sense for a prime kill, set her sights and brought the prey down. Shall we say it was a short engagement? City bred, he was interested in village life, in country life, and I suspect it was more at his insistence than Helen's that she brought him visiting. He thought the farms were quaint and wanted to try driving a tractor. Ted, and Cathy's husband, Rupert, were strained but polite. Fortunately, the tractor lark never got beyond the evening of Scotch and Roland's loud voice. Well, no one reminded him about it.

'I don't know what's worse,' Cathy said. 'A rich boor who's pompous and condescending, or a rich boor who's devoted to being everybody's best buddy.'

Still, we accepted the antique brandies, and such like,

and were always coolly friendly.

Deermount House came on the market because the Pargeters couldn't keep the place up. Sons and daughter had moved away and had no interest in the family pile; the roof was caving in. Roland fought off developers, hoteliers, theme park entrepreneurs, conference centre planners and outbid the lot. He acquired Deermount House lock, stock and barrel. The Pargeters took very little away with them, other than an unspeakably large stash and a sense of financial relief. Roland and Helen would live there. They would be neighbours. Oh, wonderful.

When Helen came to tell me the news, I couldn't stop myself saying, 'Isn't it a bit big for just you and Roland?'

Helen laughed. 'Don't be absurd, Anna! It's a fucking mansion. How can a mansion be "too big"? You simply have to live bigger.'

I could almost hear her knuckles cracking at the prospect.

The garden party recreated some idyllic post war age as Helen imagined it. It was all bunting and vicars with megaphones, that sort of thing. The gardens were a mess, actually, utterly run to seed, but Roland had had the lawns rotor scythed, so it didn't look too bad. The first thing Cathy and I noticed about the house was the new roof. It looked rather peculiar, so clean and regular, atop the sagging facade of the house. Rather like an old woman wearing a teenager's hat. We presumed the rest of the building would soon succumb to cosmetic surgery, its wrinkles nipped and tucked, so that it matched the roof.

It appeared that everyone from the village and surrounding farms had come to be nosy. Children shrieked, piped band music stuttered, vicars cajoled. The river, caressed by ancient willows, oozed slowly through the gardens, like an ancient snake that knew its own territory. There were swans, of course. Summer as it had once been, perhaps.

Then Helen came gliding up the lawns towards us from the river, backlit by gleaming water. She looked divine in a flowered sundress, required large hat, silken blonde hair and ready red smile. 'Darlings! So glad you came!' she screamed.

God, it was embarrassing. Yes, we were jealous.

'You *must* see the house!' Helen insisted, and we had to follow her inside.

Once there, the spirit of the place claimed us and envy and irritation gave way to awe.

'Helen, you've done wonders!' Cathy exclaimed, craning her neck to try and take in the appallingly massive vista of the stuccoed ceiling in the main hall.

'Oh, it wasn't me,' Helen said, almost apologetically. 'Roland got designers in, architects, the lot. I just sat around waiting for them to finish. Didn't have a word in it.'

Did she mind about that? I wondered, mentally filing the thought to repeat to Cathy later.

'But you simply have to see my new man,' Helen said, her eyes shining.

Cathy and I exchanged a glance, and Cathy shrugged. New man? Our minds were open.

Helen led us upstairs to a long, well lit gallery that overlooked the gardens. 'All the paintings have been restored,' she told us. 'I found him only a few days ago. He's divine.' She had paused before a painting, gesturing at it with some reverence.

'Who is it?' I asked.

'Rufus Aston,' Helen said grandly. We were clearly supposed to know who that was.

'A Pargeter ancestor?' Cathy suggested.

'Oh no!' Helen answered. 'He was a poet. Haven't you

heard of him?'

No, we hadn't. Had anyone? He was beautiful, I suppose, although the chins of long dead people always seem too weak for my taste. Perhaps that is the fault of long dead painters rather than their models. The poet's hair was a resplendent red, his eyes dark and limpid, the mouth a little too generous, although not that wide. I estimated, with my untutored eye, he had lived in the nineteenth century. Helen confirmed this. 'Yes, I've been researching.'

'Did he live here?' Cathy asked, politely. I dared not look at her for fear of grinning.

'No,' Helen explained, 'but he stayed here quite often over a period of several years. Best of all, he died here!'

Best of all?

'Oh,' said Cathy and I together.

'Isn't it romantic?' Helen enthused. 'I'm reading up about him like mad, though it's hard to find things out.'

Well, Rufus Aston was obviously the latest fad. Helen's enthusiasm would be poured into him, and continue to do so, until it overflowed and her attention surged elsewhere.

We didn't see much of her for a few weeks after the garden party. We were busy with the harvest, and Helen, presumably, with renovating Deermount House and its grounds. Roland had asked Ted about buying horses, hiring grooms. Cathy's aunt, Mags, had been taken on as a cook. From her came the gossip. She felt that Roland and Helen were not like real people. They never seemed to argue, and spoke to one another as if they were acting in a play about domestic bliss. Such sunshine, such idyll. Is it any surprise, then, that they were threatened by thunderstorms? The weather always has to change.

Helen came calling three weeks after the garden party. She sat at my kitchen table, while I washed the breakfast things at the sink. I thought she seemed a little on edge, which was unusual for her. 'Everything all right?' I enquired.

Helen scowled at my youngest, who was hanging on to my skirts and attempting to disrupt our conversation. She, of course, would never want children.

'Fine,' she said. 'Everything's fine. I'm a bit exhausted, naturally. The job's never ending! Still, Rolly and I wouldn't have missed taking the place for the world. We love it.' She lit a cigarette. Her nails were immaculate. I doubted she ever applied hand to paint stripper herself. 'Do you know, I think I must be luckiest woman alive.'

I winced, and smiled at her in what I hoped was a convincing fashion.

'Roland is buying me a mare,' she said.

I took a few moments to consider the wonder of a woman who had married the most incredibly rich man and was actually in love with him. It seemed that way. Her eyes went moist when she mentioned his name.

'You were never much into riding,' I said.

'I have the time now.' Helen leaned down and produced a bottle of gin from her large bag. 'Oh, for God's sake, Anna, come and sit down. Leave the washing-up. Have a drink.'

I obeyed her, instinctively sensing she wanted to talk. I even shooed the boy out into the garden. 'Well?' I said, sipping gin.

Helen laughed. 'Well, what?' She leaned back in her chair, struck a pose with the cigarette.

'What is it you want to say?'

Helen leaned forward and squeezed my arm where it lay on the table. 'Oh darling, you country women are just so intuitive!'

That was the sort of remark I was used to putting up with. I declined to respond.

'The thing is, I've discovered some magic, some real

magic.'

'Oh? Witchcraft in the old grounds, then?'

'No, nothing like that.' She adopted an earnest expression, lowered her voice. 'I think Rufus is trying to contact me.'

'Rufus?' I had forgotten about the poet, and imagined this must be an old flame.

'Don't you remember the painting I showed you?

'Oh yes.' I paused. 'Hel, are we talking ghosts, here?'

'Nothing so banal,' she answered. 'A ghost is just a picture, a memory. Rufus is stronger than that. I'm sure I've seen him.'

'Oh Helen! Where?' I am not a sceptic, but not for one moment could I imagine a worldly woman like Helen being in tune with something spiritual.

'In the gardens,' she replied. 'Anna, I couldn't tell anyone else about this. Rolly would think I'd gone mad and start to worry, and Cathy would just laugh.'

'You'd better tell me about it,' I said.

I was, as usual, curious. Helen was always interesting. She had caught sight of a man, whom she now presumed to be Rufus Aston, in one of the more tangled corners of the gardens. Every morning, she walked her new Labrador puppies in the grounds, and it was always then that she saw him. Never at night, never at dusk, but in clear morning sunlight. He would be standing amid the shoulder high grasses, as still as a stone, but with an air of absolute alertness. 'He doesn't look like a ghost, he's completely solid,' she said. 'And he watches me. The thing is, it doesn't scare me.'

'Are you sure it's not just some young man who's taken a shine to you?' I asked. 'Why do you think it's Rufus?'

'Because it looks like him, silly. The clothes, the hair, the face. It's him.' She took a drink, swallowed. 'I know it

Storm Constantine

is. But what does he want from me?' Only then did her
brow cloud, but it wasn't with fear.

We talked about further research. Even I became a little
infected with her enthusiasm. Helen didn't know where the
poet was buried, or even how he died. Only that his last
moments had been spent at Deermount House, although
whether he had expired within the walls or out in the
grounds: she didn't know. I believed her utterly. There was
no question of it.

'Perhaps I should hold a séance,' she said.

I frowned. 'Oh, I don't think... I think that's asking for
trouble. No, don't do that.'

'I trust your instincts, darling,' she said, standing up.
'Well, I must be off. Keep the gin. I'll let you know what I
find out.'

I tell Cathy everything, but I didn't tell her about Helen's
visit. Probably because I believed Helen and, as she had
correctly pointed out, Cathy would laugh about it. I didn't
tell anyone, not even Ted, who would genuinely have been
interested. Perhaps I should have done.

We held a Halloween party for the children at Cathy and
Rupert's. While the kids screamed round us in garish
costumes, Cathy and I sipped port in the flickering light of
pumpkin lamps. Our men had sloped off down the pub. I
felt warm, at one with myself. The pagan new year.

'Have you seen much of Helen?' Cathy asked.

'No,' I answered. In fact, I hadn't seen her since the
morning she'd told me about her apparition. 'You?'

'Nothing. Mags thinks she's out of sorts. Perhaps we
should visit.'

'Out of sorts? What's wrong with her?' Just for a
moment, my blissful mood froze.

'Oh, nothing serious, I don't think. Mags says she's

distracted. Apparently, she's got a new set of friends, though where she dredged them up from, heaven knows. Mags thinks they're weird. The place is crawling with them. They're ghost hunters, or something like that. Helen actually held a séance up there, you know.'

'No! Cath, why didn't you tell me?'

Cathy looked surprised at my outburst. 'I only found out today. Why? What do you know?'

'As much as you do. Remember the painting she showed us, the new man?'

'You think she's trying to call his ghost up?' Cathy, predictably, cackled.

'It could be dangerous, Cath. I think Helen's fragile, for all her panache. Deermount House is such a big old place, and she's rattling round in it, on her own with dear Rolly, who's about as sensitive as a plank. Perhaps she's becoming too imaginative. You know how easily impressed she is. What if these new friends of hers are a bit, well, shady?'

'Yeah, you're right. Shall we call on the off chance tomorrow?'

I nodded. 'Yes, but keep a zip on it, Cath. Don't ridicule her.'

Cathy gave me a studying look. 'Why is it we care about her, Annie? What keeps us there for her?'

I shrugged. 'Don't know. Old bonds, I suppose.'

'She shuts us out when she's having crises though. Remember when she first came back?'

'I remember. As I said, I think she's fragile. And, for all her ways, she's always been generous.'

'Yes, generous.' Cathy took a slug of port. 'I hope I don't want something awful to happen to her.'

'Course you don't,' I said.

Halloween, Samhain, the pagan new year, the time when

the veil is thin between the worlds. If we should have visited Helen, perhaps it should have been the night before, the time when the dead come back to commune with the living. We were unprepared for the maelstrom of energy that greeted us at Deermount House.

Helen came like a hurricane into the drawing room where her housekeeper had installed us. She seemed almost hysterically delighted to see us. She hugged us, and her skin felt feverish, hot, against our own. 'My dears, my dears!' she said.

'Hi,' Cathy said. 'We wondered how you were. Haven't seen you for ages.'

'I'm fine,' Helen answered. 'Brilliantly fine.' She looked at me and a secretive cast came into her expression. Forget the offer of tea, or anything stronger: she launched straight into her new obsession. 'Anna, I've been continuing with my research.'

'Come up with anything?' I asked.

She rolled her eyes. 'Haven't I just? I'm on a quest, now.'

Quest? Cathy and I sat down, while Helen leaned against the mantelpiece to light a cigarette. Her fever had cooled. She seemed quite businesslike.

'Psychic questing,' Helen said. 'A lot of people are doing it.' I noticed she did not look at Cathy as she spoke, although her voice was firm and confident, as if challenging Cathy to poke fun. 'I wrote to some people who are into it, and they've been helping me. It's a science, you know.'

How far had she gone that she could speak this way in front of Cathy? Her reserve had vanished, which to me spoke of a replacement mania. 'Are you questing about Rufus Aston?' I asked.

She nodded. 'Absolutely. There's more to it than meets the eye. He was involved in something, Anna, something from the past that can still affect the present.'

'Oh really!' exclaimed Cathy, unable to contain herself.

Helen gave her a hard look, the hardest look I'd ever seen her give anyone. 'You can scoff, Cath,' she said in a cool voice, 'but I know what I've seen and experienced. I was sceptical once, too. If you can listen to me with an open mind, I'll tell you about it.'

Why had I thought she was fragile? She wasn't. If anything, her experiences, whatever they were, had strengthened her. There was a new steel to Helen Marchant, almost as if she'd somehow become anchored to the earth, had slowed down, become part of real life. Absurd. But that's how it felt. And from the way she spoke, it was impossible to laugh at her, even for Cathy.

With the help of her new friends, who were thorough researchers and had recourse to documents that Helen would not even have thought about, she had discovered that Rufus Aston had been found dead in the grounds of the house, during a visit in the summer of 1883. He had been twenty-two years old. The cause of death was given as an overdose of laudanum. Well, they were all into it, then, weren't they? Poets and artists, the bohemians. The incumbent of the House at the time, Richard Pargeter, had been a patron of the arts, and much else besides, it seems. The glitterati of artistic society had regularly gathered at the estate, or so Helen said, but I must admit I'd not heard of any of the names she cited as evidence.

'They had a society,' Helen said. 'A secret society. There's no documentation about it, but Steve – he's my psychic aid - picked it all up at the... well...' She looked guiltily at me. 'We had a little session here a few days ago. I know you think it's dangerous to meddle with, Anna, but honestly, it's quite safe with people like Steve around, who know what they're doing. Pargeter was head of the society, like a kind of High Priest, I suppose. They were seeking immortality.'

Storm Constantine

'Well, at least poor old Rufus never grew old!' Cathy observed.

'Quite,' Helen agreed. 'Things got a bit out of hand, apparently. The strange thing is, there are so few records about what went on. Strangest of all, Richard Pargeter just sort of fades from history not long after Rufus' death. There's no mention of him, other than that his brother took over the estate. We can only presume something was effectively hushed up.'

'But this is all conjecture,' Cathy said. 'The facts are a man died, in not very suspicious circumstances, really, and then Richard Pargeter stepped down. Probably to avoid a scandal, or something. This other stuff, about secret societies and immortality, was only dreamed up at your séance.'

'I realise it appears that way,' Helen said. 'But if you'd been involved you'd feel the same way I do. I was there. I heard him speak. Through Steve.'

'Heard who speak? Rufus Aston?'

She shook her head. 'No, no. Pargeter. He took over Steve's body. It was outrageous!'

'His ghost came?' I said, as an exclamation rather than a question, but Helen answered me.

'Of course not! Pargeter's not dead. But he is very powerful.'

'Er... what does Roland think about all this?' I enquired, quite gob-smacked by her revelation. Neither Cathy nor I could bring ourselves to question Helen about it.

'He thinks it's just a quaint little interest of mine. Poor Rolly, he's not very spiritual!' She laughed.

Cathy wound the visit up very quickly after that, and we left.

On the way back, Cathy broke a silence between us to say, 'She's off her head, Annie, and there's nothing we can do about it.'

Was there anything I, or anyone else, could do? Perhaps we had no right. Helen did not seem ill, or even particularly disturbed. She was excited, yes, but who wouldn't be, in her shoes? Cathy didn't believe the stuff about the séance and the psychic questers. She thought they had to be charlatans. I, for whatever reason, call it instinct or gut reaction, was not convinced about that. Still, I wasn't going to admit that to Cathy. I told Ted about it though, because he has a casual interest in strange phenomena. Was waiting to find his first crop circle, in fact, although his aim would be to disprove more than prove the evidence. In Helen's case, he thought the danger of applying that much concentration, or will power, to a search, was that you tended to find whatever you were looking for, be it a demon from ages past or a pound coin on the pavement. 'It can lead to a kind of group hysteria,' he said. 'Then you'll believe, in fact, *see*, anything. And is that reality or not? It's marshy ground, I think. We don't know enough about it.' Ted reads up on that kind of thing. I asked him to find me the article he'd seen about it. I wanted to read it too. 'I'd be wary of getting involved,' Ted said, but he trusted me not to.

Helen phoned me two days later. Her voice was low, so she must have had company somewhere in the house. 'Anna, this is a secret, but I have to let you in on it. We're going to quest for his tomb!'

'Excuse me? Whose?' I'd lost track of who she believed was dead, and who not.

'Aston's! He's buried around here somewhere, but no one knows where. There's no record, but we're going to find it. Steve is absolutely quivering with vibrations.'

'Lucky Steve,' I said, and then added carefully. 'You

will take care, won't you, Hel.'

'It's all in good hands, Anna, don't worry. I'll let you know about it.' The phone went down. Just that. I was left looking at my own receiver, wondering if I should do anything, and if so, what? In the event, I did nothing.

I expected to hear something from Helen pretty soon, but then we had a crisis with our eldest, who had a messy accident with a broken limb, and blood and screams. So I was preoccupied with running backwards and forwards to the hospital in the nearest town for a while. I forgot about Helen's quest. She phoned me a couple of times to ask how we were, but didn't mention much about her new interest. I had the impression things had faded out a little. Perhaps, as they hadn't found the tomb, Helen's enthusiasm was dying.

The next news came from Cathy, via Mags. 'You won't believe this,' Cathy said, breezing into my kitchen one morning. 'Helen's buying a church!'

'What? You're joking!'

'No. Do you suppose she's found religion now?'

'What's been going on?' I hadn't heard from Helen for weeks, so had assumed Rufus Aston had gone the way of all her previous crazes. This must be a new one.

'Well the ghost hunters are out,' Cathy said gleefully. 'Mags thinks a disagreement happened, or perhaps Roland got sick of them. Anyway, Helen has done up a room in the house like an Egyptian temple or something. No one's allowed in there, but Mags had a peek when the designers were in. She says the house absolutely reeks of incense some mornings when she goes in. Can you believe it? Has dear Helen become a sorceress now?'

'God, I dread to think! But where does the church come into this?'

'Mags doesn't know exactly. All she does know is that

it's an abandoned church - practically a ruin - near Loxcombe, and that Roland is buying it for Helen. She only found out about it because Roland was bragging in front of his friends when she was serving sherry to them last Sunday. He thinks Helen's into conservation. Thinks it's a great idea. There was talk of opening a craft centre in it. Agh! It's too much! Can you imagine it? Helen in High Priestess robes, selling joss sticks and corn dollies?' She fell back in her chair, laughing helplessly.

I joined in with the hilarity, although inside I felt a little disturbed, and absurdly, somehow disloyal to Helen for laughing.

I called her in the afternoon. 'So, what's all this, stranger?' I said in a joky manner. 'Where have you been, what have you been up to, and why are you buying a church?' I expected the usual breezy answer, but Helen was reticent.

'How do you know about that?

'Little bird told me,' I replied glibly. 'Is it true?'

She didn't want to answer me, I know she didn't, but eventually she said, with utmost reluctance, 'Well, yes.'

'Why?'

I heard her sigh down the line. 'Anna, I found the tomb.'

It didn't take a genius to work out where it was. I wanted to see her. I don't know why, but the impulse could not be ignored. 'Can you come over?'

She hesitated. 'All right. Give me an hour.'

In the event, she didn't arrive when she'd promised and I had to drive to the school around three o'clock to pick up the middle child, with my youngest in the back of the Discovery, making havoc, as usual. Eldest son was prolonging his convalescence at Ted's parents for a few days.

I waited outside the school for my daughter, tapping my fingernails against the steering wheel, wondering why Helen had stood me up, and desperate to get back in case I missed her. Then coincidence spilled beans from the mouth of my lovely daughter, as she threw her bag in through the passenger door and climbed up beside me. 'Mum, there's witches at Deermount House!'

'What, darling?

'Ben said so. His brother saw them in the grounds, wearing robes and everything. There was a fire. Is Aunty Helen a witch?'

I laughed, in a brittle fashion. 'Probably just one of her parties. You know what she's like.' Already, my daughter did. Must be that country woman intuition Helen spoke about.

Helen was waiting for us when we got home, leaning against her shiny black car, which looked like a big cat, and actually was, in another, brand name sense. She was wearing a big coat and dark glasses, her glossy hair covered by a scarf.

'Don't you dare mention witches!' I hissed at my daughter as she tumbled out of the Discovery.

Daughter despatched to friends nearby for pony activities, with the firm directive, despite complaints, to take younger brother with her, I settled Helen in the parlour. I considered making tea, and then poured her a glass of wine instead. She took off her dark glasses, and yes, she looked haggard. Makeup could not conceal the dark puffiness below her eyes. Worse, her nails were lacquerless and bitten. It was too much, almost as if she'd designed herself to look like the archetype of a troubled woman. The biggest shock was when she took off her scarf and shook out her hair. She'd cut it to shoulder length and had dyed it red.

'That's a change,' I remarked, almost choking.

'Mmm.' Helen rubbed her forehead.

'You look terrible,' I said, 'although I suppose you know that.'

Helen managed to avoid my eyes by reaching down to delve in her bag for cigarettes and lighter. 'I haven't been sleeping well, actually.'

'What's going on?' I demanded.

She lit up, blew smoke at me, or rather a smoke screen in front of herself. 'It's nothing bad, Anna, honestly. Just tiring.' A monumental lie.

Is it anything to do with the tomb you found, or the secret temple in the house?'

Helen smiled wanly. 'God, you just can't get the staff nowadays, can you? I presume your information comes from the fount of all rumour, Mags Whitely?'

'I never betray my informants,' I answered, 'but what I heard concerns me, Hel. And look at you! What are you doing to yourself? What's the temple for?'

'I find comfort in it,' Helen said. 'I feel safe there.'

I shook my head slowly. 'Even my daughter talks of witches in the gardens at Deermount. Just what is going on?'

Helen considered for a moment, and then relented. 'All right. I don't want this going back to Cathy, but, well, I would appreciate a chat.'

I gave her my promise, and I meant it. She spoke at length about how much she'd found out about the secret society of Deermount House, circa 1883. The Bearers of the Old Light, they called themselves. All of the information had been channelled through Steve during psychic sittings. (The so-called witches in the garden, incidentally, had been an outdoor séance). The Bearers of Old Light had consisted of ten members, three of them women, all of them artistic or creative, but for Richard Pargeter, who called the shots. Helen said he was a vampire for the creative energy of the others, but that he also replenished them, whatever that meant. They sought immortality, through magical artefacts, which failed, and then through ritual. 'It's not magic as we know it,' Helen said, 'but a form of parascience. It's trying to make contact with a more evolved form of yourself, who of course knows all the answers.'

And Rufus? His death, Helen said, was not accidental.

'Exactly *what* it was is difficult to establish. Steve never made contact with Rufus. He thought that Pargeter was blocking him.'

'Ah, yes,' I ventured, 'I remember you saying something outrageous like Richard Pargeter wasn't dead...'

Helen nodded. 'I know it sounds crazy, I know it does. I don't want to believe it myself, but Steve was convinced. And now, I feel him myself, around the house, in the back of my head, everywhere.'

I shivered, thinking of cruel eyes beyond the window, where the afternoon was darkening. 'I hate to say this, but how... how *genuine* do you think this Steve is?'

Helen flicked me a crystalline glance. 'No one could act that well,' she said shortly.

'So you're saying Pargeter actually found immortality?' I risked a smile. 'I'm sorry, but I find that very hard to believe. What has he been doing for the past hundred years? Do his family know about him? And how on earth did he manage to live so long? Come on, Hel, you must agree it's pretty far-fetched!'

'It's not just far fetched, it's insane,' Helen said. 'But I also believe it to be true.' She leaned towards me. 'He's making his presence felt to me, Anna, he really is.' She shuddered, and looked around herself, as if a malevolent draught had suddenly chilled her.

My spine prickled in sympathy. 'Do you think you're in danger?' I asked her gently.

She gave me a naked, wild look that made me jump. For a second, something else seemed to look from the face of my friend. I remember saying her name in shock. Then she shook her head, hiding her face with that new, red hair.

'I don't know, but I feel I have to... I need Rufus' help. I'm sure he'd be able to tell me what to do.' She rubbed her face wearily with her hands. 'God, Anna, why did I get into this? Why? Now, it's too late. I'm in it!'

Sitting there, in my cosy parlour, it was hard to believe this other world existed; a world of magicians, secret societies, voices from beyond, psychic quests, supernatural threat. And yet, there was Helen before me, a ragged, haunted Helen who'd uttered the first regrets I'd ever heard from her, the first truly honest words concerning herself. I realised, with some awe, it was also the first time she had truly confided in me. No bravado, no wit, no barrier; just a frightened woman.

I'll help you,' I said impulsively. 'Whatever I can do...'

She reached to squeeze my hands. 'Darling, thank you, but I don't know what you can do, other than listen to my ravings! Steve and the others have gone now. I'm afraid I threw them out. Stupid of me! I realise I need them, and yet I don't want to be part of their world.'

'Why did you throw them out?'

She sighed. 'Two reasons. First, I haven't seen Rufus in the gardens since they came, or since Richard Pargeter made his presence felt. I believed Rufus would come back once they'd gone, but he hasn't. And second, I thought this nightmare would end if Steve and the others left. But it hasn't. I feel *he's* there with me all the time, Anna, watching me, waiting for a weak moment. He hates me.'

'Pargeter?'

She nodded miserably. 'Sometimes I tell myself it's only my imagination. I tell myself not to be so silly, to throw off these ridiculous fears. Then I'm in bed at night, terrified, and whatever I do, however I scream, and hit out, I can't wake Rolly up, and I'm alone with this...' She struggled for colourful enough words. 'With this... *evil*, cold mind. All around me. My little temple offers some respite, but not for much longer, I'm sure.'

'Perhaps you should contact Steve and his friends again,' I suggested lamely.

She shook her head vehemently. 'No. Then it would just go on and on. They love this kind of stuff. It's like a drug to them. They'd only make it worse, I'm sure.'

'Then someone else. There must be other people who deal with this kind of thing? A priest even.'

She nodded, a little distantly. 'Yes... you're right.' Then she flicked her attention back to me. 'But I know Rufus can help me. I nearly have him now, Anna, what's left of him.'

'No, Hel, no!' I insisted. 'Go home, get your spooky journals, or whatever it is you have, and ring some people. Get someone to help you. Leave it alone until then. Have you told Roland about it?'

She laughed coldly. 'Don't be ridiculous! He'd have me committed.'

'Surely not? He loves you.'

'Yes, I think he does. But he's afraid of madness, of anything he can't see and touch and control. If he could say to people "Oh, we have a ghost, you know", he'd love it, but not this, not something real and dreadful.' She took a breath and dropped her cigarettes and lighter back into her bag. 'Anyway, I must be going. Hate to sound dramatic, but I don't like being out alone after dark.'

I stood up with her, and we embraced awkwardly. 'Helen, this is vile!'

She smiled tightly and put on her coat.

'Will you call me tomorrow, after you've contacted some other psychics or something?'

'Yes, I will.'

As I watched her Jag glide off towards the road, I was afraid that I'd never see her again. I wish in some ways that had been true.

That evening, as we shared a night cap in the parlour, I told Ted everything. I watched his eyes and I could see his feelings shifting from belief to disbelief and back again. Like me, he didn't want to believe it, for believing in it meant it had to be dealt with, and how do you deal with a thing like that? Far better to ignore it, to scoff, to cling stubbornly to the mundane world, where only what you can see and touch are real, and there are no hidden powers. Perhaps it is worse for a man, because men are brought up to think they have to be in control, otherwise they're sunk. We, as women, are somewhat more attuned to the unseen, the tides of our blood and instincts. We accept the unacceptable more readily.

'Those weirdos have put these crazy ideas into her head,' my husband declared, taking a stand. 'You must see that, Annie. They've scared her to death. She lives in a huge, echoing, empty house, and she's afraid of it. You know yourself she's gullible. Now every echo is a disembodied voice, and every shadow a spook. She's conjuring things up from her own mind. You must see that I'm right.'

I looked at him steadily. He *could* be right. The explanation was rational and reasonable.

'If you want to help her,' Ted said, 'you should make her believe what I've just said. Then her phantoms will disappear, I'm sure of it.' He smiled and adopted an eerie tone. 'Whether they're real or not.'

I laughed. 'Ted!'

He shrugged. 'It's just a question of belief.'

'You're quite a little mystic in your own way, aren't you,' I said. 'So you won't mind driving out with me to

Helen's church tomorrow.'

'He pulled a comical face that was halfway to a frown. 'What for?'

'I just want to see, and I'd rather be with you than Helen. I'd feel safer with your rationality around. It would be like a shield, if there is anything nasty there.'

Ted rolled his eyes. 'I can't believe we're having this conversation, but OK, if that's what you want...'

I knew it. He was hooked.

Kids off-loaded to grandparents once more, we drove out to Loxcombe in the morning. It was a Saturday, a bright, cold day. There were two churches in Loxcombe, but it didn't take us long to locate the semi-ruin that would soon belong to the Marchants. It was a dull little place, neglected and feeling sorry for itself. Ted and I nosed around the graveyard, and squinted at the plain, weathered stones, but there was no sign of Rufus Aston.

'Surely, if his grave was here,' Ted said, 'it would be well known. He was a kind of personality, after all.'

'I don't think he was that well known,' I said. 'As far as I'm aware, there are no books in existence of his poetry.'

Ted pulled an exasperated face. 'What the hell are we doing here?' he asked the sky, throwing up his hands.

The door to the church was locked, but we found a smaller door round the back, which was open a few inches but stuck. Ted applied brawn to the wood and eventually, there was enough room for us to wriggle inside. The interior smelled musty and damp, the pews had been ripped to pieces, and the uninspiring stained glass windows broken. Still there was one wonder left. It was Ted who found it, and the awe in his voice when he said, 'Annie, come and look at this!' alerted me immediately. The tomb of the poet.

There was no legend to tell us whose remains lay

inside, but I recognised him immediately. There he lay; the stone effigy of Rufus Aston. The tomb was enormous, fit for a king. My first thought was that Rufus had been dearly loved by someone: a someone who could have afforded to pay for this monument, even if they had neglected to leave a reminder for the world concerning exactly who lay within it. The carving of the effigy was exquisite. But for the colour of the stone - a strange, shiny black - he could have been a youth lying there asleep. The long hair was not stiffly stylised, but reproduced as flowing over the stone, down the sides of the sarcophagus. One long fingered hand lay lightly on his breast, the other at his side. His shirt was open at the collar, revealing a slender throat, with the wonderful hollow that invites a finger to trace its depths. I touched him, with reverence, while Ted looked on. Neither of us said a word. If anything of Rufus *was* still there, he was certainly at peace. Even though the building was vandalised, the tranquillity seemed to flow from the tomb of the poet in waves. Helen should not, must not, violate this. Her problem was not Rufus, not now. She must not drag what was left him, essence or spirit, back into whatever filthy enterprise Richard Pargeter, alive or dead, represented. If an image of Rufus had ever haunted Helen's garden, it must simply have been a memory, a captured moment in time replaying throughout history, not an essence, or a soul. I was entirely sure about these thoughts, so sure, it was like a telepathic message. Perhaps Rufus' guardian angel was still around, keeping an eye out for him.

I took a step back, and saw the inscription on the side of the tomb. Although there was no name to the words, I knew they had once been penned by the exquisite hand mimicked in stone above them:

'Let me resist this old passion, let it pass over me.

For the flower of this love is death, which I have picked with my own hands

Pressed my own face into the flesh of it, taken the scent within.'

'Strange they should put that on the tomb,' Ted murmured.

I glanced at him. 'Not strange to whoever chose it.'

What could I say to Helen, how could I dissuade her from trying to disturb the eternal rest of Rufus Aston?

Back home, I called her immediately, but her housekeeper answered the phone. Mrs Marchant was ill, she wasn't taking calls. 'This is important,' I told her, 'very important.'

'I'm sorry, Mrs Brown. She won't come to the phone. She's in bed. Can I take a message?'

'What's wrong with her?' I demanded.

'The flu,' answered the housekeeper. 'Is there any message?'

'Just say I called.' I slammed down the phone, thwarted. Was Helen's illness feigned so she did not have to speak to me? I was getting paranoid. Still, I phoned Cathy straight away.

'Cath, will you call Mags at Deermount for me?'

'Why?' Cathy's voice showed she sensed intrigue.

'Ask her if Helen is ill, and if so, with what? I've been trying to get in touch with her, but the housekeeper isn't being very helpful.'

Cathy phoned back about fifteen minutes later. 'Madam has the flu,' she reported.

I slumped in relief. Flu might keep Helen away from Loxcombe for a while.

'However,' Cathy continued. 'Mags has news. Since the psychics were kicked out, Madam and Sir have been arguing. Apparently, Helen looks a right wreck at the moment. She's not eating, she's chain-smoking, and she leaves all the lights on in the house at night. Must be costing them a fortune in electricity, given the size of the place! And that's not all. The feudal slaves, bless them, are starting to get spooked as well. The girl who looks after the horses won't go near the stables at night now, and the housekeeper saw something nasty on the stairs. She thought it was a big stain on the stair carpet, like oil, but when she went indignantly to investigate, scrubbing brush in hand, no doubt, the stain reared up and flew off like smoke. Poor woman nearly fell down stairs.'

'Cathy,' I said. 'You don't believe any of that, do you?'

'Well it was probably a cat, or a bird, or something,' she said, 'but what a good tale, eh?'

'Has Mags told you how Roland's taking all this?'

Spending time in the city, of course! What do you expect?'

'What's Helen doing about it, the funny goings on, I mean?'

'She has the phone with her in bed, and several tons of Psychics' Monthly beside her. Soon the old pile will be crawling with fat women in long dresses and beads, and cadaverous men who've never had girlfriends. Ghosts, beware!'

'Cath, you're enjoying this, aren't you!'

She laughed. 'It's the best of her obsessions yet!'

I wanted to slam down the phone, angry with Cathy for the first time in years. Helen hadn't mentioned her arguments with Roland, or the staff's experiences. She hadn't confided in me that deeply, then. And I was right: she *was* avoiding speaking to me.

I phoned Helen every day, and after four attempts, she deigned to speak. I had resolved not to be too pushy. 'How are you?' I began.

She did sound very snuffly. 'Oh, I'm over the worst. And you?'

Once the pleasantries were over, I asked her how she was getting on with locating a suitable psychic.

'Some have been here already,' she said. 'I'm surprised Mags hasn't told Cathy.' The rebuke did not go unregistered, but I ignored it.

'Any success?'

'It's too early to tell.'

I took a deep breath. 'And the church at Loxcombe? Have you been there yet?'

'Of course. Ages ago. Did you think I'd buy it without seeing it?'

'You've seen the tomb, then?'

'What do you *think*?' she retorted.

'What's it like?'

'Just a tomb,' Helen answered. Her voice was positively waspish. 'What did you expect?'

'A gravestone in a graveyard?'

'That's exactly what it is.'

The lie outraged me. So much so I did a stupid thing and blurted out. 'Helen, that's bullshit! I've been there! I've seen it!'

There was a silence and then Helen said in a slow, chilling voice, 'How dare you!'

'You don't own it yet,' I said. 'Helen, I've got to speak to you about this. You mustn't go charging in there, desecrating Aston's tomb! Rufus is at rest. You must have been able to feel it! It would be wrong, so terribly wrong to...'

I realised I was speaking to a dead line. My friend Helen had put the phone down on me, probably right after she'd asked me how I dared.

There was silence for days. Cathy reported the comings and goings of the psychics, with one or two amusing anecdotes concerning their appearance and behaviour, but other than that, nothing. I must have picked up the phone a dozen times with the intention of calling Helen, but pride stopped me. If she wanted me, she knew where I was.

Then Roland called us in the middle of the night. Ted got out of bed to answer the phone and I followed him down, sensing trouble.

'It's all right,' I heard him say, soothingly. 'Now think, Roland, where would she go?'

Helen had disappeared. Of course, we offered to help Roland look for her. We couldn't leave the kids alone, so Ted drove up to Deermount. Later he told me Roland was in a terrible state, out of his mind with worry. He confessed his wife hadn't been right for weeks, perhaps months. He blamed himself. He should have done something, got her to see someone, anything.

They found her at Loxcombe. Ted thought it was the obvious place.

'She was lying on top of him, on top of the tomb,' Ted said to me. 'It was...' He shook his head. 'God, Annie, she's out of her mind. You should have seen her. Writhing over that effigy in her dressing gown with nothing on beneath, mud up to her knees, her face scratched. Her face. It was like something out of Bedlam! Hardly human. God, that poor man. Poor Roland.'

They'd carried her home and called the doctor. Scant hours later, an ambulance had come and Helen had been taken away. Roland, in a rare moment of eloquence, said dazedly to Ted, as they watched the ambulance disappear down the drive, 'It's as if she's no longer with us. That person, it's not Helen, it's not her.'

Ted brought Roland back to the farm. He stayed with us for over a week.

That was the end of it really. The rest was simply having the details filled in. Helen's breakdown was acute. She was going to be away for a long time. Ted, Cathy, Rupert and I did what we could to comfort Roland. He isn't really a bad sort, and he was so bewildered and lost after the event, it was pathetic. I spent some time blaming myself, thinking I could have done something, told someone, but what good would that do now? I did take some action though. First, I found the psychic Steve's number and called him. My intention was bawl him out over what had happened to Helen, but when I began telling him, he seemed genuinely appalled and asked if he could come to talk to me. Rather surprised, I agreed.

He arrived with his girlfriend, Rachel, the same evening. They were young, earnest types, and not at all what I expected. Very down to earth, in fact.

'Helen had a problem before we got there,' Steve told me. 'She was obviously suffering from some past trauma, and whatever was being repressed ignited the presence in the house. When she asked us to leave, I knew I shouldn't just let it go at that. I wish I hadn't now. I could have done something.'

'We've all been blaming ourselves,' I said, kindly. 'You're not alone in that.'

I told him about the tomb at Loxcombe and expressed my concern for Rufus Aston. We agreed to drive out there together at the weekend, to see if Steve could pick anything up. I was amazed at myself. Only weeks before I had been scoffing at the boy, now I spoke to him as intimately as to an old friend.

So, Ted and I and Steve and Rachel followed the lanes to the church on another bright, cold Saturday. I was nervous of what I might feel, and dreaded seeing some relic of Helen's dementia on the tomb, but there was nothing. Steve seemed to light up like a candle as he nosed energetically around the building. His hands skimmed the contours of Rufus' effigy. He nodded vigorously to himself.

'They hid him here,' he said. There was a weird light inside him, invisible yet entirely brilliant, that turned him into something quite beautiful.

'They?' I prompted.

'Rufus' friends. Away from Pargeter. He escaped, you see. I've always thought that. What Rufus must have realised was that true immortality means relinquishing the flesh. Therefore, we are all immortal already. Anything else is just a travesty against nature. Rufus' death was his statement to Pargeter. An escape and a denial.'

'Oh...' I traced the words on the side of the tomb. 'Were they lovers, do you think?'

'It's not unlikely,' Steve said, 'but I feel that's Rufus' business, don't you?'

I felt strangely chastened.

'But anyway, Rufus' friends must have thought it was important to hide his remains from Pargeter. There's some strong cloaking around this place. The church is almost invisible, an unattractive dump, and yet,' he gestured at the tomb, 'here it is. A hidden masterpiece.'

'Why did Helen come here?' I asked. 'Was she trying to reach Rufus' spirit?'

Steve frowned. 'I don't think Helen was quite herself by then,' he remarked, but that was all.

'Will she ever be?' Ted enquired. We were both deferring to this intense youth.

Steve shrugged. 'I can't say.' He looked back at the tomb, let his hand hover over the breast of the effigy. 'But I can reassure you that whatever Helen tried to do, our friend here didn't bat an eyelid. The love and protection around him is too strong. He can't be reached by something like that.'

Relieved, we walked back into the harsh sunlight. I felt buoyant, melancholy, but sadly happy, if that's possible.

I went to visit Helen in hospital, and I wish I hadn't. Roland was right. The Helen we knew had gone. Perhaps she was only hiding, and could be coaxed back into that limp, listless form, but I doubt it. A year has passed, and she's still there, in that hospital, sitting in the same chair, looking out of the same window, seeing nothing. I hope she's not suffering inside. Perhaps, like Rufus, she's spurned the flesh, and what lives in her body is something else, something that's trapped there now. That would be justice, I think.

Two postscripts. The first was that Roland's attempt to buy the church at Loxcombe fell through. He had no real idea what had been going on in Helen's life and mind, and entertained the wistful notion that he could buy the place and do it up as a craft shop for Helen, for when she got out of hospital, if ever. Something blocked him though, and he was very puzzled about it, because his money usually meant he got everything he wanted. I suspected Rufus still had friends around who made sure the Marchants couldn't get near him. Strangely enough, a couple of months later, the church was sold, and renovated, but who had bought it and what they wanted it for, no one knew. Workmen came and went, a high fence was put up around it, and a caretaker came to live in a caravan in the graveyard. To this day, the church is still barricaded against the world, more invisible now than it ever was. Weird.

The second postscript results from a visit from Helen's mother. She had never had much time for Cathy and I. We thought she'd considered us common and unsuitable friends for her glittering daughter. Now, she wanted to talk to me. I realised I had seen a lot more of Helen over the past year than she had. She was devastated by what had happened, naturally. Her dream girl had disappeared, as dreams do, when you wake up to reality. Rumours had filtered back to her concerning hauntings and possession, and she needed reassurance. I told her the rumours were exaggerated. 'Helen was ill,' I said. 'There were no ghosts, not really.'

Helen's mother nodded at that. Then she told me the

truth about something, which was sadly pertinent to the whole tragic drama. The reason Helen had returned to the village when she was twenty-five was because she'd had a breakdown in the city. She had, in fact, been in hospital for a month before she came home. Apparently, she'd got mixed up with some very dodgy characters, who were into a peculiar sort of cult, which involved a lot of drugs and sex and sheer debauchery. Helen must have been attracted to it because most of the devotees were very rich. She had, (perhaps inevitably, given his bank balance), fallen for the guru of the outfit, who'd used her in every conceivable way. She'd put up with this, until she discovered her Great Man was also abusing, in similar ways, most of the other members of the group, both male and female. There were complications by then, and Helen's mind caved in.

Speaking as if her mouth was full of bile, Helen's mother spat out almost indecipherable words about pregnancy and unmentionable diseases. Poor Helen. No one had realised she was in such a mess. If only we'd known about her past, we might have been more alert for trouble in the present.

Afterwards, I thought about the superficial parallels between Helen and Rufus Aston. In some ways, it had been like a replay, but it wasn't finished. There had been no solution, no true denouement.

Roland still lives at Deermount, waiting for his wife to return to the world. But it's a bad place now. You can feel it sometimes, up there at the house, so I don't go there often. Something waiting, like a nerve end, to be touched.

Just His Type

The trouble was she was just his type. Sitting at the back of the stuffy pub function room, her eyes fixed upon him, she commanded his attention, apparently without effort. He could tell she was tall, because her head was the highest on the row. Her hands were clasped in her lap and she was dressed in black.

She had come to watch the famous historical investigator and author, Noah Johnson, deliver a lecture. He found he was playing to her alone throughout the evening. He knew the talk, 'Vampires in Myth and History', off by heart, having delivered it countless times before. He updated it constantly, but essentially, it was the same old stuff: colourful but careful. He was selective about what he gave the punters. He knew how to please a mixed crowd.

The regular meetings, 'Enigmas of History', were going well. He ran it once a fortnight in the upstairs room of his local pub, The Gun and Duck, and now had a regular attendance of around fifty people. Sometimes, he had to turn some away. More than fifty and the front row started fainting. He'd started it to augment his writing income, for the periods when funds were slack – a downside of any writer's life. But it was going so well, he had planned more events; outdoors, now that summer was coming. Sarah would have loved all this. But he mustn't think about her now. She was no longer part of his life.

Noah's friend and assistant, Gary, dimmed the lights in preparation for the slide show. Some of the audience were fanning themselves with the handouts Gary's girlfriend, Abby, had placed on every seat prior to the meeting. The windows were open, but did little to improve the air quality in the room.

One by one, the slides slipped across the screen: illustrations copied from ancient texts, photographs Noah had taken himself while investigating in far corners of obscure eastern European countries. Some of them had been reproduced in Noah's best-selling book, 'The Search for Nosferatu'. The subject no longer captivated him: he'd done it and it was over, but the public were always hungry for it. Noah had moved on to other things and was currently researching his next book, which was concerned with the mythical landscape of the remote Scottish islands, and how the strange ancient structures there might have come to be built.

When the lights came back on, Noah's eyes were drawn immediately to the girl on the back row. He half expected to see that she'd left. That would be just his luck, but no, there she was, sitting straight and demure, gazing at him from beneath downcast lashes, a slight smile on her lips.

He began to answer questions from the audience, but was anxious to keep it short tonight. If people wanted to air their opinions, which most of them did, especially the regulars, they could continue in the bar downstairs. He interrupted a woman as she was speaking. 'Hey, it's too hot up here. Shall we move down?'

Most of them would go home, but the ones who saw themselves as the core of his group would remain until closing time. It was only nine o'clock.

People started getting out of their seats, apparently as eager as he was to escape the hot function room. The woman who'd been interrupted looked crestfallen, somewhat confused.

Gary and Abby began clearing up, gathering the dropped leaflets, packing away the slide equipment. 'Good turnout,' Gary said.

'You could hire a bigger place,' Abby suggested. 'You'd still pack it.'

Noah was looking at the crowd shuffling out. He saw that the girl in black had remained in her seat. He smiled at her and she stood up. He went towards her.

'Excuse me, Mr Johnson, would you mind if I asked you something?'

'Of course not,' he said. 'Come down to the bar. We usually stay on for a few drinks.'

'Thank you.'

He put his arm behind her proprietarily to guide her to the door.

'Thanks, Noah!' Abby called behind him. 'We'll just finish off, shall we?'

He grinned back at her and she shook her head in mock disapproval. Abby was used to him and he knew how much he could get away with.

Downstairs, punters insisted on buying Noah drinks, but he bought one for the girl himself. 'I haven't seen you here before,' he said, leaning on the bar.

She pulled a face. Her features were delicate, mobile. 'No, I've only just moved here. It was great to discover this group, especially that it's run by you. I've got all your books.'

He laughed. 'Thanks.' In his mind, he could hear Abby's warning cry of: 'Noah! She's a fan, OK? For God's sake, be careful.'

The girl brushed strands of dark hair from her eyes. Her well-shaped lips were painted perfectly in a dark purple. Her dress was of black lace and velvet, down to the floor. She was virtually the same height he was. 'I'm Lara, by the way. Lara Hoskins.'

Noah handed her a vodka and tonic. When she took it from him, he saw that her lace cuffs came right down to her fingers. The nails were painted black. 'So, what did you want to ask me?' He was conscious of the eyes of his 'core group' upon him, their resentment at a newcomer monopolising him. Normally, this was the time for Noah to hold court.

'Well, I have to admit it was the subject of the talk tonight that most attracted me,' Lara said. She laughed nervously. 'Not that I wouldn't have come anyway, of course...'

'And?'

'Why don't you talk about the origins of the vampire myth?'

'I do. You heard it.'

She was silent for a moment. 'I think we both know there's more to it than that.'

'Essentially, it's European, although there are parallels in Mesopotamian and Judaic mythology.'

'But where do those myths come from?'

'There are recurrent themes in every mythology. People the world over have the same fears, the same desires. There's no reason to think the vampire myth comes from a single root source.'

'But in 'Nosferatu', you implied differently.'

'What are you getting at?' Noah said, grinning. 'Don't tell me you're a vampire searching for your roots!'

A vampire would certainly not colour up the way she did then. 'I have a serious interest in the subject,' she said. 'I'd hoped you'd take me seriously too.'

'Look,' he said. 'If you want the truth, I think people can become obsessed with certain myths, especially the vampire ones. It's dangerous.'

'How?' She looked hungry.

'Any obsession is dangerous. I don't like to encourage it.' He was thinking of Sarah. Her face was before his eyes, sad and despairing.

'What happened?' Lara asked in a low voice. It was as if she knew already.

He could tell her easily. She could be his confessor. 'I knew someone,' he began. Then a hand slapped his back.

'Hey!' It was Abby. 'Don't tell me you haven't got drinks in for us!' She smiled at Lara. 'He treats us like lackeys!'

'Sorry,' Noah said. He turned to attract the attention of the barman.

For the rest of the evening Abby refused to leave Noah's side. He knew why. Abby knew him too well. She was good company and gave no indication to Lara that she was suspicious of her, but Noah was well aware of his friend's feelings.

After last orders, when the group was breaking up, Noah said to Lara, 'There's an event next Sunday. We're going on a tour of local ancient sites, churches, springs and so on. Should be quite a convoy. Would you like to come?'

'Well...' Lara put her empty glass down on the bar. 'Might be difficult. I don't have transport.'

'I could pick you up,' said Noah.

'Great!' Lara opened her bag and rummaged in it. 'I'll give you my address. What time?'

'Oh, about mid-day.'

'It'll cost a tenner,' said Abby, somewhat darkly.

'Good value,' Lara said, taking the lid off a fountain pen.

Outside, in the car park, Abby started on Noah. 'What are you up to?' she demanded. 'I thought you'd decided to leave punters well alone.'

'What do you mean?' Noah countered, fiddling with his keys.

'I mean that you fancy her. It's obvious. But you've been down this road many times before. You know where it leads.'

'She's just coming to the event,' Noah said. 'What's wrong with that? Lots of other people are going and they're all punters as well.'

Abby folded her arms belligerently across her chest. 'I'm not stupid!'

'Give him a break, will you,' Gary snapped.

Abby was not to be deterred. 'She's a fan, Gary, and she's got her sights set. There's something a bit odd about her. I can just feel it.'

'He's a grown man,' Gary said in a tired voice. 'For Christ's sake, Ab, you sound like his bloody mother.'

'I'm the nearest he has to that,' Abby said, getting into the front passenger seat of Noah's car.

For the next few days, Noah couldn't stop thinking about Lara Hoskins. Abby was wrong to be so suspicious. Of course, he *had* met Sarah at a lecture, long before he'd begun the regular meetings, and perhaps this was why Abby was so scared for him. He'd dated lots of girls since, some of them plucked from the 'Enigmas of History' group, and he was the first to admit that none of them had worked out particularly well, but he was sure this was different. Lara was bright and had an enquiring mind. There were no warning signs. Her hands had been steady on her glass all evening. She'd been open and sociable.

By Sunday morning, he was buzzing with anticipation, and spent more time than usual on his appearance. Lara was probably about ten years younger than him, in her mid-twenties by the look of her, but that didn't matter. He looked young for his age. All his life, women had flocked to him.

When he drew up outside her house, she came through the front door before he'd even turned off the engine. She was dressed in black jeans and T-shirt, with a black hooded fleece tied around her waist, presumably in case it got cold later. Her long black hair was caught up in a severe pony tail but swished provocatively around her head and shoulders as she ran down the short drive to the road. She was as slim as a boy and looked athletic. Noah's heart turned over. She was gorgeous.

'Hi!' she said breathlessly as she virtually threw herself into the car. She smelled strongly of an oriental yet floral scent.

'Hi,' Noah echoed. 'I like a woman who's ready on time.'

Lara laughed. It was a bright, free sound, devoid of artifice. Of course, she'd been ready for hours.

When they arrived at the meeting point, Noah was pleased to see there was a good turnout – about seven packed cars. Abby was going round collecting money and distributing maps.

At each site they visited, Noah had the group sit down and meditate to see if they could pick up any information from the past, such as what the site might have been used for in ancient times. He never did this at the indoor meetings. This was his select group, with whom he was prepared to try more 'weird stuff', as some referred to it.

During the meditation, Lara saw a great deal of detailed and pertinent imagery.

'I think you're psychic,' Noah told her privately.

'Oh, I know *that*,' she said.

'You couldn't be more perfect,' Noah said.

Lara smiled. 'When can we continue our conversation?'

'Later. How about dinner?'

'Sounds great.'

Noah had to lose Abby and Gary for the evening, which was not easy. He didn't want Abby to know he was taking Lara out, sure that she would insist that she and Gary went with him. Fortunately, they'd brought their own car that day, so at the last site, Noah whisked Lara off quickly, virtually without saying goodbye to anybody. He knew he'd have to pay for it later and could anticipate Abby's terse message that would be waiting on his answerphone when he got home. But for the time being, he didn't give a damn. Both he and Lara were giggling as his car skidded away in a cloud of dust and gravel.

'Why do I get the feeling we're playing truant?' Lara asked.

'Sometimes, I want a bit of privacy, that's all,' Noah answered. 'The trouble with these events is that people want it to carry on till all hours. Sometimes, that's fine, but tonight...' He glanced at her and she smiled.

He took her to a Thai restaurant he'd never visited before, secure in the knowledge that none of the group would track him there. The food was rather lacklustre, but it didn't matter, because Lara was sitting opposite him and her smile seemed to enfold him in a hazy golden mist. They were both high on the sense of being secret conspirators. They were high on the potential of what might happen later.

Lara seemed content to listen to Noah talk about his new book, and it wasn't until the coffee arrived that she broached the subject she'd brought up after the meeting last Tuesday. 'Why did you react so badly to my question?'

'I don't think I did. Some things I just steer clear of.'

'So what's the story behind it?' She took a sip of coffee, smiled disarmingly. 'Or is it a secret?'

Noah leaned back in his chair. 'It's no secret. If you become part of the core group – and I'm sure you will – anyone would tell you about it. Basically, while I was writing 'Nosferatu', I was involved in more than the obvious method of research. The problem came from that.'

Lara put her head to one side. 'What do you mean?'

'You saw what we did today. People are keen on the psychic stuff. On one level, it's harmless, and most people never go beyond that. But on another, it isn't. Sitting outside an old church and trying to visualise images of the past can't hurt anyone, because it's dead and gone. It's nothing more than a psychic photograph. But other things, well, they're more alive, still around, so to speak.'

Lara laughed, lit a cigarette. 'Are you trying to tell me that you contacted a vampire psychically?'

Noah hesitated for a moment. Part of him didn't want to say more, but Lara's wide eyes were fixed upon him with a bright, intelligent gaze. He felt safe with her. 'I worked with a girl called Sarah. People don't realise it, but a lot of the information in my books comes from what I call 'inspired' sources, from psychics. Most of what I find out can't be used in a serious book, because it can't be checked out and verified as fact, but it gives me a feel for and understanding of the subject. Sarah was my assistant and also my partner. She was very psychic.'

'*Was*,' Lara said, her chin resting on her hands. Smoke curled around her in slow tendrils. 'That sounds ominous.'

'Let's just say that I was interested in the origin of the vampire myth, like you are. I'd investigated all the legends of blood-drinking demons, from medieval Europe, right back to Sumerian times. Somewhere along the way, the flavour of the subject changed.' He gestured with both hands. 'It's difficult to describe, but the idea of the vampire as unfortunate undead – perhaps a victim of their circumstances – mutated into the idea that the original vampires were very much alive and that their vampirism was by choice, a necessary facet of their belief system.'

Lara nodded enthusiastically. 'That's my thought also.'

'It all seemed very academic to us. We called them the vulture people, a shamanic tribe who indulged in blood drinking and sacrifice. Sarah picked up some interesting stuff that pointed us in the direction of certain ancient sites in Turkey. The imagery she saw could be verified. These places existed and there was archaeological evidence that a shamanic culture existed there, who had worshipped vultures. They believed that drinking blood gave them superhuman abilities. Whether that was true or not, we thought that other tribes would probably have regarded them as supernatural, as demons, even, because of their bloodthirsty habits. We believed that there was a diaspora and that factions of this tribe might have moved gradually into Europe, eventually giving rise to the vampire legend.

'Every evening, I'd have Sarah go into a kind of trance, guiding her further and further back into the past, seeking the true story. It seemed we were meant to discover all this, to make the link. The vulture people became more real for us: powerful shamans, who used the rites of blood to change their world. As time went on, Sarah started to get jumpy about it. She said she sensed little dark things that scuttled in the folds of these creatures' vulture wing robes, that they had begun to touch her. She wanted to stop, but I persuaded her otherwise. I thought we were getting close to something that would prove my theory incontrovertibly. We had to continue. But then, one night, Sarah brought something back with her.'

There was a silence, while Lara took a long, meditative draw on her cigarette. Then she said, 'And Sarah couldn't cope?'

Noah pressed the fingers of one hand briefly against his eyes. He could hear her screams even now. 'It was too overwhelming, too *alien*. We always did these sessions by the light of one candle, so we couldn't see much, but it was as if the night just surged into the room. We were surrounded by a presence, not evil exactly, but beyond good and evil. It was amoral, and we were *nothing* to it.

Even I could sense it, and I'm no great psychic. In moments, I realised how we'd been playing with something inconceivably huge and beyond us, something immeasurably powerful. We'd pulled at its skirts too insistently and now it had noticed us.'

'What happened?'

'Well, once Sarah started screaming, I just leapt up and put the lights on. If something really had been there, it disappeared.' He finished off the warm lager left in his glass and shook his head. 'Sarah was writhing on the floor. I didn't know what to do. The noises were hideous. In the end, I slapped her. It's what you're supposed to do, isn't it? And she kind of came out of it. But even if the thing had gone, it left a taint behind.'

'Did it kill her?' Lara asked bluntly.

Noah detected a faint note of scorn in her voice. 'No, no. Of course not. Sarah was an experienced psychic, but she was damaged by what she'd felt and seen. It changed her and there was nothing I could do about it. Nothing. She became paranoid, jealous and afraid. It destroyed us.'

'It wasn't your fault,' Lara said, reaching out to touch one of Noah's hands.

He laughed cynically. 'They all said that, but it's not true. I was so eager to discover the truth, I didn't think about the dangers. I just kept pushing and pushing. After we split up, Sarah lost her job. She just lost it, big time. The last I heard she'd admitted herself to hospital. She dropped all her old friends.'

'It wasn't your fault,' Lara insisted. 'Sarah just wasn't strong enough.'

'She was,' Noah said. '*It* was stronger than both of us.'

'I don't believe that.'

'You weren't there. Even as a writer, I don't have the words to describe to you how terrible that night was, how real the entity that came to us. This wasn't Christopher Lee in a silk cape, Lara. This wasn't a nice, safe little meditation like all those we did today. This was the most raw and primeval energy; it could snuff you out like that!' He snapped his fingers before her face, but she did not flinch.

'I want it,' she said.

He laughed shakily. 'What?'

'It's what I want. I need to know the truth. I'm not afraid.'

Noah raised his hands and shook his head emphatically. 'No. You don't know what you're asking for. The vampires you're so enamoured of, they're just fashion accessories, a romantic myth. You don't want the truth of it, believe me.'

'How dare you!' Lara snapped. 'You make me sound like some stupid little girl who's just into looking weird. I'm not enamoured by anything.' She thumped her chest with a closed fist. 'I've lived with this stuff all my life, felt it tugging at the corners of my mind, trying to make itself known to me. Their carrion smell has always been strong to my senses. When I read 'Nosferatu', I thought I'd found someone who would understand, who wouldn't think I was mad.' She put her hands against her head, scraped them through her sleek, confined hair, pulling strands of it free. 'If you really are so against it, why did you put all those coy clues in the book?'

Noah thought she now looked demented, with her hair beginning to fall over her face, a hectic flush along her cheekbones and those wild, wide eyes. But she was breathtakingly beautiful and, in those moments, he could believe she was as strong as she claimed to be. 'You'd better tell me what you mean by saying you've lived with it,' he said.

Lara ducked her head in assent and then summoned a waiter to order more drinks.

'No,' Noah said. 'I'm driving. Let's get the bill. We can

talk at my place.'

They were silent in the car on the drive home. Lara sat with her hands folded in her lap, staring through the windscreen. Noah wondered what he was doing. He guessed what would come. In was as inexorable as a tidal wave, and he could already see it massing on the horizon. He could stop it now, take her home.

They passed the turn off that would lead to her road. His hands tightened on the steering wheel. In ten minutes, he was parking the car outside his house.

Inside, Lara wandered around the living-room, touching lightly the ancient artefacts that clustered on every available surface. Sarah had collected most of them, but hadn't wanted to take them with her when she left. She hadn't taken anything, or exercised her rights to have half of the house. She'd just wanted out, to cast off any vestige of her life with Noah, desperate to live in the here and now, in safe mundaneity. But it was denied her. No one else should go to the place where Sarah was. No one.

Noah made coffee in the vast silent kitchen, where modern appliances gleamed on the spotless work surfaces. Sarah had had the kitchen installed, paid for it herself. The cutlery and crockery Noah had used for his lunch still lay in the sink, but generally he kept the house tidy out of respect for her, as if she was still around in an etheric kind of way, and might disapprove of clutter and mess. On the way back to the living room, he took a bottle of brandy and two huge globe glasses out of his liquor cupboard and placed them onto the tray next to the cafetiere and mugs.

Lara was curled up in the big leather armchair by the hearth and had lit the log effect gas fire. She had also managed to find the tiny ashtray that Noah kept reluctantly for guests. 'You're so lucky,' she said, as Noah came into the room. 'This place is great. Tons of books and things.

How many bedrooms has it got?'

'Five,' Noah answered.

'I'm in the wrong job!' Lara said, laughing. She seemed just like an ordinary girl now, gamine and flirtatious.

Noah set down the tray on the coffee table and set about pouring drinks. 'We got this place for a song,' he said, rather apologetically. 'It was a dump. Sarah did it up.' He looked around the room. 'It's worth a bit now, of course, but all I'd need is a couple of bad years and I'd have to sell it. Writing is not the millionaire's game it's made out to be, you know.'

'I'm surprised to hear you say that,' Lara said.

'Most people are. They think we all live like Jackie Collins.'

'No, I meant that you know how to change fate, how to make things happen. Why don't you use it for yourself, so that you don't get any of those "bad years"?'

'You've lost me,' Noah said, pushing a glass of brandy and a coffee across the table towards her. 'I'm a writer, a researcher, not a bloody magician!'

Lara smiled, turning in her fingers a lock of hair that hung beside her face. 'Oh, come on! What about the "weird stuff"?'

'If I knew how to meditate money into existence, I'd be rich. But I don't. I just use the "weird stuff" to delve into the past.'

'But the vulture people knew how to change their world. You said so.'

'Strangely enough, I have no compelling desire to drink blood and murder people.' He was enjoying their exchange, sure that the undercurrent was sexual.

Lara picked up the brandy globe. 'You've contacted them,' she said. 'How many people have done that? If you weren't scared shitless, you could use that energy for yourself.' Slowly, sensuously, she drained her glass.

Noah knelt back on his heels, his hands braced against his thighs. 'I think you are a dangerous young woman,' he said.

'You wouldn't have to kill anybody,' she said, holding out her glass for more brandy. 'I'm sure the smallest of blood sacrifices would do.'

Noah poured out a generous measure of the golden liquor. 'I'm not going back there, Lara. I got burned and sensibly pay attention to what hurts. You don't put your hand in the fire twice.'

'When people have no fear, they can walk across red hot coals,' Lara said. 'I'm scared of madmen with knives, and perverts hiding in alleys. I'm scared of people, because they're shit. But etheric entities don't frighten me. They don't have hands of flesh and blood. They can't fire a gun. The only way they can hurt you is through fear, your own mind. You must know that.'

Noah hesitated. He could feel the conviction pulsing from Lara's body. 'You are a witch,' he said and took a long drink of his brandy. It burned his throat, felt good.

Her eyes were hooded now. 'Take me there, Noah. I'm not afraid to go alone and I won't freak you out by having the screaming heeby jeebies. Just take me there.'

'Why?' he said.

'Because they want you to,' she said. 'I've heard their voices whispering in my dreams since I was a child. I've seen their shadows in the curtains of my bedroom every night. I've felt their carrion breath on my face in the dark. I'm one of them, Noah. Not in this life perhaps, but I *know* them. I want to go home.'

The silence in the room was absolute and the atmosphere had become still and watchful, as if vulture shamans were already gathering round them. It was as if Lara had conjured something into being through the passion of her words. There was no way he could disbelieve her. She looked remarkably sane, but driven. He could not speak.

'I'm not some sick cow who wants to drink blood,' Lara said in a conversational tone. 'I don't have a black bedroom or collect horror films. I don't want to be a vampire in the traditional sense. I just need to know what it is that has been trying to get through to me, that's all.' She smiled. 'God, I must sound mad. What else do I have to say to convince you I'm not?'

He stared at her, wrestling with himself, thinking of Sarah.

'I'm a bloody good psychic,' she said mischievously, cocking her head to the side. 'You can always use one of those, can't you?'

'Then why do you need me? If you're that good, do it yourself.'

'You have the map,' she said. 'You are the guide. It's that simple.' She adopted a mock serious tone. 'I'll look after you, Noah, don't worry. You'll be *perfectly* safe.'

His meditation room was at the back of the house on the second floor, overlooking fields and a small wood. As he'd always done with Sarah, he kept the curtains open and lit a single candle. His heart was beating fast, but not through fear. He was not sure exactly what he felt. As he prepared to light some loose incense, to help conjure the right atmosphere, Lara said, 'Have you got a pin?'

'What?'

'To prick our fingers. We should put our blood into the incense.'

'Lara...'

'*Noah...!* She was laughing at him.

It took some minutes to find a pin, by which time Lara had consumed another globe of brandy. Noah himself was beginning to feel the effects of the alcohol. Perhaps it was numbing his sense of apprehension. He let Lara prick his thumb and squeeze a bright droplet of blood from the wound, which she shook into the incense. Then she put his thumb into her warm mouth and sucked it. 'Scared?' she said.

'Horrified.'

She pricked her own thumb, but didn't offer to let him taste her blood. It was a slight disappointment.

Lara lay down on the rug before the cold hearth, while Noah sat crossed-legged beside her, and took her gently into a light trance. The words were soporific. His own eyelids began to droop. He led her back through time, made her watch the centuries fall away, until he told her to visualise herself standing at the mouth of a cave amid high, wind-sculpted crags. Beyond the threshold, all was dark.

'This is the Shanidar Cave,' he murmured. 'Home of the vulture people. Walk into it.'

He paused, listening to her light breathing. 'Tell me what you see,' he said.

'Darkness,' she replied. Her brow had creased into a frown. 'But I can smell...'

She would say blood, he thought.

'Flowers,' she said faintly. 'Everywhere, flowers. They've placed them over the bones. I see them. So many bones. There are wings...'

'Is anyone there with you?'

'Yes.' Her voice was like that of a child, young and tremulous.

'Do you want to leave?' Noah said. 'You can leave at any time.'

'No. He knows me. He wants to give me something.'

'What?'

'The talking bone...'

'What does he look like?'

Storm Constantine

Suddenly, Lara gasped, her eyes flew open and she sat bolt upright. Noah reached out to steady her. 'It's okay,' he said.

She turned her head slowly and when she spoke, her voice was deep and rasping. 'Keep me not from her, son of Lamech. Her laughter filled the mountains and bowed the heads of the wild beasts. Shame took her from me. Shame!'

Noah could smell carrion, the reek of her breath.

Abruptly, Lara sighed and fell back gracefully onto the floor.

'Lara,' Noah breathed, leaning over her. 'Lara. Are you all right?'

She laughed and wriggled her body on the rug. 'Oh *yes*.' Without opening her eyes, she reached up for him, dragged him down. When he kissed her, he tasted brandy, the flame of it.

'Thank you,' she murmured, between kisses. 'Thank you.'

Her skin was hot beneath his hand, exuding the last warmth of her perfume. He made love to her where she lay, wondering if she was fully in this world or not. It didn't matter. She was a dream come to life, a woman who could walk alone into the dark and come back laughing and smelling of flowers.

Afterwards, she lay naked beside him, smoking a cigarette. 'What the hell was there to be scared of?' she said. 'Have I brought anything back with me? No. And believe me, I willed it.'

Noah lay on his side, stroking her taut belly. 'What did it – he – look like?'

She grimaced. 'Pretty much how you'd think. At first, he was crouched down, wrapped in this immense cloak of black feathers. It looked like it had been made from the whole wings of a single vulture. I could just see the slits of his eyes peering over the top. He looked like a vulture himself... like a vampire! Although he was crouched down, I could tell he was a giant; magnificent, wise and savage.'

'That's pretty powerful imagery,' Noah said.

'Then he stood up and opened his cloak of wings. Beneath it, he was dressed in animal skins. His body was covered in some kind of paint, but it wasn't blood. There were patterns in it like primitive cave paintings. He did have bones in his hair and wore a necklace of bones. Bird bones, I think. You'll be pleased to know he had pointy teeth. All of them.'

'Filed down?'

'Probably.' She took a fierce draw off her cigarette. 'Oh, I don't know. Maybe I saw what I wanted to see, or was influenced by what you said earlier.'

'What about what he said through you?'

'I don't know. It was as if he'd known me before, obviously. He seemed to know you too, in a way. Lamech was the father of Noah in biblical myth, wasn't he?'

Noah nodded, uncomfortable with the idea that the entity might be aware of him.

'If the whole thing wasn't subjective,' Lara said, 'maybe I lived in his time once. Maybe we were lovers. I certainly felt really horny when I came out of it.'

'He doesn't sound very attractive!'

Lara stubbed out her cigarette and reached for Noah's crotch. 'Oh, but he was! Beautiful, in fact. His eyes were amazing, this deep piercing blue. Christ, I wanted him to possess me. Utterly. It was the archetypal thing.' She laughed huskily. 'I'd have been quite happy for him to sink his teeth into me.'

Noah leaned over and nipped the skin of her throat. 'Come on, let's go to bed. It's getting cold in here.'

They made love several more times. Noah felt

euphoric, hardly daring to believe a woman such as this could come into his life. She was full of humour and warmth, serious about her ability yet amusingly irreverent. She was uninhibited, open, mysterious and fey. A witch woman. A priestess.

'Where have you been all my life?' Noah said.

'I bet you say that to all the girls,' she replied, and they giggled like children at the stupid clichés for several minutes.

About four o'clock, Lara said she was tired and turned onto her side in the bed. Noah studied her for some time, drinking in each detail of her smooth contours, the spill of dark hair upon the pillow. He passed his hand in the air above her body, and she squirmed and made a sound of pleasure as if she felt him stroking her aura.

'Beauty,' he whispered. 'Love.' He lay down to sleep, closing his eyes with the after-image of her white flesh burning in his mind.

Waking came with a shock in the grey of predawn twilight.

He was aware at once of cold, and saw that the bed beside him was empty. A terrified pang of loss coursed through him, then he saw her clothes still draped on the pale wicker chair by the window and told himself she had gone to the bathroom, or else to get herself a drink.

He lay on his back and pulled the duvet over his chilled torso. A hiss in the corner of the room made him start.

'Lara?'

He sat up. Most of the room was still in shadow, but he thought he could make out a dark shape hunched in the corner near his clothes rail. 'Lara...'

He reached to turn on the bedside lamp, but the switch did not respond. The bulb must have gone.

Again, a hiss, low and sibilant.

Something moved in the shadows, sidled forward. He

saw the eyes clearly first: a deep piercing blue. She was naked and had covered herself in what looked like dark paint, which was possible because there were a few tins left in the garage. Her hair was wild and straw-like, filled with a sticky substance. Her tongue protruded unnaturally from her mouth, like that of the destroyer goddess, Kali. Her teeth could not possibly be pointed. There were no tools in his house she could have used to do that. She hissed and stamped with one foot.

'Lara.'

He got out of bed slowly. This was so different to the time before with Sarah. Lara wasn't screaming. She wasn't raving or weeping.

Her eyes followed him as he skirted the room.

He held out his hands in the universal gesture of peace. 'Lara, wake up. You're dreaming. It's not real. Lara.'

She made a threatening lunge towards him, growled and stamped both feet. He jumped back. It was unreal. He couldn't feel anything, because it was so unreal.

The night had come into the room. Not darkness, but the essence of night, the absence of light. The cold of the Earth before the first dawn rose.

'Lara...'

She came for him then, scuttling with crablike speed across the room. She grabbed him by the shoulders and he felt the sharp prick of her fingernails. She stank of rotten meat and there was a crust around her lips. She was bleeding from the mouth. Her teeth were filed away to ragged points.

What pain she must be in. What pain...

He fought back. This wasn't Lara. This was the darkness he had hidden from for so long. Perhaps it had always been here, lurking in the shadows of his house, in his memories.

She was so strong, like a tigress. She pushed him back onto the bed and straddled him. Her breasts looked heavier than they had been earlier, scored with the marks of her own fingernails. She uttered a shriek and lunged for his neck.

He should be afraid, shouldn't he? This *thing*, this monstrous abomination dredged from the primal soup, was feasting on him, tearing at his flesh, kneading his skin with its claws, sucking the life from him. It stank of Hell. Yet he was aroused by it. He wanted her and she let him do it, her body bucking in frenzy.

And he saw it then, the tunnel into history. The rivers of blood that carried the memories of humanity. *It is within all of us,* he thought. *We have tamed it and dressed it up in a silk suit. We have made it dead. We have contained it in books and films and lascivious dreams. We have contained it in nightmares. But ultimately, it is within us all the time. And it is alive, pulsing, warm and wet, stinking of musk and spoiled meat.*

Lara wasn't stronger than Sarah. The opposite was true. Because Sarah had rejected this. It was what she had seen and felt and had never spoken of. The search for Nosferatu didn't begin in the grave, but in the reptile brain, the primordial remnant of beast within every human mind. It was demonic. It was divine.

In the late morning, with bright sunshine coming into the kitchen, they were politely formal with each other. She said she had badly chipped a tooth falling over in the dark. They didn't talk about how she'd decorated her body. The mess in the kitchen had been cleaned up by the time he had come downstairs and she was freshly showered, smelling of his patchouli body wash. She joked about her loathing of dentists as she carefully drank hot coffee. He made toast, then apologised and offered something softer: scrambled eggs perhaps? She wasn't hungry, she said.

He rubbed his neck. 'Ah well...'

She had to go to work at two. Worked part-time in a local shop. Perhaps she could get an emergency dental appointment before she went in.

He had work to do too. The book would be late to his publishers otherwise. Nice day, though.

Yes, nice day.

At the door, she pecked his cheek in a brief kiss. 'We must do this again,' she said.

'Must we?' Many words hung unspoken between them.

She smiled. She looked very tired and there were purple rings beneath her eyes. 'I think I got what I wanted. Didn't you?'

'Lara...'

'You can call me. Or not,' she said. 'I don't need you now, Noah, but I kind of like you.'

He watched her run down the path to the road. She had rejected a lift. He leaned his forehead on the doorframe. Once your eyes are open, you can never close them. Sarah knew this.

He shouldn't see Lara again. He should attempt to forget all that had occurred. They'd been drunk. She'd broken one tooth, that's all. It had been less than he'd imagined. As if to remind him otherwise, his neck twinged painfully. He felt light-headed, sick, suddenly able to imagine the future, the long, slow, agonising stretch of it, the descent into realms he dared not think about.

He shouldn't see her again. But she was just his type, wasn't she? Just his type.

Remedy of the Bane

The immensity of the city unnerved him at first; the height of its walls that contained as much as excluded. Once within their protecting stones, he felt swallowed: the training barracks beyond the city, with their ranks of guards, manifold rules and restrictions, seemed less enfolding.

His name was Orlando Pepper. He was a young man, from a good family, and very handsome. He was also a new soldier, meticulously trained, and because of his father's connections, if not his own good conduct, had secured a position in the palace guard in the city of Kadrid. His leather gleamed, his dark eyes shone with optimism, his devotion to his King was keen and passionate. It was an honour to be assigned to the palace guard, even though his function would be essentially decorative, and bar unforeseen invasion - which was of course unlikely - lacking action of any kind.

In the royal barracks, Orlando Pepper was given a new uniform with tassels and an ornate sword. On active duty (standing on guard at various stations around the palace and its environs, or parading up and down for the citizens), he wore a splendid helm adorned with horsehair dyed to indigo. He was allotted a servant to see to his polishing, light his pipe, or whatever other duties he might require, and had recourse to the services of painstaking whores who lived in a house, which was painted red, but discretely positioned behind the royal barracks, and shielded by tall trees.

Orlando felt as if his circumstances could not be improved in any way. His demands from life were modest. He wrote letters to his mother in the country, describing the disturbing opulence and bulk of the city, Kadrid. He sent his sisters trinkets bought from the markets, amulets impressed with the image of the King, the silent Queen, or their daughters, Seramis, Thirza and Phedra. 'One day,' Orlando wrote to his mother, 'the Princess Seramis will be queen, and I hope to serve her, for she is a woman of great beauty and kindness.'

Seramis, gifted eldest daughter. Gentle, popular, white of skin, with a mane of glorious black hair, her eyes dark as shadows, but with a warmth within. In mid-winter, when the city stood stark against the wilderness of ice and famine beyond its walls, it was Seramis' habit to solicit donated goods from the rich of the city, which were sold at a colourful winter market, held in the outer garden of the palace. The professional classes would clamour to buy a ticket for the market, would spend their money generously, afterwards boasting of a walk upon the royal lawns, of nodding at sovereign figures at close quarters. All the proceeds from the market, distributed by Seramis' own white hand, via her sweeping signature upon papers of recommendation, went towards relieving the deficiencies of poor people's lives: a softening of winter's clutch. The people loved Seramis. Whenever she inspected the guard, she would smile softly and incline her head. They, of course, could make no response, but she left flowers for them; small, compact roses of aching scent, which they could pick up from the ground when they went off-duty, and take to place beneath their pillows. Everyone loved Seramis. One day, she would become a legendary queen.

Thirza, the youngest daughter was still a child; boisterous and plump. She rode her ponies in the palace gardens, with her own guard, for all of whom she had invented pet names. She gave them gifts, pictures she had drawn, or little models of clay and straw she had made, and chattered gaily to them as they rode, bringing light and happiness to their hearts. Thirza too was loved.

Then the middle daughter, Phedra. She was beautiful, as her mother was beautiful. Pale yellow hair like a bolt of unravelled silk, slim as a reed, with slanting cat's eyes, unusually dark for her colouring. But where Seramis had a sweetly-scented blossom beneath her tongue, and Thirza a bubbling, aromatic stream, Phedra had a blade. When she spoke, it was as if she spat poison. Her voice was low-pitched but deadly. She had no interest in the citizens, and indeed seemed impatient with them. When the royal family gathered for some public occasion or another, and Seramis touched brows with cool fingers and uttered soft words of hope and inspiration, and Thirza bounced around making people ache with delighted laughter, Phedra stood back, tapping her toes, yawning, turning away from earnest faces. The King would flick admonishing glances at her, the Queen might scowl very slightly in disappointment, and later, in the royal apartments, sharp words might be exchanged on the subject, but Phedra seemed immune to criticism. Many rumours were circulated in the city concerning other aspects of Phedra's behaviour, which were deemed unsuitable for a princess. She got through ladies-in-waiting faster than they could be dragooned into her service. It was said her venom occasionally manifested in more physical outbursts, and ladies had been sighted fleeing from Phedra's apartments, tears on their faces, the red flowers of sharp slaps upon their cheeks, or bruises upon their arms. It was also suggested that Princess Phedra had rather too eager a taste for wine, which only served to exacerbate her temper. Someone had fallen downstairs once, broken a bone. Perhaps an accident.

Orlando Pepper heard these rumours, but his superior officers advised all the soldiers to ignore such gossip, and warned them not to repeat anything that they might hear.

Orlando agreed fervently with this directive. The royal family, in his opinion, were above reproach. Therefore he closed his ears, and even offered a short rebuke, to the colleague who whispered to him about how the Princess Phedra had taken to spending most evenings away from the palace. Of course, there was nothing that unusual in this. Princess Seramis also made many excursions into the city at night, accompanied by her personal guard, her retinue of ladies, and her bevy of castrated pages. She would always return before midnight, pausing only to scatter flowers at the guards on duty before the main doors of the palace, after she had alighted from her carriage. Princess Phedra, however, rarely returned before dawn, and often she had managed to shake off the attentions of her personal guard, her ladies and pages. Orlando's informant claimed that one of the guards had reported that Phedra had come stumbling up the main driveway alone, only two nights previously, so drunk she could barely stand, with her boots in her hand and her fur wrap lost. She had even paused to utter lewd remarks at the guard, and, horror of horrors, though perhaps this was an exaggeration, had lifted her skirts to display her underwear. 'At least she was wearing some,' said the informant gleefully, 'otherwise the poor man's eyes might have had to be put out! Such a sight is not for commoners, after all!'

'I don't believe any of it,' said Orlando, loyally, with a stern glance at his colleague.

'It is absolutely true,' said the informant, who then shrugged. 'Who cares? The woman's an evil bitch. If you don't believe that little snippet, you certainly wouldn't believe other tales I could tell you, of incidents that have occurred involving members of the palace staff.'

'I don't want to hear them,' Orlando said, stiffly, and he didn't.

The time came for Orlando Pepper's first night on sentry

duty outside the palace. He was not stationed at the grand main portico with others, but at a lone sentinel's post behind the main building, where the lawns yawned downwards in moonlight. Unseen by human eyes, Orlando stood to attention, frowning sightlessly at the garden, but his senses alert for untoward noises that might advertise intrusion. Twice a night, once after midnight, once before dawn, two senior officers patrolled the gardens, ostensibly to inspect the sentries. As the Witch Star fell in the sky, exhausted after her hectic rise to midnight, Orlando heard the crunch of booted feet along the gravel pathways, the murmur of the officers conferring softly in the moonlight. Orlando's spine stiffened, his lower lip stuck out, his breast bone also. The officers flicked him a glance, said nothing, strolled on. Orlando heard laughter over some private joke or another. He felt they had not really seen him, nor appreciated his meticulous attention to his duties. Still, he was aware of his own devoutness, and that was enough.

The night poured on. The moon sank dreamily into the arms of the tallest trees.

How beautiful the gardens as the white ghost-light faded; the heavy drooping branches, the night-scented flowers hanging over the great stone vases, the fountains that glinted distantly between the tangled boughs of ancient trees. Peacocks called, as they dragged their folded tails through the wet grass; nervous foxes ran across the lawns. From some far window came a thread of music, quickly silenced. Orlando felt the dew fall upon his face, but he did not move. A moth alighted on his cheek. He did not move.

There was laughter in the distance; a female sound. She came into view around a corner of the palace. Gargoyles and the death-masks of martyred virgins looked down through stone eyes, their expressions weirdly censorious, even outraged. Her hair hung around her shoulders, darker because it was not entirely dry. She looked, in fact, drowned. She was not alone, but

97

accompanied by a whinnying young man who was having as much trouble controlling his feet as she. They stumbled, leaning on one another, giggles smothered by fingers and a pantomimed 'Sssh!' Then she saw Orlando.

Orlando had recognised the Princess Phedra immediately, even if her hair was in disarray. It was clear that she was drunk. He stood to attention sternly, his eyes focused straight ahead, down across the lawns. In some perverse fashion, he was glad to witness the truth of the rumours, because it meant he could seal his lips for her sake, for the sake of her father and royal honour.

Phedra eyed the soldier. For a moment, she stood swaying on the gravel. Then she walked towards him, or rather sashayed wantonly across the space between them. 'Soldier,' she said, 'look at me.' Her hands defined the lithe contours of her body in its sheathe of dark silk. She shook her hair and tendrils of it clung to her damp face.

Orlando knew he must make no response. As a sentry, he had no other choice.

Phedra leaned close. He could smell her breath, smoky and sweetly rotten with too much liquor. She was a blurred shadow before him, while the lawns stretched away in sharp focus. 'Soldier, I gave you an order! Look at me!'

Orlando's face began to burn. He was torn. Should he obey the princess and desert his duty? Did the royal word come before the offices of sentinel? No, he knew his obligation. He had learned that a sentry must not flinch, must remain still and unmoving, alert only for danger to the palace, no matter what other distractions arose.

Phedra laughed. She reached up with a hot, moist hand and stroked the soldier's cheek. 'You're just a boy,' she murmured. 'Come now, look at me. I demand it.' Then she stood on tiptoe and put her lips against his.

Orlando pulled away. 'Your Highness, I beg you!' he exclaimed.

'Oh!' said Phedra. 'Well, well, well! Am I not good

enough for you? Are the whores they give you more beautiful than me, is that it?'

'No,' Orlando said miserably. 'Forgive me, Your Highness.'

Phedra pulled a sour face. Her companion still stood swaying behind her, offering encouragement. 'Grab his balls, Pheddy!'

Phedra turned away. 'There are only one set of balls I'm grabbing tonight, Taristo! Come along!' She walked unsteadily away along the path, in the direction of a back entrance to the palace, and with a final sneer at Orlando, her companion followed her.

Orlando was left dazed, feeling as if he'd suffered some ghastly hallucination. Still, his lips were sealed, his eyes were blind. As his heart slowed down, and his brain denied the verity of what had happened, he gazed once more upon the spreading lawns, and the night continued.

At dawn, Orlando went off duty and returned to his room in the barracks to sleep. After a scant two hours' slumber, his door was thrown open and three men marched into the room, one of them a senior officer of the guard. 'Out of bed and on with your trousers,' he said.

Orlando was confused, but obeyed. He had been trained to obey. He asked was what wrong, but the men would not tell him. They dragged him out into a yard beyond the kitchens, where he was surprised to discover most of his colleagues were gathered. None of them, he noticed, looked very happy. All of them were in full uniform, while Orlando wore only his trousers.

The officer produced a paper and read from it. Orlando was so shocked by what he heard, he felt he might faint, and that would be a terrible thing for a soldier to do. Princess Phedra had reported him for neglecting his duties. He had spoken to her, she said. He had broken his silence.

Orlando tried to utter an anguished explanation, but

his words were ignored. He was told to be silent. His sentence, for his misdemeanour, was six strokes of the lash.

After he had knelt in the dust to suffer the blinding, scalding pain of his punishment, two of his friends helped him to his feet. 'You are not the first,' one of them said, but that was all.

It was a test, Orlando thought to himself. *A test, and I failed it. I deserved my punishment.*

He convinced himself he was grateful to the Princess for underlining his weaknesses. It would not happen a second time. The incident was not mentioned by his superiors again, and if any of his friends wanted to speak with him about it, Orlando discouraged them by keeping a distance.

Among themselves, but excluding Orlando, the palace guard talked about how the Princess Phedra had taken to sentry-baiting as a new sport. The example set by Orlando, the scapegoat, encouraged them all to ignore the Princess' advances. She was aware of this and tormented them cruelly. One said she had even stripped naked before him, then danced upon the lawn like a harlot. Perhaps some wild elaboration entered their tales.

Orlando was on night sentry duty again a couple of months later. If there was any trepidation in his breast as he exchanged with the soldier on duty before him, he kept it hidden even from himself. The summer was turning and the garden seemed too ripe, too heavy. Heat hung above the royal lawns, and the peacocks drowsed beneath the spreading cedars. Orlando was hot in his uniform, and sweat ran down beneath his helm. This time, he was stationed at a point where two other sentries were visible to his left and right. In that, he might have felt safer.

Still, she came. Alone, this time, and her hair pinned up. She did not seem quite so drunk, but called out a bright hello to the first soldier she passed. His apparent ignorance of her presence did not appear to offend her. Then, she saw Orlando.

'Why, it's you!' she cried, and then laughed.

It was Hell in its truest form for Orlando as he suffered the predations of the Princess Phedra. She goaded him, she kissed him, she pawed his face, fondled him through his clothes, whispered lewd promises. He felt as if his soul might break, as if he might die, as the heat pressed down like a fist from the pulsing dark sky and the woman writhed like a succubus around him. He found himself thinking that she was mad, and perhaps to be pitied, and this thought strengthened him. Then an unexpected stab of anger passed through him, hotter than the night. He wanted to push her away, spit on her, tell her she did not deserve the title Princess. She dishonoured the ancient noble house of her ancestors. But all this took place only in his mind.

Eventually, Princess Phedra tired of her sport. She sighed, and for a moment, leaned against the soldier, feeling for that moment like a sad, lost creature, without weight or substance. Then, she retreated. 'You must join my prissy sister's retinue of lovely catamites,' she said, 'for clearly you have no interest in women.' She called to the sentry standing rigidly to attention some yards away. 'Take him indoors and see to him, soldier. It's what he wants, I'll wager.' Then she hiccuped and walked away along the path, disappearing round the corner that led to the place where she had first accosted Orlando.

Silence descended, and the soldiers did not look at one another, not once throughout the long, hot reaches of the night.

In the dawn, when the change came, Orlando's confederates of the night came to offer support, a hand upon the shoulder, quiet words. Orlando shrugged them off. He felt numb yet invigorated. He went straight to his superior officer. The man listened in silence as Orlando related what had happened in the night.

'I would not have come to you and told you these things if there was any other way,' Orlando said with dignity, standing straight. 'But we cannot endure this treatment for much longer. It is inhuman.'

'Do you suppose I'm unaware of what happens around here?' drawled the officer.

Orlando shook his head. 'No sir.'

'And will you be the one to go to the King and report what is happening?'

Orlando stuttered. 'It is... it is not my place, sir.'

'No,' replied the officer, dryly. 'In fact, it is not anyone's place. The King would order you hanged for treason. The royal daughters are beyond reproach, you must know this. They are inviolate, and their ways are not to be questioned. That is an end to the matter.'

'But...' began Orlando.

'It is to be hoped Her Highness will presently tire of her little games,' interrupted the officer. 'The best way to deal with it is to ignore it.'

'Yes sir.'

'And if you mention this matter again to me, I will have you flogged.'

'Yes sir.'

'As far as you're concerned, it did not happen.'

'Yes sir.' But Orlando knew that it had. His faith in his work had been shaken. He no longer felt loyal, only abused.

As the leaves upon the cedars turned to the brazen hues of death in the palace garden, Orlando went home to the country on leave for a few days. Although the officers of the guard had not mentioned the antics of Princess Phedra to their men, it must have been discussed among themselves, because certain precautions had been introduced. The guard now changed more frequently, so that the sentries were not obliged to endure long hours of motionless torment after surviving the attentions of the Princess. She generally appeared in the garden between two or three hours before dawn. Naturally, this shift became unpopular among the guard. Certain soldiers, she clearly singled out for special attention. Orlando was one of them. He rarely found himself on sentry duty after one o'clock in the morning, or before dawn thereafter. Still, it was impossible to avoid Princess Phedra completely. Often, she would walk in the gardens in the afternoon, with her sister, Seramis, and her mother. If Orlando, or any of her other favourites, were on duty, she would stare at them beneath the brim of her sun-hat, and smile a wide, predatory smile. Once she sauntered past Orlando on her way into the house and said, 'Why, I believe you are avoiding me, soldier!' Then she laughed. 'But it won't be for ever.'

Orlando burned with an emotion so complex he could not name it. In some ways it was flavoured with a perverse desire, in others a lust to kill. Phedra was lovely in her wantonness. Her defiance of convention held its own wicked allure. She tempted, and should anyone succumb to that temptation, she betrayed. None of the guard entertained any doubts she would report them if one of them ever broke their silence before her again.

So, Orlando went home. His mother remarked that his letters had become infrequent over the past couple of months, and that he had lost weight. Was all well with him? Orlando, naturally, had not reported the happenings at the palace to his family. He muttered excuses; work was hard.

'You seemed so glad to be there,' his mother said, undeceived. 'It was a stroke of luck you got the post, and you trained so hard for it. Other boys at the barracks envied you, because palace duties are less onerous than others. Were you all so wrong?'

'We have heavy responsibilities,' Orlando answered. His lips were sealed now, not by loyalty to the crown, but because he knew to speak the truth could cost him his life. Privately, the situation obsessed him; he thought of it constantly. If he were Phedra's father, he would have her beaten naked before the whole guard, whether she was a princess or not. A whore who accosted guards on duty would be hanged or burned. Phedra was no better. And yet... He thought of her in the garden, the afternoon gilding the trees, her misty smile beneath her wide hat. He thought of her low laughter, the flash of her eyes, the intelligent humour there, and something sharp twisted inside him.

He visited his grandmother, his mother's mother, in her attic room in the house. Here a huge stove kept the draughts at bay and Granny's collection of arcana cluttered the walls and shelves. She was considered to be eccentric, but forgiven for her age, for she was very old. Her eyesight and her intuition, however, were still keen.

'So, who is this woman who's breaking your heart?' she demanded when Orlando sat down on the rug before her chair.

Orlando glanced up, stunned. 'No-one!' he declared, but a burn came to his cheeks.

Granny flapped a disbelieving hand. 'But it is written all over you, as if her claws had scratched it into your skin. Don't lie to me, Olly, my sweet. You never could lie to Granny.'

Orlando stared at the carpet. 'I know what you see in me, but it is not what you think,' he said. 'Neither can I explain it to you.'

'Try!' said the old woman.

Orlando shook his head. 'No,' he said. 'I don't need to *try*. I could tell you in simple words quite easily. It's just that I am honour bound to silence.' He looked up. 'My life depends on it.'

Granny frowned. 'And who will I tell? The wind, to spread it around the world? The birds to fly it here and there? Bah!' She laughed and threw up her hands. 'Who will I tell, little Olly, who might threaten your life?'

'I would prefer to keep silent,' Orlando answered. 'In truth, I would feel soiled speaking of it, for it is terrible.'

Granny narrowed her keen eyes. 'Hmm. You are just a boy. You need help. I won't have you thinning away in your grief. You must tell me something, just a little something, so I might help you.'

'I don't see how you possibly could.' His head came up and fire came into his voice. 'It is a torment that is clawing me to rags! It will not let me be! I cannot see how it will end! If I succumb, I am lost, but my strength is failing...' He shook his head. 'It is a great evil, a spirit of evil!'

Granny narrowed her eyes and made a suggestion. 'In the form of a woman?'

Orlando nodded silently. He felt his eyes grow hot, and suddenly he was weeping against his grandmother's knees. In his mind, he was thinking this was not the way a soldier should behave, certainly not a soldier of the palace guard, but he couldn't help it. Granny patted his head and hummed to herself. Orlando wondered whether he'd said too much. Granny was astute. Perhaps she'd guessed some of the meaning behind his words. Presently, she said, 'Dry your tears, my lovely boy, and help me up. We have to delve in my trunk.'

Granny's trunk was a vast thing, bound in iron, and off-limits to other members of the household. Orlando had never seen inside it, although, as a child, one of his sisters had told him their grandmother kept the mummified corpse of a former lover inside it. This, Orlando had believed, for Granny seemed capable of anything like that. She was, after all, eccentric. Now, he scorned such fancies, but he still felt breathless as she wrestled with the fastenings to the iron bands. But when the trunk was opened, it was only full of the usual items that comprised her 'collection': bottles, jars, powders, twigs, leaves, dried mice and lizards, glass marbles, broken clocks, hanks of hair, skeins of silk, bright necklaces of glittering jewels, folded gowns rusty with age, boxes of candles, and the like.

Granny delved. 'Ah, here we are!' she declared and kneeled upright on her creaking knees. She held an elegant little glass vase up to the light. It was brown and opaque, but something seemed to shine within its depths.

'What is it?' Orlando asked.

'Take it!' ordered Granny and thrust the vase into his hands. It felt warm to the skin. Presently Granny re-emerged from the depths of the trunk holding a companion vase of blue glass. This was clearly filled with liquid. 'One to remedy, one to bane!' declared the grandmother. 'Help me up now!'

Orlando did so.

'You must take these,' Granny said. 'In the brown vase is a powder. This you must dust upon your lips - or indeed any other place you deem suitable! But before you do this, you must dab three drops of the liquid from the blue vase on your tongue.'

'Why?' Orlando asked, nervously shaking the blue vase and looking at its contents.

'Because the powder will kill you unless you prepare yourself against its effects with the liquid.'

'A poison,' murmured Orlando.

'Oh, wake up a little, Olly!' snapped Granny. 'If you powder your lips with my bane-dust, whoever kisses you is dead within a week! If a she-devil harrows your shadow, then poison it.'

Orlando swiftly put down the vases on his grandmother's table. 'No,' he said, shaking his head vehemently. 'I can't do that! It's absolutely impossible.' His Granny had not guessed the truth of his dilemma, then.

'Nonsense,' admonished the old woman. 'The poison

is undetectable. I paid a great deal for it once. Its effects mimic a clench of the heart, and as I said, takes some days to work. No-one will suspect you! If the recipient should also have drunk a little wine, or some other liquor, before you apply the powder, all to the better.'

'That would not be difficult,' said Orlando, and with those words he realised he was seriously considering the idea.

He could tell no-one, of course, but then he had a reputation for being reclusive among his peers. Would anyone suspect? Surely not. Who would dare to poison a princess, however cruel and wayward she might be? His life was dedicated to protecting her and her family. At this thought, he felt a twinge of self-rebuke. How could he, a man of honour, even consider stooping to murder, for murder it would be? Phedra was a high-spirited girl, who did not, could not, comprehend the effects of her conduct on the sentries. You could not kill a person for silly behaviour. And yet, some part of him suspected Phedra knew all too well what she was doing, and that her antics were leading to a grisly climax. She was pushing the situation further all the time, pushing it as far as it would go. He felt that if nothing were done about it, someone would die because of her. No. Ridiculous.

He pondered the matter all the time he was with his family. His grandmother did not mention his visit to her again, and the subject of the vases was not raised. His mother continued to criticise his appearance and mien, and tried to improve his mood with large meals. His father simply regaled him with tales of his own days in the army, while his sisters languished for local young men, and did not really notice him.

Soon, his period of leave was over and it was time for him to return to the city. As he packed the night before leaving, the vases stood on the window-sill in his room. It was only as he was about to lock the case that his hands reached nervelessly to push them inside among his shirts.

By the time he reached Kadrid, and the reality of the city grew before him, in sight and in presence, Orlando had abandoned the thought of poisoning Princess Phedra. The idea seemed absurd now, dangerous even. He was a creature of order and correctness, and must not let his grandmother's eccentricities affect him. Then he heard the news.

While he'd been away, Phedra had reported one of the night sentries for indecent assault. 'He didn't have a chance,' said Orlando's informant. 'She was a she-demon. Others saw it, and were powerless. He cracked. Simple as that. It had to happen eventually.'

The King had ordered the assailant to be hanged. The execution had been carried out only two days before.

'They gave him the poppy at the end,' Orlando was told. 'They did that much for him. He died dreaming.'

Orlando went numb. That could have been him kicking air, dying cruelly in the arms of Lady Morphia and the rope. Perhaps only a timely holiday had saved him, passed the death card along to some other wretch.

He went to his room alone, and locked the door. For some moments, he sat upon his bed, his hands hanging limply between his knees, his mind empty. Eventually, he roused himself and set about unpacking his case. The shirts around the vases felt warm as if they'd been hung next to a stove. He stared at the glass vessels for a short while, before gently lifting them in turn, opening their stoppers and sniffing the contents. *Kiss this bane*, he thought. *Kiss it with your sly smile, and your clever, cruel laughter. Die as he died, kicking...*

The only time he could do this terrible thing would be at night, but he was never on duty at the crucial hour nowadays. Then, he remembered Phedra's words, that he would not be able to avoid her forever. She, he felt, was waiting to hunt him down, and weirdly, because of that, he trusted her. It also gave him an advantage she did not suspect. The prey, when it was driven into the open, would be stronger and fiercer than she imagined.

The following afternoon, Orlando was on sentinel duty in the gardens. Phedra spotted him the moment she walked across the upper lawn behind her mother, but waited for over an hour to launch an attack. She strolled along the gravel path, pausing at his station to gaze haughtily up at him; a beautiful, exquisite, evil thing. 'I have missed you these past days,' she said. Her voice was a sweet poison. 'Missed your pretty face. Where have you been? Off with your lover? Is he pretty too?'

For a fraction of second, Orlando flicked his glance towards hers. It was, he hoped, an enigmatic look, yet charged with intention, so brief, the Princess might believe she'd only imagined it. He knew it would not be enough for her to report him, but enough for something, *something.*

She raised her brows, but said nothing, and walked on.

Orlando was confident the challenge had been recognised. He was filled with an intense and dark excitement.

Dead of night, and the harvest moon hung low behind the barracks. Like a ghost she came along the corridor, where the long windows overlooked the parade yard. Like a ghost in her floating white linen, with her unbound harvest hair, her naiad's eyes. No-one saw her moving from moonbeam to shadow, no-one heard her silent feet. But she came, nonetheless. Hunting.

Orlando had not expected such an obvious move. When the door to his room opened and he awoke to behold a slim silhouette in the pale light at the threshold, he thought one of the whores had come to him. Then she came inside, shut the door and leaned against it, gripping the handle behind her. Corn-coloured hair spilled forward over her shoulders, her face was heavily shadowed, almost demonic. Orlando was not on duty now, nor bound to silence. At once, every nerve in his body became alert. He sensed her weapons, the lashing tongue, the mordant eyes, perhaps, at last, the claws. Yet he did not speak.

'Soldier,' said the Princess, conversationally. 'Here I am. What will you do?'

Orlando was half sitting up in the bed, crouching, like some cornered thing. He pulled himself upright. 'What would you have me do, Your Highness?'

Phedra narrowed her eyes at his tone, but chose not to comment on it. 'Whatever your imagination can come up with,' she answered.

'I don't think so,' said Orlando.

Phedra padded into the room, her robe - a night-gown - aswirl around her thighs. 'Oh, don't be dull! This is a private time. Are you afraid of me?'

'Your word is law in this place.'

'Then I could claim you raped me!'

'In my own bedchamber? What would you be doing here?'

Phedra narrowed her eyes again. 'I would say you'd crept into my room. Who would be believed?'

'We know the answer to that.'

'Then throw dice with the gods! Dally with me! Of course, I *might* have you punished severely! But, then, you'll not find out till dawn. That should lend spice to your performance!' She paused. 'If you refuse me, I shall be piqued, and in that mood, more likely to cause trouble for you, surely.' She sat down on the end of his bed, reached for his feet through the bedclothes. 'Anyway, you desire me. I know it.'

How could he deny it? She was there before him, a primeval thing, an essence of woman; dangerous and lovely, caressable and fanged. Here she was, in his room, and the door closed against the world. The vase of blue and the vase of brown resided warmly in his trunk beneath the window. She was here.

'You did a terrible thing,' he said.

'And what was that?' She combed her hair with her fingers, smiling sweetly.

'A man died.'

Phedra wrinkled her brow. 'And that was terrible? You don't know the meaning of the word. He broke the rules. An animal...' She grimaced, and then reasserted the smile. 'You know the rules, and I don't even know your name.'

'Neither will you,' retorted Orlando. 'Once a demon knows your name, it gives them power.'

Phedra laughed. 'I, a demon? How droll! How flattering!'

Could he poison such a senseless child? It seemed unthinkable. And yet the vases called to him. He could almost hear them clinking together amongst the linen in the trunk. In the silent, isolated world of night, anything was possible, any unspeakable act. Reality was a changed thing in the dark. Surely she must realise he was aware of what she could do to him, simply because he'd spoken to her? Didn't she consider he might be afraid, and capable of anything? But there were thoughts, too, of taking what she was offering. He could not deny it. How confident this female creature was not to realise all these things, and to come here alone. And yet, some part of him, remembering daylight, wanted her to explain her behaviour. He wanted to find the woman within the demon. If she existed, the vases could lie cold among the linen.

'Why do you do it?' he asked. 'Why torment the men? What have they ever done to you? Their lives are given to protecting yours.'

Phedra frowned. 'They are fools,' she said, 'As you are! What is there to protect me from? You stand there like little mannikins of tin, with you silly, stern expressions, fawning over the royalty.' She stood up, gestured abruptly.

'It's pathetic. What are we, but privileged by accident of birth? Why *should* you serve me?'

'The royal family serves the country,' Orlando said lamely. 'Another king might not be so benevolent to his people - or another queen. I think that's worth protecting.'

'Pah!' spat the princess. 'I despise you! I despise all of it! You are men as well as soldiers.'

'Then why do you report us to our officers?'

Phedra shrugged. 'It should show you how stupid the rules are...' She shook a rigid finger at Orlando. 'And don't think I'm not as constrained by them as you are! I would give anything for the life of your sister, or your mother, or even your whore. I have no life, but a predetermined pageant. I cannot love anyone but whom my parents decide. I cannot run free, anywhere. I cannot wander through the markets, I cannot choose my friends. In short, I am in prison, with a life-time's sentence! And Seramis... hah!' She pulled a sour face. 'I will always be second fiddle to her. I expect you think she's an angel. Yes, of course you do. But she's rigid, soldier, rigid as a pole, regarding conformity, and etiquette and all that muck! Life beneath her rule will be hell for me.' Phedra sighed and sat down again, her hands laced between her knees. 'She will marry me off to a proper sort of minor duke, who will no doubt be ugly and old and want hundreds of children. I shall be confined in another splendid palace, and my life will be over.'

'Then you might as well end it now,' said Orlando, and the space between them seemed to condense, become cold.

There was a silence - strained - and then Phedra laughed harshly. 'I sometimes think of it,' she said. 'Then I decide I don't want death, just a different life. Something I can never have.' She leaned towards him. 'Do you realise I have never spoken this way to anyone?' She paused. 'Well, at least not to anyone who's actually listened or who's not tried to shut me up with platitudes after the second word.'

'Why choose me?'

She turned away. 'I don't know... It must be your looks. I like pretty things.'

'And did the soldier who went to his death really attack you, or did he die because you just decided to despise him that night?'

Phedra clearly did not anticipate the question. She looked, momentarily, nonplussed. 'He would have killed me,' she said at last. 'You were not there, so you cannot judge me.'

'You drove him to it!'

'Humanity are worms!' declared the princess. 'I, as much as any other. It makes no difference when a life flame is quenched. There are always plenty more. None of us are precious, none of us! I don't care about it! Fate made me a princess, a woman screaming inside, and him a soldier. Fate made our paths cross, to his misfortune. That's all there is to it!'

'You have no regrets,' Orlando said, even now surprised. 'Not one.'

She shrugged. 'It is hard for me to feel anything at all. Why should I? Who feels for me, *my* torment? I am a prisoner wielding what little power I have. If that is cruel, then so be it. I will at least leave my mark upon the world. Don't you see how insane it all is? My parents must be aware of everything I do, yet they will not stop me. Why? Because princesses don't do wicked things. We are supposed to be sainted creatures. I am not a living creature to them, but a symbol. If I yawn at a parade, they punish me. Send a man to his death and eyes are turned away. Who are the real demons, soldier, answer me that?'

'You have gone too far,' replied Orlando. 'You have excuses for your behaviour, but they are not enough to comfort the kin of he who died.'

The Princess threw up her arms. 'Oh, stop talking

about it! Enter the real world with me, soldier. Why do you think I'm here? We could be a team, you and I. Explore the excesses of experience. Imagine it! I saw it in your eyes today. Break away from the herd, and join me. It is easier than you think.'

'Very well.' There, the offer had been made. It created a strange irony. Smiling briefly at the Princess, Orlando got up out of the bed and walked across the room. Speaking of the dead man had strengthened his resolve. He would not deliver himself into her clutches, but he was prepared to join her dark world. She had invited him in, hadn't she?

Phedra, encouraged by the smile, eyed his naked body. 'You are very beautiful,' she said. 'What are you doing?'

He did not answer, but knelt down before his trunk and opened the lid.

Phedra admired the curve of his back, the knobbed protuberances of his spine, his hair spread over his shoulders. It is likely she felt a quickening, then, sure that she had him.

The blue vase was warm in his hands. He did not shake as he prised out the stopper, nor as he swiftly placed three jewels of the bitter liquid within on his tongue with the dropper attached to the stopper. Phedra stood up and went over to him, attempting to peer over his shoulder in the faint light coming through the window.

'What are you doing, soldier?' Her voice was sharp.

He looked up at her. 'Where I come from, we have potent aids to pleasure,' he said smoothly. 'You do want pleasure from me, don't you?'

Phedra frowned slightly. 'What aids?'

'There is a special powder that my grandmother mixes.' He held up the brown vase. Phedra took it from his hand, wrenched out the stopper, and sniffed the contents.

'What about that other bottle, the one you just took something from?'

Orlando felt his face grow hot, but surely she couldn't

see that in the colourless light. 'A man's potion,' he answered smoothly. 'Of no use to you. Whereas the powder...' He gestured at her hands.

She was silent for a few moments, and Orlando's heart contracted. Did she realise what the stuff was? Then, she drew in her breath and smiled a brittle smile. 'Well, what do you do with it?'

'It sensitises the skin. Taste it and see.'

Could it be that easy? The moment hung in silence. Then Phedra narrowed her eyes. '*You* taste it!' she said and thrust the vase at him, adding sourly. 'Or is it just a *woman's* potion'?'

'No, not just that.' Orlando put a finger against the lip of the vase and tilted it. A soft rain of sparkling grains fell out, some of them onto the floor.

'It is pretty,' said Phedra. 'We must use it lavishly. If it acts as you say, we must use it all over our bodies.'

Orlando said nothing, but dusted his lips with the powder.

'Your lips are shining,' said Phedra. 'How strange it looks. Will I taste it, do you suppose?'

'Let me kiss you, and we'll find out.' He stood up.

Phedra was a pale shape before him, diminished by his shadow. She hesitated. He reached for her. For a moment, she resisted, then let him draw her body against his. They clung to each other for a moment, shuddering, then Orlando tried to lift her chin with his hands. He looked into her eyes, which were wide and dark, wondering. He couldn't do it. No. Yet if he didn't, now, what would be his fate? *Oh misery, woman, why have you done this?* he thought. *Why force me to this?* He closed his eyes and bent his head to hers.

But before he could kiss her, she pulled away, and said, 'No.'

Orlando felt as if his heart would burst. He was suddenly afraid, yet filled with a profound relief. 'No?' he said. 'Isn't this what you came here for?'

She gazed at him steadily. 'You know that it isn't.' She made to turn away.

Panicked, seeing himself dead by noon, Orlando grabbed her arm. 'You cannot leave,' he said, as calmly as he could manage. 'You might regret it.'

Phedra went limp in his hold. 'You are right,' she said. 'I might, but that is my decision. I order you, as your princess, to let me go. Don't be afraid. No harm will come to you, I promise.'

'Am I to believe that?' Orlando said bitterly. He tightened his grip.

'Yes.' Phedra looked him in the eye. 'You have my word.'

Orlando wasn't aware of releasing her, but soon she was gone, the door closed again. He furiously wiped the powder from his lips, which felt numb. *I am insane,* he thought. *Insane and weak. Now I will die for my weakness.*

Later, as he sat awake on his bed, waiting for dawn, for the summons he dreaded, he remembered her words *You know that it isn't.* Why would she say that? Could she have known what the powder was? Surely that was impossible. How could a royal princess know of country poisons, the shadowed province of wise-women and witches?

Orlando waited so long for his superior officers to charge into his room and carry him off to execution, he was almost late for breakfast. When the cock had crowed four times, and no-one had come, he dressed himself in a daze and went down to the mess. Colleagues hailed him cheerfully enough. His superior officer, passing, nodded curtly in greeting. Orlando was confused. He felt in a dreamlike state, but as the day progressed, and nothing untoward occurred, he dared to believe Princess Phedra had meant what she said.

Only one thing happened of any import. When he returned to his room later in the day, and by some instinct went to check the vases, they had disappeared from his trunk. In their place, was a single compact rose, of the kind Princess Seramis cast at the soldiers' feet.

Phedra never bothered the sentries again, although tales of her wild exploits continued to filter through as gossip among the men. As the years passed, Orlando rose up through the ranks, and was well thought of by his superiors. Sometimes, he thought of the night when Phedra had come to his room, but as time went on, the incident became hazy in his memory. He began to wonder whether he'd dreamed it all.

Almost ten years to the day Orlando had come to Kadrid, the King died and Princess Seramis was crowned. As had been predicted, she was a popular and gracious queen, who took for herself a handsome husband from the royal family of a neighbouring kingdom. Almost immediately, she began spawning children, who never seemed to drain her youth and stamina, who grew up as beautiful as she.

Thirza, still boisterous and cheerful, took to travelling, representing the royal family abroad.

And Phedra? Seramis found a husband for her, a local duke who was pleasant and avuncular, although not greatly favoured in appearance. At the wedding, he pawed his new wife continually, who stood rigidly beside him, sour in nuptial green, her hair pinned up with flowers.

Orlando, resplendent in his uniform, watched her through the day. At dusk, she was taken away in a carriage drawn by six white horses. She was rarely seen in the city again.

Orlando had kept the flower that had come to replace his vases of remedy and bane in the trunk. Often, he had wondered about it. The flower was Seramis' mark. Had she taken the poisons away? He thought he would never know.

Rumours came to Kadrid, passed down by the servants of the royal household. Princess Phedra was not happy in marriage. Orlando was not surprised. Events had transpired almost as she'd predicted. He thought of her in her magnificent prison, and wondered whether she still hungered for freedom. She was married only a year and a half when her husband died. A clench of the heart, they said. Orlando thought nothing of it. The man had been fat, given to excess in food and drink. His death was not unexpected, given his lifestyle.

Then, a package came for him. It came at dusk, delivered by a white-skinned page, a beauteous boy, perhaps one of Seramis' creatures, though maybe not. He waited while Orlando opened the package, even though Orlando had attempted to dismiss him with hard glances. Inside, wrapped in white linen was a single rose, compact of flesh and highly-fragranced. It lay in a dusting of sparkling powder. There was no letter with the package, no other sign. Orlando was at first puzzled, then rather outraged. Finally, he laughed.

'I am to say "is there any message"?' said the page.

Orlando looked at the boy. Still laughing, he said, 'Only that the offer is still there, without bane, without remedy.' He was older now, of high rank, and could say the words with authority, and without recrimination.

The page repeated the message, and left.

Orlando went into his apartment - several rooms were his, now that he was an officer. He sat on a window seat and, covering his fingers with the clean side of the linen wrapping, turned the rose in his hands, making it glow in the light of the rising moon. The fatal powder rained off it like tiny fires. He could so easily have touched the powder as he opened the package. He could have died. A dark and searing thrill awoke in his belly. Soon, she would send for him.

Sweet Bruising Skin

My critics have often said - though never to my face - that I overindulged my son Marquithi. Some people believe that because his poor father, the late king of Gordania, succumbed at a relatively young age to a morbid excitement of the brain, Marquithi is heir to an undesirable malfunction. Myself, I blame the premature thrusting of a responsible position on the boy for his witless behaviour. It is certainly no fault of mine, for I have always maintained the highest standards of discipline, from the nursery to the exalted chambers. Still, it is easy for others to criticise. I would have liked to see them cope as efficiently as I did in such a crucial situation. In any case, madam, the night is young, your mead flagon full, and it is a propitious time for a story. It is my privilege to tell you all.

Everyone in the palace was still wearing their mourning weeds and chewing the berries of grief-tarry-not when my late husband's chamberlain, Tartalan, came to me in my rooms of resiance. Although my husband had been removed from our marital quarters for some months prior to his demise, I had since been haunted by a restless ghost of sickness-stench and, for that reason, had ordered the place to be thoroughly fumigated by the perfume of burning stomach-mint and pine. Everyone moved like phantoms through the antiseptic fusc, and it did little to lift their spirits, which had understandably been rather low over the past obsequy-heavy days.

I myself felt less than joyous as, far from being allowed the limpid sighing and aimless preoccupation of a widow, I had been subject to callous antagonism from the King's Councillors. They were impatient to inaugurate some in-bred relative of my late husband's as regent until Marquithi reached his twentieth year, being blind to the fact that despite my son's relatively coltish nature, he was more than capable of administering the land. I, as Queen Mother, was incomparably qualified to assist him in his new duties. For some reason, the Council objected to this. I suspect that financial inducements originating from the estates of my late husband's kin were responsible for this dreary obstinacy. However, following the King's funeral, I had efficiently lambasted all the Council's feeble propositions.

Beneath the palace lies a vast catacomb - much of it flooded - which is stuffed with the rotting and mouldering remains of the state archives. A thousand years of judicial silliness reposes there in corruption; laws that refute previous laws, labyrinthine edicts, and a host of contradictory narratives of Gordanian history. I had directed my personal staff to scour the archives for material that might serve to promote my cause. Being a foreigner, I was unfamiliar with the early history of this barbarous country, so it was with great rejoicing I learned that four centuries previously, some other King had been crowned at the age of twelve; a boy who had gone on to survive a productive if rather unmemorable reign. As Marquithi was eighteen years old, the Council's argument was effectively boggled. However, I was aware they would continue to obstruct me until the moment Marquithi took the crown. The fact that they had sent the obsequious Tartalan to interview me personally oppressed me with foreboding, but I received him courteously, nevertheless.

'Your highness,' Tartalan said, pausing to indulge in a sequence of rather outlandish bowing and scraping, 'I regret there is a matter of some delicacy to be discussed.'

I had never known the man to be capable of delicacy in any situation before but, because I am groomed for my role, I murmured some suitable response and bade him be seated. I myself remained standing, in order to peer down at him. He is a cadaverous yet handsome man of some forty years, but frightened of women, I think. His eyes were running because of the fumigation, a circumstance which he lost no time in employing to lend an emotive tone to his discourse.

'Prince Marquithi,' he said, blinking rapidly.

I did not respond verbally, but raised an eyebrow. The chamberlain's goatish eyes slithered away from mine.

'The Council feel - *know* - that in order for the Prince to assume the crown, the population of our country would be more comfortable with - would prefer him to be married.'

I sighed. 'My dear Tartalan, as you know, this is a matter close to my own heart, one that I am currently intent on resolving. No-one wishes more than I to see my son happily wed, but neither will I permit him to be persuaded into an alliance with which he feels uncomfortable.'

'Of course, we all realise the industry you have applied to the subject,' Tartalan gushed, 'but, with regret, I must remind you that the waters of time trickle ever to drought... In short, your highness, we respectfully suggest that Prince Marquithi take advantage of the offer tendered by the House of Crooms, and accept the hand of Lady Selini.'

I had to sit down abruptly. It was common knowledge that the Lady Selini was subject to fits and constant drooling; her father had despaired of ever marrying her off. 'My lord chamberlain, I must *respectfully* disagree! As long as I live, I will not see my son wed to a woman with more than one chin! I beg you to remember his status. How would our people react to the proposition of such a homely queen?'

'With favour, I suggest! A homely queen is better than none!'

121

'I would agree, but you seem to have forgotten this realm already has a queen: myself. For this reason, I feel we can be lenient with Marquithi's desire to find a wife whom he finds both attractive and companionable.'

Tartalan rubbed his face in apparent agitation. 'We are rapidly coming to the conclusion such a woman cannot possibly exist!' he said. 'Do you realise how long Council agents have now been scouring every known land for ladies of adequate breeding? Four years! And every girl - all of them eminently suitable as prospective brides - has been summarily rejected by the prince! In fact, I will confess that standards have lately been compromised in the hope of unearthing, in some desolate spot, a woman Marquithi will consent to wed!'

I closed my eyes for a moment and took a heavy, shuddering breath. 'Can you not, for one moment, put yourself in my son's position? Not only has he recently lost his father, but is being harried by insensitive fools to deny himself the chance of love! I can assure you, Marquithi will not be persuaded into accepting the Crooms lump as a wife!'

'By his advisors and councillors maybe not,' Tartalan agreed, 'but I cannot imagine him countermanding the desires of his mother.'

'You already know my views on the subject.'

Tartalan nodded. 'Indeed. However, it might interest you to know that I myself have been combing the judicial archives. I have discovered an ancient edict relevant to this situation. As I hope you know, my loyalty lies unfalteringly with you and the Prince, your highness, which is why I feel compelled to warn you...'

'I am afraid you will have to remind me of the contents of this edict,' I said. Of course, I knew there was treachery afoot, but what Tartalan related still dismayed me profoundly.

'In short it states that should an unmarried heir to the

crown fail to wed within two months of the King's demise, the regency falls automatically to the next of kin, in this instance Lord Romolox of Brude.'

'What!' So they had managed to raise the head of that moronic oaf again.

Tartalan raised his hands. 'Believe me, it pains me to inform you of this edict, and I am sure no-one of this House would happily welcome the scion of Brude as King, but you know how some of the older councillors are sticklers for procedure. Therefore, I and my immediate colleagues beg your cooperation. After all, if memory serves me correctly, I recall there is little affection between your own family and Brude. I am not sure how effective the Council's influence would be should Romolox act imprudently and decide to remove you from the palace.'

My first instinct was to strike the sly beast with the nearest sharp object, but, because I am queen, I collected myself. Anger would have to be vented later. Some years previously a cousin of mine, having been sold into a marriage alliance with Brude, which she bitterly resented had, through deft application of toxins, reduced her husband's intelligence to something less than that enjoyed by a vegetable, and had also rendered all children of the family under the age of ten incurably insane, before escaping the Brudish demesne with her maid. Consequently, I had scant appetite to be under the control of that family. 'Your words do indeed stimulate my thoughts,' I said. 'Perhaps you would be so kind as to deliver a message to my son, requesting his presence here immediately.'

The Chamberlain stood up and bowed. 'I felt sure we could rely on you,' he said.

Marquithi had always been a compliant and sensitive child: I had made sure of it. It is imprudent to let careless Fate have too strong a hand in the fortune of kings, so I had always ensured my son's temperament remained equable, through practical employment of certain philtres. Likewise, I had made sure my late husband had lived a serene and tranquillised life. Therefore, I was discomforted by the tantrum Marquithi manifested once I informed him he should marry the daughter of Crooms.

'My darling, it is quite bad for the complexion to work yourself into such a rage,' I said. 'Remember that being royal precludes displays of a brutish nature.'

'I don't want to marry such a sow! I won't marry her!' Marquithi declared, gesturing widely with stiff, angry arms. His slim, delicate frame was visibly shaking, his dark hair tumbling into disarray. I had to turn away. The sight of so much indiscretion alarmed me. Naturally, I shrank from explaining our predicament in too much detail. I had no wish to frighten him, his being such a dainty constitution.

'I fear I must order you to concede, my lamb,' I said.

'No!'

'Oh, do you want to hurt your mamma?' I appealed to him with open arms.

'I won't do it,' he said, stepping back from me. 'If I can be pushed around in this manner now, it hardly bodes well for my future as king. I know my youth is against me, Mother, and that many of this court would prefer to see another in my place. Therefore, I must remain steadfast over this matter. It is the only way to gain respect.'

Poor deluded boy! Still, it was hardly gratifying for me to discover he had acquired a will from somewhere.

One thing I had learned from the women of my own family in far Loolania; as a lady of standing and therefore vulnerability to the spite and jealousy of other, less important mortals, I should never be without recourse to a competent alchemist. In comparison to their Loolanian contemporaries, the alchemists of Gordania were grievously incompetent, and for most of my married life I had been forced to rely upon my own resources. However, the previous year my sister had sent me a recently graduated student from the Alchemical Academy in Panossos as a birthday gift. Anguin was a serpentine young man, with yellow eyes and an eerie fondness for bones, but who was nevertheless canny and discreet. I kept him in a suite of rooms, high above my own, and now consulted him regularly on matters of dire significance.

His apartment was approached by a narrow dusty stair, beyond three locked doors. Only Anguin and myself possessed keys to these doors. Coming up the last of the stairs, I emerged through the floor of Anguin's workroom. It was an arcane place, the ceiling strung with bizarre devices, some of which were astronomical, some decidedly necromantic. His worktables were littered with parchments, books, alembics, athames, roots, herbs, and brass dishes in which he burned his substances. The air reeked of the various fluids and powders he employed in his art; musty, half pleasant, half sour. An enormous open chest stood against the far wall, filled with a muddle of broken bones, all of which I knew to be human despite Anguin's claims to the contrary.

Anguin was so engrossed in his work, he did not hear me approach. The sound of my feet was quite drowned out by the angry hissing of a sparking substance he was holding in a small metal tray. I watched him for a moment or two; his faded yellow hair, tied at the neck, the sweet knobs of vertebrae pressing out against the tawny skin above the collar of his shirt. He had an iridescent pile of dismembered damsel-flies beside him, which he was dropping one by one into the blue sparks.

'Anguin, if I may disturb you?'

He turned and looked at me slyly over his shoulder. I had to repress a shudder. Sometimes he can look so menacing.

'Your wondrousness, I am ever yours to disturb,' he

said. There is a slight hiss to Anguin's voice, which is not a lisp exactly, but something distinctly more reptilian. I had never had occasion to inspect his tongue minutely, but it would not have surprised me to find it forked.

I sat down upon the only chair that was not occupied by boxes, manuscripts, fusty animal pelts, or piles of thin, jointed metallic arms. 'Anguin, I have a problem which I feel you may be disposed to solve for me. I need a wife for my son. Speedily.'

Anguin was familiar with this subject, since I had previously consulted him about it. Knowing that all the simpering females of aristocratic birth my late husband's sycophants had so far presented to Marquithi were all unsuitable to share his bed, never mind his throne, I had commissioned Anguin to concoct an elixir that would make all females unattractive to Marquithi's eyes. The only good wife was a wife chosen by a loving mother. Preferably, she should be a girl whose like mind would make her a reliable accomplice to the mother, well versed in the arcana natural to womankind. If such a female proved unobtainable, a cowering mouse should be procured; a girl who could be confidently ignored. Intelligence would only be tolerated in examples of the former. Under no circumstances should a son's wife be in love with him, because she might become prone to acting unwisely. Husbands, like horses or dogs, should be admired for their conformation and, when they have it, their kind nature. As with domestic beasts, they should be cared for with consideration and gentleness, but one should not become too attached to them because then they are likely to take advantage of the situation. Also, you never know when they might die unexpectedly.

'Do I detect a change of circumstances?' Anguin enquired.

I nodded. 'Quite so. I want a girl who is beautiful but mindless, someone of royal birth, but without a royal family behind her. She must be controllable, yet charmingly capricious. She must be an accomplished courtezan, yet a virgin. She must be at our threshold within a few days.'

Anguin stood up and cupped his chin, tapping his lips with long fingers. 'Hmm, this is a challenging request.'

'But not, I trust, beyond your capabilities.'

He grinned, displaying his small, white teeth. 'Certainly not. In fact, one of my final year projects at the Academy involved a similar difficulty, which I solved with honours.'

'I am relieved to hear it. Will you require any special equipment for this task?'

He pondered for a moment. 'There are one or two items which might prove difficult to procure in this region. That is, at their proper value.'

'I shall consult my personal treasurer immediately,' I said. 'Come to me when you have finalised your costings.'

'Also, I shall require the prince's foreskin.'

It was lucky that my late husband had allowed me observe the custom of my native kingdom whereby all male infants are circumcised at birth. I had, of course, kept this scrap of skin as both a memento and insurance against any future filial intractability. It seemed my prudence had been justified.

I glided through the next few days with calm detachment, confident of my alchemist's art. I had discontinued the use of Anguin's elixir in Marquithi's food and had satisfied the subsequent gust of libido with a stream of catamites who were members of my personal staff and thus to be trusted. Women, I kept far from my son's apartment, in order to prime him for his bride-to-be.

One afternoon, the late summer balm turned sour in the sky, and heavy purple clouds bustled in from the west. From my window, I could see that the greenery in the garden glowed unnaturally lush beneath the murk, and the air was full of powerful scents; the loamy earth, voluptuous late flowers, recently-cut hay beyond the palace grounds, putrid offal from the slaughter-houses. I had a slight headache. By dinner-time, the clouds had burst, and a wind had arisen to drive the rain into hard spears that came down at a slant over the gardens. The temperature dropped so dramatically, everyone was forced to don extra clothing in order to withstand the chill in the dining-hall. Rain came down the great chimneys to drip upon the blackened tiles of the hearths. Dogs moaned and licked their paws beneath the tables. Marquithi, dressed in midnight blue, seemed feverish, his pale skin flushed along his cheekbones, his black hair strangely lank about his shoulders.

Thunder growled like the nightling shades that exist at the boundary between our world and the next. Crooked tridents of sulphurous lightning flashed beyond the windows, while nervous servants hurried wraith-like from the kitchens to load the table with rich viands and wine. The storm was uncommonly violent, indeed almost predatory in tone. Windows rattled, candelabra shook, the air was oppressively damp. One or two of the less spirited courtiers were beginning to look greatly alarmed. I myself felt only a momentous thrill building up within me, similar to how I'd felt when the obsequy-horn had bleatingly announced my husband's death. Fate was turning a page in her Book of Delusions. I wondered whether my loyal Anguin, having slipped out through the lichened slates, was presently poised atop the palace roof, conjuring up these fierce elements of storm and light. Elaborating upon this fantasy, I imagined him naked, his wet body lissom as a river snake's, his genitals swinging heavy and fat between his thighs.

'Something amuses you, your highness?'

I was dragged from my pleasant reverie by Tartalan's stiff, nasal voice beside me. 'A private matter,' I said, dabbing my mouth with a napkin. On my other side, Marquithi stared at me narrowly but did not speak. I forgave him his continuing unfriendliness. Soon, all the knots in our relationship would be cut away.

'Your highness,' Tartalan murmured, bending towards me. 'If I might remind you of our conversation the other day...'

I raised my left hand a fraction and glanced significantly at Marquithi. 'Being attended to,' I whispered.

Tartalan opened his mouth to deliver further indiscretions but, as that precise moment, the thunder suddenly abated. Diners blinked at each other, dazed by the abrupt stillness as much as they had been deafened by the former noise. For a few long seconds, nobody so much as murmured. The only sound was that of the rain patting softly at the windows, like little fingers seeking ingress. Then, the great doors to the hall swung open and a solitary liveried steward, puny in the immensity of the storm's departure, minced hurriedly towards the high table. He went directly to Tartalan, and whispered in his ear. Everyone had stopped eating, and all eyes were directed towards the high table. It was as if they had all experienced some dire precognition and were waiting for terrible news.

'Well?' I said to Tartalan. 'Has some catastrophe occurred to the fabric of the palace? Has someone been killed?' My voice, which was usually low and musical, sounded loud and harsh in my ears.

The Chamberlain looked thoughtful and spoke with some reluctance. 'No, your highness. It seems a stranger has presented themselves at the gates, most insistent upon speaking to the Prince.'

'Oh? Who?'

'A *girl*, your highness. She says she is a princess.'

At a brief inspection of the girl, it was hard to imagine why any of the palace staff had entertained her claim, and had not propelled her instantly back into the storm. From her apparel, our little visitor hardly resembled a princess. However, a longer glance at her face and hands revealed she was no gypsy scrap. I had expected some ploy of Anguin's to come into manifestation, so therefore I was less perplexed than the Chamberlain by the news of this female's arrival. Indeed Tartalan was clearly astonished when I ordered the steward to accommodate the girl in one of the staff sitting-rooms until I could interview her myself.

'Is this wise, your highness?' he inquired. 'Doubtless we are host only to some wandering mooncalf.'

I shook my head. 'Instinct, my dear Chamberlain, speaks to me most emphatically at this time. I feel we should indulge the girl's request.'

He shrugged. 'As you wish.'

Both Tartalan and Marquithi accompanied me to the staff quarters to interview the girl. Under normal circumstances, I'd have never set foot in the servants' domain, simply because many unprepossessing sights could greet the unwary there. I had little interest in the procedures that ensured a comfortable life in the higher apartments of the palace, because most of them were grossly repulsive. The servants' quarters were a hot dismal warren of steaming laundry, greasy smoke, and hump-backed scullions, and there seemed too many rooms dedicated to the disembowelling of carcases for my liking. Marquithi berated me during our passage, declaring it was beneath our royal dignity even to view this unprecedented guest, never mind speak to her. I had been encouraged by the way he'd demanded to accompany me though. It was not a response I would have expected from him, and I suspected it might have been involuntary.

'Have a little faith, my lamb,' I said. In truth, I was beginning to realise there were few lamblike qualities left in my son. Once this matter was resolved, I would have to direct Anguin to concoct a more potent philtre to restore Marquithi's docility.

The girl had been accommodated in a small room

dedicated to the maintenance of royal footwear, and was seated in a high-backed chair, beside an open fire. She was surrounded by a tumble of boots and shoes, through which the steward made a path for us. The slim little storm-maiden, who did not look up as we entered the room, held my entire concentration. A sodden cloak hung along the back of her chair, and her hair drooped down over her face and chest in damp tendrils. Her gown was torn and muddied, her shoes split along the seams. As I approached her, I noticed that, despite her frail body and sodden condition, she did not shiver. Her body was surrounded by a fragrance of crushed, wet flowers, quite at odds with the odours of starch and cooking meat that predominated in this area.

'What is your name, girl?'

She looked up at me then. Her face was utterly white and her eyes seemed overly large within it. She had the most astounding eyes. I was reminded of black poppies. She squinted at me only slightly before she spoke. 'I am Papavera,' she said. 'I am a princess.'

'A princess of where?' demanded Tartalan, sidling up beside me. His voice was hardly friendly.

The girl screwed up her face. 'I cannot remember,' she said. 'I am lost.'

Tartalan glanced at me with a sneer, which I divined I was supposed to return. 'Poor child,' I said, pulling a sympathetic frown.

'If your memory has gone, it is astounding you can still remember your status,' Tartalan said in a sarcastic tone.

The girl shrugged. 'It is the truth. I am royal.'

'Why have you come here?' the Chamberlain snapped.

Again, a shrug. 'The lights in the high towers drew me.'

Tartalan sighed and leaned towards me. 'Well, what are we to do?' he whispered. 'I am loath to accept her claim simply because, having recently become familiar with all royal ladies of nearby kingdoms, I have not come across this girl before.'

'I am from a far place,' the girl murmured. She must have had extraordinarily acute hearing.

Tartalan visible jumped and then fussily collected himself. 'Tch! I say we send her to the local nunnery in the morning. They can care for her there, until the time some person comes to claim her as kin.'

I was about to remonstrate with him when my son, with unprecedented conviction, spoke before me. 'No, my Lord Chamberlain. Any person can see this poor girl is of noble birth. Look at her skin, listen to her voice! Are these the attributes of a drab? No doubt she has become estranged from travelling companions. Perhaps suffered some accident, which has addled her mind.'

I was astonished by his interest, even though I should have perhaps anticipated it.

He turned to me. 'Mother, I recommend we have our guest conveyed to the visitors' suites, where she may be attended in proper surroundings. Perhaps you would lend a couple of your women for the task?'

I raised my hands. 'Well... if you wish, my son.'

Spots of colour bloomed along his cheekbones. He dropped his eyes. 'I do. It is only polite.'

Of course.

It will come as little surprise that Marquithi, beloved innocent, found himself the victim of an irresistible attraction to the so-called Princess Papavera. She, like a dark velvet bloom with an intoxicating scent, pervaded the palace with her alluring presence. She had a slow, halting gait, as if she had recently awoken from a daze. Her skin glowed pellucidly along the darker passages of the upper suites, where she roamed continually, one white hand held out from her side, touching the dusty drapes, the dimmed brass candelabra, the goblin carvings on the walls.

Marquithi also took to haunting these upper apartments, dancing attendance on eager feet to the fey princess. I myself interviewed her several times during the following two days, subjecting her to a gentle yet relentless inquisition. She slumped blinking in a chair as I spoke, responding slowly but without displeasure. She could remember nothing about her origins; the only memories being those of waking on drenched ground into the fury of the storm, with the slim yet consistent conviction that she was a princess. Her name, she confessed, she only remembered at the time it was asked of her. Papavera came into her head, so she naturally assumed this must be the correct epithet. She was a lovely misty creature, languid and graceful in all her movements. Her voice was soft as a dove's and her face ever reposed in a timorous smile. To my pleasure, she also appeared quite stupid.

Anguin proved annoyingly obtuse when I went to congratulate him on his success. All my questions concerning the origin of Papavera were met with grinning silence. 'I have no proof that the lady you describe is actually attributable to my influence,' he said eventually. 'It might be coincidence.'

'Then perhaps we shall end up with two winsome beauties in the palace!' I said. 'And my dear Marquithi will have a choice! Really, Anguin, I can't understand why you don't want to view the girl yourself. I am not averse to bringing her here. She is vague and largely witless.'

Anguin shook his head. 'No,' he said. 'It is not necessary. If the Prince is enamoured of her, it hardly matters who or what she is, does it?'

I shrugged. Perhaps he was right, but I felt uneasy.

The creatures of the court were naturally most inquisitive about the Princess, and I had to fend them off from plaguing her with their boisterous company, claiming she was feeling ill and weak, and needed some time in which to recompose herself. Their pique at this response was further augmented by a reckless declaration Marquithi made at dinner one evening. We had finished our repast and were drinking port while supervising a few floggings of recalcitrant serfs between the tables. Marquithi looked flushed and excited. The last groaning carcase had barely been removed from the hall, when he suddenly stood up and commanded silence.

'Friends, lords and ladies of the court, I have great news!' he said, beaming. I noticed he was rather unsteady on his feet. 'I have found the woman I wish to marry!'

The Councillors all rose to their feet like a flock of aged birds and hooted in unison: 'Who?'

Marquithi's face was positively glowing. 'The Princess Papavera, of course!'

Well, I was hardly surprised, although a little concerned he had not voiced his conviction to me first.

A low roar of grumbling voices greeted this announcement, as the Councillors predictably objected to Marquithi's choice.

'It's infatuation!'

'Folly!'

'Totally inappropriate!'

'Grossly improper!'

No-one knew who Papavera was, or even *what* she was. She could be an actress, a mad-woman, a bastard daughter. She had no pedigree, and no dowry. She might be diseased, barren, or host to a hereditary peculiarity. I myself remained silent while the storm of voices raged above my head. In fact, I poured myself some more port and sat back to enjoy the proceedings. Still, I foresaw difficult days of persuasion ahead.

Tartalan caught my eye and shook his head, sighing. At that moment, we were in total accord.

As soon as Marquithi and I had retired for the evening, the

Councillors scurried to Tartalan to persevere in their complaints. However, having anticipated this reaction, I had already sent the most intelligent of my servants - a dashingly attractive northern girl named Vienquil - down to the archives. Having supervision over a team of six others, she was instructed to scour the ancient documents for anything I could employ as artillery in my battle with the Council. 'Bring me anything, however bizarre, that I might utilise in this instance,' I had told her. 'And, on no account contemplate returning from the catacombs until you have found something.'

Despite the efficiency of my swift-fingered operatives, and the familiarity they had recently acquired with the archives, it still took them nearly two days to uncover something of use. This, my servant Vienquil brought to my apartment the next afternoon.

The poor creature looked exhausted; her clothes, her skin, even her lustrous, black hair fouled with reeking dust and cobwebs. In her hands, she held the friable remains of an ancient parchment, which she had soaked in oil in order to prevent its utter dissolution. 'The search was hard, your highness,' she said. 'And I'm afraid this was all we could find.' She did not sound at all confident I would be able to use it.

I took the parchment from her and carefully laid it out on a table. Together, we scanned the faded lines of text. 'Hmm, I am having trouble convincing myself the Council will accept this,' I said.

Vienquil shrugged. 'We found nothing else down there remotely connected with your dilemma, your highness.'

I sighed, and patted her arm. 'Well, a law is a law, however ancient or peculiar. Thank you. You have done well under extenuating circumstances. Take this coin.'

I carried the parchment to Anguin right away.

It took him some time to read the document and I was

forced to wait impatiently as he did so. He grinned to himself as he perused the lines and then laughed openly when he had finished reading.

'I agree the content is amusing,' I said, 'but would value your opinion as to how I might successfully invoke this law.'

Anguin narrowed his eyes at me. 'Didn't I promise you a princess?' he said. 'Simply follow the instructions in this document.'

'It is preposterous!' I cried, and gestured at the parchment. 'No-one could be affected by that. Flesh bruised by a handful of dried peas beneath a score of mattresses? If I attempt this procedure, I will be laughed out of Gordania!'

'You must trust me, your highness.'

'Trust you?' I paused to consider. 'Well... obviously you will have to medicate the girl in some way.'

'Oh, that won't be necessary!' he said.

I blinked at him in disbelief, on the verge of losing my temper. 'I suspect you are being rather too flippant, Anguin! If this plan fails, which I am sure it is doomed to do, I will appear foolish, if not deranged, and Marquithi will lose his opportunity to marry.'

'Have I failed you before?' Anguin asked. 'Have a little faith in me, your highness.' He handed me the parchment. 'Prepare the bed as instructed.'

Tartalan shook his head gloomily when I showed him the parchment. 'A desperate measure,' he said, 'destined only for failure.'

I patted his arm. 'I think we shall both be surprised.' It was strange how the Chamberlain and I had become allies, albeit reluctantly. He had no love of Brude either and felt, as I did, that only by Marquithi becoming king could the comfortable stability of the kingdom be ensured.

'I wonder what circumstances inspired this paper,' he said. 'Are there no historical records giving explanation?'

I shook my head. 'Regrettably, no.'

He frowned. 'But it is so bizarre! Can a royal integument really be so sensitive?'

'We shall have to hope so.'

'The Council will contest this action.'

'Of course they will... until my experiment proves successful.'

Tartalan sighed heavily. 'I wish I had your confidence.'

I smiled at him in encouragement, even though I still harboured the greatest of qualms myself. 'Don't fret, Lord Tartalan. Convene the Council and have the scullions search the store-rooms for the hardest dried peas they can find.'

The bed in question was an enormous construction, whose canopy brushed the ceiling of our highest chamber. Onto this framework, I ordered a score of mattresses to be piled. The stuffing for these was varied; some were to be of horsehair, some of feathers, some of straw. The topmost mattress had to be filled with lavender and dried basil, in order to ensure the slumber of the person who lay within the bed. In the centre of the base mattress, with due ceremony and before witnesses, I placed a handful of small, dried peas. Then, I stood back to supervise the placement of the subsequent mattresses. If the ancient text was accurate, after sleeping upon this bed for a single night, the royal flesh of Papavera would be bruised black and blue by the peas, because the skin of a *real* princess was so delicate, it was sensitive to the slightest pressures. It is hard to believe that such absurd trials must once have been conducted on a regular basis. I pondered the fate of those unfortunate princesses whose skins had proved unsatisfactorily resistant. The Council were naturally sceptical about the test, and demanded to inspect the bed themselves, thereby indicating they suspected deceit on my part. I happily allowed them their examination, after which they had to admit there was no sign of trickery at work.

'Do you agree,' I inquired, 'that if Papavera's sweet skin is indeed bruised after a night's repose upon this bed, you will accept her claims and allow Marquithi to marry her? After all, the parchment was taken from your own archives. It *is* genuine.'

'Madam,' said the oldest of the Councillors, eyeing the mountain of mattresses, 'if the girl's skin is marked by the peas to the slightest degree, I will be forced to re-evaluate my whole philosophy on life and creation. Assenting to her marriage to the Prince will be a minor concern, in comparison.'

'Well, that's settled then.'

At sundown, the girl Papavera was escorted down from the guest's suite by a retinue of ladies, and taken to a room on the main floor in which the bed had been built. It was a cold, dark and unfriendly chamber whose windows faced an overgrown, neglected courtyard that was forever devoid of sunlight. I noticed that the upper walls were lividly stained by aged patches of mould. In these less than savoury surroundings, Papavera was subjected to a minute examination by the wives of the Councillors, who confirmed her skin was unmarked by blemishes of any kind. As the women poked and prodded at her body, the mysterious princess stood swaying, as if in a daze. Her expression reminded me of those found upon the countenances of marbled saints in the ruined cathedrals dotted around the kingdom; imbecilic yet uplifted. She had made no objection whatsoever to the outrageous test of the peas, and after the inspection, climbed the ladder propped up against the bed, as if she was ascending an angels' stair to paradise.

The Councillors' wives had arranged to keep a vigil over the girl as she slept, patently to prevent one of my staff slipping in halfway through the night in order to inflict bruises upon the girl.

The night passed without incident, although one or two of the invigilating ladies claimed Papavera sighed very deeply occasionally. In the morning, they all converged upon the bedroom in a bustling throng, myself among them. When Papavera descended the ladder, I was alarmed to see there were dark circles beneath her eyes, which were scarcely open. On the removal of her white night-gown, as she stood quivering and naked upon the hard, balding carpet, it was easy to see her soft skin was marked with the most appalling contusions all around her lower back and belly, even along the tops of her thighs. The Councillor's wives were aghast at the injuries, as indeed I was myself. I hastened to cover the poor girl with a gown, keeping my arm around her shoulder. 'I feel this is conclusive evidence,' I said.

'It is unwholesome!' declared one lady.

'An abomination!' whinnied another.

'It is as the law decrees,' I reminded them, and led the girl from their presence.

When examined by the physicks, Papavera repeated the same words, 'There were stones in my bed. They made me sleep on stones.' She was restless with discomfort in a strange, disquieting manner, rather like an animal who, suffering from some internal impairment, can find no position in which to assuage the hurt.

Marquithi was at once furious that his beloved had been damaged and ecstatic that she appeared to have fulfilled the requirements of the law. He held her hand as they sat together in my rooms after the physicks had left, and while he crooned devotion into her ear, she ignored him and blinked dazedly at the floor. My approval of the girl increased immeasurably.

Papavera and Marquithi were married in the autumn, an event preceding their coronation by only five days. By this time, having become inured to the idea, the Council grudgingly allowed themselves to celebrate both occasions in the proper manner. All the guests, from every neighbouring kingdom, complimented Marquithi on his choice of bride. Papavera floated throughout the proceedings like the phantom of an opiate dream, as if unaware of her surroundings, smiling at Marquithi occasionally. Being such a modest and winsome creature, she could not fail to glide her way into the hearts of all the court. Following the coronation, she assumed her role in an appropriate manner. She worked with a deft hand upon tapestries with the other ladies, took protracted and aimless walks in the palace grounds, and attended executions without complaint. When we had foreign guests, she danced enchantingly every night until dawn. She smiled continually in the presence of others, nodded often, but spoke little herself. This made her a much sought after companion, and many ladies of the court considered themselves to be her confidante. She was trustworthy because she never repeated anything she was told. In the palace, this was a refreshing novelty.

Prudently, I had urged one of the catamites, Eluski, to continue visiting Marquithi, in order to discover how the marriage was progressing in his eyes. The knowledge I gleaned was intriguing. Typically, my son did not consider Papavera's silence and lack of female curiosity as unusual, although he was concerned about the delicacy of her skin. Once, he had pulled her towards him playfully, without violence of any sort, and her arm had bloomed purple to the shape of his demanding fingers. Yet as a lover she, in her silence, became a succubus. Marquithi was astounded by the intensity of her interest in the marriage duties, and confessed it was the only time she made much noise. However, driven to disclose further confidences by the vigilant Eluski, my son admitted to a certain distaste that his wife's body was so cold within. Sometimes - and he thought this might be connected with her female cycles - it felt as if his member was grabbed by cold, wet meat. Eluski faithfully reported all this to me. I began to wonder exactly how, and from where, Anguin had procured the girl. More to the point, *what* was she? Very soon, these questions became more urgent.

There was some fuss one afternoon, when Papavera was found lurching around the palace gardens, her garments in some disarray, her voice a moaning and relentless lament. Servants carrying her back into the building claimed she appeared extremely unwell, and that thick hanks of her hair had fallen out into their hands. Alarmed, I went to inspect her in her chambers, and the sight that greeted was far from appealing. Papavera lay virtually motionless upon the bed and her appearance reminded me horribly of some dreadful ghoul unearthed from a desecrated grave. Her normally translucent skin had turned a dull grey-white. Her gums and eyelids were unnaturally red, and her tongue, which reflexively licked her cracked white lips, was a strange bluish colour. The odour she gave off was sweet yet corrupt. I fled to Anguin's rooms immediately, so unnerved I actually grabbed his arms and shook him wildly.

Shrugging off my assault, he appeared unconcerned about Papavera's condition. 'Simply have her brought here,' he said, fiddling with some equipment on his bench, 'and I will do what I can to ameliorate her condition.'

Normally, nobody but me ever visited Anguin's resiance, but on this occasion I was forced to secure the services of Vienquil and Eluski to carry the young queen up the stairs, because I was loath to touch the girl myself. Despite their unflinching loyalty to me, they still complained in the most forthright terms about the disagreeable odours and liquids emanating from the queen's body. At Anguin's direction, they laid Papavera on the largest table in the room, which the alchemist had cleared of debris. I had to hold a kercheif to my nose, for the stench was indeed terrible, although Anguin hastened to assure me this was only because the poor girl had soiled herself. My servants and I were then asked to depart, which we did without question.

Back in my rooms, I poured us all a stiff tincture of narcoceine, which we drank in silence with shaking hands.

'Your highness,' Vienquil ventured. 'If I may speak plainly, I feel there is something quite seriously amiss with the young queen.'

'Something rather more than a simple illness,' Eluski added.

'A deduction I share, my dears!' I said briskly. 'However, I feel it is a subject we should not discuss at this point, at least until Anguin has reported back to me.'

Both servants assumed a mulish expression, sensing my refusal to include them in my secrets. 'Come now,' I said in mild admonishment. 'No need for hard faces! Vienquil, massage my shoulders, if you would. I feel quite shaken!'

As the girl's long, agile fingers plunged with shuddering accuracy into my muscles, I was beginning to question whether I had done the right thing in commissioning a bride for my son from the alchemist. Perhaps it would have been wiser to have asked him to concoct a philtre whereby Marquithi would have become so senseless, he'd have married a sheep if I'd asked him to. Still, it was too late for regrets. We could only live with the results of my actions and trust that Anguin knew what he was doing.

At dinner-time, when Marquithi returned from a tour of the neighbouring estates, he came rampaging into my rooms, demanding to know what I had done with his wife.

'Mother, Papavera's ladies claim you had Vienquil and

Eluski carry her off this afternoon! They say my beloved was quite ill! Where are the physicks? Where the sickroom fumes? Where, indeed, is Papavera?'

'Calm yourself, my pet,' I said. 'The girl is in good hands.'

'Those of your slithering wizard, no doubt!' he cried. 'Take me to my wife at once!'

I regret that we fell into serious dispute at that point, resulting in my having to physically restrain Marquithi from barging to the secret stairway and breaking down the doors. I don't know what would have happened if, at the climax of our altercation when the exchange of blows seemed imminent, the door to Anguin's stairway had not opened and Papavera herself walked into the room.

Marquithi let go of my hair and arms immediately and swept across the room to smother the girl in a fond embrace. 'My love, my dear sweet love,' he cooed. 'What have they been doing to you?'

There was not the slightest trace of illness lingering about Papavera's body. Her pale skin had resumed its limpid translucency, her long, black hair its lustre. She smelled so strongly of honeysuckle that the air in the room was drenched in perfume.

'Mother, what has transpired here?' Marquithi asked, his arm protectively clutching the slim shoulders of his wife. 'There is nothing wrong with Papavera.'

The girl caught my eyes with her own, and gently, imperceptibly, inclined her head. A weird intelligence sparkled in her gaze which I had not recalled seeing there before.

'Indeed not,' I said, patting my hair, which had come quite adrift from its tressure in the struggle. 'Happily, your illness seems to have been of a temporary kind, Papavera.'

'I am quite well,' she said softly.

An idiot light bloomed in my son's face. 'A temporary sickness? Mother, call the physicks at once! Can it be my beloved is with child?'

I shuddered and turned away. Somehow, the prospect of that was distinctly gruesome.

Mercifully, Marquithi's blithe assumption proved incorrect. Physicks examined Papavera and could find no trace of sickness, but neither any trace of pregnancy. It was decided her condition had been caused by something she'd eaten, or else a twist of the gut from some female complaint. Whatever the cause, she now appeared to be in the best of health and as vibrant as she ever could be. However, I could not dismiss a feeling of unease.

Anguin again manifested infuriating obstinacy when I attempted to question him about the girl.

'You saw her condition!' I said. 'She appeared dead, indeed half rotted! Yet, hours later, she trips into my chambers as lively as a doe! What was wrong with her, and what did you do about it? I demand to know, Anguin. Remember, I am your mistress!'

Anguin waved aside my outburst. 'The puissance of my work is ensured only by its secrecy,' he said. 'Therefore, I regret I cannot comply with your requests.'

'At one time you doubted you were responsible for Papavera's presence here at all,' I reminded him.

He grinned; an expression one would expect to find upon the slack-jawed face of a slaughtered dog. 'Did I? And you believed me?' He laughed. 'Do you think a person who can induce an ancient parchment, as authentic as the hair on your head, to manifest spontaneously in the archives would encounter any difficulty conjuring up a princess?'

I narrowed my eyes at him. 'What are you saying? The document was genuine. It bore an antique seal no-one from Loolania could possibly have known about, but which the Councillors vouched was official, if rather outdated. You could not have created it.'

He shrugged. 'True... perhaps. Anyway, you must

smother your fears about the young queen, your highness. The lady Papavera has a very delicate constitution and is therefore prone to minor maladies. It is nothing beyond my adroitness to handle.'

'You mean this might occur regularly?' I had to sit down. The prospect was not pleasant.

Anguin shrugged. 'To preclude such inconvenience, it might be best if the young queen visits me regularly, so that I might attend to her needs.'

'Did you foresee this, Anguin?' I demanded.

He turned away. 'It is impossible to anticipate the outcome of any experiment in fulness,' he said.

After her illness, the character of my daughter-in-law seemed subtly to change. There was less evidence of vacuosity, although she remained as mute as ever. I perceived a calculating glint in her eyes as they gazed, downcast, at the floor. Her followers and sycophants seemed hysterical in their desire to ingratiate themselves into her favour, and she seemed to grow taller from their attentions, trailing them behind her like the hem of a sumptuous gown that is worn for effect, but has become quite invisible to the wearer through its utter familiarity. Marquithi, on the other hand, shrank before the eruption of his wife's dark glory. He locked his door upon Eluski's requests for entrance, and I could no longer glean any information as to his condition or thoughts. Every night was spent with Papavera, and all that Eluski could report was that upon pressing his ear to the King's bedroom door, he heard the sound of a woman's laughter and the moans of a man in ecstasy - or torment.

I never encountered Papavera in my rooms on those days when she went to visit Anguin, although I always knew when she'd been through them, because the scent of honeysuckle hung heavily on the air. Anguin must have cut another set of keys for her, because she never had to request entrance from me. I gradually realised that the palace and its occupants had all become subject to Papavera's power. She had grown from a pathetic scrap of a girl into a creature of insidious strength. All were besotted by her. All, that is, but for myself and my immediate staff.

One evening, I instructed Vienquil and Eluski to monitor the young queen's behaviour, as I knew the time must be approaching when I would again encounter the flavour of honeysuckle lingering in my rooms. 'Watch her with great care,' I said, 'and report.'

Neither of them returned to my rooms that night, nor even in the morning. I believed them to be engaged upon some course of investigation, trusting their intelligence and survival skills would ensure their safety.

At noon, I was aroused from the contemplation of a book by a faint, high-pitched scream that emanated from some distant corner of the palace. Later, two of the post-prandial guard came to my rooms and reported that my beautiful Vienquil and Eluski were dead. Vienquil had been found spreadeagled beneath the royal bee-hives, quite stung to death, her body unrecognisably swollen in the most hideous fashion. The bee-keepers were aghast and could not imagine what had impelled the swarms to behave in such an uncharacteristically aggressive manner. Eluski, having met the Black Summoner in an even more grisly way, had been found dead in a well, his genitals and his eyes having been brutally torn from his body.

Upon receiving these unwelcome tidings, my body went into spasm and two of my maids had to beat my chest fiercely to force my lungs to draw breath. Emotion overtook me and I succumbed to a fit of weeping. The sensation of it was curious, for I had never suffered it before. How vile to be subject to such uncontrollable convulsions on a regular basis!

Eventually, however, after a large dose of narcoceine, the reaction abated, and I was able to examine the situation with a placid eye. It seemed obvious to me who was responsible for these repulsive crimes. Papavera was clearly of my particular female clan, yet she was far from an accomplice of mine. How dare she despatch my favourite retainers with such aplomb! I was in the process of formulating a suitable response, when the bitch pre-empted me. Even as I reposed in my bed fashioning a wax poppet, she swept, without knocking, into the room and posed, hands on hips, at my feet. The scent of honeysuckle was so strong, it almost made me gag.

'I can't recall inviting you here to see me,' I said, covering the poppet with a corner of blanket. 'Neither did I hear you knock.'

Papavera ignored my remarks. 'I take exception to the eyes of spies,' she said. 'Do not presume to have me watched again.' I don't think I'd ever heard her speak so many words at once. She seemed like a towering column of evil vapour, as beautiful as she was wicked.

'Papavera,' I said, attempting to sound tranquil. 'Would I be correct in thinking you are attempting to lock horns with me in some way?'

She did not answer.

'Look,' I continued, 'if any of my staff *have* been observing you, it was simply through my concern for your welfare.'

'Pah!' she spat. 'I don't need your concern! I am quite capable of looking after myself.'

I could see that, and it vexed me greatly. I attempted a rueful smile. 'My dear, I do not wish us to become enemies. We are sisters, after all, in a way.'

Papavera flexed her narrow shoulders, and pulled her mouth down into a sneer. 'Sisters? You attempt to amuse me, obviously. I am not your sister, I am your son's wife. I am the Queen of Gordania, and you are the widow of a dead king. I have no intention of becoming your creature, like Marquithi is - *was*. I value my independence. All I have

Storm Constantine

to say to you is this: leave me be, and I shall leave you be. This seems a sensible and workable arrangement.'

'You have murdered the most valued of my people!' I cried.

She shook her head. 'Indeed, I have not! Whatever gave you that idea? The beasts were punished in a just and fitting way, but not by me, I assure you.'

'By whom, then?'

Her face assumed a dreamy expression. 'My kin are vigilant on my behalf,' she said.

'Your kin?' A cold, dark shadow smothered my heart.

'Quite so,' she replied with a crooked grin. 'Now, no more pretty boys sent to my husband's room, no more spies, and I promise there'll be no more unfortunate accidents. Are you agreeable to this?'

My hand, beneath the coverlet clutched convulsively around the wax poppet. I opened my mouth to speak, but Papavera interrupted me.

'And images of wax will certainly have no effect upon me,' she said. 'Of this you can be sure. Now, comply or suffer. It is your choice.'

She mocked me. I had no choice.

The sinister turn events were taking would have be dealt with immediately, I knew that. With Vienquil and Eluski gone, I realised how alone I was. Marquithi was lost to me, a paralysed insect in the web of the dark queen. Anguin, I felt I could no longer trust. In desperation, I appealed to the Chamberlain. For all his faults, I had realised Tartalan was no fool. Surely, he, of all the court, could discern the malevolent aspect of the young queen? He came to my rooms at nightfall, obeying my furtive summons.

'Tartalan, there is something diabolical about Queen Papavera,' I said. 'She is dangerous and wicked, indeed possibly inhuman. It is imperative we do something about her.'

Tartalan screwed up his nose in vexation. 'Diabolical? Dangerous and wicked?' He shook his head. 'Why should you think that?'

I took a few deep breaths to calm myself. There was no way I could convince Tartalan of the truth with an hysterical tremor in my voice. 'My Lord Chamberlain, I beg you to listen to what I have to say. Every word is truth. Will you believe me?'

He studied me profoundly for a few moments, and then nodded. 'Of course. I believe you to be many things, my lady, but a liar is not one of them.'

'I am glad to hear it. Your credulity may indeed be stretched by what I have to relate.'

Because I needed an ally so badly, I gambled with Fate and told the Chamberlain everything, from the moment when I had approached Anguin with my dilemma. He listened in silence to my words, one finger pressed against his thin mouth. Near the end of my narrative, he was beginning to cast nervous glances over his shoulder. I have a gift for story-telling. Even I felt a little frightened.

Tartalan shook his head, and rubbed his face. 'This is a startling tale,' he said and then peered at me sideways. 'Still, it could be said you have brought this misfortune on yourself.'

I made an exasperated sound. 'I know! Don't you think I haven't admonished myself severely for that? Anyone can make a mistake. I did it for the sake of Gordania, not just for myself.'

He nodded vaguely, apparently deep in thought. Then he said, 'I will need proof of Papavera's malignance before I dare approach the Council.'

I gasped in horror. 'Approach the Council? Are you mad? No, no! We must see to this abomination ourselves! But of course I respect your desire for tangible evidence...

'So, what do you suggest?' he inquired, as if we were discussing some trivial issue of palace etiquette.

'We must observe what transpires in Anguin's chambers on those occasions when Papavera visits him for her... treatments,' I said. 'It is to be hoped we should gain the knowledge of how to deal with her.'

Tartalan looked doubtful. 'With respect, I have no desire to suffer the same fate as other members of this household who have observed Papavera's behaviour,' he said.

'Neither have I! But it seems to me that the young queen is at her least powerful when she needs Anguin's attentions. It is the obvious time to set about dealing with her.'

'I hope you are right,' said the Chamberlain.

It was a sentiment I shared.

Papavera now visited Anguin once a month. I was unsure whether this was because her descent into illness had begun to occur on a more regular basis or simply because Anguin had stepped up her treatments in order to avoid any serious relapse. I was distinctly nervous of interfering. Anguin had withdrawn from me and I no longer enjoyed visiting him in his workroom. I realised I had badly underestimated his personal strength and overestimated his loyalty to me. He had created his own queen. Who really wielded the power in this House?

As I counted the days to the dark of the moon, that time when the scent of honeysuckle invaded my rooms, I thought wistfully, even affectionately, of the doltish Lady Selini of Crooms. Perhaps there was still room for manoeuvre in that direction - should Queen Papavera be removed from Marquithi's life. This thought cheered me a little, as I wrought what sorcerous protection I could to provide Tartalan and myself with at least a measure of security.

On the evening in question, a chill mid-winter night, Tartalan came to my chambers dressed in black. I myself donned the apparel of a man, so that I should be able to move quickly if the occasion merited it. Ever since my initial talk with the Chamberlain concerning this night's venture, I had been considering how this might be the only chance I would get to rid myself of the presence of both Anguin and his creation. Consequently, I had armed myself with razor-edged metal crescents and topical poisons. Tartalan, as my witness, would be my only defence against any legal unpleasantness which might follow. We hid in one of the ante-rooms, and waited for the scent to reach us. At the hour when evening turns to night, all the lamps in my apartment became weirdly dimmer, and the appointments took on a vigilant, breathless appearance. Power sizzled invisibly in the air, raising the hairs on my arms and neck. I glanced at Tartalan as we crouched among the curtains. 'Do you feel it?' I asked him.

He nodded.

'She is coming,' I said. 'We will not see her, but she is coming.'

A faint breeze that held the promise of snow lifted the golden fringes of the curtains, and I shrank back against the window casement. I was terrified that, at any moment, Papavera would swoop into the room and throw the curtain wide. She would stand there, tall as a tree, with her black hair whipping round her colourless face, and she would point a finger right at me, utter some fatal words... No, no, I must not direct my thoughts along such a fell avenue. I had charms aplenty around my neck, my skin had been anointed with an essence of protection. Papavera did not consider me a threat. As she glided through my rooms, she would not even give me a single thought. I pressed my hands against my mouth.

The scent came insidiously, trickling like smoke into the room. At first, I thought I was imagining it. Then, Tartalan said, 'It smells like early summer.' He began to stand up.

151

'She is here,' I hissed, putting a restraining hand on Tartalan's arm. 'Keep down.'

'I feel ridiculous,' Tartalan whispered back. 'This is a child's prank!'

I shook my head. 'No!' I clutched Tartalan's arm for several minutes, until the overpowering scent faded a little and I was sure the dark queen had entered the locked doors. My body felt hot and yet I could see my breath steaming on the chill air.

Stealthily, I led the Chamberlain into the main room. The fire was a dull, angry glow in the hearth and the lamplight looked weak and sick. The very air felt polluted. With shaking hands, I took the keys to Anguin's doors from my trouser pocket. For a moment, I considered abandoning this course of action, packing my bags and fleeing back to my parents' estate in Loolania that same night. Then, a shred of dignity reasserted itself. Had I not held sway in this kingdom for the last eighteen years? I had been a mere child, just past her first bud, when Marquithi's father had taken me to wed. And that child had been afraid of nothing. If she could have looked forward in time, she would have been ashamed to see the woman she was to become hesitating and shying like a skittish mare. Straightening my back, I strode towards the secret stairway, Tartalan padding along behind me.

The stairwell to Anguin's rooms was in darkness, and we could hear no sound. I had to remind myself to breathe as we advanced cautiously up the dusty treads. I pulled one of the crescents from a leather pouch fixed inside my shirt, and with my free hand unstoppered a phial of caustic bane. If there was trouble, I intended to attack immediately.

Anguin's workroom was lit by the flickering, yellow glow of a single candle. As I poked my head through the floor, I could see he was busy working on something on one of the tables. He wore a refracting crystal on a metal band around his brow, which directed beams of the guttering light onto whatever lay on the table. Because of the design of the room, it was impossible to enter it and hide without being seen, so with a last prayer to my grandmother's spirit, I walked over the wooden floor, straight towards my erstwhile alchemist. He looked up with alarm when he realised he was no longer alone, and I experienced a swift thrill of satisfaction to see the expression of shock on his face.

'Yes, it is I, your mistress,' I said. 'I have come to inspect your work.'

I went to stand beside him. 'My Lord Chamberlain,' I said, without looking round. 'If you would be so kind as to examine this... handiwork.'

Papavera lay on the table, split open from breast to groin. Where one would expect to see entrails and blood was only a jumble of thick purplish juices. There was evidence of bone, but it was strangely jointed together with gnarled sticks and metal rods. Undulating bags of soaked cloth approximated the position of stomach and guts. As for her face, it was an eerie caricature of her normal beauty; the mouth hung open, the black tongue lolled, the clouded eyes stared at the ceiling. A more repulsive sight was hard to imagine, neither was the odour of this operation particularly benign. Anguin had not spoken at all. He looked distinctly sullen.

'Perhaps you can explain what it is you're doing,' I said to him.

Tartalan stood behind me, making small anguished noises of disgust, a kercheif held to his nose.

'Well, as you can see, I am working upon the queen,' Anguin said lamely.

I folded my arms and nodded. 'Indeed. Now, you will destroy the monster.' I picked up a sharp tool from beside the body and began stirring one of the bags of fluid in Papavera's torso with it. 'If you do not, Anguin, I shall rip this abomination apart myself!'

'My lady, I am most reluctant to do as you ask. There are certain implications of which you are unaware...'

'Such as?' I raised the dripping instrument and pointed it at his face. 'Hurry, Anguin. Your explanation would indeed gratify me.'

'Her kin,' he said flatly. 'I fashioned her body from whatever materials I could lay my hands on, but her soul was not created by my acts. It was quickened by nightling energy.'

I blinked at him, aghast. It is no coincidence that, in some places, nightlings are called the Devourers. 'Destroy it!' I hissed. 'For the love of all things lit, Anguin, I will discount your insubordination and add my strength to yours against any eventuality, but destroy this creature now!'

His mouth opened and closed a few times. I think he would have complied with my wishes, but at that point, the sound of splintering wood and heavy feet came from below. Seconds later, the chamber was suddenly flooded with light and filled with palace guards, who were pouring through the floor brandishing weapons. Then, Marquithi himself leapt through the trap-door. I don't think I'd ever been so pleased to see him. My pleasure, however, was short-lived.

Upon seeing my son, Tartalan jumped backwards a few steps and raised his hand, pointing at Anguin and myself. He waved the kercheif at us like a flag. 'Arrest these traitors!' he cried.

Anguin and I exchanged a shocked glance. Angrily I turned to my son. 'Marquithi, restrain the Chamberlain. He has lost his wits!'

Marquithi was staring at the table where the parts of his wife lay in disarray. His face was unreadable, but he would not look at me. 'Take them away!' he said to the guards and left the room.

You can imagine that the shock of Marquithi's action quite

drove me senseless. I was utterly benumbed; mercifully, even to the point where I was unaware of my surroundings. I was incarcerated beneath the palace in a secure lodging best described as squalid, although that conveys little of the true horror of it. One of the Councillors came to see me, to explain that I was to be put on trial for treason, along with Anguin and the young queen, whom Marquithi had demanded be reconstituted to meet her fate. Till that point, I had not enjoyed a warm relationship with the Councillor, but I felt he sympathised with my position and perhaps felt uncomfortable with Marquithi's harsh treatment of me. They are sticklers for tradition, these Gordanians, and my blood, after all, was quite royal. I told him I'd acted in good faith, admitted I'd miscalculated, and he seemed to accept this explanation. However, it appeared Tartalan had reported everything I had told him to the King, and in a particularly venomous manner (how could I have misjudged him so!). Therefore, on the night when he and I had crept up to Anguin's room, Marquithi had already been alerted. It had been prearranged that the three of us should be caught *in flagrante*. My son knew everything: how I had kept him docile, how I had arranged for Papavera to be created, everything. I suppose in his position I too might have felt somewhat chagrined, but blood is thicker than water, as they say, so he really was going a little too far by persisting in keeping me in detention.

The hours passed interminably. To this day, I have no way of telling how long I spent in that abysmal hole. Sleep evaded me, and I could not eat. I realised that, should Marquithi stick to the letter of the law, I was finished. I only hoped the method of despatch would be painless, if it came to that. How ungrateful a son can be! Had I acted in any way but to spare him pain and bother? He did not even come to speak with me.

At some point, Queen Papavera was brought in to share my cell. She had indeed been restored, although her face was tight with some unnamed emotion. At first, she did not speak, while I, upon seeing her, desired only to execute the plan I'd had in Anguin's chamber, namely tear her to pieces. We sat upon opposite sides of the small cell, glaring at one another. Eventually, because of my breeding and innate gentility, it was I that broke the silence.

'Look at me in that way if you wish,' I said, 'but the fact is we are both in error. I, for having Anguin conjure you in the first place, and you for becoming too ambitious. Together we could have lived in harmony for many years and, I might add, in rewarding control of this country!'

Papavera made a guttural, hissing sound. 'Empty comfort!' she said in harsh voice. 'I anticipate an ignoble end to my reign.'

Having made communication, my mind had begun to stir itself from torpor. I tapped my lips thoughtfully with my fingers. 'Papavera, we are both in the direst of predicaments. Marquithi is a fool. However, if my memory serves me correctly, you at least have recourse to assistance.'

She growled dismally. 'Hardly! Once Anguin finished his ministrations upon me, Marquithi had the soldiers cut off his hands. I expect he is already dead.'

'I did not mean Anguin,' I said. 'I was referring to your kin.'

She looked up at me sharply. 'Do not think I haven't tried to petition them,' she said. 'The fact is they are contemptuous of my ineptitude at manipulating my circumstances. They believe I deserve to lose this human form and revert to my true state.'

'Is that a sentiment you share?'

She looked thoughtful for a moment. 'No,' she said at last. 'There are certain enjoyable aspects of this incarnation.'

'In that case, it is obvious what we have to do,' I told her.

'What?' I was gratified by the ignition of hope in her eyes.

'First, you must give me your most binding vow you will not desert me, betray me or harm me in any way.'

She nodded. 'Excise me from this mess, and I shall shower you with devotion for eternity.'

'Very well, we shall see to the solemnising of that vow presently. First, I will tell you this. In order to attract the assistance of your kin, we must have something to offer them in return, for even though I am unacquainted with the customs of your people, I know there is no form of life in existence that does not respond to the prospect of gain.'

'True enough,' said the young queen. 'But what do you suggest?'

I reached over and patted her clenched hands. 'My dear, there is not one bumbling foreign nobleman who is not slave to your charm and beauty. Should we escape our distress, I am convinced we will find succour somewhere else beyond Gordania. It seems to me that your kin would welcome ingress into some area of human activity. Perhaps we could facilitate that.'

Papavera smiled. 'With your knowledge of the human condition and my access to nightling caprices, it does indeed seem a workable plan.'

The trial was a farce, although I must admit it gave me some satisfaction to hear my crimes recited. Papavera was declared demonic and would be burned at the stake. I, as conspirator in diabolic practices and consequently a traitor to the crown, must also be executed but, because of my rank, I would be allowed to drink poison. Anguin, already half dead and mutilated, would be thrown to the royal hounds and be devoured alive. Marquithi maintained a pale, cold distance while the fates of the women in his life were proclaimed. It was almost as if he'd never loved either of us. It was very strange, but I could not hate him. He simply could not understand our female ways, which seemed very ordinary to myself. Still, it was a mistake to let a man witness the true nature of our power, and if anyone deserved to die that day, it was Tartalan.

As a formality, I was allowed to speak in my own defence; a procedure I knew would have no effect upon the outcome. I spoke plainly, remarking that, as I saw it, the only problem was a disagreement between Papavera and myself, and that I could not imagine why it had reached the grand court of Gordania. These comments caused a rumble among the spectators' gallery, where the dim-witted Councillors' wives flapped themselves with fans and gorged their spirits on my humiliation. I refused to be penitent or cowed. At least Papavera gave me her support through her gentle smile across the court. She was allowed no defence, poor creature. At length, after all the talking was done, the judge donned his black cowl and named the time of our executions. Sunfall. Papavera held my eyes as she was taken from the room. I had to trust her; not just her intention, but her ability. I prayed for her success.

Papavera and Anguin were returned to the dungeons, whilst I was escorted to my former rooms to await the hour when the physicks would bring me the deadly cup. I sat in my favourite chair by the window, watching the shadows lengthen. No-one came to tender their farewells. My servants were all gone. Only a couple of whiskered slaughter-house women kept me company, and a brace of guards beside the door. I reflected how badly my life had gone awry, and yet, given the time again, would I have acted differently? It was difficult to tell. As the dusk stole quietly towards the windows, I heard their steps outside the door. My heart began to beat much faster. I saw the night-black shadow of an enormous wing across the sill.

So you see, that is my story, that is how I am here beside

your fire, and my fellow travellers asleep in your hayloft. What? Oh do not be afraid, our unseen companions will not attack you, or your animals. Although I must admit the ferocity of their attack, when the mood takes them to indulge in violence, is quite incredible. Did I tell you how quickly it is possible to shred the bodies of two guards, two large women and a brace of physicks? No? Well, perhaps I had better spare you the details.

We had to bring Anguin with us, of course, in order for my dear companion to retain her physical splendour on a long-term basis. To date, he has been teaching me some measure of his skills, although - please don't tell him this - my lady and I are considering allowing him to build himself a pair of hands. He did so well with Papavera's bodily equipment after all, and, well, he is so tractable nowadays.

Anyway, I've kept you awake long enough. So gracious of you to offer us accommodation. Now, I must sleep. Tomorrow, we have business with the squire of this parish. Madam, you are too kind, but I insist you accept my coin as payment. Are we not sisters, after all, sisters of a certain persuasion? Before bed, I would walk in your mandrake garden. So fortunate we saw you weeding it from the road as we were passing, so fortunate. I have longed to share my story with a woman of like mind. A night of blessings to you, madam, a night of blessings.

Curse of the Snake

Lyye was lost. The last of her defenders had been trampled beneath the hooves of the enemy's war-horses; smashed carrion meat across the fields of death. The thousand turrets of Lyye, once a wonder of the world, had been toppled by the marauders, who cared nothing for their beauty and impossible convolutions. Decapitated, the towers were a litter of shattered debris, amid the ruins of desecrated temples. The idols of Lyyrian gods, whose names were unknown beyond the city walls, lay like slaughtered giants in the rubble; an imperious arm pointing up at the sky here, a grimacing face peering through corpses there. The ground in those places was scarified with blood; later it would be sown with salt.

The massive city walls, which had stood for centuries uncounted, had been breached and tumbled. The titanic blocks of marble, each anointed long ages past with the life essence of a sacrificed priest, had crushed the last desperate defenders, even as they had attempted to repel the invaders, who clambered over the rubble like ants, swinging their great weapons, dismembering anyone in their path. The Lyyrians had never been fighters and, unused to war, could do little to save their city or themselves. Their weapons were ornaments, worn at the hip to accentuate the lines of a costume. None of them were blooded; their blades were virgin, witless.

In the past, only the Lyyrians' reputation as sorcerers had kept enemies at bay - ambitious conquerors, outraged neighbouring states, greedy rabble. The city had been impenetrable, hiding its supposedly dark secrets within. Only the hint of sulphurous flame playing about the towers on certain nights of the year hinted at the activities that took place within the walls.

The people of the Wolf Kings, a coalition of neighbouring kingdoms, avoided the area. It was considered the safest course. But then the nomad hordes of the Fenilix, having been driven from their far northern lands by a hot-headed warmonger, had sought passage through the swamp plains of Giddian. The Wolf Kings of the Twenty Cities, who met often to discuss the bane of Lyye, but never to plan action, had held counsel with the Fenilict leaders. The Fenilix were fearless and only dimly aware of the Lyyrian reputation. For a price, they were prepared to attack the dreaded sorcerer princes of Lyye. Their gods, they said, rode with them into battle and no man, mage-wise or not, could withstand their righteous wrath.

The Fenilix had gathered upon the swamp plains beyond the white city. Votive fires had been lit, the throats of youths ritually cut, to invoke the presence of the gods.

Sentinels upon the walls of Lyye had observed these procedures with interest. After aeons of unmolested privacy, they could not believe that some lesser race was preparing to attack them. In any case, the walls of Lyye were too thick and too high to succumb to invaders. In retrospect this had proved short-sighted.

After long months of siege, while the Fenilix besported themselves before the walls, swigging wine and conducting feasts in full sight of their rapidly famishing enemies, the walls had proved as much a prison as a refuge. One drunken night, the Fenilix had poured forth across the plain, shouting war hymns and anointing themselves with fresh blood. It was through accident rather than strategy that they discovered the walls of Lyye, though thick and towering, were as friable as chalk, owing to their immense age. Encouraged by their first assault, the Fenilix clawed and battered the massive stones, and the walls crumbled.

The Lyyrians were a beautiful, fragile race, but doomed

to extinction. Inbreeding had thinned their blood, whereas the Fenilix were young and hardy, and familiar with the art of war. As the palaces fell, the weary citizens were herded from the ruins to be raped and massacred upon the blood-soaked plazas. Priceless artefacts were looted, burned or broken. Whole libraries, where the knowledge of millennia was stored in ordered ranks, were ransacked and despoiled. If the Lyyrians had recourse to magic, it was not strong enough to repel the brutal physical force of the Fenilix.

The advocates of the Wolf Kings sat astride white horses at the edges of the battle, watching. When the last defenders were slain, they rode forward to inspect what was left of the city. Cautiously, they investigated the subterranean labyrinths, whose entrances had been exposed by destruction. What they found in these places confirmed their fears and suspicions concerning the Lyyrians' true nature. They could not fathom what the bizarre machines and tools could have been used for exactly, but they reeked of torture, of pain and perversity.

The advocates of the Wolf Kings quickly sought the open air once more. Hurriedly, they gathered spoils for their lords, who had not deigned to leave the safety of their fortresses across the plains. They took precious metals, they took jewels, but all the books and machinery were left behind to be destroyed. Once the carts were loaded with treasure, the advocates ordered that every surviving inhabitant of the city should be put to the sword. All should be destroyed. All, but the hard, cold, unforgiving treasures of metal and stone. These things had no memory and no volition, or so the advocates thought, whereas flesh was dangerous. The smallest child held within it the seeds of power. None must live.

Hailaz, Prince of Lyye was perhaps the member of the royal family least deserving of being spared. On that final day, he spent the entire battle hiding behind sacks of flour in one of the palace basements. As screams and the thunder of toppling stone resounded overhead, Hailaz knelt on the dusty flour, praying fervently for deliverance to his goddess, Meluvia, but painfully aware of Her absence. The gods, he knew, had abandoned the city. But perhaps Meluvia was not as distant as she seemed. A group of courtiers, charged by the King to take the most precious and powerful artefacts from the city to safety, had been crossing the basement on their way to the sewers, where a team of horses awaited them. Hailaz had been discovered, cowering amid the flour. He had begged them to help him, a request that at first had provoked only outraged refusal. In Lyye, Hailaz enjoyed a less than savoury reputation. His cowardly disposition was legendary, as were his petulance and his licentious behaviour, which were considered excessive, even in Lyye. One of the courtiers had even said to him that in her opinion he did not deserve to be saved, especially as his brother, Liraiz, far braver and more respected, and certainly far worthier of escape, had just been disembowelled by a Fenilict sword. Liraiz had never lifted a weapon in defence in his life, but nevertheless had attempted to help defend the city, paying with his life. Why should Hailaz, grovelling and snivelling in the cellars, be spared a similar fate?

Hailaz had implored and wept.

Finally, one of the men, an old friend of the King, suggested that any member of the royal family should be saved, even if it was Hailaz, and reluctantly the others had agreed. With scant consideration for his rank, they bundled him between them into the evil-smelling dark beneath the city.

Although the impartial Fates had granted Hailaz a questionable character, they had at least bestowed upon him the gift of beauty, which was his greatest, if not his only, asset. Well moulded of body, he was accustomed to carrying himself with arrogant dignity. He had a lean, sculpted face and a mane of wild white hair. Like his entire race, his eyes were orange, resembling the eyes of the great spoiled lynxes that had once lounged carelessly around the palace gardens.

Hailaz had been petrified to a kind of mindless numbness, and let himself be pushed in whatever direction his rescuers pleased. Several times, he had fallen face down into the noxious runnels, to be dragged up, retching and gasping, and pushed onward. Eventually, the company had emerged into daylight, stinking, filthy, and in fact not that much different in appearance from the Fenelix. By this time, most of the invaders were within the city walls, and the three soldiers with the party were able to steal several mangy-looking pack-horses, who were guarded only by what appeared to be a gang of imbecile children.

With four of the party riding two to a horse, they galloped downstream, fetlock-deep in the foul shallow waters.

Hailaz was not aware of their plans, but soon realised they were heading in the direction of the wilderlands that lay beyond the fertile plains. He knew little of this place, other than that it was an infertile and arid territory, flanked by peeling, scabrous mountains. Fairy-tales, which he had heard as a child, suggested it was an area inhabited by monsters, both supernatural and human. If anyone should be stupid enough to brave venturing across the wilderlands, they could look forward only to a terrible death, made all the more terrifying because so little was known about what could kill a person there. Hailaz' nurse had once told him that whatever life stirred in the dust was warped and hostile. The only water that flowed there was thick with poisonous salts or blanketed with sour scum. Because it was this shunned place, Hailaz could understand the logic of fleeing there, but surely such a route would only serve to delay an inevitable extinction. Perhaps the swords of the Fenilix would be preferable.

The Lyyrians rode through the night, pausing only at dawn to rest the horses, which showed symptoms of imminent collapse. It was then that the signs of pursuit were noticed, far nearer than was thought possible. It was clear that the urchins guarding the horses had alerted the Fenilix to the theft. Now the pursuers, catching sight of their quarry, increased their speed. Even from a distance it was possible to hear their yelling and perceive their waving weapons. Hastily, the Lyyrians remounted their exhausted horses and lashed them into a stumbling gallop, towards the first humped foothills of the Mountains of Morstar, which surrounded the wilderlands and hid them from the outside world.

Hailaz did not think they would escape their pursuers, but once the Lyyrians ventured into the shadow of the rocks, the Fenilix gave up the chase, contenting themselves with a few last, shouted insults before heading back to the devastation of Lyye. Later they would joke about the slow deaths that waited for the pallid Lyyrians in the wilderlands. No one could survive long in that place, especially weaklings.

Hailaz had enough sense not to complain too much as the party descended into the gloom of Morstar, but despite this restraint, the atmosphere was a glowering, simmering one, cored by terrible grief. Hailaz, being sensitive, was well aware of the barely veiled hostility the others felt for him. Once it became clear they were no longer being pursued, the party paused in their flight again, and an argument began.

The woman, Hailaz's main detractor, claimed the cowardly prince might prove a hex upon their progress and should be abandoned.

Hailaz's defender, the friend of the king, repeated his solemn words concerning the succour of the last heir of Lyye.

At this point, the woman had uttered a claim that had

turned opinion in her favour. It seemed she was carrying the child of Liraiz, Hailaz' brother, who was of course the true heir of Lyye, and guardian of the artefacts.

Wearily, Hailaz realised why she had been so furious he had lived while Liraiz had died. In his heart, he could not blame her for her feelings. As time went on, he was beginning to sympathise more and more with way the others saw him. He hated himself, and could hardly censure others if they shared his opinion.

'Leave me here,' he said. 'I will only impede your flight.'

He meant these words, but nevertheless felt very hurt that no one tried to argue with him.

At the injunction of the king's friend, they left him one of the horses and a small supply of water, before riding off without a backward glance.

For several hours, Hailaz sat in a dazed stupor on the damp sand of the canyon floor. He could not imagine that he had a future, and in this bleak prospect, he discovered a kind of courage. If he was to die, then he would do so in the wilderlands, at least discovering what they were like before he died. He harboured a faint glimmer of hope that he might find something completely unexpected beyond the mountains; water, food, friendly faces. It was not impossible, only very unlikely.

Little daylight ever found its way down to the sandy path where Hailaz crouched, but he could tell by the deepening gloom that the sun was sinking. The expanding shadows seemed thronged by unseen eyes, and Hailaz noticed the bony nag, who waited patiently beside him, was casting nervous glances around herself. Shuddering, Hailaz forced himself painfully to his feet. His body ached and his head throbbed with pain, but he was filled with an urge to escape the canyon.

It took him some minutes to hoist himself onto the saddle, and once there, he had to vomit a dark brown liquid, which undoubtedly he had imbibed during his torment in the sewers. Perhaps he would die of poisoning before any monster of the wilderlands attacked him.

As he rode out from the clutching shades of Morstar's rocks, into the pebbled lip of the waste, Hailaz looked wholly unlike a prince. His argentine hair was matted and dulled, his posture slouched and defeated. The sight of the wilderlands did nothing to lift his spirits. It was, as had been rumoured, a dull and lonely landscape. There was no sign of any vegetation, just a spreading vista of tumbled rocks, that might, in daylight, reveal themselves to be ruins. Hailaz let the pony have her head. Maybe she could scent water or life. Of his erstwhile companions he could find no trace at all. He muttered a brief prayer to Meluvia, knowing even as he intoned the sacred verses, that Her patronage was utterly lost to him in this place.

Whatever spirits or malign deities held sway among the bare rocks hid themselves in the silence, but Hailaz could feel their scrutiny. What genuflection, what prayers, could buy him passage across the land? He had no idea.

It seemed he rode for many hours, half drowsing in his saddle. However, the swollen yellow moon never passed her zenith, and neither did the air grow colder with the expected first hours of the dawn. A pallid glow continued to flood down from halfway up the sky, and constellations Hailaz did not recognise pulsed across the velvet vault of night. Endless night, thought Hailaz. Perhaps the sun never rose over the wilderlands.

The soaring barrier of Morstar disappeared into the distance. Now, Hailaz faced a limitless sea of grey stones, which stretched to all horizons. He could perceive no plant life, never mind buildings or roads. Even the stones were all of a similar size; that of man's clenched fist.

After a few hours, Hailaz considered that perhaps he

had died, either during the sacking of Lyye or else later during his flight from the city. Perhaps this was a kind of eternal underworld, and his punishment for his cowardly ways would be to travel it endlessly, not even haunted by the ghosts of the slain for company. The only reassurance came from the regular crunching of the nag's hooves upon the stones. Hailaz buried his frozen hands in her rough thick mane for comfort.

Just when he thought he would fall from his saddle, unable to remain upright because his limbs were so cold, Hailaz suffered a fit of panic. He lifted his arms above his head and shrieked out a wordless invocation to the spirit of the land, promising his body, his life, his soul, to anything or anyone who could end his torment now. Presently, he exhausted himself; the horse still plodded on relentlessly, seemingly unmoved by his outcries. Tears fell down Hailaz' face to freeze upon his cheeks. Eventually, he dozed, his dreams filled with screams and smoke.

When Hailaz awoke, he thought he must be hallucinating, for upon the far horizon rose the stately spires of some forgotten city. Had he crossed the wilderlands, then? Was this the beginning of the other side? The spires rose black and lightless against the sky, but, whatever they might hide, Hailaz was relieved to see them. Even if monsters lived within its walls, their company was preferable to the pressing desolation of the waste. With a boyish whoop of delight that echoed in the silence, Hailaz kicked the mare into an exhausted canter.

Strangely, the alien buildings wavered before Hailaz' eyes. As they drew nearer to the ponderous walls of the city, the young prince could not be sure whether those lofty minarets were fabulous examples of opulent luxury or but a sad, skeletal ruin of what once might have been. There was insubstantiality like the flicker of bat's wings that hovered half-seen beyond his vision. He pleaded aloud, 'No, let it be

169

real, Nameless Spirits of the Waste. No matter what lies beyond its walls, let it be real.'

He screwed up his eyes and clasped his hands, allowing the reins to flap unheeded as he prayed. When he opened his eyes once more, the city seemed surprisingly nearer than he had thought it to be and undeniably real. Its walls were constructed of black and gleaming stone, with porphyritic glisterings caught by the moon. Beautiful and sombre, it reared against the sky, cloaked in a breathless, waiting silence. Surely that was uncanny for a town so large? Even at night, there should be some sign of habitation. But the lofty walls kept their secrets, revealing nothing of what lay behind their cyclopean stones.

Hailaz could see no way into the city and rode a little way round the wall, seeking some mode of ingress. Suddenly, without warning, his mare stopped dead. The prince could see a great portal hanging open a little further forward, and no guards, who might challenge his entrance, appeared to occupy its wreathing shadows. Hailaz' mount seemed strongly against the idea of entering the doorway, and it was with a great deal of goading and cursing that Hailaz tyrannised the poor beast into hesitantly braving whatever she felt lay beyond.

Hailaz passed beneath the musty gloom of the overhanging eaves and found himself in the centre of a small cobbled square, flanked by brooding black-stone dwellings and barred shop fronts. He drew in his breath as his benumbed brain took in his surroundings. The city towered over him, so that its tall and exalted towers seemed to scratch the stars. Perspective crushed him with the illusion that the buildings leaned right over him. Tearing his eyes from the soaring summits, he stood up in his stirrups, comforted by the familiar squeak of the worn leather. He attempted to discern some sign of life down any of the labyrinthine streets that swept away like snakes into shadows. He hoped to find a friendly inn, whose proprietor might be kind enough to accommodate him, perhaps in exchange for one of the heavy jewels that still adorned his fingers. But the city was sepulchrally quiet, and a blanket of darkness lay over the houses; it crept in black tendrils through the columns of the mighty temples and assaulted the alabaster caryatids that sneered down from the fronts of hilltop palaces. Darkness. Deep and rich as the thick black oil that once burned in the lamps of Lyye. Even the water in the fountains was stilled here.

Hailaz shivered. Obviously, this was no normal city. It seemed completely deserted and pregnant with a terrible atmosphere, that of an expectant hunger. Hailaz' mare danced upon her black hooves, as if a pack of terriers were snapping at her heels, and thick, frothing sweat bubbled behind the leather at her ears. Her fear was infectious; terror gripped Hailaz' heart with gelid claws. He also became aware of the pangs of discomfort in his body: howls of hunger and the dull ache of fatigue.

As he contemplated his discomforts, a thread of sound impinged itself gradually upon the air. It was a thin and plaintive melody that insinuated itself all along the stilled and darkened lanes. As its subtle fingers closed about the mare's ears, she quieted strangely and ceased to shiver. Hailaz tried to trace the source of the bewitching strain, but it seemed to come from every direction at once.

The mare began to walk again, head lowered almost to her knees. She made her way into a tiny, overhung street that was totally shrouded with blackness. Not a single rat scuttled in the gutter. In fact, the utter cleanliness of the pathways was uncanny. No rats ran here because there was no human waste for them to explore, not even an occasional twirl of fruit peel. The streets were meticulously clean, almost polished.

Eventually, after riding through a labyrinth of alleys, Hailaz found the spectral melody had lured and delivered him to the forecourt of a great white palace, set high above the rest of the city on its own hill. A forest of thick snowy pillars, in whose pristine depths dwelt traces of scarlet fire, fronted it. The formless melody that had seemed to direct the mare's footsteps had now changed into a sweet and simple song that was full of sorrow. The song conjured images in Hailaz's mind, and he fancied it was the lament of some wretched creature, who was doomed to live forever alone, a prisoner of the silent city. He tried to dismount from his horse, but his legs were weak and he fell heavily to the floor, cracking his head upon the huge flagstones.

Groaning, Hailaz crawled slowly forward, towards the columns. He was driven to enter the palace. As the shadows closed over him, the song slowly died away. Behind him, the mare pricked up her ears. Following an unseen call, she walked away into the night.

Hailaz found himself kneeling in a gargantuan hall. It was so immense, his senses could barely take it in. He looked back at the entrance, and it seemed to be incredibly far away. Hailaz wondered how he could have dragged himself so far. Still, for all the palace's silent strangeness, he could not perceive any threat. The air was hushed and still and smelled of nothing. The floor was constructed of enormous slabs, carved with unearthly runes and symbols. Flickering roches of amber light illumined a festival of bizarre carvings on the wall. They seemed to be lewd; strange beasts cavorted with one another. Around them, drapes of inky velvet that were fringed and tasselled cascaded from the high shadows to the floor. Otherwise, the hall was completely devoid of furniture. Hailaz sensed it was a sorry, empty place that once had witnessed great merriment and flooding light. It seemed as if a sad receding echo of those times still bounced from wall to wall.

Hailaz curled up on the floor, and a strange and dreamless sleep came at last to his tortured frame.

'Hailaz, prince of Lyye, awake.'

Hailaz woke up at once, and in panic attempted to rise. Someone was here, someone who knew him. He looked up and saw a small figure, silhouetted between the sparkling pillars, against the rosiness of dawn. Its appearance was concealed in shadow, and he could not really tell if the voice was male or female. But he was still flooded with relief. Whatever phantoms had tortured his mind during the night, the glorious reality of day swept the cobwebs from his eyes. The city had just been asleep. With the advent of day it had clearly come alive once more. He could sense movement and noise beyond the obscuring columns.

The person who had spoken advanced into the hall and stood over him. 'I am Lord of these halls, prince. Do you have reason for seeking my hospitality?'

'Forgive my audacity,' Hailaz begged obsequiously. 'Yesterday, my father's city was razed to the ground by the Fenilix from the north, and I was driven into the wilderlands by the same fiends who butchered my people. I have ridden long and have injuries. I seek only sanctuary.' He paused and remembered, easing himself up onto one elbow. 'A strange singer lured me to your home in the night.' He could see now that his host was hardly more than a boy, clad simply in hugging deerskins, not unlike the many wide-eyed slaves that once scampered through his father's palace. Not unlike his own attendant Xal-Liha, whose probable fate could only cause him to wince in pain as he gazed upon this lovely youth. Poor Xal, whose huge and tender eyes had never mocked him, most probably lay dead and broken amidst the carnage of his home. 'You knew my name,' the prince wheedled. 'Has news reached here already of Lyye's untimely fall?'

173

'Untimely? Hardly. And yes, I know of you,' said the boy, with only a hint of contempt. 'All things witnessed by the hills of Morstar are known to me. You are in the ancient city of Vaengir, and this is my revered Hall of Ages you violate with your self-pity. Get to your feet, Prince of Lyye. As you are here, I can afford you aid, for well you need it. Follow me.'

The proud boy stalked towards the end of the Hall without another look behind him, and Hailaz had no choice but to stagger after.

Hailaz was led through many fine and sweeping halls, eventually being ushered him into a splendid chamber. He leaned against the doorframe, and examined the sumptuous luxury of the room. A doorway to the side revealed a bathroom, where scented steam rose from a bath, ready drawn and presumably for his use. What good fortune this was! He pushed from his mind the strange fact that nowhere in the palace had he seen any servants going about their duties. But for his exotic host, the place still seemed deserted.

The boy aided Hailaz across the room to the great tapestried bed that was set into the wall by tall windows of pale yellow glass. Hailaz lay in an ecstasy upon the soft coverlet, all his pains aching gloriously. He looked forward to a warm soaking. The boy knelt at his side and made to draw off the prince's stained and shabby boots.

'No,' Hailaz said, 'you are master of his palace. It is not fitting that you attend upon me. I have thrust myself upon your hospitality without invitation. Leave me be, and I will presently find the strength to attend myself, I assure you. I do not deserve even the attentions of your meanest slave, for if you know me, you will know the curse and revilement I carry. Do not soil your hands that others may shun you also.'

The boy sat up on his heels and laughed merrily. 'Poor fool, Hailaz. You are truly a mean individual caught up in your own misery. Believe me, you know little of curses. Also, the song that brought you here belongs to me. It is the spirit of the Falls. You had no choice but to come here. Therefore I will attend you. My servants are sullen and unpleasant. As a prince, you deserve more than that.' And he carried on with the business of peeling off the well-used boots.

Hailaz regarded the boy thoughtfully. He could not tell what blood ran in those tender veins. The small face was inhuman, beautifully alien, sallow-skinned and almond-eyed, with a mouth curved in a perpetual smile, but hardly of mirth. His head was framed with serpentine hair, multiply braided, so that it seemed a hundred black snakes hung from his head. Looking at those black-irised eyes, Hailaz thought that the creature was far older than the appearance of sixteen years or so bespoke. There dwelt in his eyes a perverse humour, a patient irony, laced with such a vengeful bitterness that Hailaz was unnerved by his unobtrusive touch.

Once bathed and clad in a nightgown of soft cloth, Hailaz sought the comfort of the bed, feeling wonderfully at peace and secure in his new-found haven. His mysterious host promised to bring him sustenance shortly, and he fell into a slumber. But strange phantoms arose in his mind, twisting his sleep to fearsome nightmare, so that he woke raving and fevered to find the boy gazing into his troubled face with an expression akin to amusement. It filled Hailaz with a greater horror than he had yet known, realising that in his recumbent position he was completely at the mercy of this strange being.

'You are fevered,' the boy murmured. 'Drink of this broth.'

Fighting the nausea that rose in his stomach, Hailaz obeyed, fearful of arousing the boy's disapproval.

'Tomorrow, you will feel so much better, Prince of

Lyye. I will release the Spirit of the Falls to woo you in your sleep with pleasant song. It is very healing.'

'My mare, did you find her?' Hailaz asked suddenly, remembering the faithful beast.

'Rest easy, Hailaz, she crops the sward above the Falls. All animals are welcome here.'

The boy left the chamber, leaving Hailaz alone, and not unafraid, for the space of one day and one night.

At the end of this time, as the boy had predicted, the fever and pain had left Hailaz completely and he felt better disposed towards the strangeness of his circumstances. Fresh, well-made clothing had been left out for him, and he rose from his bed in a mood of happy congeniality.

Once Hailaz had dressed himself, his host appeared and accompanied him to a pleasant dining room that looked out over a sunny patio, beyond which the marvellous gardens of the palace could be seen. The room was light and airy, decorated with vivid green plants that trailed from baskets down the walls and sent ferny tendrils out into the room. For the first time Hailaz had the chance to see two of his host's servants and they did indeed appear to be a pack of lack-lustre individuals. Their movements were sluggish and clumsy, their eyes glazed, as if they were under the influence of some potent philtre. But the food they served was well-prepared and mouth-watering, and after all his previous hardships Hailaz found the meal invigorating.

The boy sat opposite him, and though he scarcely nibbled at his own food, seemed content to watch his guest heartily devour great portions.

'You said you are Lord of all this city?' Hailaz asked out of politeness, thinking it was quite possible that the boy's father had once ruled here, and dying while his son was still young, had caused the youth to inherit the title before his time.

'Yes,' the boy replied with a sharp-toothed smile. 'I am Gahrazel and this is my city.' He gestured widely and laughed. A discomforting note of insanity rang through it.

Hailaz began to wonder if he had fallen into the hands of a lunatic. He wiped his mouth fastidiously on a napkin, searching for a suitable topic of conversation. None came.

'You observe me very strangely, Prince Hailaz,' said Gahrazel. 'Does it disturb you to think someone so young as I can rule a city? Do you look upon youth with contempt? Maybe I remind you of the young slaves within your own lost home, whom you treated ruthlessly, without thought for their own sensibilities. You know, of course, what I mean?'

'Yes,' Hailaz answered, wincing at the smouldering fury in the boy's eyes. 'But do not think I thought that of you. I am thankful for the kindness you have showed towards me, and moreover I do not think you are as much of a child as you would have me believe.'

The boy smiled.

At that moment, another servant entered the room. He bore a silver charger on which reposed a carafe of wine. Hailaz uttered a startled cry and dropped the napkin he still held in his hand. The servant was one of his own company, who had so mercilessly left him for dead beyond the wilderlands. 'Mahor!' Hailaz cried. 'Do you not know me?'

The man ignored him and poured out a goblet of wine. He never looked up once nor acknowledged Hailaz' presence.

'Speak, Mahor,' Hailaz urged. 'Did Gahrazel bring you here too? Why do you wait upon his table?' He touched the man's arm to attract his attention and was horrified to find the flesh was cold, and dull as clay, as if no life moved in his body. It seemed his eyes were filmed with the nacre of the tomb.

'What have you done to him?' Hailaz screeched at the boy. A terrible inkling of the truth stirred in his blood.

177

Gahrazel was smiling, lazily and cruelly, smoothing the kingly robes he wore. Hailaz felt a shock course through him as the almond-shaped eyes fixed him in a cold gaze.

'Have I not rescued him from the desolation of the wilderlands? It amuses me to have new faces around the palace.'

Trembling, Hailaz challenged him. 'That I do not believe! I would say, Gahrazel, that this man is lent a horrible animation, when in truth he should be mouldering in his tomb.'

Gahrazel speculated upon the Prince's ashen face and damp brow. He threw back his head and laughed. 'I choose to keep him in this state, because humankind are otherwise difficult to manage. They are too eager to create trouble and attempt petty heroics. This way, they accept my dominion without question.'

'What kind of a fiend are you?' Hailaz said in an outraged, low voice.

'Do not fear,' spoke Gahrazel placatingly. 'If you would know the truth, come with me.'

He rose, ophidian, from his chair. Hailaz saw that the costly robes he had worn had vanished, as if they had never existed at all, beyond illusion. Gahrazel stood naked before him, clothed only with anguine ropes of midnight hair. But this was not the only transformation. Hailaz shuddered to see that the youth's skin was scaled like a reptile. The scales were smooth and pale, and glistened like pearl. There was no indication of a sex; he seemed neither male nor female. 'This is the truth of me,' Gahrazel said. 'I do not need the constricting vestments of a human being.' He indicated his strange, supple flesh. 'This, my integument, is my kingly robe.' He walked out of the room without a further word, and Hailaz followed mutely, filled equally with curiosity and dread.

They came to a great balcony that overlooked a bustling

market-place, filled with people. The shrill cries of darting children mixed the homely sound of barking dogs. Stall-holders cried out to advertise their wares. Women in colourful robes moved among them, examining the produce. There were no beggars to be seen – a common sight in Lyrrian markets – and all the people, including the merchants, appeared healthy and well dressed.

'My people,' said Gahrazel quietly. 'In thrall to me, yes, but their lives are perfect. At night, I bid them sleep without dreams until the dawn, but at daybreak, I bring them alive again. I find silence very... sad.'

Hailaz peered over the balcony and saw that all below was not, as first appeared, quite all as it should be. There was something heavy in the smiles, something dead in the lithe limbs of the young women. 'If there is sadness here, it is the state of these poor creatures,' Hailaz observed. 'They are walking dead. Truly you are a monster, Gahrazel, and have killed all these people.'

'You are ignorant,' Gahrazel said and taking one of Hailaz' hands, pressed it against his squamous hide. 'This is what I am, Prince of Lyye. I am of the Colurastes, the serpent people.'

The flesh was strangely warm; Hailaz did not expect that.

'These animals,' the boy continued, with a grimace and a gesture at the crowd, 'deserved all they got from me. It was just punishment. But come, you shall hear the tale from he who shall tell it best, the erstwhile king of fair Vaengir, Lord Arax. He shall recite it. Come.' And still holding Hailaz's hand, he dragged the prince back into the palace.

In a curtained throne-room, long deserted, and cloaked with a pall of thick, grey dust, King Arax brooded in the silence on a mighty throne, his body swathed in dust. Here, Gahrazel had not arrested the machinations of time; it had worked its chaos of decays upon the once magnificent apartment.

'Here sits the king of Vaengir in his rubble,' the snake-boy said delightedly. 'It still pleases me to see him like this. He was such a proud man, proud and selfish. Always wanted his own way, as kings do. I keep him alive, so that he may contemplate his sins. He has been given eternity to repent. One day, I might even release him so he may see what I have done to his fair city. How he hated dirt and disorder. That is why I keep his city spotless - except for this room.' He laughed, a sound that Hailaz found quite manic.

The whole scene and atmosphere was so oppressive, Hailaz needed to sit down. Carefully, he negotiated the accumulated detritus that had once been splendid carvings and decorations, and eventually found a seat on a crumbling divan.

Ensorcelled Arax scowled down from his throne. He was still handsome, even though he might have been frozen in that way for centuries.

'Awake, Arax,' Gahrazel commanded. 'Awake and tell your sorry tale, for here is one who would like to hear it.'

Slowly, Arax lifted his head, and a gleam of life entered his grey eyes. Dust trickled down from his hair and brow. Mournfully, he gazed upon his keeper.

'Speak, Arax, speak,' said Gahrazel. 'Tell Prince Hailaz here how you came to be in this pitiful condition.' He sat down on a moth eaten chair, a perfectly bestial smile upon his curving lips.

Like an automaton, the wretched king turned his eyes on Hailaz. His voice was faint, as if his throat was full of dust. 'Long ago, this city fair, Vaengir of the Singing Falls, was the capital of a great kingdom that was known from Morstar and beyond as Tinsantrel. Of great power were the cities of Tinsantrel and, most of all, the jewel of her hills, fair Vaengir. Her people were strong and healthy, and summer lay long over the green and gentle flanks of Morstar. Happy people raised their sheep and cattle there, and wealth poured out of the land.

'Of all the inhabitants of this forgotten country, none was more contented than I, its king. I had three beautiful wives, who bore for me incomparable children. The rooms of my splendid palace were stacked high with jewels and treasures from far, exotic lands. The Singing Falls filled my spirit with joy and my heart with peace. I enjoyed nothing more than to lie in the spray of the Falls and listen to the sweet voice that sang from its shimmering droplets. No, I lacked for nothing. My country was strong, and but for one calamity, might have lasted for eternity. Even now, Vaengir could still be a queen of cities; my sons and their sons ruling here in wisdom. But doom came to Vaengir, upon a summer's day, when two foreign merchant-adventurers rode into her streets.

'These travellers visited many of the city taverns, where they boasted of their exploits, and of the strange and wonderful things they had brought with them from far, unmapped lands. Eventually, they came to the palace gate and requested an audience with me, professing they had in their possession a thing that would interest me greatly. I had already heard of these travellers and was curious about what wares they might offer to me.

'I gladly received the men and offered them hospitality. They spoke to me of a strange creature they had caught in a land far southward, which was unknown even to the wise scribes of Vaengir. In return for this fabulous creature, they were willing to accept gold and jewels. They said they knew I had a love of unnatural wonders and liked to collect them. And so, they brought forth the snake-boy, Gahrazel, he of the Colurastes.

'All of my wives gasped at the creature's loveliness. They exclaimed over the nacreous lustre of his scaly skin and yearned to stroke his braided hair. The snake boy would be a wonderful adornment for the court, they said. They had never beheld such a bewitching creature.

'To please them, and also myself, for I could see that here was a rare prize, I paid the merchants what they demanded, and then bid them on their way. Oh, how blind I was to the truth! I thought that Gahrazel, though strange, was nothing more than an innocent boy. I could not see I had accepted into my royal house an ageless lamia, who was furious at being entrapped.

'The merchants had bound his body thrice with the magical twine of the wolf-hemp, a ritual act that had nullified the creature's powers. In ignorance, I cut those restraining cords with my own, jewelled dagger. Whereupon, the creature could once again speak.

'He said to me, "Let me go free from this house, Great Arax. I see you are a fair man, and you know you have no claim over me. I hail from the Colurastes, and even now my siblings weep for me upon the flat, wet rocks beside the speaking river of Shyya. Let me be free, so I may rejoin them. I am not meant to dwell within the halls of humankind."

'I refused this request resolutely, for I had just paid a great sum for him. Also, he was the most beautiful and unusual creature I had ever seen. I had to own him. My wives were in accord with me, and nodded their heads vigorously when I told the boy there was no question of his leaving.

'Gahrazel contemplated my words for some moments, then said, "You have indeed paid a great many jewels for me. I can see that you appreciate me in an aesthetic sense. As I said to you, I cannot dwell in a place such as this for long, but in goodwill, I elect to stay here in your palace for five years. But, in that time, neither you, nor any of your people, must contemplate even to lay a finger to my flesh. Should any of you violate my wish, fair Vaengir will suffer my curse and the whole of Tinsantrel shall perish."

'I was amused by his words. He was just a boy, yet he spoke as if the might of my guards could do nothing to prevent him leaving should he decide to do so. As I said, I was ignorant of his power then, but in amusement agreed to his terms. I let him have his dignity.

'Gahrazel dwelled in the palace for four pleasant years, never appearing any older than when he first arrived. I know he found us as fascinating as we found him, and perhaps had events occurred differently, he would have decided to remain here even after the five years had ended. In Vaengir, he was treated as a prince, and had the freedom of the city. Among his siblings, he would again be only a lowly hunter who procured food for their great serpent king.

'Then, one evening, the first barrels of new wine were delivered from Morstar's vineyards. The entire court drank heavily. Some strange magic had wormed into the grape that year. The wine was potent but induced a kind of madness. I drank as heavily as anyone else did. A fire ran through my veins, and conjured ill thoughts in my head. I became lustful, but at the same time spawned a terrible contempt for my wives and even my accustomed concubines. I sprawled in my throne, while my courtiers cavorted around me, and I could not fight the vision of Gahrazel's inhuman beauty, which arose constantly and provocatively before my inner eye. I considered what a new and stimulating experience it would be to touch his scaled flesh. I would find a way to slake my lust upon him.

'I went at once to the shrouded apartments of the lamia, and here informed him of my desire. As I spoke, his pale flesh turned an even deadlier white, like that of the blind, white cobras, which crawl the tombs of kings. He hissed and rose up from his couch, and said to me, "Remember your promise, Arax. Remember the words I spoke to you. Once you have taken hold of my arm, I am as good as yours, for that is the way of my people. I cannot resist it, but I beg you to resist, for once you have touched me, I may never go back to the cool green caverns of the Colurastes. I will be doomed to slither through the world of humankind, devouring in a lust of hatred. Know this, and leave me be."

'But I was a drunken fool, and Gahrazel's advice was wasted upon me. I reached for his arm, and once my fingers had curled around his warm flesh, he uttered a shuddering hiss and threw himself upon me.

'That night, I learned of things no man could, or should, imagine. But in the morning, the green of the land curled up on itself and fled away, from the borders of Tinsantrel to the far foothills of Morstar. Every tree became a stark skeleton and every field a barren waste. The hills themselves crumbled into tiny stones. All the people and creatures of Tinsantrel began to wither and die. This was because the dreadful lamia feasted upon their souls. He was right: he could not contain his evil cravings. The Singing Falls became still, and their song, made homeless, haunted the streets, wailing dismally.

'Eventually, even the name of Tinsantrel faded from the lips of the people beyond the hills. It was nothing more than a dead wasteland, its former glory forgotten by all.

'This then is the curse of Gahrazel, the potent, devastating curse of a true Colurastes. Not only did he kill this land, but also erased its memory from history. Neither did his vengeance cease there, for the people of Vaengir are in his thrall, and daily must emerge from death to enact a meaningless life for his entertainment. But Gahrazel too is a prisoner here. Any stray soul he senses abroad in the wilderlands is subject to his will, owing to the power he has over the land. He waits for a deliverance, of which I cannot speak. When he attains this freedom, Tinsantrel will live again.'

Hailaz watched in amazement as Arax's head drooped back

towards his breast and his spell-bound body froze once more.

Gahrazel stretched and stood up again. 'The air in here is foul, Prince Hailaz. Let us return to my balcony.'

Numbly, Hailaz obeyed. He was torn by the story he had heard. Gahrazel's spite was fearsome, but then he had warned Arax of what would happen.

When they were once again in the sunlight, overlooking the market, Hailaz said, 'And what is to happen to me, Gahrazel? Will you feast on me too, so I'll become a mindless hunk of clay like Mahor and the rest?'

'Sometimes, I take pity on the most wretched and weak of this world,' Gahrazel answered. 'I pitied you even as you tried to cross the wilderlands. Therefore, I will give you a choice. You may either resume your journey, in an attempt to reach human civilisation or you may stay here with me, but I will not take your life. I have to say that it is impossible for you to survive the wilderlands. You would starve and thirst before you could find your way out. Far better you resign yourself to your fate and remain here.'

'But this city is hideous!' Hailaz cried. 'A place of the dead. The wilderlands can be no worse. I found my way here and I can find my way back.'

'I lured you here. You would require my complicity even to reach the country now dominated by the Fenelix, who incidentally would slaughter you immediately you set foot on their soil. They watch the border, for they know no-one can live in the wilderlands, nor cross it.'

Hailaz considered this information. 'Can you really not reverse your own curse? Leave this place. Together we could journey to a new land. With the aid of your powers, surely we could succeed?

'And leave my people?' Gahrazel said bitterly. 'I have nowhere to go in this world, Prince of Lyye. As I have lain with a son of man, the Colurastes would not have me back to taint their blood. I would be doomed to haunt the shadowed corners of the world, preying upon the hapless travellers who came within my power. There is no escape for me. At least here I can curb the vile desires that would consume me completely once I left Tinsantrel's boundary.'

'But do you really have to become this predatory thing?' Hailaz asked. 'What happened here was not really your fault. Is there no way you can be freed? You were the victim of a bored king. Kings consider themselves above all other men. They can often seek their amusement in cruel ways. I know this only too well from what I beheld with my own eyes back in the Halls of Lyye.'

A troubled look crossed Gahrazel's face. 'Hailaz,' he said, 'I would welcome your company. There would be much for you to study here. Stay with me. I beg you, do not ask how I might be freed.'

'But why not?' Hailaz asked. 'It is a living death for you here. I would gladly free you if it were in my power to do so. Why do you not desire it?'

Gahrazel sighed. 'Because, if you offered, I would accept it.'

Hailaz leaned against the sun-warmed balcony, and gazed down at the bustling scene below. 'There is nothing for me beyond the wilderlands,' he said, 'but I have no wish to live the rest of my days in a city of the dead. Together, we could travel to far lands, and see many wonders. I feel that surviving the fall of Lyye was a preordained event. I have been given another chance at life. Gahrazel, tell me the secret that I may release you.' He did not look at the lamia, but could feel those strange eyes beating upon his turned back like a physical force.

'Give me your soul,' Gahrazel whispered. 'If I take it without your consent, the curse continues. But should you give me your whole essence, willingly, I shall be free of it.'

Hailaz went cold and the sun seemed to darken. He turned round and gazed into Gahrazel's black eyes. He could not look away; his strength seemed to run out of his spine like a hot fluid. *What have I to lose?* he thought. *What good is my soul to me? I am unsure I even have one.*

Hailaz felt as if he was sinking into the lamia's enormous black eyes. They were ready to engulf and devour him with an ancient hunger. 'Take it then!' Hailaz blurted. 'I will accept the consequences.'

Gahrazel's eyes leapt like jewels in the sunlight and with the speed of a striking snake, he did not question Hailaz's offer, but dragged him down to the marble tiles. His body transformed, so that from the waist downward he became a mass of glistening coils that wrapped themselves around Hailaz's body in constricting strength.

Hailaz expelled a moan. He felt that every bone in his body would be crushed. The lamia fixed his lips upon the prince's own, and breathed into him a toxic sigh. Hailaz's body jerked within the coils. His whole being was lashed by waves of ecstasy, pain, lust and revolting horror. Gahrazel was no longer remotely human in appearance. He had no real gender. He was simply a purpose, and the purpose was to devour, to suck the life and soul from his prey. After that, would come darkness and cold for eternity.

Hailaz screamed, and Gahrazel swallowed the sound and its terror. In his mind, Hailaz begged for release. He withdrew his offer. He would take his chance in the wilderlands. But it was too late, for by that time he was already dead.

Gahrazel lay beside Hailaz in the late afternoon sun, panting and bloody, his eyes shining in repletion. Impotent whimpering fell from Hailaz' bitten lips as the city began to crumble. Time swept back like a tidal wave over the land. Life stirred in the sleeping soil of Morstar, as in a lazy, green undulation, a mantle of verdure crawled towards Vaengir's fast-falling stones. Skeletons, long blown to dust, caused a thick miasma on the air, the fire died in the palace columns and, in his ruined apartments, a mad imprisoned king bubbled out his last words.

Wrapped in Gahrazel's embrace, Hailaz breathed deeply. In the air, carried far, was the faint scent of burnt flesh and timber. It was the perfume of the ruins of Lyye.

As the sun sank on that first day of the reawakening of Tinsantrel, a small brown mare kicked up her heels and galloped among the powdering blocks of a dead city. As she left the fallen roadways in the direction of the city gate, she shied. Slithering along the grassy path, strangely entwined, two serpents wound their way out of Vaengir.

Carmia secretly despised Jeanette, and was perplexed as to why she was so popular with the Crowd. Jeanette, in Carmia's opinion, strove to appear mystical, but failed abysmally. She was drunk most of the time and this did not help the image of neo-Egyptian Queen. It took more than make-up to be exotic. Sometimes, Carmia felt sorry for Jeanette, although Jeanette's witty, if cruel, observations concerning the other girls in the Crowd were always entertaining.

'I heard that Maggie found out Anton's been seeing another girl,' Carmia mentioned in a casual manner. The sharing of gossip was a currency among the Crowd.

Jeanette smiled. 'Old news, sweetheart. Of course Maggie's upset about it, but their relationship hasn't been right for weeks, has it? She really is a most *whining* girl. Never could see what Anton saw in her. She's hardly attractive, after all, and makes the most abominable noise when she's eating.'

Another girl joined them, having overheard the remarks. She was spangled, slender and blond and her eyes shone with the fanaticism of the apprentice vampire. 'That reminds me, girls,' she said in a high voice. 'Did you know Shirley's parents have kicked her out of home? She's been staying at my place this week. Gone over to her sister's tonight to fix up a bed for a few months. She's not working, you know. Can't say I blame her parents, though. A week was enough for me! Stroppy little cow! I shan't be sorry to see the back of her.'

'That Marina is as bad,' Jeanette commented, her face lighting up in preparation for a full-scale assault.

'She's really pretty,' Carmia said, regretting the words the moment they left her lips. She quite liked Marina.

'Can't stand her!' Jeannette snapped. She thinks she's God's gift on high heels! As if smoking those expensive cigarettes impresses anyone. She makes out she's Val's best friend, but all Marina wants is that emaciated little creep of a boyfriend of hers. Mind you, Marina's never had any taste concerning men.'

Carmia found her attention drifting. At one time, she'd felt proud to be part of such conversations, but tonight, she found the mean attitude stifling. She let her eyes wander around the bar. Familiar faces. Her lip curled, showing her trim white teeth. She saw men she had slept with, others she had tried to seduce. Of the latter category, there were few. She was not exactly proud of that fact. She was disappointed that none of her romances had ever lasted. The initial delicious spice had always faded to leave behind a thing that was like tasteless meat. These men could not really inspire her. They were only interested in the possessions they could acquire, and they boasted too much about nothing. In fact, they were embarrassing, for all their fashionable clothes and cool demeanour.

Carmia shuddered. A changing wind swept silently over the heads of the throng. Carmia felt it. Deep inside her, a primal instinct sniffed the air and noticed something that left an uncomfortable impression in her psyche. She felt hungry, dry-mouthed hungry. In her soul. She felt like she wanted to run and scream, barefoot, naked. The jumbled images in the bar bucked before her eyes. Shocked, she shook her hair, cleared her head, feeling in a far away place in her mind that she must be sickening for something.

She raised her eyes. Everything still seemed the same. Jeanette and the other girl still barked and jabbered behind her, their eyes and their glasses of wine sparkling, catching the light. The noise in the bar hadn't changed, but the atmosphere had - subtly. Something had arrived. Carmia could not tell what it was, nor interpret the tingling in her toes and fingers, but she looked around calmly, waiting.

And there it was.

Across the room, leaning on the bar, crumpled money in his hand, a man she had not seen before was purchasing a drink. He became aware he was being watched, because his eyes flickered quickly in Carmia's direction.

He's a god, she thought, staring. She had sampled and smoothed the bodies of every fascinating male who frequented the place, but now she had discovered someone new. She had never encountered such perfection. He was everybody's idea of perfection. Should she go over to him? No, the others! She almost growled in her throat. A quick glance over her shoulder reassured her. They still chattered, hadn't noticed. She glanced back at the bar. Yes, he was still there. Tall, straight-limbed, a golden aura round his head. He had thick hair the colour of corn sheaves and agates. Carmia whined softly and ran her tongue over her lips. The man stared back impassively. Man? No, too young - he was merely a boy. Fresh and clean, untouched. Perfect. Carmia wanted him. More than she had ever wanted anything in her life. The thrill of the chase was upon her.

'Carmia!' Jeanette shook her. 'You've gone pale. What's up? Are you feeling OK?'

Carmia looked round into Jeanette's cruel, amused eyes and the red, red smile that was equally cruel. 'No,' she answered. 'It's just hot in here, that's all.' Turning away, she took a hasty swig from her glass and almost choked, which prompted a sly sneer from Jeanette. 'This wine is vile stuff,' Carmia said, wrinkling her nose. 'Think I'll buy something else, otherwise I *will* be ill before the evening's out.' She pushed her way to the bar.

Where had he gone? Anxiously, Carmia looked round the crowd. Damn, damn! No sign of him. Oh, nobody else had got to him yet, surely? He was hers now. She had marked him. Petulantly, she ordered a whisky; straight with ice, feeling angry and cheated as she threaded her way back to the others. Men smiled at her and addressed her in coaxing tones, but they were not her prey, and she hardly noticed them.

* * *

Later that night, after a disappointing evening that had fallen flat on its face, Carmia dreamed. She dreamed while her parents still watched the late movie on the television in the room beneath her own. Dreamed while Jeanette got picked up by some of the Crowd and swerved drunkenly off to a party. Carmia twitched and whined in her sleep, perceiving snippets of faint movie sounds and moulding them into her dream.

She was running along a great flat expanse of ochre sand that spread to the horizon all around, punctuated by faraway dots that might have been trees, scrub or rancid pools of water. The sand was firm and pleasant to the touch of her bare feet. Bare feet, bare hands. She realised she was galloping bizarrely on all fours. Her gait was at once awkward yet speedy. She was an animal, surrounded by others of her kind, who pushed, jostled, bayed, snapped and howled. Their presence annoyed her. She wanted to be alone with the sand-spiked wind in her hide, but the others were close and hot. Stabbing lights shot out from their wet steaming mouths and wet steaming eyes, into her head. White lances of pain. Why were they running? What were they pursuing? There was no quarry in sight, yet Carmia had no doubt they were hunting.

Glancing aside, she noticed something bright running alongside her, but a fair distance off. Its jaws were more dazzling than anything she'd ever seen and strangely, they seemed to laugh.

In the morning, Carmia woke unrested. Her body ached with exertion, and she knew she must wait for the night.

The following evening, a Saturday night, Carmia was ready to go out earlier than usual. Tonight, she would not miss her bus. Tonight, she would be at Batwings first. As she sat painting her nails in her bedroom, making mistakes because her hands were shaking, she was pervaded by the impression that something immensely ancient was drifting in the air. It was a vague smell or a strange feeling. She did not feel at ease.

Once she reached Batwings, she felt uncomfortable sitting alone at one of the small tables in the front bar. The place was nearly empty at this hour. When she lifted her wineglass, she noticed that her hands were still shaking. Why had she come here at this absurd time? She was acting like a fool. Her memory of the day was hazy. She felt it had taken effort to survive it. Everything around her had seemed blackened by the frantic thumping of her blood. She did not understand this feeling. It was as if a deep inner part of her was looking out, over which her conscious self had no control. Something inside her was waiting; she sensed it whining and scraping to be let out.

The bar was just beginning to fill up with people when he arrived. Alone. He paused at the doorway like a cat, mere feet from where Carmia sat. He looked round carefully before entering the room. Carmia thought his sleek muscles were set as if ready to spring, yet he appeared lithe and relaxed. The world dimmed around her. The noise in the bar was eclipsed by the pound of blood in her ears, and the boy was a straight reed of light in the dimness. Carmia was transfixed by instant passion. She did not move, but with her eyes pleaded for him to turn round. When he did, his eyes were golden-green. Laughing eyes.

'Hi,' he said

Carmia opened her mouth to speak, suddenly devoid of poise and confidence. She felt tiny, too young. She must say something, a witty remark, a warm remark, anything at all. No sound came. Feelings boiled within her as if he'd conjured them from her: anger, desolation, courage, freedom, fear, confusion and helpless sadness. In her mind, she saw an image of ochre sand running between her fingers. The boy did not look away and neither did his expression change. He reached out and patted Carmia on the head as if she were an animal, not a she-wolf, but a homeless dog begging in the gutter, craving affection. Involuntarily, Carmia made a noise in her throat that came out like a whine.

'Hi, Carmy!' The voice intruded upon her thoughts. She blinked, but the impossible, incomparable boy had gone. The bar heaved before her eyes, heaving with hot milling bodies and their hundred incompatible perfumes. Jeanette's face leered over her, like a gargoyle disembodied in the air. 'You look ill,' Jeanette commented, without apparent concern. 'Let's go to the loo. There's something I just have to tell you and you never know who's listening out here.'

Crouched over the toilet bowl, half listening to Jeanette's cackling speech, half listening to the sound of the comb being dragged endlessly through Jeanette's wild hair, Carmia retched until she felt her stomach must bleed.

That night, Carmia's dreams were more vivid than before, unhindered by the fact that Jeanette, owing to a drunken stupor her parents would not have tolerated, slept restlessly in the same bed. In the dream, Carmia raced alone with the wind across the great wide plain of ochre sand. Far to her right, ragged grey and black peaks now soared frighteningly high, unearthly structures, like the houses of gods, ringed with vulture-wing clouds and vast black wings that only she could hear. She was quite happy running alone: inexhaustible energy thrummed through her veins. Her fur felt hot, the sun was very bright, but she was not uncomfortable. If only it could have lasted like that. She loved the feeling of freedom, the strangely comfortable solitude, but then a shuddering howl filled the air behind her and a stench of stale musk invaded her muzzle. Soon a hundred pushing, shoving grey bodies pressed around her, froth flying from their gaping jaws, fur matted by the undergrowth of some far-off chase.

They seek my prey! she thought in a panic, and began to snap at the lean, hairy flanks beside her.

Baying carelessly, they ignored her attack.

A great shaggy beast with an abnormally large head jostled up against her, gripping her shoulder in its maw. 'Do not desert the pack,' it snarled between its teeth, spraying her with rank saliva. 'Run with us! We know best.'

Growling, Carmia managed to wriggle free. She heard a hollow barking laugh behind her and flung a glance over her shoulder. Fangs bright, Jeanette gambolled along effortlessly at her tail. Even in an animal form, she was instantly recognisable. Her wide jaws were stretched in a humourless grin. Carmia let out a dismal howl and increased her speed. The she-wolves gave tongue and matched her pace.

I am not one of them, she thought. *If I am a she-wolf, then I am a loner. I'm not part of the pack.*

She wanted to be a beautiful wild animal, as free as the elements. Her fur would be the silver of the moon, and the lunar light would shine from her eyes. These creatures around her were a pack of stray dogs, muddied, lice-ridden and mindlessly vicious. They had lost touch with the astounding wonder of existence. They could not comprehend the true light of the moon, so could not be wolves. Their petty spite infected Carmia, tainted the beauty of her soul. She was learning something important, but the din of their howling made it difficult to think.

Desperately, Carmia tried to evade their company, weaving, turning and snapping. But they were too strong and too many. Exhausted, she let them steer her body in the direction they chose, only half aware of the golden thing, loping, thwarted, beside the pack, as if waiting for the moment to strike.

* * *

The following week seemed interminable. Carmia yearned for the weekend when she might be able to see the boy again. Maybe even speak to him. But she was so tired. Her sleep was troubled and did not seem to relieve her any more. Nightmares plagued her tumbled bed, nightmares of unattainable gold, and of hot, feral breath and cruel, yellow eyes. Jeanette called her a few times, and carefully Carmia asked questions to discover whether Jeanette or any of the other girls had noticed the new boy in Batwings. She could not believe she was the only one to have noticed him, and yet her inquiries elicited no information. She became afraid. Perhaps all the others knew about him and were deliberately excluding her from talking about him. They would have seduction plans of their own. The thought of it made Carmia feel sick. She was the silver wolf, they were the yapping dogs. He must see her light, not their shadows.

Friday night arrived, hot and sultry. From her bedroom window, Carmia could see the lights of the town shimmering in a haze. All day, she had felt fevered, planning what she would do later when she went to Batwings. The boy would be there again, she just knew it, and this time she would impress him, show him she was different from all the others. Therefore, Carmia was horrified when Jeanette called her in the afternoon and told her she'd be round in a couple of hours. 'I want to walk into Batwings with you tonight,' she said. 'I met this guy the other day and he's going to meet me there. I'm not going in on my own.'

Carmia knew that Jeanette lacked confidence until she was drunk. She couldn't think of an excuse to put Jeanette off.

When she arrived, Jeanette complained about how early Carmia wanted to go out. 'What's the rush?'

'I want to get a good seat.'

'Since when have you cared about that? The place will be dead until nine. I've bought a bottle with me. We can take our time getting ready and have a few drinks. I want to look my best.'

Carmia gritted her teeth. 'We're going out at half seven, OK? We can drink when we get there.'

Disgruntled, Jeanette spent hours in the bathroom applying her make-up, while Carmia, ready and itching to be off, stood rigid and angry in her bedroom, staring fixedly into the full-length mirror, but taking no comfort from her reflection.

Eventually, Jeanette glided into the room, where she squeezed her reflection into the glass, patted her hair, twisted, grimaced, and announced, 'OK, I'm ready.' It was eight o'clock.

Barely containing her fury, Carmia flung a silk jacket round her shoulders and they left the house.

At the bus stop, Jeanette said, 'so what's eating you, then?'

Carmia squirmed. 'Nothing.'

'Look, I'm supposed to be your friend. Tell me.'

Carmia stared at Jeanette for a moment. She did not see friendship in the face looking back at her. 'Don't you sometimes wish there was something else to do?' she said.

Jeanette laughed. 'You what?'

Carmia shrugged. 'We go to Batwings all the time. There must be other things to do.'

Jeanette narrowed her eyes. 'It's our place. It's where we go. You spent enough time lurking around waiting to be let in, so why moan about it now?'

'I don't know. If we're she-wolves, then we're not running free. We're in a zoo without knowing it.'

Jeanette made a disparaging sound. 'Who says you're a she-wolf? More like a hyena to me.' She expelled a sound, which was clearly meant to be a hyena.

Carmia winced and wanted to say, 'you and are your

Storm Constantine

friends aren't wolves, you're just stupid dogs', but she did not want to deal with the reaction these words would invoke.

Once they reached Batwings, Carmia noticed the boy the minute they stepped through the door. He was leaning against the bar: drowsy, powerful, beautiful. It had been worth the wait. He was more splendid than she remembered, and strangely, she felt as if they were friends already. It was no longer difficult to go up to him and speak. Surprisingly, Jeanette did not follow and for a brief moment Carmia wondered why she seemed to be the only one tracking this paragon. Were they all so blind? It was unreal. He was alone.

'Hi,' he said, as before, half smiling.

'Hi,' she replied, trying to sound husky. She sat down on a stool and leaned her elbows on the bar.

He laughed. 'You don't have to try so hard,' he said.

She felt herself redden. 'Excuse me?'

He shrugged. 'You know.' He put a drink into her hand and reality faded for her. It had all been so easy.

'Why me?' she heard herself asking. 'You could have any one of us.'

'Because a good huntress always demands the best trophies,' he replied.

She laughed coldly. 'You think that much of yourself?'

'Don't you?'

She shook her head. 'This is weird.'

He smiled, but said nothing. She felt comfortable with his silence. Where was Jeanette? Why hadn't she come over? Carmia studied the boy's profile. He was really the most exquisite creature she had ever seen, but it went beyond the physical. He had a shine to him, an aura she could almost see. All the usual trivialities of Batwings conversation seemed inappropriate. She could think of nothing to say, simply because, for those few minutes, there *was* nothing to say.

Carmia finished her drink and put down her glass. 'I love you,' she said.

'I know,' he replied. His voice was like honey being poured onto pure marble. 'That's why I've come. Look into the mirror.'

His arm curled around her shoulder, warm and pliable. She looked into the mirror on the wall beside them. 'I'm beautiful,' she said. 'So are you.'

He did not comment. The mirror was misty, ochre-coloured, fading, shifting, glittering, spitting scenes. Carmia tore her gaze away from it and stood up to embrace the perfect boy. She pressed her body against him, smothered his lips with her own. Her hands clawed his body, coveting his litheness. He was a wolf, like her, an animal of the night, full of secrets. They would snarl together, run together, but free of the pack.

He pulled away from her, and examined her with depthless golden eyes. He breathed on her, and his breath carried the ghost of a snarl. Then he took her hand and led her into the mirror.

Onto the ochre sand. They were running wildly with the wind, his great golden body seeming to skim the ground. His limbs devoured space and time. No wolf, but some other creature. He leapt and twisted his body, coming to a halt in front of her so that she was forced to skid on the shifting sand that puffed up around her in a choking cloud. For some moments, she could neither see nor breathe and writhed on the ground, coughing. When the air cleared, she saw an immense golden shape crouching over her. It breathed an aurous light down on to her, watching her placidly. The light filled Carmia's body, reached into every cell of her being. He did not touch her at all.

Two golden lions loped silently away from the body of the wolf that lay half buried in the sand. Their gold-green eyes scanned the horizon as they ran onto the savannah where the deer herds grazed. The deer were tranquil, their damp black muzzles thrust into the rattling grass. The lions crouched among the concealing stems. *There are too many wolves,* they decided. *Too many, and they take the best. But not for long.*

Night's Damozel

On the morning of her arrival, Samuel wandered out into his garden. Already the sun was blistering and the still, clammy air threatened later storms. He walked along the shaded walkways where, as it dripped through the dense canopy of leaves, the burning yellow light turned to cool amber. His heart felt too large within its cage of bones. Where was the joy with which he should be greeting his new bride? Standing in the sunlight, he shivered.

Samuel was a quiet man with few friends, and those who had somehow stuck to his life since childhood now lived far away. He saw them only once a year, in early summer, when for a month, he would travel overseas. His life was marked only slightly by the presence of others; he had a single servant, a bad tempered woman named Hesta, who lived on a nearby farm. She visited him daily, but Samuel rarely saw her. He left her coins as wages once a week and consumed her indifferent cooking with neither relish nor disgust.

Few other visitors ventured up the long, tree-shuttered drive-way to the house, yet Samuel never felt lonely. He had companions. His garden was full of them: nearly a hundred different species of rare and exotic plants. They were his passion. They spoke to him without words, and listened to his most secret confidences without interrupting. They indulged him with gifts; dark, sticky fruit and flowers whose petals felt as soft as the skin of children. Their names were beautiful: Dancing Bride, whose spray of small white blooms concealed a bitter nectar that stopped the heart; Severia, whose juices thinned the blood so effectively, a simple scratch might result in slow death; Lady Anne's Pearls, whose dull-bloomed berries nestled in a grey-green nest of prickled leaves, whose taste was sweet yet paralysed the lungs. There were many more languishing in darkness beneath the evergreens, hugging their secret lives to themselves, or wantonly sprawling over the lichened walls of the sun garden. Often Samuel would lie among them and inhale their narcotic scent until his head throbbed and pulsed. During his annual travels, he had gathered his dark ladies from every corner of the world. But this year, he had journeyed to the hot land of Mewt, where he'd cut for himself a different kind of flower, and soon she would be here.

Samuel's steps were slow, even dragging. He wondered how he would tell the green ladies of his wife's arrival. He should have spoken before, but had sensed the displeasure his news would invoke. They would be anxious, for they were used only to his company.

There was a queen to Samuel's kingdom and her name was Night's Damozel. Her velvet blooms, of imperial purple, reared on tall, slender necks from a coronet of long, silver-furred leaves. Her pollen could be deadly, yet to one familiar with her charms, it imparted a sweet euphoria. Samuel had long acquaintance with the Damozel and spent many a balmy evening with his head in her royal lap, inhaling the sparkling dust that drifted down from her open hearts. Now, he came again to her court in a grove of ancient yews. Little sun-light reached her, yet her bower was always temperate. Her maids of honour were a riot of cobalt ground poppies. Swollen bees hung drunkenly above her blooms, droning low and deep.

Samuel knelt before her, his head bowed. He felt the sun reach down with attenuated fingers between the needles of the yews and touch his neck. He told the Damozel his news.

He had first seen Xanthe in twilight, standing above him on a balcony at the villa of one of his acquaintances. Framed by tall, sputtering candles, she had been holding a long-stemmed glass to the side of her face, gazing out at the dark sea beyond the villa gardens. The ocean breeze had lifted tendrils of her hair and they had coiled around her face and shoulders like questing vipers. She was lovely: tall, slender, her body swaying slightly as she meditated upon the approaching night. Samuel's heart had at once been captivated for he'd seen within this woman a similarity to the green ladies who populated his garden. Like them, she had seemed remote, silent, rooted to the spot.

On the terrace near the cliffs, where a host of people mingled, and food and wine grew damp and warm respectively in the heavy air, he had sought out his hostess, a duchess named Sythia. She had been standing at the centre of a group of guests, amusing them with gossip. Samuel had sipped his wine and made what he hoped were discreet enquiries about the woman on the balcony.

Sythia had smiled conspiratorially and led Samuel to one side. 'You speak of Xanthe. You like her? Of course you do. She is charming. A temptation to many men.'

Samuel, unused to such direct words, had felt himself grow hot. 'She is interesting,' he'd replied, which was exactly what he'd felt.

Sythia's smiled had widened. 'You would like to meet her, of course.'

Samuel had been irritated by Sythia's demeanour. He knew the people who thought themselves his friends had despaired of him ever finding a mate. Well-meaning older ladies had often told him he was a well-favoured man and had many admirers, but once he saw the women whose eyes he'd caught, he had to flee. They seemed so pink and fleshy, so clumsy. Now, his fumbling enquiries about Xanthe would soon be known to all the company. The

morsel of information would be relished as much as the
rare, salty shell-fish that lay dismembered on the duchess'
table.

'In truth, I know very little about the lady,' Sythia had
confessed as she cut through the throng of guests that
cluttered her garden. 'I met her at a soiree some weeks
back, and like you, felt my curiosity stir. Nobody knows her.
She is an enigma, and a lovely complement to any
gathering. I have invited her here three times already.'

Sythia had paused beneath the balcony where Xanthe
still contemplated the scenery. The duchess called her name
and, languidly, Xanthe directed her attention towards the
sound. Her face had remained expressionless.

'My dear,' Sythia had said, in a voice of constrained
excitement, 'would you come down here for a moment.
There is someone who wishes to meet you.'

With neither words nor smile, Xanthe had put down
her glass on the rail of the balcony. She'd descended the
steps that flanked the house, her movements precise yet
elegant. Then she had stood before them, towering over
Sythia, looking Samuel directly in the eye. She'd been
dressed in a long, finely-pleated garment, the colour of
ripened corn, which clung to her body like scales. Her dark,
straight hair had hung lustrously over her shoulders. Her
skin had seemed dusty, and Samuel had known instinctively
that it would feel smooth and dry to his touch. He'd wanted
to shrink from Xanthe's overt scrutiny, yet simultaneously
wanted to drown in her unwavering gaze.

He could no longer remember how Sythia had affected
introductions. His memory had discarded any words that
had been exchanged beyond that initial overture, but he
could still recall in detail the smashing of the sea below, and
the scent of the night-blooming vines, and Xanthe's private
smile as she observed, through her dark, slanting eyes, his
developing infatuation.

In a dry, barely interested kind of way she apparently

decided to collude in his desires. Later that same night, after most of the guests had retired to bed, or else had fallen where they stood among the empty glasses, she had led Samuel to a bare promontory and here, beneath the swelling moon, had discarded the sheath of her dress, to reveal a long, sinuous body whose flesh was cool yet supple. She'd had no inhibitions whatsoever, although Samuel, being devoid of experience in these matters, had wondered whether all women were so open in this regard.

There had followed a week of intoxicated passion, of fever and of joy. In the mornings, Xanthe would leave Samuel's bed and go to sun herself upon the balcony, kneading into her skin fragrant oils that were absorbed almost immediately to leave a matte sheen. In the afternoons, while the other guests dozed after lunch, she and Samuel would walk into the nearby town, and drink cold, tart wines beneath the shade of awnings outside sleepy inns. She'd talked of herself, of her dreams and expectations. Her voice had been low, husky, with a slight lisp. Her family were rich, she'd told Samuel, and she was an artist. She was amused by Sythia's patronage, but was happy to enjoy the benefits of the friendship. 'I love her house,' Xanthe had said. 'The rocks around it retain such heat.'

At the end of that week, Samuel had made up his mind: he wanted Xanthe as a wife. One afternoon, as they paused in their daily walk at a shore-side inn, he'd become emboldened by wine, and had taken hold of her hands across the table. 'Xanthe, be my bride.'

She'd looked at him inscrutably for a few moments, then said, 'If you like.'

Just a few days later, they'd married in a small, mountain temple, and afterwards Sythia had thrown a banquet in their honour. Then, Xanthe had returned to her family estate to organise the packing of items she wished to transport to her new home, while Samuel had travelled back across the sea to his homeland of Tarbonnay, where he would prepare his demesne for her arrival.

'And today she comes,' Samuel told the Damozel. 'I pray you will love her as I do.'

The afternoon had dulled and seemed to fall silent; the bees had tumbled away, and not even a leaf stirred in the bower. Then, as Samuel raised his head, the sun reappeared from behind a cloud and the Damozel's stately blooms turned slowly away from him. She seemed to gaze haughtily at the sky.

'Fear not, my lady,' he murmured. 'My consort will attend you as I have. She is eager to meet you and tend you. She will be a mother to you. It is a wife's duty to love all that her husband loves.'

The sun rolled behind the first black cloud of the approaching storm, and stayed there. First the Damozel, then her hand-maidens, slowly bowed their heads once more and stared at Samuel with the blind eyes of their velvet hearts. He had never lied to them before.

Samuel did not bother to make any special effort over his appearance to greet his new wife. He spent a few hours tending his plants, then, pausing only to wipe his hands on a dirty rag, bound back his long hair with a piece of twine, and positioned himself in his gloomy study to await Xanthe's arrival. His eyes skittered with discomfort over the disarray in the room, as if becoming aware of it for the first time. Perhaps he should have hired a team of cleaners to prepare the house for her arrival, but it was not his habit to fuss about his environment. After the last of his parents' retainers had left, complaining the house was too large for so small a staff to cope with, he had never engaged anyone but Hesta, who in fact did very little for her money. Still, domestic matters would be Xanthe's province. He smiled to himself. Previously, he had not considered that particular benefit of taking a wife.

After Xanthe did not arrive at the expected hour, Samuel started to feel impatient. Rain began to fall heavily upon the garden, which did not improve his mood. Hesta presented herself at the doorway of his study. She was a large woman with resentful eyes. 'Is she here yet?' she enquired rather disrespectfully.

'No,' Samuel answered shortly. 'Prepare a cold supper and leave it in the kitchen.'

Hesta grunted and departed; perhaps relieved she would not be required to stretch her culinary talents for the benefit of a new wife.

Samuel waited for the storm to pass, then went outside, where the air was cool and damp. He resolved to walk down the long, winding driveway and if Xanthe had not made an appearance by the time he reached the road, he would lock the gates. It was as if the events of his recent holiday had been a dream, a pleasant dream, but one ill destined to continue. Now, it seemed inconceivable that Xanthe, with her foreign air, would settle successfully in his home. He must have been bewitched in Mewt; lulled by the hot, perfumed air and the long, lazy nights.

At the gates, Samuel put his hands upon the wet, rusty rods and peered down the road that led to the nearest town. He saw her then, walking ahead of a wagon like a common farm girl. She wore a sun-coloured, loose dress that brushed her ankles, and her face was shadowed by a wide-brimmed hat. She walked languorously, clearly in no particular hurry to reach her destination. Sometimes, she paused to sniff a road-side flower or turned to say something to the wagon driver. Not until she'd nearly reached Samuel's gates, did she look ahead, notice him and raise a languid hand to wave.

'You are late,' Samuel said churlishly.

'Yes,' she agreed and came forward to lay a cool hand on his arm. 'Open the gates then, Samuel, so the wagon can carry my effects to the house.'

The wagon heaved past them; it was not heavily laden. Xanthe hooked her hand through Samuel's arm and they strolled up the driveway behind the wagon. Their feet crunched upon gravel that was softened by clumps of dark moss. 'This is a rich and fertile land,' she remarked, 'but I trust it is not too cold in winter. I thrive only in heat.'

Samuel ignored these words and snapped. 'You are now the lady of this house, Xanthe. You should have hired a proper carriage in the town, rather than arrive here on foot like a slattern.'

Xanthe laughed and squinted at him sidelong. 'Why, Samuel, you look like a farm-hand yourself. There are seeds in your hair and dirt beneath your nails. Cheer up. Don't be irritable just because I chose to enjoy a walk and acquaint myself with the land. I am here now.' She leaned over and kissed his cheek.

Her touch kindled heat within him. 'This is your home now, my love. We shall be happy here.' The dream took on flesh once more.

Xanthe uttered an appreciative murmur as the house appeared around a bend in the drive. The garden at the front was rather neglected; a sweep of waving grasses, hedged by willows. The house itself lay like a sleeping lizard in its grounds; a grey sprawl of wings, buttresses and towers that had formed over the generations, from architectural additions by Samuel's ancestors. It was scaled with a myriad tiny windows and its walls were lazily uneven, corseted with immense wooden beams. The late afternoon sun, still watery from the storm, washed the lichened walls with rusty light and gilded the window panes. 'So warm,' Xanthe breathed. 'So warm.'

The heat of summer, however, seemed not to have penetrated the hall of the house, and here the air felt uncomfortably cold and damp. The house smelled of its own age - once a familiar, comforting odour to Samuel, but now somehow repellent. He noticed his wife shiver a little. 'The place needs a good airing,' he said lamely. 'It was shut up while I was away.'

Xanthe glanced at him, but made no comment, even though Samuel could guess she thought the house had been neglected for rather more than a month. The wooden panels of the hall, which once had burned with the sheen of bees' wax, now looked dull and sticky. The floor tiles were obscured by years of accumulated mud, trampled in by Samuel from the garden. Xanthe ventured forward cautiously, apparently to examine her surroundings.

Samuel called, 'Look out,' but it was too late. Xanthe had stepped into a tray against the wall and had scattered its contents.

'Oh, I'm sorry, I've spilled all your seeds,' Xanthe said, adding pointedly, 'I didn't see them.' She bent to brush them up but Samuel hurried to her side and stopped her hand.

'Don't touch it, my love!'

Xanthe frowned. 'Why not?'

Samuel took her hand in his. 'It's poison. A hazard of living in the country, I'm afraid. We have a problem keeping these old places free of vermin.'

'Vermin,' said Xanthe, flatly, straightening up.

'Mice,' Samuel explained. 'Even rats - not that they often come this far into the house, of course, but the cellars, the old larders... I have to keep poison down.'

Xanthe raised an eyebrow. 'Don't worry. Rodents don't scare me. They are too small to inspire fear.'

Samuel smiled at her. What an admirable quality in a woman, this fearlessness where vermin were concerned. He'd always believed women screamed and fainted at the mere mention of them. He led her through the dark passages of the house, into the old kitchen, where he suggested she should wash her hands. Xanthe went to the great, white sink - which was not as white as it could have been - and turned on the cold water tap. 'Poison is dangerous,' she said. 'We might have children one day, Samuel. Why haven't you got a brace of good cats to deal with the problem?'

Samuel did not wish to mention that the poisons growing in his garden were lethal to dogs and cats, while at the same time oddly attractive to them. The thought of children made him go momentarily cold. He imagined little hands reaching for the tempting, deadly fruits. He laughed too heartily and made a feeble joke that animals did not like him.

'Do they not?' Xanthe said coolly, looking for something on which to wipe her wet hands, and finally opting for the front of her dress.

As the sun sank, they went into the dark, dusty dining-room and there consumed the modest repast that Hesta had left for them; cold meats, cheese and thick, heavy bread. Samuel had found a bottle of wine that had not gone off, but it was thick and red - nothing like the light, acid wines he had enjoyed with Xanthe in Mewt.

Afterwards, Samuel showed Xanthe around the more habitable areas of the house, finally leading her to his bedroom. Xanthe's nose wrinkled fastidiously, but she seemed relieved to discover that at least the sheets were crisp and clean. Spiders bred in the dusty, faded folds of velvet drapes around the bed, and the windows were opaque with grey-green grime. Samuel had made a small effort at decorating the room, however, and had filled a number of huge, antique vases with garden flowers - not the children of his ladies, but some lesser blooms left over from the days when his mother had tended the estate.

Xanthe sat on the bed and said, 'I may have to make

changes here, Samuel.' She leaned back on stiff arms and looked around herself. 'You've had dire need of a homely touch, it seems.'

'You may do what you like to the house,' he replied.

Xanthe nodded and silently smiled. Standing, and fixing him with her slanting eyes, she peeled away her dress. Samuel went to her, eager to touch her smooth skin once more, to breathe in her intoxicating scent. Pulling away from him, she walked, naked, to the window and wiped the glass. The moon was rising above the trees, sailing high. Xanthe struggled to open one of the windows and, at last, with a scraping creak and a fall of dead insects and spider webs, it released its hold on its frame. Xanthe stood tall, taking deep breaths. Samuel put his hands upon her smooth, bare shoulders and kissed the cool flesh. She buried her fingers in the thick velvet drapes and sighed like the night.

Below them, in the pale moonlight, the flowers had turned their heads towards the ground. But for the rustling of rats in the grass, the gardens were silent.

The following morning after breakfast, Samuel took his new bride into the garden behind the house. He had decided there was no point in delaying a certain crucial introduction, although his heart beat fast.

Xanthe stepped down the shallow steps led to the lawn and shaded her eyes. 'It is so bright out here after being inside. The house needs light, Samuel.'

Samuel took her elbow in a firm yet gentle grip and ushered her over the grass to the first walled garden. Herbs grew here, surrounded by granite pathways. In the centre, was an ancient grey sundial, almost like an altar. Beyond the herb garden, steps led down into a shaded avenue of stately poplars, with lawns to either side, bordered by mature roses of dark red and startling white. Behind them, lush green ivy tumbled over crumbling walls.

Xanthe examined her surroundings with apparent pleasure, complimenting Samuel on the variety of the plants and the secluded mystery of the linked gardens. 'Is that water I hear?' she asked. 'Oh, Samuel, do you have a water garden?'

Breaking away from him, she ran down a path-way, her swift body dappled by sun-light. Samuel was forced to run to keep up with her, slightly annoyed by her wilfulness.

He found her by the fountain, where a voluptuous stone mermaid held up her hands to release a stream of cold, clear water. The pond was greened with the leathery saucers of water-lilies. It was surrounded by a circular path, around which grew a tall juniper hedge.

Samuel once again slipped a hand beneath Xanthe's elbow. His voice was hushed. 'This way.' He put a finger to his lips.

Xanthe frowned quizzically, but did not speak. She went compliantly into the yew walk that led to the court of the queen. Samuel saw her studying the strange plants that grew in the gloom, some with long, white heads like trumpets and others with purple spikes. Later, he would regale her with their secret histories. Then, the narrow opening in the hedge was ahead, and he allowed his new bride to go before him.

Night's Damozel reared imperially in her green bower. Xanthe paused at the entrance to this hidden garden, and Samuel heard her draw in her breath. She seemed almost shocked.

He hurried past her, smiled encouragingly and urged her forward. 'Come, come, this is who I've been waiting to show you.'

Xanthe's eyes were wide; it made her look peculiarly sinister. 'It is a creature of enchantment,' she breathed, and then flicked him a narrower glance. 'Where did you get it?'

'A corner of the world,' Samuel whispered, 'but hush.

Stand before her, but not too close. Her pollen is toxic.'

So the new bride was introduced to the queen. Their beauty seemed to complement each other; both so tall and still. Samuel could not detect any sense of rivalry or pique in the Damozel, but perhaps the presence of another human being stifled his communication with the flower.

'I can see,' Xanthe said softly, 'that all other flowers in your garden are but a screen for this priceless bloom. You keep her secret, of course.' She nodded gently to herself. 'But that is only right.'

'Well, I wouldn't go so far as to say...'

'No!' Xanthe interrupted. 'I can see the truth of it. Thank you for bringing me here.'

Samuel felt oddly uneasy. He wasn't sure what reaction he'd expected from Xanthe, but it wasn't this.

As they walked back to the house, Xanthe was silent. Samuel asked her what she thought of his garden.

'It is a wonderland,' she said. 'Your haven of myth and dream.' A certain gleam in her eyes made Samuel wonder whether she'd divined the nature of his relationship with some of the more narcotic plants. He did not like her thinking that. She seemed to be laughing at him.

It is my hobby,' he said stiffly. 'I have spent a lot of time on it.'

She smiled. 'Oh yes, I can see that. I have some small knowledge myself, for my father is something of a horticulturist.'

'Really.' This was news to Samuel.

'Indeed. I think I can say that although you cultivate many rare species, there is only one of true value - your maiden of the night. The others may be seen commonly in many Mewtish gardens.'

'Is that so?' Samuel felt nettled, annoyed that someone, who herself had confessed to having 'small knowledge' would dare to comment on the value of his collection. It would take some getting used to - living with someone else, who was full of opinions of their own. Still, she was indeed beautiful, and he was gratified she shared his respect for the Damozel. He bent down to pluck a delicate blue flower, a species of orchid. 'This reminds me of you. It is named Velenia, after a bewitching woman. This flower is yours, my love.'

Xanthe took the bloom and stared at it bemusedly. 'It has thorns, tiny thorns,' she said, twirling it in her fingers.

By the time they reached the sundial, her fingers had begun to itch and sting. She dropped the flower on the lawn.

At mid-day, Hesta arrived for work, and disappeared with Xanthe into the kitchens. Samuel felt strongly that he was excluded from their domain, but was relieved that Hesta seemed not to resent his new wife. Later, he questioned Xanthe on how Hesta had behaved.

'We will have an understanding,' Xanthe replied. 'She is a strong-willed woman, who expected trouble, I think, but I trust she is as pleased with me as I am with her.'

This answer seemed ambiguous, but it was clear Xanthe did not intend to expand upon it. Samuel, a stranger to the ways of women, reluctantly accepted that it was beyond his comprehension.

On the morning of the second day, Samuel said to Xanthe, 'You have brought the sun from Mewt with you.'

By ten o-clock, the gardens had begun to simmer in the heat.

'Aah, this is the weather I like,' sighed Xanthe, padding on bare feet out from the house to the lawn.

Samuel glanced at the sky. A heat-wave, or worse, a drought, would mean a lot of work for him in the garden. All the plants would need to be kept watered. He felt exhausted. Tonight, he must try to get more sleep.

Xanthe on the other hand seemed full of energy. She made her way to the sundial garden and there composed herself on the ancient grey flag-stones, fanned by the scent of baking herbs.

At noon, Hesta stamped out from the house, carrying a tray of refreshment. Samuel, working on a flower-bed nearby, saw her disappear into the herb garden. She did not come out for some time. It was strange how Xanthe seemed to have cultivated a friendship with the dour Hesta so quickly. They seemed unlikely companions.

As the weeks passed, this friendship developed. Xanthe apparently encouraged Hesta into cleaning some of the rooms, because the house became a lighter, airier place that smelled of scent and polish. Xanthe seemed to respect that Samuel needed time alone with his ladies, for she rarely went into the garden after sundown, having spent most of day sunning herself by the sundial. She really was quite a lazy creature, but her presence inspired Hesta to work hard, despite the uncomfortable heat, which seemed now to have invaded even the shadiest corner of the house.

Samuel was concerned by the persistent lack of rain; the more delicate of his plants were already beginning to suffer the effects. Fortunately the shady bower of Night's Damozel seemed to suffer the least effects, and it was here where Samuel concentrated his greatest efforts at keeping the soil moist. He always watered the Damozel in the sultry evenings, and after his task was complete, disrobed himself, confidant he would not be disturbed. Then he would lie down on the drenched leaves of the Damozel, while a mist of dream dust shimmered down from her open hearts. Sometimes, in his intoxicated state, Samuel could almost believe that the Damozel was indeed a female of flesh and blood. A spirit lived within her, who manifested into his dreams as a soft-fingered lover. It was as if he had two wives; one of the sun and one of darkness. The night was so serene and comfortable, whereas the scorching day made him irritable and anxious. In these tranquil moments, Samuel found uncomfortable thoughts forming in his head. Had he made a mistake in bringing Xanthe here? She was lovely, but a foreigner, and despite their weeks of passion in Mewt had very little else in common. She was here now, installed. He would have to live with her forever. Yet she was compliant, soft-footed and unobtrusive. The only changes she had made to his life had to be seen as positive. Why did these doubts come to plague him? All the while, a soft drift of pollen fell from the blooms of the Damozel, like words into his ears.

As the summer scorched the lawns, Xanthe basked in the herb garden, while Samuel toiled to keep his ladies alive. The work was really too much for him, the garden too large. At first, as he struggled around his domain carrying heavy buckets of water, he thought Xanthe might offer to help, but when no suggestions were forthcoming, he stomped over to the herb garden, intent on complaining. Wasn't a wife supposed to assist her husband in all his duties? He found her lolling prostrate in the sun, soaking up its heat like a reptile. At his approach, she rolled onto her back on the flag-stones and squinted up at him. Her dress had fallen from her shoulders, where her skin was as dry as paper and studded with tiny pebbles and strands of moss. 'You are sweating on me, Samuel. What is it you want?'

'Some help.'

She frowned. 'To do what?'

He gestured angrily. 'My garden is dying and you just lie here all day, every day. Help me carry the water.'

Xanthe laughed and raised herself onto her elbows. 'You want *me* to help? What on earth for? Get a boy from the town, or one of the farms. You surely can't expect *me* to lug carriers of water about.'

'You know I don't want strangers here.'

Xanthe shrugged. 'You are a fool. Keep your dark lady secret, by all means, but there's no reason why some local boys shouldn't attend to the rest of the place.' She smiled. 'Samuel, I am not a big, strong man and that's what you need for this. See sense.'

'What about Hesta? Get her to help me.'

Xanthe shook her head mildly. 'No, the garden is not Hesta's province. She has too much to do about the house.'

'I noticed!'

Hesta's hours had increased over the weeks, as had her wages - at Xanthe's insistence. It was as if the women were somehow building a new house around Samuel that no longer belonged to him.

'Are you complaining that I have turned your ruin of a house into a home?' Xanthe said, her voice cool.

'No, no...' Samuel wanted to abandon the conversation. He backed away from his wife until the hedges hid her from view. Pausing beyond them, he heard her sigh, then imagined she just settled herself back to drowsing, dismissing him from her mind.

Disgruntled, Samuel sought the sanctuary of Night's Damozel's bower. He couldn't help unburdening himself of sour thoughts about his wife. 'Sometimes, the mere sight of her makes me angry,' he confessed. 'Yet she is exquisite - submissive and calm. What she said about hiring boys from the village was right, of course, and yet...' He shook his head. 'There is something wrong. Something.'

The queen of his garden listened patiently. She alone seemed unaffected by the heat. Around her, her maidens lay swooning on the soil.

Later, when Samuel returned to the house, Xanthe was there with her serpent smile and cool, welcoming hands.

'Samuel,' she said, 'we must not argue about petty

things. Of course, I shall ask Hesta to give you an hour of her time every day. I'm sure she won't mind.' She bathed his brow and kissed his finger-tips. She was his wife, his beauty. He felt ashamed.

Now, every day, Hesta, apparently without grudge, tramped back and forth from the kitchen to the gardens with water. She was a strong, steady worker, but even her help was not enough to slake the thirst of the parched soil.

'The garden is dying,' Samuel told Xanthe in anguish. 'I am helpless.'

'There is more to life than gardens,' Xanthe said. 'And anyway, what is lost can be regained. Your precious Damozel won't wither. I know you make sure of that.'

Samuel did not like her tone. She often seemed to make innuendoes about his relationship with the Damozel, but not enough for Samuel to challenge her outright. He wondered whether in some way, Xanthe actually enjoyed watching him panic as his ladies succumbed to the drought. Perhaps she was jealous.

Every day, Samuel examined the rat-traps he kept in corners of the house to augment the poison trays. For the past few weeks, he'd been surprised to find all the traps empty, although on one occasion he'd thought he detected a smear of blood, some hairs. It was strange there were no kills. Had the vermin become wise to his precautions, or was the continuing hot weather responsible?

He mentioned it to Xanthe, who replied, 'Are you complaining? I'd have thought you'd be glad to see the back of them.'

Again, that sharp tone, an implied criticism. 'But they are not gone completely,' Samuel said, 'I hear them walking beneath the floor-boards at night. Don't you?'

Xanthe shrugged. 'I hear many strange things. This is an old house. What do you expect?'

Anger burned through him. He wanted to strike her. Relations between them were becoming more frequently tinged with what Samuel perceived as sniping comments, yet at the same time, he found his desire for Xanthe increased. His lovemaking became urgent and unsophisticated, although Xanthe remained unruffled by his lust. Samuel always felt drained and exhausted afterwards, usually falling into a deep sleep within minutes, while he suspected that Xanthe remained awake for hours. More often than not, he would wake in the morning with a pounding headache, as drained and groggy as if he had hardly slept. The heat was oppressive; he felt feel weak and sickly.

As the weeks of summer rolled on, it seemed that Xanthe's initial interest in renovating the family pile had been short-lived. Hesta, no longer confined to scrubbing away the past in the house, was now Xanthe's constant hand-maiden, sitting beside her in the herb garden, shelling peas for dinner, or skinning rabbits. Xanthe's sole occupation was to lie in the sun, and when she entered the house at night, she seemed to burn with her own light. She and Hesta murmured together. Samuel could hear their soft tones in every corner of the garden, and occasionally a husky laugh. Hesta brought gifts for Xanthe from the farm, some of which were distinctly strange: a dish of goat's milk, what appeared to be a withered umbilical cord, some dried poppy heads, a dead bird. Samuel supposed this was some traditional thing that once his mother must have enjoyed with the local women.

One day, in the kitchen, he said, 'She seems to think you are a cat.' He gestured at the milk Hesta had left out in a dish on the table.

'No,' said Xanthe emphatically, 'she does not. The milk is for my hands and arms.' She began to rub it into her dry skin.

'But the other things...' He wrinkled his nose in distaste.

Xanthe examined him blandly. 'Alkanet root, poppy seeds, feathers? They are ingredients for a herbal concoction. I have trouble with my skin.'

Samuel shook his head. Xanthe increasingly unnerved him. She was attentive in their shared bed, but during the day seemed distant and indifferent. Also, Samuel noticed that she rarely seemed to drink. It was unnatural. As he watched her dipping her pointed fingers in the milk, he had to suppress a shudder. It was more than being unnerved; he felt a wave of revulsion.

Xanthe looked at him, alert, as if his mind was her garden in which to walk. She smiled at him, perhaps with a hint of cynicism. He felt dizzy; the heat was getting to him. There was so much to do, yet he had little energy. Xanthe had come into his domain and had made it hers. She had brought searing equatorial heat with her, and both he and his garden were withering in it. She will be the death of me, he thought.

That evening, Samuel wearily carried water to the Night's Damozel's bower. Her blooms reared into the darkness, releasing a drizzle of shimmering pollen. He held out his hands to it, let it run over the backs of his hands.

Xanthe left dust wherever she lay. In the mornings, their bed was full of it, a pollen of her own, faintly soapy against his fingers.

Groaning, Samuel threw himself into the lap of the Damozel's leaves. 'Help me,' he said. 'I am invaded!'

The Damozel could not speak. She only gave him visions.

As the pollen settled over him, seeped down into his lungs and melted through the pores of his skin, he saw Xanthe stealing through the house at noon, when all was still and drenched in heat. He saw her stoop over the rat traps and take the soft corpses from them. He saw her eat. In his stupor, his stomach roiled. She had what she wanted: this house, these gardens. She would turn them into a barren desert where her unnatural hunger for heat could be indulged. She was a witch who influenced the weather, killing all that he held dear. Hesta was her creature now; bewitched and pliant. What a fool he had been.

The blooms above him looked like fairy faces. He fancied he could almost see thin lips mouthing silent words. 'Listen, my beloved, listen...'

Later, Samuel crept in from the garden, and went to the room where his wife lay slumbering. He stared at her for a few moments, noticing the faintly luminous sparkle on her skin, which might be an effect of the oils she used. He dreaded the powdery touch of her flesh against his own, yet when he slid beneath the covers beside her still form, he could do nothing but take her in his arms, inhale her strong, musky scent. She had that power over him. He resented it. *Do not think. Act now or it will be too late.* Carefully, he rolled her onto her back. She made a small sound, but did not wake. Her lips were slightly parted.

Samuel dribbled a shining stream of motes down into Xanthe's mouth. The Damozel's pollen could be rubbed into the skin, inhaled or ingested, the latter being the most effective method. The gate of dreams or the portal of death: only long acquaintance with the lady made that distinction. A dust glistened faintly at the corners of Xanthe's lips; Samuel covered them with his own, her body with his.

The funeral cortege milled around the front of the house. There was Sythia, imported from her summer home of Mewt, holding a scrap of black lace to her eyes. She was surrounded by others of her tribe, profligates, counts and divas, debutantes, artists and concubines. The majority of them had been summering at Sythia's estate, and once the news of the death had arrived by swift courier, the group had flocked to accept the invitation to the funeral. They were a mass of tall, nodding feathers and rustling costumes of black silk. Jetty horses stamped and snorted before the hearse, tossing their girlish manes, their hooves polished to a sheen. The day should have been overcast and grey, the trees weeping tears of rain. Clouds should have occluded the sun. The brightness and heat of late summer seemed an affront to the occasion, and several ladies were already feeling weak in their tight stays.

Sythia spotted a tall figure emerging from the shadows of the hall and swept up the worn front steps. 'Oh, but I shall ride with you in the foremost carriage. What a distressing time, for you, dear heart. How terrible. How cruel.'

Xanthe paused to pull on a skin-tight pair of black gloves. She inclined her head coolly. 'I shall be grateful for your company, Sythia.'

Together, the women descended the steps, and the mourners drew apart to give them passage.

On the boat over, one of Sythia's friends had divulged an alarming revelation. Although information concerning Xanthe was scant in Mewt, the informant had discovered that Samuel's death occasioned the fourth time Xanthe had been widowed. 'It seems, my dear,' the confidant had said dryly, 'that the lady has a distressing propensity for losing husbands.'

'Sad coincidences,' Sythia had said coldly, for she admired Xanthe greatly.

'Perhaps so,' the companion had continued, 'but this is certainly the shortest marriage of her history. The other three husbands at least survived the wedding for several years.'

'You should not say such things,' Sythia had retorted. 'That is how ugly rumours start.'

Her friend had raised an eyebrow. 'But I heard this

from the second cousin of her last husband, who was Cossic. What do you think the talk of the coast is at present? There were rumours already. Some have said that Samuel had the spectre of death at his shoulder even as he spoke his marriage vows.'

'I won't countenance this nonsense,' Sythia had said. 'Xanthe is a lovely woman. She comes from a rich family, and lacks for nothing.'

Now, as she climbed into the sombre carriage, with Xanthe so self-possessed beside her, suspicions flitted across Sythia's mind. The widow seemed very little marked by grief. Her eyes were clear, her face set in its usual enigmatic expression. 'It was very thoughtful of you to wait so long for the interment, my dear,' Sythia said. 'This heat...'

Xanthe flicked her a glance. 'Poor Samuel has no family. It was the least I could do to gather his friends for this occasion.'

'But three weeks...'

'The coffin is sealed,' Xanthe said. 'And we have stored him in the cellars, which are cool.'

Sythia shuddered. The frank details seemed indelicate. 'Of course, we came as soon as we could.'

Xanthe patted Sythia's hand. 'I know. Please don't trouble yourself.'

Sythia paused for a moment, then said, 'The contents of your message were scant. How exactly did Samuel die?'

Xanthe closed her eyes for a moment, the first signal Sythia had seen that the widow suffered any twinge of emotion. 'This may be distressing for you to hear,' she said, 'but the truth is, Samuel has long been addicted to intoxicants extracted from certain exotic plants he grew at the estate. I'm afraid he poisoned himself unwittingly.' She seemed to sense her companion's troubled thoughts and fixed her with a guileless stare. 'The family doctor from the town has identified the plant responsible, and we made upsetting discoveries in my husband's study - equipment to distil the essence of the plant, and so on.'

'Oh,' said Sythia inadequately.

Xanthe sighed. 'I have little luck where husbands are concerned, it seems.'

'You poor creature,' Sythia murmured, but still her heart beat fast.

At the graveside, while the mourners sweated uncomfortably in their ornate costumes, Xanthe stood cool and tall, staring down into the gaping earth. She seemed at least melancholy.

'What will you do now?' Sythia asked her as they returned to the house. 'Come home to Mewt?'

'No,' Xanthe answered. 'I shall remain here for a while at least.'

'Alone?'

Xanthe smiled. 'Yes. Alone.'

In the humid evening, Hesta reverently sponged Xanthe's skin with milk. The moon was rising behind the trees and the gardens lay in silence. There were no rats out there, nor in the house; no small creatures at all. All the guests had gone.

Xanthe rose from her bath and Hesta wrapped her in a towel. 'I will never marry outside my own kind again,' Xanthe said.

Hesta made a small, comforting sound. 'It was not your fault, my lady.'

Xanthe shook her head. 'This time... this time, it seemed so right. He accepted me as what I am, did not question my behaviour.' Her voice was low and uninflected, her gaze steady. She glanced down at Hesta. 'But what I am has followed me from Mewt. It was waiting here, but twisted.' She sighed and touched her belly. 'It is time now for me to settle this matter.'

Hesta dropped a small curtsey. 'I will await you, ma'am, in the kitchens.'

Xanthe smiled. 'I will not be long.' She clad herself in a long sheath of fabric, the colour of the moon, opalescent and oily. She glided through the house and out through the long back windows, down across the yellow lawns, past the sun-dial, the mermaid fountain, deeper, deeper into the garden to the court of the queen. In the outer courts the ladies of venom lay desiccated in their beds, petals strewn around them like papery jewels. Xanthe paid them no attention.

The queen, Night's Damozel, still reigned in her bower, despite the fact that Xanthe had denied her water for three weeks. Her leaves had withered and the tall stalks of her flowers were wrinkled like the skin of a crone. The purple flowers were splayed open, like dying tulips, revealing black and golden hearts. Xanthe crept through the yews on silent, naked feet and stood before her.

'Greetings,' she said. 'We have commerce to conduct, you and I.'

A single, damaged petal fell from one of the flowers, and the stillness of the night was absolute. Xanthe began to circle the central bower. 'Your lover is dead, and your minions have either perished or retreated into a death-like sleep. How much longer will you stand, dark lady? I admire the way you cling to life, even though half your roots are now nothing more than lifeless twigs.'

Night's Damozel seemed to shudder in the moonlight and another petal fell.

'Come forth,' Xanthe hissed, her eyes like slits, her elegant hands clenched into fists at her sides. Her narrow body swayed before the Damozel, and her will pulsed out of her like steam.

Again the plant convulsed.

'Do you hear me?' Xanthe said. 'I order you to come

227

forth. If you savour life, then obey me. If not, I shall trample your crippled body into the earth. I am not afraid of you, dark Damozel, for my poisons are greater than yours.'

The image of the plant seemed to ripple, and a stream of vapour exuded from the earth. It coiled at ground level, and then puffed upwards, resolving at last into an indistinct, female figure.

'But you must show me more,' Xanthe said. 'I do not believe this wisp, this ghost!'

The emanation gradually became more solid, until it was clear that a strange woman stood upon the withered leaves of the Damozel. Her skin was pale with purple shadows. Her heart-shaped face was alien, horrifying, yet peculiarly alluring. She had barely a nose to speak of and her eyes were feathered slits.

Xanthe shook her head. 'He never had the power to conjure you, did he,' she murmured, 'but then he knew so little of what he had.'

The Damozel fell to hands and knees upon the soil, her pale downy hair falling over her face. She looked starved, nearly dead.

'You know I could have come before,' Xanthe said, 'and perhaps you were waiting for me. If I had succumbed, would Samuel still be alive?' She put her head on one side to study the spirit of the flower. 'I could destroy you now,' she said. 'And should. Poor Samuel. He sought to kill me with your pollen, and woke in me the instinct to survive. What could I do but strike? I had no choice, for my nature overcame me. Didn't you think of that? I found him dead upon me. You are a jealous mistress, lady, but I know your measure.'

The spirit of the Damozel lifted her head. Her eyes wept an indigo steam.

Xanthe extended one slim foot until it nearly touched the Damozel's fragile, splayed fingers. 'I have loved and lost too many times, but in Samuel found peace. In his innocence and inexperience, he lacked the brutal qualities of men who awake the beast within me. Noxious flower, you have destroyed my haven, for now I am alone again!'

The Damozel's fingers flexed in the dry soil.

Xanthe folded her arms. 'In my land, you are known by a different name, Ophidia. You are the serpent flower. They say in Mewt that the serpents who doze among your leaves leave you the gift of their poison. It is said that this is how you able to concoct your seductive venoms.' Xanthe laughed coldly. 'We know better, don't we?'

The spirit raised its head and opened its mouth, the interior of which was black. No sound came out.

'Oh, you are parched, of course,' Xanthe said. 'Do you choose death or life, dark lady? You see, I am merciful. I give you that choice.' She squatted down before the spirit. 'As I know your kind, Ophidia, you must know mine. We have a long history between us. I walk the land, but you cannot. You are the cauldron of venom, and I am its channel. Together we become greater than our separate parts. You have killed my love, and made me all that I sought to forget. So, we must revive the ancient contract. Refuse me, and you die.'

The Damozel's eyes were black holes in her pale countenance, without expression. Then, with painful slowness, she attempted to crawl to Xanthe across the crumbling soil.

Xanthe smiled to herself and stood up, retreating a few steps. She gestured with both arms. 'Come, come to me, serpent flower. Get to your feet.'

Stumbling, the Damozel lifted her body erect. It seemed she was unused to it, for her limbs moved awkwardly. There was a hunger in her posture, in the curve of her spine.

Xanthe put her hands upon the mushroomy flesh of the Damozel's arms and lifted her as if she were a child.

Xanthe opened her mouth wide and lifted her tongue. In the moonlight, two dark glands that leaked an inky liquid extended over her lower teeth. Even before the Damozel's lips met her own, a spray of venom jetted out of her mouth, smelling of burned feathers. 'I know you,' Xanthe hissed. 'Take my bane.'

The house was a cool now, a shadowy sanctuary from the sun. The gardens below simmered and seethed in the last of summer's heat; the grass now parched and crisp, the flowers brown and withered. Xanthe looked out upon the garden from her bedroom window as Hesta busied herself stripping the sheets from the bed. Summer was breaking now. It would not be long before the cold came creeping across the land, bringing with it the desire for sleep.

'My lady,' Hesta said.

Xanthe turned and found the woman holding out the folds of white bed-sheet to her. They were filled with a fibrous dust. 'Yes, it is time.' She stroked her swollen belly, where the heart of a daughter beat and grew. Xanthe's kind rarely had sons. She took some of the dust in her fingers, then let it trickle away. Her skin itched, and now her face looked grey and tired.

'It has been a long summer,' Xanthe said. 'I will be glad to cast it away.'

She removed her dress and went naked through the house, down long stairs, through the drawing-room and out into the sunlight, moving stiffly. The desiccated lawn crunched beneath her feet. In the herb-garden, the soles of her feet burned against the flagstones, yet her face registered no pain. Deeper now, into the court of the queen. The bower thrived in a tropical lushness, and a single flower remained in the midst of the Damozel's leaves. Here, Xanthe lay down upon the soil. She closed her eyes and arched her back, her brow wrinkled in a frown. She touched her throat, and then pressed one finger-nail, the colour of dried blood, against her flesh. The skin parted with a soft popping sound. Slowly, she drew the nail down her body, opening herself up like a flower. Pollen drifted down from the Damozel; the last of it. No blood beaded along the deep scratch in Xanthe's flesh. The skin simply lifted away, like old paper, crumbling with age. Beneath it lay clean, virgin skin already coloured a deep honey gold, glistening as if kneaded with rich oils. Softly, the last petals of the Damozel fell down upon Xanthe's body and veiled her eyes.

The Heart of Fairen De'ath

Filerion had dwelled in the heart of the forest, in the house of black stone, for two years. Other people lived among the trees, in dark and hidden glades, but Filerion rarely saw them. It was a lonely life he led, and one quite different to that he had left behind in the lakeside town of Celestia. Filerion was not upset by this; his seclusion was wholly voluntary.

One night, what now seemed such a long time ago, he had sat outside an inn along the Avenue of Red Eyes and, over his sweet but vicious cordial of direthorn and spice, had faced the sadness and disappointment that had become the sum total of his life. His mother had recently died – there was no father he could remember – and had left him worse than penniless. More creditors than friends had attended the funeral and, to satisfy them, Filerion had been obliged to sell the lease to his mother's spacious rooms and millinery workshops. He had then moved all the possessions he could not sell into smaller and meaner accommodation. But it had not been enough.

There had been a series of jobs, each more poorly paid than the last; most of what he earned passing straight to the purses of the merchants and storemen to whom his mother had owed money. Filerion wished he'd paid more attention to family finances in the past, and considered bleakly that luck must have fled along with his mother's spirit. If luck was currency, perhaps the dead woman had owed more than earthly debts.

Barely more than a boy, Filerion's only recourse to survive had been to open his cloak along the dark alleys of

233

the Footways of Perfect Desire, and receive coin for the brief pleasure his flesh could bring to others more financially fortunate. The reality of this trade revealed itself less dreadful than the intention of it, Celestia being a town where courtesans were respected rather than reviled. They could earn themselves legendary status if they were clever.

Furtive, masked gentlemen, whose breath smelled of cloves, enticed Filerion into their carriages, where they fumbled through cramped couplings. Sometimes, pairs of pampered, spoiled boys would come giggling to the Footways and Filerion would take them to his lodgings to join in their laughter and offer them the delicious, dark pleasures they yearned. Also, sleek young daughters of wealthy houses sought his services, all claiming, in bored voices, they were there because it was necessary to sample all of life's spices; it was merely curiosity.

Filerion did not care about their reasons. He took the money and walked away. It was not important. He never experienced shame or self-hatred, but knew that his youth, however fresh for now, would not last forever, and when it left him, he would have to think of a different way to earn his coin. Affairs of the heart, though plentiful – for many of his patrons were intrigued enough by his mystery to become regular – had always ended in sorrow. It was a game to them, an act of rebellion and daring. Should wives, lovers or parents ever begin to suspect, they fled, never to return. Filerion was tired of trying to convince himself he did not care. Resolve hardened within him. He must seek a new life, elsewhere.

Perhaps crazed by the moon, for it was full and powerful that night, he gathered up his belongings, left a brief, vague note in his lodgings, and walked northwards out of the town, through the shuttered merchant quarter, past the low, sprawling temples, whose chimneys gouted the smoke of burnt offerings and incense. He wondered how long it would take for him to be missed. Tonight's regular patron would undoubtedly already be fractious at his absence from his usual corner, beneath the magnolia trees. He wondered whether he'd miss the generosity of his customers. No, he decided. All they'd given him was coin and material things. Filerion suspected there was more to happiness than that.

Without planning a destination, he eventually found himself upon the road that wound along the edges of Coolcandle Forest. The dark between the trees seemed to beckon him; he felt soothed by it. By the roadside, he came upon an old, wooden barrel that appeared to act as a post box for lake-bound mail, and here there was a track, leading into the forest. Filerion followed it. The strong scent of the foliage enveloped him like the water of a scented bath. He felt comfortably drowsy. Now, he would rest, shaded and fanned by fragrant ferns. Tomorrow, he could plan his future.

Filerion woke with the dawn. He stared up through the shivering fronds, arching over him protectively and decided he could not bear to set foot once more upon the hard, open road. Let the forest take him. He sat up, ate some food from his pack, drank some water and ventured further into the trees.

He travelled this way for three days. To complement his meagre food supply, he ate berries and nuts he recognised as edible. Later on, he unpacked his slender knife and confidently, if inexpertly, killed and skinned a small animal. He changed direction many times, doubling back, leaving the paths, investigating each intriguing sound. At no time did he feel in any danger. At first, it seemed he was the only human creature in the forest, but as time went on, he scented smoke and once passed a camp of charcoal-burners, who paid him no attention. At night, resting in open glades, he patiently persisted in the art of making fire. During the day, as he wandered, he was wooed by the low, enchanting song of hidden life, and entranced by the stranger places that seemed to vibrate with sentience, and where there was no sound at all.

On the morning of the fourth day Filerion discovered a brown, dusty pathway shadowed by ancient trees. Short, dark green grass grew between the massive, moss-carbuncled trunks. In the distance, he could hear the sound of water running. Filerion felt a quickening of excitement within him. The track appeared to have been beaten down by human feet. Perhaps it would lead him to a deep forest settlement. What kind of people would live there? Would they be friendly or hostile?

At length, the trees thinned and a large glade was revealed, overlooked by a soaring, crag that reared above the trees. Filerion immediately recognised the marks of cultivation in the glade. Against the dark rock at the farther end stood a tall, black house.

Filerion froze, staring. The house exuded a powerful air of great age, its eccentric design suggesting someone quite apart from conventional thinking had built it. There was no sign of life, however; no curl of smoke, no sound, no open window or door. Brooding eaves overhung the dark bricks. Grass and moss mantled the sagging roof. A weather vane poised motionless among the tall, narrow chimneys. Every bit of the building showed signs of neglect and decay.

After maybe half an hour of cautious scrutiny, Filerion convinced himself that if the house did have inhabitants, they must be old or dead. Summoning courage, he walked up to the front door, which swung open when he knocked on it. Filerion paused at the threshold, then entered the building. What had he to lose? A search within revealed the place deserted.

Dusty furniture stood disintegrating beneath shawls of spider-web. In a spacious, low-ceilinged kitchen at the back of the house, Filerion found a large, cracked sink filled with leaves. There were corridors and passages to explore, scurrying things darting from his sight as he crept through the silence. There were stairs to climb; stairs that wound, stairs that swept purposefully straight, stairs behind doors, stairs down to darkness. And there was a multitude of rooms; big rooms, small rooms, empty rooms, rooms with books, rooms with torn, heavy curtains, rooms with bare, high window-frames, rooms with beds. The place was enormous. Enormous and unused.

Filerion found himself once more in the kitchen, after having carefully made his way down a narrow, dark stairway with a door at the bottom. He dropped his bags upon the large central table, tested the pump above the sink and was eventually rewarded by a trickle of clear water. It was obvious no one had lived in the tall, black house for considerable time. Filerion took a drink of the water, found it good, and straightened up to assess his find. He breathed deeply. Yes, he thought to himself, the house had a good feel. Solemnly, he spoke aloud, introducing himself, asking if he might be allowed to stay for a while. Silence. But not a menacing silence.

He decided to stay there for a couple of days until some plan presented itself for the future. In the meantime, he thought, he could tidy the place up a little. He took off his thick cloak, bound up his glossy black hair and rolled up his linen shirtsleeves. Brooms were found in a cupboard and he tore down some of the ragged curtains to use as cleaning cloths. By mid-afternoon, the kitchen was almost habitable.

Pausing to refresh himself, Filerion heard an eerie scratching at the back door. Suppressing a tremor of apprehension, he wrenched open the protesting door and looked out. At first nothing. Then: 'meow.' Filerion looked down. A small grey cat sat upon the doorstep, smiling.

'Meow, pee-urr, yeowrrr!' it said, and to Filerion it sounded as if the cat was saying, 'At last, you've finally arrived.'

The couple of days extended into a couple of weeks. Treasure after treasure revealed themselves in the tall, black house. Not jewels or gold or rare paintings, or any such riches, but useable crockery; packets of seeds; a keg of salt; bales of twine; bottles, some still full of wine; a chest crammed with blankets packed in lavender and sage; baroque mirrors; bolts of cloth; jars of beeswax; dried herbs hanging like mummified limbs in a closet, and many books.

The cat, whom Filerion named Segila, followed him from room to room, jumping onto the windowsills, whispering cruelties at the birds outside, jumping down again to wash herself and generally keep him company.

Time sped by; a holiday of exploration and renovation. Gradually, Filerion accepted the fact that some part of him had decided to stay indefinitely, and he gave in to that desire with little fight. The house seduced him, constantly leading him to find things of use, to bring comfort to his life. There were caves in the cliffs behind the garden, some with pools of sweet, clear water. At one time, someone had constructed a plumbing system, using as supply a natural reservoir found within the caves, and had connected it to the house. Filerion inspected the pipe-work and found it sound. A survey of the garden and orchard revealed overgrown vegetable plots, masses of riotous, giant herbs and fertile fruit trees. There were hives for bees, sadly empty, but, Filerion reasoned, if he could restore the garden, he could grow things to sell in the villages that punctuated the road to Celestia and Grote. Maybe he could buy some bees one day.

Buy bees he did. And a goat, some hens, grain, meat and white, glistening sugar in a sack. The garden responded to his attentions and even the first harvest, only months after he'd begun work, rendered a pleasing income.

Sometimes, Filerion wondered who had lived in the house before him, why they had left it, and whether they'd been as contented as he was now. Surely, countless lives before his own had whiled away the dark, green hours beneath this roof? Many of the books he'd found had been written by hand, in graceful, curling script. The subject matter was often esoteric and strange, as well as being practical and eminently useful. Since studying them, Filerion had learned how to heal his body, whether of disease, wounds or spiritual ennui. He could treat his animals effectively. All of the plants required were on hand in the garden, waiting to be discovered and nurtured once more as Filerion cleared the ground of weeds. The strength of will to empower the remedies he drew from the trees themselves.

There was only a single stain on his happiness. One afternoon, in summer's full heat, Filerion took mop and brooms to the uppermost floor of the house. It consisted of a single passageway, with three doors leading off it, and had the feeling and smell of a place that had not been disturbed for years. There was almost an air of resentment at Filerion's intrusion. Summer was shut out there. Filerion did not like it. He turned to say to Segila, 'Perhaps this part can wait...' and then noticed Segila was not behind him. A shiver of unease slipped up his spine. Usually, the cat followed him everywhere. He stepped backwards, not through feeling threatened, but wanting to avoid something he thought would be unpleasant, sickening. The house would not allow that. It was quite emphatic. As if dazed, Filerion let it show him a small, dismal room at the end of the corridor.

Afterwards, he could not remember clearly what he had seen; only a feeling of depression had remained, but words whispered through his head for the rest of the day, faint yet persistent: *This is why, this is why, this is why...*' Filerion avoided that area of the house thereafter.

Two years passed and during that time, Filerion devoted himself to repairing the tall, black house and its gardens. His old life seemed a hideous, tawdry, contemptuous existence in comparison to what he had now. It was very rare he missed the town, although one damp, winter evening, when his spirits were low, he found himself thinking about old friends and, perhaps unwisely, wrote a couple of letters to people he knew. He remembered the place at the edge of Coolcandle, where the woodcutters, charcoal-burners and local villagers left items they wished to be taken to the towns. A man on a grey pony came regularly to collect them, leaving behind any mail or packages he'd picked up. Filerion went out into the drizzly night, swishing through the trees. He began the journey to the edge of the forest, unable in his sudden anguish to wait till morning. By that time, he'd learned a quicker route to the road and had reached the collection bin by the following afternoon. He left two dozen eggs with the letters and hoped that would be enough payment to cover their delivery.

The morning after his return dawned bright and optimistic and Filerion's brief depression passed. The flight through the wood, the burning desire to communicate seemed a silly, feverish thing to have done. He did not need anybody. The advantages of his new life far outweighed the ephemeral loneliness he experienced. After all, here in the forest, the only twittering was that of the birds, not of gossips and quick-tongues. The only harshness that of the elements, never of a human temperament.

Not long after he had taken up occupation of the house, Filerion had drawn himself a likeness of Celestia, to serve as a reminder and perhaps a warning. It hung on the wall in the kitchen, in an old, wooden frame he had found. That evening, as he sat in the kitchen after his meal, relaxing, sipping herb wine and smoking one of his green cigarettes, he gazed at the picture thoughtfully. It seemed he'd poured all the filth and subtle cruelty of the past right into it. A purge. He was truly rid of it. The letters would reach the town and people would laugh at his strangeness, and think him mad. No one would come to find him and that was for the best. The pangs of lust and hopeless love would never touch him here. All he needed now was that which the tall, black house had given him. All the company he needed was that of Segila, his hens, his rather sour-tempered but amusing goat and the spirits of the forest itself, never seen but often felt. In time, he completely forgot he'd sent the letters.

One day, as a summer evening bloomed around him like a late flower, Filerion sat outside his house, taking a glass of wine fermented from honey and elderflower, when he heard the unmistakable sound of human movement through the trees. Very occasionally, other wood-dwellers crossed Filerion's glade, but they travelled with the silky, silent ease of the wilderness-footed. An understanding existed between all forest natives; contact was minimal unless invited, and respect for privacy observed. This movement was accompanied by the warble of voices, the sound of iron-shod hoofs, the swish of outraged branches, pushed to the side. The noises came from the south. Whoever travelled towards him must have come upon the wide, dusty road from the direction of Celestia and Grote.

Filerion watched with a mixture of fascination and fury as horses burst from the trees. He stood up and put down his glass of wine. The horses trotted nearer, two of them; one spotted grey, one dark dun. Filerion wasn't sure whether to be pleased or annoyed when he realised he recognised the person riding the dun. A hand was raised in a splash of yellow silk. A voice cried 'Yo! Filerion, you imp!' and an old friend urged his horse into a canter, spewing up clods of turf behind him.

Filerion felt weak. He remembered the letters; more

than twelve months' sent. Finally, it seemed, someone had decided to sniff him out.

Filerion had known Ricardo Neathtree since they'd been children. Their careers had diverged somewhat over the years – Ricardo had nestled comfortably into his father's merchant business – but, up until Filerion had left Celestia, their friendship had remained constant, if rather shallow. Ricardo, after all, had never considered their relationship close enough to offer Filerion the funds he'd desperately needed after his mother died. And Filerion had had more pride than to ask for it, although he'd fought resentment at the time. Ricardo liked having a courtesan as a friend, rather like he enjoyed owning exotic, foreign pets. In all the years he'd known Filerion, Ricardo had never suggested their friendship change its platonic state. Filerion had never desired Ricardo either, and even though the pair of them behaved as if they were brothers, Filerion was secretly glad Ricardo was not a relative. As he watched the expensively-clad Ricardo spring down from his horse, Filerion considered that he still harboured a vestige of feeling for his friend, but it was faint.

Ricardo's companion – a young man, silent and unremarkable in shadow – was overlooked during the first flurry of greeting, the inevitable shower of city gifts, the exclamations, comments, mandatory viewing of the tall, black house and the gardens beyond, the quickly offered refreshment, quickly prepared. Ricardo's companion kept his head hung low, shuffling behind the others, quite invisible, a satellite in orbit round Ricardo's sunshine.

'You have yourself a palace here!' Ricardo declared, nodding round the rooms.

It would cost a fortune to own such a place in Celestia or Grote, even more to build one. Filerion thought waspishly how Ricardo would probably go and commission himself a copy of it immediately when he got home, using his father's money, without a second thought.

'I would have come before if I'd known you lived like this!' Ricardo said.

Filerion flinched. 'I prefer to live alone,' he said, and then added hastily, 'but it is good to see you, Rico, after all this time.'

Filerion laid out a table with white linen in the porch. He set a bowl of smouldering resin by the door, which exuded a delicious smoke into the heavy, sensual evening air. He carried out bowls of salad chopped freshly from his garden and arranged one of the cooked fowl, which Ricardo had brought him, on a plate. The little group sat down to eat.

Ricardo smiled at Filerion's exquisite, delicate wines and then shook his head. 'Delightful! So clever! But tonight, a treat!' He had brought expensive liquor with him from Celestia, fiery with spice, smoky as the town itself on Fall nights. It did not taste of the green forest at all.

As they sat down, Ricardo indicated his companion and said, almost as an afterthought, 'Ah, this is Fairen De'ath. He had a whim to accompany me here. Needed a rest too, I expect.' He laughed heartily, offering no more explanation or introduction than that.

Fairen De'ath ducked his head and shrank into a seat.

Filerion thought it looked as if the young man was shrouded in smoke, as if he was somehow fuzzy at the edges. How strange. He blinked quickly and the smokiness vanished. Perhaps a trick of the light, something in his eye...

Ricardo didn't stop talking, throwing his arms about, indicating further gifts he'd forgotten to mention. Filerion wondered if Ricardo was faintly embarrassed coming to a place like this where the silence of the forest was so huge and its strength so pure and near. 'So how is your life going now?' Ricardo enquired boisterously. 'Quiet, eh?'

Filerion smiled sweetly and replied that all was going very well, thank you and, yes, it was quiet, but he liked it that way, having got used to it.

Fairen De'ath sat silently, his head bowed as if in timidity. Filerion was reminded of the boys and girls he had known in the town, too young to solicit alone, too desperate not to, who had fallen under the protection of older men and women, who undertook to manage their business. They too used to sit bowed and humble, deaf to the haggling that occurred over their heads. Was Ricardo Fairen's patron in some way?

The moon rose over the chimneys of the black house, which stood nearly as tall as the tallest tree. Nimble bats flitted in and out of the eaves, peeping out their high, navigational squeaks. Below, sitting comfortably in the glow of a lighted globe of glass, the three talked long and deeply. The presence of the forest stole over them, seeming to bring the mysteries of life very close to hand. It was inevitable the conversation should turn towards the mysterious, the baffling, the arcane.

Ricardo Neathtree squinted nervously at the black, rustling forest and said, 'It must unnerve you often, Fil, living here.'

'No,' Filerion answered, 'I am never afraid.' It was true. He feared what he had left behind in the town more.

'No ghosts then? Not even in this dark old house?' Ricardo's smile held an edge, as if he had only just realised he too would be spending a night inside it.

Filerion grinned. 'No ghosts,' he said, sipping his glass of liquor. Had it tasted this harsh back in Celestia or had his palate become refined these past two years?

'You don't get lonely?'

'Only once.' Filerion remembered, with mixed feelings, that sad, cold night he'd sat and written the letters telling people where he was. Thank All That Breathed Ricardo had been the only one to respond. Ricardo shrugged petulantly, perhaps affronted his old friend didn't seem more relieved to see him. Filerion hoped this presaged no further surprise visits and then silently reprimanded himself for being so anti-social. He smiled at his friend. 'I'm glad you came,' he said. 'Really.'

Ricardo grinned roguishly. 'I half expected to find you'd already know I was coming!' He indicated their surroundings. 'You were always mystically inclined. I was not surprised when you left so abruptly, or at your letter telling where you'd decided to root. No, not at all. You are a proper witch now, of course. Did you sense me coming? A scrying ball wouldn't be out of place here. Do you have one hidden away perhaps?'

Filerion shook his head and laughed. 'I cannot read the future,' he said.

Fairen De'ath, nudged from his silence by alcohol, said suddenly, 'Upon the table in my house there stands a sphere of perfect crystal. I look into it often.'

'And does it tell your future?' Ricardo asked, winking at Filerion.

The brow of Fairen De'ath, which was pale and high, wrinkled in thought. 'Sometimes. I have seen hints, presentiments perhaps.

Ricardo laughed. Though he would not dismiss the existence of sorcery, he clearly doubted whether his young companion had any knowledge of it.

Filerion merely looked on warily.

'So tell us, tell us,' Ricardo chided. 'What hints present themselves to you? Daughters of rich houses clad in jewels, I should hope!'

Fairen De'ath shook his head seriously. 'No, nothing like that. Other things.' He looked up.

Filerion was shocked from a lazy comfort by the glance. Dark eyes in a pale face, wistful as a slave, perhaps lovely. What had Ricardo brought here, and why? Discomfort pooled itself in Filerion's breast. He felt as if a rushing wind, foul with destruction, had come gusting up the south road, and not two travellers on iron-shod horses. He sensed turmoil.

After a moment, Filerion excused himself, rose, and went into the shadows of the house. He let its cool, sinuous presence invade his troubled mind and closed his eyes. Balm. Security. Sighing, he padded into the kitchen and poured himself a long, cold glass of clearest water to rid his palate of the sting of Ricardo's liquor. His brain seemed full of the echoes of past noise; voices, laughter, hot, smoky taverns, yellow light and stale air. He did not want that here, in this house. He would be glad when Ricardo and his strange companion left him alone, to bask in the luxury of solitude once more.

Fairen De'ath, he considered; even the name inspires fear. Loveliness he disguises with smoke. A trickster. No, a boy, shy and faltering. Pretty boy. Dangerous. Like all those pretty boys who'd come to the Footways, their brief attraction to his light. And yet... A look? Desire? Was it there? No. No. Too long alone here. A mistake. He is Rico's plaything. Must be. A mistake...

Then, in the darkness behind him, there was a movement, so slight Filerion wondered whether he had really perceived it.

A voice came out of the darkness, a furtive whisper. 'In the crystal... It was you, Filerion. Just a moon ago, the crystal showed me, told me. You, you, you.'

Filerion turned and saw the pale shape of Fairen De'ath, standing in the doorway. 'I beg your pardon?' False confidence. False cool. It was an angel gliding towards him.

Fairen De'ath advanced into the room, his hands wrestling each other in discomfort. 'The letter you sent. I read it. Months ago. And then, in the crystal, I saw you. I saw all of this!'

'You must have been mistaken,' Filerion said coldly, filled with dread. 'I do not know you at all.'

Fairen still crept forwards into the moonlit room, still

wringing his slim, pale hands. 'No, but I know you,' he said, babbling, almost incoherent. 'I've seen you. Before. Many times. If only I'd spoken, but you seemed so distant, so aloof... I watched. I saw. Others came, others touched you. But not me. Not me. And then you were gone, vanished. It was like the light went out of the town. When Ricardo showed me the letter, months after you'd sent it, I wanted to come then, but I was nervous, shy. Ricardo kept mentioning he would visit you one day, but that day never came. I waited and waited, and then... the crystal. I had to act. I was out of my mind. I persuaded Ricardo to come here. He was tired. Needed a rest. The forest, I said, would do him good. I asked him to bring me with him, introduce me to you. Two years. I have not forgotten you. I had to see you. I had to tell you this. You are my life!'

Filerion made a dismissive gesture. 'This is... a shock. What you are saying sounds like madness.'

'It is!' Fairen agreed. 'I had no alternative but to obey the call of this insanity.'

'You don't understand,' Filerion said. 'I have chosen this life, this privacy. I have no desire to share it with anyone, no desires at all, in fact. I am touched by your feelings, it's very flattering, but...'

Fairen came and put his hands on Filerion's arm, and oh, how cool that touch was, so cool yet vibrant with promise. How dark were the eyes that implored to be recognised, how winsome the face. Filerion could smell the maleness of him, young and vibrant. He looked away, pierced by a swift, insidious spear of lust. He'd forgotten the bittersweet poignancy of such attacks. 'I have no wish to share my life with anyone,' he repeated and paused before adding, 'not even someone as lovely as you.' The words hung like crystal in the air between them.

Then, Fairen De'ath made a bitter sound. 'I will not leave here,' he declared fervently. 'Do not underestimate my feelings. I will stay until I make you want me to stay.'

'Does Ricardo know of this obsession?'

Fairen shook his head.

Filerion sighed deeply. He felt as if he was being offered a flaming torch and, although the torch could give him light, it might also burn him fearfully. In the past, such offers had been made before and from accepting he had only brought himself pain.

'You are not of my world,' Filerion said gently. 'I am here in the forest to escape civilisation. Do you really want to cast off the luxuries of your life and live here, in this quiet place, for the sake of desire?'

'If it means I will be with you, yes!' Fairen replied without a pause.

Filerion sighed again, prompting Fairen to say, 'It is more than desire, I swear it.'

'You might find, if your desires are satisfied, your feelings are not as enduring as you presently believe,' Filerion said dryly.

Fairen made an angry sound. 'I should hate you for that,' he said, 'insulting my love for you, because it *is* love. Can't you imagine the risk I've taken approaching you like this? Would I do such a thing lightly?'

Filerion looked at the glowing, pale form of Fairen De'ath. Had the house brought him this final, complete miracle? He had everything now but human love. Was it possible he was now being offered that too, in the shape of this pretty, effeminate boy? Impulsively, he held out his arms. 'It may be you are simply mad, or misguided, or even lying to me, but for tonight at least, then I am here for you,' he said, and in the moonlight, they embraced.

When they went back to Ricardo, it was to carry an air of celebration with them. No more talk of dark mystery. Now Ricardo regaled them with ribald tales of his experiences and the glade rang with the sound of laughter, the clink of glasses being refilled. The air was redolent of the smoky thrill of anticipation. When at last, they all retired for the night, Fairen De'ath crept to Filerion's room, his voice hot with the passion of his desire; his hands, his eyes, his lips. Filerion swam in a sweet delirium of ecstasy. So long since he'd touched warm skin, so long. Fairen De'ath told him a hundred times with what impatience he'd waited for this moment, with what dread it might never be fulfilled. Filerion's happiness was so exquisite, it almost made him afraid.

So followed a blissful week. Ricardo was content to drink his liquor in the porch of the house and in the gardens all day, reading some of Filerion's books, so that Filerion himself was free to initiate the fey Fairen De'ath into the mysteries of the forest. Filerion showed him the icy pool where he bathed in the light of the sickle moon, obeying a suggestion one of his books had mentioned. *Have I ever wished for love on those nights?* Filerion wondered silently, thinking about all the wishes he had made, while sluicing himself with the water. Hadn't they all been for good harvests, for health, for more rain, for less rain and such like? Never this, surely? And yet... *This feels like heaven. If I didn't wish for it, I should have done.*

He and Fairen made love in the pool and Filerion marvelled at the svelte contours of Fairen's body, the cleanness of limb, the sweep of hair, the deep, sulky eyes. Perfection.

Fairen kissed him saying, 'Never have I seen such beauty as you. You are a gypsy raven! Say that you love me!'

'You are a silver wildcat,' Filerion answered. 'Yes, I love you.'

Whether Ricardo Neathree guessed what was really going on, Filerion did not know. He certainly never professed a desire to accompany the others on their forest walks, but his eyes and smile were free of innuendo. 'I have had such a holiday here!' he cried. 'I feel renewed. Thank you Filerion.'

'Thank *you*,' Filerion said, with a smile.

He and Fairen had not spoken of the future, but Filerion had no doubt that when Ricardo returned to Celestia, he would return alone.

At the end of the week, Ricardo said, 'Tomorrow, I'll have to get back to town. But I'll return one day for another refreshment, never fear!'

Filerion smiled and squeezed Ricardo's hand. 'You cannot guess what pleasure your visit has given me,' he said.

When morning came to the black walls and the black chimneys of Filerion's house, Fairen De'ath rose alone from the shared warmth of Filerion's bed and went to the open window. He could not see the wide road leading south through the trees from there. And the air was cool, too fresh for him. He shivered.

Filerion awoke, smiling into the dawn sunlight, savouring the crisp, perfumed air.

'And now I must go,' Fairen De'ath said, without looking backwards. He closed the window.

'Go?' Filerion felt the shining cocoon of happiness around him crack. He felt blood must surely pour from the wound. 'What do you mean?' he asked. 'Only a week ago, you were begging me to let you stay here!'

Fairen shrugged awkwardly. 'I know but...' He looked around the room.

Filerion's shock expressed itself in anger. 'You virtually forced me to love you!' he cried. 'What is this talk of leaving so soon?'

Fairen still stared southwards through the window. 'It is not right,' he said. 'One day I shall have to return to Celestia and, when I do, I do not want to have to hide from knowing eyes. If I stay here when Ricardo leaves, he will know why. I realise now I do not want that.'

'Because of what I was?' Filerion asked bitterly. 'Is that it? You don't want people to know you lived with a whore?'

Fairen De'ath did not answer. He put his fingers on the window glass, long, slender fingers.

Filerion's heart turned over. 'Haven't I pleased you?' he asked softly. 'You said you loved me. You made me feel that too.'

Fairen shook his head. 'I know. You have pleased me, you have been wonderful and I do... feel for you, but... We achieved the miracle, didn't we? We fulfilled my prophecy, and it was good. But now it is done. Such affairs as this can only be brief.'

Filerion was stunned. Fairen De'ath had broken his defences, every one. He felt naked and wretched and helpless.

'I'm sorry,' said Fairen De'ath.

By mid-day, Ricardo Neathtree, still blissfully unaware of what had transpired, oblivious to any dark atmosphere, set his horse once more upon the path that led to the wide, dusty road, taking Fairen De'ath with him.

Filerion steeled himself and mouthed goodbyes, smiling; stood on his porch and watched them go. Only once the leaves had hidden them completely, did he allow himself to fall down upon the grass outside the tall, black house and surrender to bitter, silent grief.

'What have I done to deserve this?' he raged inside, bewildered. 'Why did he do this to me? Why did I let him?'

Fairen De'ath had destroyed his contentment. Filerion had not needed company, but now Fairen had gone, after bestowing that brief, vicious gift of lust and heat, Filerion felt he could not live with the weight of solitude any longer. All the things that he most enjoyed seemed blighted. Where was the delight in bathing in the forest streams if he had to bathe alone? Where the delight in discovering the dens of the wild creatures, spilling tumbling mounds of cubs and kittens in the sunlight, if there was no one but the grey cat to show them to? Was the sense of satisfaction in a job well done valid if it was not shared? Could he live knowing he would not touch Fairen's skin again, nor hear his voice and bask in his radiant smile? A torment! Unbearable! Filerion's heart felt broken. He was sure it could never heal. Not now. Not this time. Never. Everything was gone: light, hope, happiness. He could not escape the past. He was a whore. Used for sex. Simple as that. Even here. He did not want to be this thing.

As the afternoon sloped towards sunset, Filerion picked himself up off the grass and went back into the tall, black house. With bowed posture, he slowly mounted the steepest flight of stairs and ventured deep into the shadowed corridor beyond them. This was the house's most secret place. Filerion went to door at the end of the passage and turned the handle. Beyond lay a small room, brown with age, lit by a single, dusty skylight. The room reeked of sadness, of betrayal, and had been used before. It was completely empty, but for a slim, silver dart hanging from a nail upon the wall. Filerion had only been here once before, and that just to acknowledge what lay within and why. The house had granted him permission then to see. It had said to his heart, without words, 'Remember this, but be wise'. It had intimated the power of what lay within the room, its varied uses. It explained something of why the house had been unoccupied, but not everything.

Filerion felt he had no choice now but for a certain course of action. He knew what use to make of the slim, silver dart, kissed with poison. Numb, he lifted it down from the wall, turning it in his hands. A beautiful thing, smooth as satin. It felt good to the touch. And so sharp! He raised his face to the evening sunlight coming in through the roof light and held the point of the dart against his throat. It was as cool as a sliver of ice. He knew it would take very little effort on his part to ease it right into his flesh. Such is the way of deadly things, he thought. So little effort. A piercing. Then darkness. He took a deep breath, prepared to push the dart and then...

Then, through the dusty window, he saw the moon sailing high into a dark blue, lustrous sky. He smelled the perfume of warm earth drifting in from outside and heard the echoing calls of the night creatures, stirred from rest, slithering forth into the pale light. Coming in through the door behind him, the grey cat mewed for her supper and wound her long tail around Filerion's legs. If Segila sensed her master's distress, her own comfort was obviously more important.

The moment cracked; cracked like ice. The dart felt cold and wicked in Filerion's hands. He dropped it, uttering a soft cry of distaste.

'Meow?' said Segila.

Filerion rubbed his face, smiled and bent down to caress the furry head.

'You are right,' he said, and then to the room, 'I misunderstood.'

He bent down and picked up the dart. Holding it loosely, carelessly, he spoke six precise words of power over it and carried it downstairs. Laying it carefully on the kitchen table, he gave meat to his cat, went outside, threw corn to his hens and cabbage leaves to his goat. Then he fetched the dart and held it up to the moonlight. The silver glinted icily. A purposeful, condensed thing it was. Filerion closed his eyes and threw the dart high, high into the air.

Twisting, turning, glittering, it seemed the dart would fall back to earth, but then, with a strange shiver of a song, it paused and flew, point first, southwards, above the trees. Filerion wiped his hands, smiled into the moonlight and went back inside. He made himself a fine supper of the food that Ricardo had brought him and then sat down to read, smoking one of his favourite blends of herbal cigarettes, Segila purring happily in his lap. After a while, he shuddered, got up, removed the picture of Celestia from the wall and put it outside. Tomorrow he would bathe in the clearest, coldest stream he could find and it would all be gone from him. Forever.

Outside, the silver dart flew southwards, towards the city. It reverberated to one, single, burning, inexorable sentiment. Filerion had breathed six words into it. Six to make it live, to instil its one true purpose. The room in the secret place of the tall, black house was completely empty now. Nothing would ever come to fill it but the silence of peace. Six words. All the hurt condensed. Six words.

'Pierce the heart of Fairen De'ath!'

Oblivious of the fiery, white progress above it, the forest continued as always, a surge of silence, and the tall, black house, as always, looked after its own. It may be reached from three directions, that house, but few who follow the paths will find it.

Poisoning the Sea

(or Circe Invidiosa)

I have proved them all to be fools! Not that there was any doubt in my mind that my father, his scheming lackwit underlings and indeed all men on this world, were anything other than that to begin with, but this most recent victory has a delicious sweetness on my tongue.

I have just left him: once man, now animal. I left him fawning on my chamber floor. His name is Aertes. He was a poet. He is a dog, now.

Oh, beloved father, did you really think to pull my claws by expelling me into this isolation? I cannot believe you underestimated my intelligence, but then, you are a man yourself and therefore lacking in wit of a sharper nature.

As I descend the cold, white stairs to the terrace, I can see, through the open shutters, that the sister ocean is choppy today. I will pour blood into her waves, as a blessing and in celebration of my triumph. There is little else to do upon this blasted rock. Then, I shall speak to my domestic, Baucis, and tell her to remove the beast from my rooms with a brief ritual; no doubt he will still be whining there among the curtains when I return from the sea.

Beyond the garden walls of my palace, there is a cluster of dwellings that hug the cliffs, inhabited by the rough folk who farm the waves beneath. These creatures, my royal father thought, would be my only companions until I learned humility. Imprisoning me upon this backward isle, secured by the prowling ships that haunt the horizon, he seeks to break my spirit, to imbue me with remorse for an act I can only regard as expedient. As I would have said to my dear sister, whom I miss intolerably, despite her limper nature: 'It is beyond our beloved sire to penetrate the whims and desires of his female relatives, let alone their skills and caprices.'

The path to the ocean is steep and winding, hemmed by stiff herbs of a thorny nature and shivering with green and turquoise lizards. The air is scented by a sharp, leafy reek that mingles with the smell of brine. The day is shaking to the sound of roaring waves and from beneath my feet I hear the brisk crunch of the shells that litter the path like little white flowers. I am wearing my favourite cloak of finely spun wool, dark in colour as befits my mood, and am accompanied by black Ishti, who is the largest and most splendid of my companion cats. Ishti, perhaps unusual among his kind, loves the sea. In fact, I took him half-drowned from the wreck of some vessel that had spewed lolling white corpses upon the beach some seasons back. Baucis maintains he is not a cat at all, as he is rather too big to fit comfortably into that category but, to me, anything that purrs so divinely must surely be a scion of the tribe of the Egyptian Bast. I treat him as such, for which respect he repays me with touching loyalty.

We wind our way down through the black, damp rocks. At high tide, there is no beach at all on this side of the island and, when the sea draws back her foamy skirts, there are pleasing pools full of unusual, twisted shells and weed that streams like long switches of green hair. Sometimes, we find richer treasures, but I am not beachcombing today. Ishti has brought me a white cockerel from the village, which I drained into a bowl, ultimately transferring the blood to a stoppered vial. The villagers are afraid of my Ishti and never interfere with his excursions into their territory to bring me the things I need. They are also rather afraid of me, which effectively prevents them from taking the law into their own hands concerning Ishti. I give them things in return that my father has sent me – items of clothing, meaningless baubles, certain foods I dislike – so they cannot really complain.

Mad Helen is on the rocks today, an eerie figure amidst the foam. She is staring out across the grey waves, her pale hair blowing right over her face, standing still as a stone. She, of all the peasants, I find intriguing. Her people believe her to be simple-minded, yet I know she is merely stultified by the life she leads upon this rock, and would blossom away from it, if she could only find a place to exercise the skills with which I have acquainted her. An eager student, Helen. When I am allowed to return home, I have a mind to take her with me. It would serve my father right.

'Good day to you my dear!' I announce.

Helen does not move. She is thinking deeply. Sometimes I pinch her sharply to make her share her thoughts with me, because they can be so interesting.

'I have some blood to cast!' I tell her.

That wakes her up a little. She turns her small pointy face in my direction, her narrow grey eyes screwed up against the wind. 'Have you, Mistress? May I watch?'

'Of course.' I take the vial out of the pocket of my cloak and begin to wrestle with the stopper. The vials I use are quite old, and the only vessels suitable for this type of task I can find among the rubbish of my equally old palace. I am always concerned they will spill their contents onto my clothes and consequently tend to stopper them too tightly.

'Allow me, Mistress,' Helen says, and I hand the vial over to her clever fingers, surprisingly brutish and thick members, on such a fragile body.

'There is talk that raised voices were heard coming from your windows last night, my lady Circe,' she says.

'Indeed,' I reply, as perhaps question or exclamation. Helen does not understand the difference, but she eyes the vial with greater interest.

'A cockerel,' I say.

Together, smiling each our different smiles, we turn towards the sea.

It was not a grey day when the *Persephone* came towards the island but, like this day of wind and clouds, I was standing on the rocks at the half tide, casting something – I have forgotten exactly what, perhaps an entrail or two – into the receding waters. Ishti was with me, as always, poking his long, stiff whiskers into the rock pools, sniffing for crablets and vulnerable fish spawn.

Helen came sliding over the wet, weedy stones towards me from the direction of the village, her dripping skirts tucked up into her belt, her feet encased in sopping animal skin slippers, tied at the ankle. She had her enhancing vitrine with her, something her grandmother had fashioned, she being a woman of invention and devices. The ignorant populace of the village believe Helen's grandmother to be a witch, but I know better and have used her inventions in many ways from time to time. The vitrine is a cleverly fashioned glass lens set in an embellished metal frame. Looking through it, things far from the eye appear close, and interesting details can be discerned. Helen, I am sure, has many clandestine uses for this device – if she has not, she is no true disciple of mine! – but sometimes, on clear days, we take it in turns to squint through the vitrine at the distant waves. It is possible to distinguish the eyes painted on the hulls of my father's guardian ships on the horizon; a dull view, it is true, but I like to peer at the tiny figures of the men on board, wishing them various misfortunes such as love and marriage.

Helen put the vitrine against her eye and described to me an elegant ship she perceived against the blue sky.

'Which direction is it taking, dearest?' I asked her.

She bared her teeth and said, 'To the east, my lady, her sails are full of wind.'

'So beyond the net of our influence,' I said pensively, wrenching the vitrine from her hold. I was thinking about how many vessels sailed along the invisible ring-pass-not that surrounded my place of exile, all of them quite ignorant of the treasure that lay so close. Occasionally, I indulged in fantasies of ships bulging with creatures uneducated in my history, who might blunder in innocence towards the island. Unfortunately, my father – damn his seed – lavishes great care on advertising what he perceives to be my dangerous nature. He is superstitious and blind, but I cannot forgive him his childish misapphrensions. The murder I committed was necessary and just, in my eyes.

I adjusted the vitrine against my brow and peered into the blue. The ship was beautiful, a mere speck, like a model created by a craftsman, each detail precise and tiny. If only it would turn its slender prow towards the rocks. If only it would come to me. Who knows what secrets it might spill among the weeds and shells? Rather wistfully, I handed the vitrine back to Helen.

'Perhaps, one day, we shall both sail away upon such a ship,' I said, because the girl liked to hear fabulous stories. We often invented new futures for ourselves, our words blown away by the sea winds, hopefully into the ears of some benign, indulgent deity.

'Perhaps we could sail away upon this one,' she replied.

I laughed gently and laid a hand against her bony shoulder. 'Perhaps, in dreams,' I said.

'No, really,' she replied, and I noticed a certain fervour

in her tone.

Without words, I snatched the vitrine away from her eyes, causing her to yelp unnecessarily as her cheek caught a blow from the metal frame. It took only a moment to confirm my hope; the ship had turned towards the island. It took a further moment for me to control myself. With vile, girlish stupidity, I had allowed the prospect of visitors to excite me. This was the kind of weakness I would expect my sweet, simpering sister to display and, having recognised it, stemmed it immediately, swiftly invoking a sense of weary nausea instead.

Owing to the fact that my father's navy patrols this stretch of water so assiduously, few vessels come to invade our privacy. Those that do are generally filled only with priests who come to pay visits to the lustreless shrines on top of the island. This rock was once the summer retreat of a noble family, who have since seen sense and built for themselves a grander retreat in more clement circumstances, but their ostentatious shrines still remain, though I suspect empty of divine presences. Occasionally, instead of priests but only barely more tolerable, a shoal of slippery courtiers from my father's court might come to peer down their elegant noses at us, but these men are always decrepit and of little interest to me. Also, they carry lies back to my father, if they get the chance. I knew that whoever sailed towards us could only be further dregs of religious society or telltale buffoons. Still, it was possible I would have to receive one of them in my abode, which at least promised a minor diversion for the day, so I called Ishti from his explorations and, gathering up my skirts, hurried towards the cliff path.

I composed myself upon my sea terrace, had the tiles strewn with crushed blossom and pungent torn ferns, and saw to it that Baucis and her crones had chilled the wine in spring snow, gathered from the higher slopes. I had dressed myself in a maidenly colour – pale saffron, I recall – and reclined limpidly upon a couch; Ishti and his smaller companions arranged around me on cushions and rugs and fleeces. I had tied back my hair – a style I loathe as it reveals the height and breadth of my forehead – and had donned some of the jewellery my father had sent me. Most of it, I throw into the sea or give away to the peasants, but I do keep a few choice items around me for occasions such as this. I never know who might come to me, with the express purpose of compiling an unflattering report of my mien and appearance to deliver to my father.

Baucis had scuttled out onto the terrace. She is like a spider, having bent hairy limbs but an alarmingly quick gait. 'Well, is it priest or sycophant this time?' I asked her, in a languid, bored voice, just in case there were ears pressed to the drapes beyond the terrace doors.

'Neither, mistress,' Baucis lisped.

'Then what?'

'A man, mistress.'

I sighed. 'Naturally.'

'A young man.'

I raised an eyebrow. 'Different!'

Baucis grinned. 'An *attractive* young man.'

'An occasion for grateful sacrifice! Is he gelded?'

My retainer grimaced. 'Does not strike me as so,' she said, 'but perhaps it is difficult to tell.'

I sat upright. 'Well, I must confess to being intrigued as to why my beloved father should send such a creature to our island, but you must show him to me immediately.'

Baucis hesitated. 'Mistress, he does not claim to have come from the king.'

I could not help gripping my own throat: excitement had leapt in it like a caged bird who spies the cage door open. No, no, I must not vault to conclusions that might lead to disappointment. 'His name?' I asked.

Baucis bobbed a curtsey, still grinning. 'Aertes of the house of Parmon,' she said. 'He is a poet of renown.'

This man intrigued me from the start, but you must understand that the intrigue of a pretty face is commonplace and it was the deeper allure which manifested later that had the strongest hooks. In appearance he was almost unkempt, his dark, gold-shot hair ungroomed and hanging nearly to his waist. He looked like some bedraggled satyr, although his cloak was spun of finest wool and edged with gold thread. The face was bare as if scoured by the salt sea. Indeed, I was reminded of bone; in shadow, he could resemble a skull, although he was undoubtedly attractive. 'My lady, Circe' he said, and swept a bow. He had come to me seeking inspiration.

Well, I was more than prepared to give him that. Demurely, I allowed him a few minutes' audience as he extolled his own virtues in what he designed to be a modest manner. Smiling sweetly, I allowed him to exercise his vanities before dismissing him by claiming I had tasks to attend to, and that I would be unable to lavish more time on him until the following evening. This, he took in good part, *disappointingly* good part, I thought, but never mind, he had one foot in the web at least, if only by being here.

Later, as Baucis brushed my hair before bedtime, in the low, captured sunset light of the lamps, within a veil of sweet, cedar incense, we made a small wager as to how long it would take me to ensnare him. 'A day,' I said. 'All poets are romantics.'

'No, he has a wolf's eyes,' my faithful crone replied, skilfully unknotting a persistent tangle. 'I'll give it a week.'

We were both in error.

I had agreed to speak with Aertes at dusk, for that is my time, when I feel my strength most potent. Also, it becomes a woman to court the evening light. It is like a veil;

you are seen through it only dimly. From Baucis, I had
learned the poet had spent the day showing himself off in
the village, escorted by a gambolling herd of coltish
followers he had brought with him off the ship. Through
Baucis, I had made it plain I would only interview him
alone. Youths annoy me.

When I drifted out onto the terrace, Aertes was sitting
on the stone wall that overlooked the sea.

'You like my palace?' I asked him, lifting back my veil
and padding over the marble. Baucis had permeated the
whole building with overwhelming fumes, supposedly as a
mark of welcome, although I suspected she harboured fears
about disagreeable odours escaping from the kitchens. In
truth, my eyes were stinging.

Aertes laughed softly, leaning forward, his forearms
resting carelessly on his knees. I perceived a bloody scratch
upon his bare shin. Perhaps he'd blundered through the
thorns along the cliff-top. 'The palace is graceful, but in a
way, disappointing,' he said.

'Oh, I am humbly shamed! Why so?' The answer was
no great surprise.

'Well, I find no skulls, no blood upon the floor, no
tortured statues suggesting men turned to stone and no
animals wearing the tatters of human clothes.'

'Perhaps you have not looked hard enough,' I said,
favouring him with a gentle smile. 'I trust your day has been
enjoyable, although I regret there is little upon this hump of
rock to entertain.'

'I visited the village,' he said. 'The people here are
starved of culture.'

'I have noticed this, too,' I said. 'Perhaps you should
perform for them.'

He pulled a face at me, hoping to draw me into some
private humour. It struck me how similar he was to all the
men I had known about my father's court; confident of his

innate splendour and unafraid. He saw me as a simple woman; a mistake all men make when viewing the female form. They think of their poems, but not the reality. They cannot see into the dark.

'You are a legend,' he said to me, gesturing abruptly with outstretched fingers. 'Forgive my intrusion, but I was interested in finding you.'

Clearly, he believed I would be delighted and grateful to have his company. It would not have surprised me to learn he had made wagers of his own concerning conquest and ravishment. 'How brave you are to dodge my father's ships,' I said.

He grinned, looking up at me with lowered head, expecting me to see the face of a boy interested in wholesome games. What I saw instead – the truth of the matter – was the face of a dog; it was not that far below the surface. 'It was no difficulty,' he said. 'I go where I please.'

I sat down upon the stone shelf below him, and composed my body into a demure maidenly posture. Sometimes, I convince even myself I am what I pretend to be. 'So, having found me, what do you want of me?' I asked him dulcetly, gazing at the floor.

'I would like to talk to you,' he said, magnanimously.

'Then please do.'

I watched him out of the corner of my eye as he rubbed his upper lip with a finger and picked up some parchment leaves he had beside him on the wall. 'I will not waste time with foolish pleasantries,' he said, 'because I respect your station. I am most interested in knowing the details of how you killed your husband.' He had a charcoal poised above an empty page.

'Quite simply,' I told him, staring him in the eye. 'I fed him certain evils.'

'How?' he asked, eagerly.

I curled my arms around my knees. 'It is hardly an

interesting story! My father had made me marry the man, after which I suffered his malodorous abuse for a week. Very soon, I became tired of his behaviour and, one evening, administered a bane mixed with his wine.'

'Because he abused you?' Aertes' eyes had assumed a hero's glint.

I shrugged. 'Yes, but I didn't like him anyway, and neither am I any man's property to barter. It was a lesson to my father. He will not sell me again.'

'Yet you are here alone, imprisoned on this island.'

'Unmarried,' I reminded him.

Aertes made a flourish on his page with the charcoal. Black splinters flew everywhere. 'Among the greater islands there are stories of you being an enchantress. It is said that you can turn men into beasts, and in fact took pleasure in doing so regularly about your father's court. Some say this was why your father was anxious to secure you in marriage to a man of strength. Is this true?'

I wriggled my shoulders. I could have told him then that all men are essentially beasts – some of them more personable than others – and that a clever female can easily draw out the feral element for display. There is no magic involved. However, I never divulge my knowledge to others and merely said, 'If I were an enchantress, I would hardly be stuck here, would I?'

He smiled at me. 'There are other legends,' he said, 'which present you in a less than kindly light.'

'All princesses are the victims of other people's legends,' I replied. 'It is an inevitable consequence of being royal.'

He nodded, grinning. 'Of course, but if I may quote just one. It concerns how a certain young princess was approached by a woman of her father's court in order to dispense a gratuity upon this woman's sons. Apparently, the sons had recently performed some service for the king.

The woman asked the princess to bestow upon her sons the greatest gift a man could have. It is said the princess agreed to do as much, and subsequently had the youths put to death in their sleep.'

'It is a legend,' I said, 'perhaps a fable, the moral being it is advisable to be precise when asking boons of those in power. The greatest gift a man can have is to die in his sleep, feeling nothing. The woman should have anticipated this. I feel it is a lesson all should learn. The gods take the easiest path in granting wishes and it is the duty of their earthbound representatives to educate the people in this matter.'

'A harsh judgement.'

'Not at all.'

'Then I am relieved you are not in the position to pass judgement on myself!' He laughed loudly.

Fool.

Adopting the role of The Maiden was ineffective on Aertes. I felt as if a veil of ice was between us; that, or he was made of ice himself. I extended all my subtle charms, gentle persuasions, movements of the body, the eyes, all designed to inflame his lust, but he did not respond. Obviously, I had chosen the wrong mask to wear that night. But there would be other nights. Sad that Baucis might have already won her wager though.

The following day, I worked upon another of my personae: the Victim of Cruel Fate, whom I intended to present to the cool Aertes at sundown. This, a lady of more mature mien, was someone who had suffered upon life's path, yet whose bitterness was tinged by wry humour. The scenario in which this lady felt most comfortable was the long and shady hall that overlooked the hill behind the palace; a room I hardly used. Here, I had Baucis set out the supper; the fruits of the vine were frosted with sugar and all the tableware was white. Everything echoed around us. Again, I commanded the poet's presence alone and made sure his company were fed in the kitchens.

Having taken good care to make sure that Aertes would already be present in the shadowed, white hall, so that my entrance would take best effect upon his senses, I emerged between the columns, amid a cloud of incense more subtle and flowery than the previous night's dousing. I had dressed in black, and coiled my hair atop my head, allowing it to fall from this confinement in inky waves over my shoulders. The poet was again scribbling with a splintered stick of charcoal on one of his parchment leaves.

'This room: amazing!' he said, without looking up. 'So full of atmosphere!' He paused then, and grinned at me. 'Perhaps a hundred souls have met their unhappy end here, at your hands.'

I was affronted because he clearly did not believe this was possible. 'It is a joy to me you are finding so much to stimulate your imagination in my home.' I hoped to sound cold.

'I walked to the top of the island today,' he said. 'Tomorrow, I may walk with my company to the farthest shore. It shouldn't take more than a couple of days, should it?'

'How can I say?' I answered waspishly. 'Generally, when wishing to make that particular trip, I anoint myself with the blood of virgin boys and fly there!'

He laughed, and I realised, with chagrin, I had been careless enough to let my mask slip a little.

'I have already composed a few verses,' he said.

'Oh, and are they about me?'

He grimaced. 'Well, not exactly. I have been travelling around collecting the stories of many infamous females. You are the last, but I already have a lot of material. I'm thinking of turning you all into a kind of composite; a

267

goddess, I suppose, but a dark one.'

'A goddess against whose powers you appear inviolate,' I observed, smiling and helping myself to a frosted grape. Soon, Baucis would bring in the roast birds.

Aertes shrugged. 'Perhaps I am too interested in the phenomenon to fall under its spell.'

'What phenomenon?' I disliked the implication of being part of something common, or widespread.

'Well, it seems to me that women, such as yourself, are merely icons of men's fear of femalekind. In a way, I feel you are created by the men who fear you: idols of perverse desire; malignant, destructive, frigid, yet ultimately fascinating.'

'You flatter me!' I said.

Aertes raised his hands in apology. 'Forgive me, I did not mean to imply I believe you to possess these attributes, but hearsay certainly suggests they are among your characteristics. Having started out with the intention of risking death to interview women such as yourself in the hope of discovering witches and monsters, I found an entirely different phenomenon.'

'Oh? How different?' I had taken another grape and found, to my consternation, that it was sour.

'I wonder why you, and other women, have been deified in this dark way,' Aertes said.

'Perhaps because we *are* the witches and monsters we're supposed to be!'

Aertes shook his head. 'Sadly, I disagree. For example, I came here looking for an evil enchantress and what I find appears to be only an isolated and perhaps disillusioned woman, someone whose sole crime could be said to have appreciated freedom in a world where the freedom of daughters was denied. You are not a compassionate creature, exactly, and I suspect never have been, but as I said, it is men – your father's chroniclers and lyricists perhaps – who have created your legend.'

'Your theory is interesting,' I said, 'but personally I believe I was created, not by men's fascinated fear, but by their insensitive and brutish self-interest.'

'You are bitter.' He smiled at me sheepishly.

Well, bitterness was certainly what I had intended to portray that night. Perhaps my mask hadn't slipped as much as I'd thought.

I shrugged. 'Some wounds take their time to heal.'

He nodded thoughtfully.

At that moment, Baucis scurried in with a retinue of hags to serve us our repast. Despite appearances, her coven are accomplished cooks. Denying me stimulation of more intriguing kinds, my father saw to it that my palate was satisfied at least.

'So, tell me,' I said as I neatly removed the legs and wings of my small, roasted bird, 'what of these other fascinating goddesses you have investigated?'

He laughed in a vaguely apologetic manner. 'You want stories? Well, I have plenty!' He rested his elbows on the table, one hand waving the leg of a bird like a baton to emphasise his speech. 'Have you heard of the Siren Sisters of Anthemusa?'

I shook my head.

'These ladies are priestesses of the river god Achelus and are reputedly monsters; half woman and half bird. Their temple stands at the place where the river flows into the sea. Their vows to the god insist on chastity and, bitter at this restriction, it is said they vent their frustrated wrath upon the male species by crouching on the rocks outside their temple at sundown. Here, they play upon lyres and double flutes, singing songs of lust and desire; their voices are reputed to be most enchanting. Men on passing ships overhear the songs and, espying the limpid maidens draped over the rocks, believe them to be hierodules offering their services to the worshippers of Aphrodite. Naturally, the men hurry towards land in order to take advantage of the situation and inflict advances upon the priestesses. Whereupon, male priests, espying what they believe to be severe violation of the sacred virgins, rush out of the temple and slay the importunate wooers immediately. The Siren sisters continue to sing while this slaughter is underway, and some say there is a note of triumph in their warblings.'

'A pretty story,' I said, thinking I could do with such company myself to draw some entertainment to my rock. 'And you have met these bloody ladies?'

Aertes grinned. 'Yes. They were, as priestesses should be, retiring and modest creatures.'

'And which half of them was avian?' I inquired.

He shook his head. 'Neither. They wore sumptuous cloaks made entirely of the feathers of swans which, when they made their evening devotions, they raised about them with their arms. The cloaks did resemble wings, I suppose, but the ladies' limbs were entirely human and not one of them had a tail!'

'How grossly disappointing!' I said. 'So none of it was true?'

Aertes shrugged. 'Well, one of the priestesses did tell me that another of her sisterhood had indeed once sat upon the rocks beyond the temple and sung pretty songs into the sea breeze. A stray fisherman had been attracted by the lovely voice and had come to investigate.' He sighed. 'Human nature being what it is, the two unfortunates fell in love. When their alliance became news to the priests – which was inevitable, given that the girl's sisters must have envied her relationship – they killed the fisherman. And that gave rise to the legend.'

I pulled a sad face. 'Is that all? How lamentable!'

Aertes gestured with open hands. 'You see? But perhaps you have more in common with the lady Atalanta, daughter of the King of Arcadia. Her father never forgave the fact she was born female, apparently, and sent his hunters to expose the babe on Mount Parthenius. Luckily, one of the men's wives had recently lost a child and was fretful and milk-bound because of it. He took the girl home and the couple raised her as theirs. As a young woman, Atalanta sorely resented the treatment meted out to her by her parent and took solace in hiding among the rocks and trees of the mountain so that she could fire arrows at passing courtiers. Legend has it that she was an accomplished murderer of men. Despite these unfriendly tendencies, her father eventually recognised her as his heir and wanted to marry her off. It is said Atalanta would only submit to marrying the man who could beat her in a race and, being a fleet athlete, was never beaten. Apparently, all the failed suitors were despatched by her in a grisly manner. At length, a man came to Arcadia equipped with golden apples, supposedly given to him by a goddess. By dropping these glittering fruits in Atalanta's path, he tempted her to pause in her running, thereby winning the race and claiming her hand in marriage!'

'What a shame!' I said, hoping she went on to murder the cunning beast.

Aertes shrugged. 'Recently, I went to Arcadia and met the lady. She now rules there, a stately matron, with her husband. I asked her about the murders – especially those of prospective suitors – at which she laughed. She admitted having once caused a superficial cut on the head of one of her father's courtiers, however. As to her husband's deception, she confessed that she found him attractive from the start and merely used the apples as an excuse to lose the race. I found her a very kind and sweet-natured creature. She reminisces wistfully of being rather boyish in her youth...' He leaned back in his chair, blinking languidly into the soft lamplight. 'I have a host of stories such as

271

these, and have found that every one of them has a fairly mundane explanation. It seems that an attractive woman of noble birth only has to have a small tantrum, or a fit of pique, to be elevated to the status of goddess. I suppose fabulists need these legends, and people find their tales more interesting if they are based on fact, but in reality, there is never much truth in them.'

I grimaced. 'So now you hope to deflate my legend, do you? It might be difficult. I did kill a man.'

Aertes raised a finger and stared at me smugly. 'Yet you yourself denied ever having turned men into beasts! That's one rumour cankered already!'

Anger was building up within me. Not just for myself, but for all these other women whom Aertes was determined to reveal as ordinary and dull, destroying their magic, which was theirs by right. How dare he! Resolve settled within me; I made a vow to veiled Hecate that this insulting little scrap of humanity would not leave my island in the same frame of mind as he approached it! Let him take on the might of female mystery. He thought to find a whinnying criminal, racked by shame and misery. What he had found was the very thing he thought could not exist. Only he did not know it yet.

The following day, Aertes set off as he had promised to explore the island. I paced up and down my chambers, trying to think of a way to penetrate his armour of protection, his scornful disbelief. All my attempts to attract him seemed to have no effect, and I knew, having heard his disrespectful 'stories', that any mask I fashioned to wear in his presence, no matter how mysterious and alluring, would fail to impress him in the manner I desired. His smug confidence infuriated me immensely.

Before he left, I inspected his retinue from behind my chamber drapes. What I saw resembled nothing more than a tumble of young pups; boys of impoverished noble families, no doubt, that could not afford to send their sons on expeditions with a more prestigious figure. It seemed incontrovertible to me that, having this giggling troupe of Ganymedes about him, he was impervious to feminine wiles. Perhaps a fatal dish of local banes served to his puppies might discommode him in a satisfying manner, but that plan was distressingly crude and ultimately would not directly affect the man himself.

Depressed by a heavy, black humour, I whistled to Ishti and set off for my favourite haunt among the sea rocks. It is a place where I always formulate my most effective schemes.

As usual, Mad Helen was sitting on the rocks, humming to herself and stirring a pool full of weed with her toes. 'Good day, my lady,' she said, smiling at me widely, with genuine welcome. A little warmth came into my frozen heart at the sight of it. I sighed and sat down beside her.

'Not a good day, Helen, my dear,' I said.

The girl frowned. 'Oh, my lady, what ails you?'

'The ship that sailed into our landing bay two days ago...'

'The *Persephone*!' Helen interrupted. 'Yes, the beautiful man who owns her came to the village yesterday. He told us funny stories and sang a few songs. What a lovely voice he has! And what a gorgeous face! He sang of distant lands, where ladies clad in the feathers of swans...'

'Vile beast!' I cried, interrupting her recitation of Aertes' impertinent story, which I simply could not endure to hear again.

At my outburst, Helen's smiled hovered uncertainly around her lips. I realised she must be quite taken with Aertes. I laid a gentle hand upon her arm. 'You do trust me, my dear, don't you?' I asked.

She nodded. 'Without question, my lady.'

I closed my eyes and sighed. 'I am relieved to hear that. Listen to me: the poet Aertes is a cruel and dangerous man. Do not be deceived by his pretty little tales and gauche cavortings.'

'Dangerous in what way, my lady?' Her eyes had gone quite round.

I leaned close to her ear. 'He ruins women!' I hissed. 'He has come here to destroy me!'

'No!' Helen gasped. 'How awful! What will you do?'

I shrugged. 'As yet, a stratagem eludes me...'

'Could you not attract the attention of one of your father's sea patrols?' she asked. 'And let them deal with the scoundrel in the proper manner?'

I shook my head. 'You do not understand, my dear. The destruction he wreaks is that of severing a lady's cord with her goddess, leaving her alone and soulless in the world. And I suspect there are few men of my acquaintance who would willingly interfere with such a plan. A woman without her goddess is a tractable creature, easily controlled. This is a woman's matter, and only women may take action against him.'

Helen's eyes had now become quite dark with passion. I saw an underground light in their velvet depths that reminded me of a spear of starlight falling through a cavern roof into a still pool. Goddess light. She was thinking deeply, I could tell, and for that reason, I kept my silence to facilitate her musings.

'Last evening, before he returned to your palace for supper, he performed for the entire village,' she said.

I nodded encouragingly, aware that some deep intuition was struggling up through Helen's mind into the light.

She looked at me with earnest eyes. 'He spoke with such ardour! He strode about in the dust, throwing out his arms, grimacing, mimicking a weeping woman, talking in a voice like a child. These were all characters in his epic. Should I have given that performance, it would have been absurd, and made people laugh. Aertes has a gift. He can make you believe you really are listening to a woman, or a child. And the truth is that it really is vital to him that his audience become enthralled by his performance. When he wants to make them laugh, he can, but laughter intruding into one of his tragedies would be, for him…' –she smiled – '… a tragedy!'

I squeezed her arm. 'I feel your instincts have just spoken to me, and that they carry a message from my goddess, shadowy Hecate!'

She screwed up her nose. 'It was just an impression of mine. Perhaps of use, perhaps not.'

I mulled over Helen's words in the privacy of my chambers. My intuition told me that within them lay the seed to a promising plan. Aertes was due back at the palace in a couple of days. I called my steward to me, a withered, half-crippled veteran of my father's army, and instructed him to deck the palace with garlands, to sweep out the enormous yard behind the building, where empty stables gaped and chickens ran about without restraint. 'Scatter some sweet straw, for which I give you leave to barter with the local herders,' I said. 'String lanterns round the walls, and transform this place into an area fit for theatrical displays.'

The steward bowed. 'Certainly, my lady. Might I ask whether you intend to entertain here at the palace?'

'Indeed, Loxos! We have a poet among us, whose performances, I understand, are superb. My staff, and the gentle people of the village, lead a life bereft of whimsical distractions. I have a mind to host a celebration for their benefit. Have your menials convey my tidings to all upon the island. Upon his return, I shall implore the gallant Aertes to indulge my whim. I will suggest that three nights hence, he should perform his most rigorous tragedy, which perhaps he might be civil enough to follow with a few conceits of a lighter nature.' Warming to the idea, I arose from my couch, and paraded around in front of the stunned Loxos, throwing out my arms, my robe aswirl. 'We shall have music and dancing! Wine shall be drunk in quantity beneath Selene's light! Have the shrine of Dionysus cleared of rubbish, light the votive lamps therein, and adorn the god's image in garlands of the vine!'

Loxos appeared quiet overwhelmed by my enthusiasm. A hectic flush bloomed along his ancient, raddled cheeks, and he bobbed out of the room in an unprecedented lively manner.

I was unsure how the spirit of the god Dionysus might react to my reanimating his rather neglected icon. His little shrine had once been frequented regularly by the family who used to live upon the island but now it was no longer visited, never filled with the songs of adoration and sacrificial offerings so essential to divine well-being. At home, I had once been an avid devotee but, devoid of Dionysian delights as my existence now was, I had little occasion and even less desire to confront this particular god. Contemplation of his attributes would only serve to remind me of the paucity of my social activities. Hence, shunned in favour of the charcoaled walls of Hecate's fane, the shrine had been untended and left open to the elements. The nose of the statue inside had been broken off by a flying tree-branch during a winter storm, and its fingers were badly crumbled, but I hoped the god would forgive me this delinquency. An attempt to invoke his ecstatic influence could only prove beneficial to the coming event.

Aertes returned in the afternoon, his advent heralded by a great deal of noise emitted by his bouncing followers.

Spring seemed to have fallen in a soft, sweet haze over the palace while he'd been away. Already the air was scented with blossom and the heady fragrance of Dionysus' incense – crushed ivy, pine resin and fennel seeds – floated through the chambers of my abode in a silvery mist. My servants had begun unaccountably to sing during their daily labours, and the ancients with which my father had equipped me had adopted an almost jaunty gait. Baucis' crones were already engaged in preparing a splendid feast for the coming celebration and the odours of their efforts mingled pleasingly with the offertory fumes.

Aertes found me on the sea terrace, where I sat with a loom, engaged in what he would see to be a proper womanly pursuit. The loom had been left behind by one of the palace's previous occupants. Scant hours before, I had had Baucis lug it out of one of the attics. A quick dusting down and a brief rub with beeswax had restored its wooden frame, and Baucis had appropriated some yarns for me to tangle on it.

Aertes came marching towards me, his hair tied back, his head crowned with a garland of twisted ivy leaves – sadly omenic, perhaps – which his puppies had obviously woven for him.

'The palace is decked as if for a wedding!' he exclaimed. 'To what happy occasion have I returned?'

I smiled at him graciously. 'That, my lord Aertes, rests entirely with you. I have heard talk of your bewitching performances in the village and wondered whether you would endow us with a major recital here at the palace.'

He appeared rather surprised. 'I cannot say this was expected, my lady,' he said.

'I hope that doesn't mean you cannot comply.' I stood up and approached him, even dared to place light fingers on his arm. 'It is not for myself but for my people here on the island,' I said in a confidential tone. 'I have a retinue of thirty staff, all of whom are, through no fault of their own, in exile as I am. All I wish is to provide for them an evening's entertainment. We shall invite the local people, and have a lively celebration of your visit.'

Aertes sighed. 'Well, you certainly exhibit the caprices of the female spirit, lady Circe. Before I left the palace, I could have sworn you'd strike me dead before you'd show interest in my work. I seem to recall you had little sympathy with my themes.'

I raised my arms, turned away from him, shrugged, looked over my shoulder. 'I was impressed by what I heard of your performances in the village, as I said.' Crossing to the pale stone wall, I sat down, supporting myself on straight arms in a girlish manner. 'Aertes, at home, I drowned in entertainment, music, dance and song. Here... I am shrivelling up into a sour and joyless hag. Indulge me; bring a little life to these empty, sorrowing walls.'

Aertes gave me a sidelong glance, and my breath was stilled in my chest. Would he give in to my demand? I hoped his egotistic desire to posture and display himself might silence his perplexity at my apparent change of heart. He looked around himself, at the ropes of spring flowers draping the terrace walls, the dishes of crushed herbs smouldering beside the door. 'Well, you seem confident of my co-operation, having already done all this work; I can hardly refuse, can I?'

I exhaled gratefully. 'Thank you. I've arranged everything for tomorrow night. Will that provide adequate time for preparation?'

'I know all my work intimately; there is no need for rehearsal,' he said.

'Excellent!' I said, standing up. 'Would you take a little wine, lord Aertes?'

He nodded and sat down upon the wall, while I busied myself filling a goblet from the flagon Baucis had left me.

'One thing has always puzzled me,' I said, as I handed him the wine. 'Would you appease my curiosity and enlighten me?'

He took a mouthful of the drink. 'By all means.'

I sat down beside him. 'Well, having seen many poets, actors and musicians perform, I have regularly pondered about what it must be like standing up there before so many people.'

'What do you mean, lady Circe? It is our way of life, our daily office.'

'I mean, how does it really *feel* to have all those eyes centred upon you, hanging onto your every word, your every gesture? What do you think about? As you utter those words you know so intimately, what passes through your mind? Do you recall some menial uncompleted task half forgotten through the day? Do you think about how your feet are aching? Do you wonder whether anyone has fed your animals, or paid court to your charming followers? Please tell me, I am fascinated to know.'

A strange thing happened to Aertes' face. As I spoke, I watched it darken, until he was scowling openly. He put down the goblet quickly. 'Lady Circe, I don't think you realise that, when I perform, I am held in the spirit of my art. I transcend the mundane world, swept aloft to the realms where the gods walk. My mind soars in beatific bliss, as the words fall like gems from my lips! There is no consideration of inconsequential, petty issues!'

'Forgive me; I only wondered,' I said, pleased at his irritation.

'Then I hope I have dispelled your silly ideas! When I perform here for your people, take a look at their faces! Pay attention to their rapt contemplation of my words! Will they be thinking of trivial things, of animals and unwashed dishes and aching feet? No, I think not! They will be transported upon the wings of my oratory.'

'It sounds enchanting,' I said. 'Indeed, from this moment forth, I shall regard each performer I meet with a new and deferential eye. I had no idea such lofty elements were involved in the act of reciting poetry, or lines of plays. Indeed, I feel inordinately educated! Thank you, Lord Aertes.'

He flexed his shoulders, attempting to calm himself down. I sincerely had not expected so fiery a response. How gratifying. 'One thing I shall pray for,' I said, steepling my fingers against my lips, and gazing at him with apparent reverence.

'And what is that?' he asked.

'That, in the midst of your performance, you do not recall this conversation.'

He smiled a little, tightly. 'That is hardly likely.'

'Good. I would hate for you, in the midst of your transportation, to be brought down from the realms of the gods. It might mar the performance.'

'Lady Circe, I am a seasoned professional,' he said. 'There is no danger of my being distracted during a performance.'

Before the recital, I made my way to Hecate's fane, my place of private devotion. It is a short walk's distance from the palace, nestled in a grove of cypress trees, one of Her sacred plants. It was not Her time, because the moon was waxing full, but I still sought to invoke Her distant presence, burning a dish of sandalwood chips and dried mint, lubricated by the resin of the cypress. Prostrating myself before Her cruel countenance, I called Her presence into me. 'Dark Lady, occupy my flesh this night,' I implored. 'Lend to me Your shady powers!'

The fane was silent, but for the spitting of the cypress resin as it burned. It seemed a black wing was cast over everything, eclipsing all but the eager hearts of the flames of the charcoal-powdered candles burning beside the statue. I felt Her there, hanging in the shadows, and among the thick spiders' webs of the blackened rafters above. Perhaps She was affronted I had made devotions to fair Dionysus these past few days, but I hoped She understood my intention, which was ultimately of Her design. 'The man seeks to disempower Your handmaidens,' I whispered. 'I would avenge this abuse!'

At these words, I felt Her approach me. If I opened my eyes, I would have been able to see Her dark hand extended to touch me. A black flame ignited in my heart and it seemed, behind my closed lids, as if the whole fane was suddenly alight with deep red flames. The candles roared and spat above me, the incense filled my body with a potent, earthy scent. For a few moments, I too was transported to the realm of gods, but my performance was yet to come.

The winding path up from the village was filled with people making their way to my palace. Torches flickered and sizzled through the night, voices were raised in cheery anticipation of the celebration ahead. Muffled and disguised by a heavy black cloak, I entered the building through a rear entrance as if I was a servant, and hurried to the rooms on an upper storey that overlooked the bedecked yard. Already it was teeming with noisy peasants; herders who had been drawn down from the higher slopes by the promise of free wine, villagers in their colourful best clothes, vintners from further round the coast. It seemed Loxos had spread the word efficiently and nearly every occupant of my little isle had converged on the palace that night.

Lamb carcasses were turning on spits over a fire near to the gates, beside trestles laden with Baucis' delicious fare. Crones in clean robes were stationed behind the tables, ready to serve the gathering with food. Huge pitchers of wine sweated in ranks along the wall, and through the open shutters, I could see my balcony further along was festooned with flowers, the couch upon it spread with fleeces for my comfort.

In the centre of the yard, a raised platform had been constructed, from where Aertes would present his entertainment. Loxos was already distributing cups of wine to the crowd, so that everybody would be in a relaxed and cheerful mood by the time the performance began. A few of Aertes' creatures were posturing beside the fire, although I knew the majority of them were presently engaged in preparing their lord's costume for the evening, fawning over him in that singularly tedious, grovelling manner employed solely by youthful males in the service of a man they admire. Soon, the gathering would expect me to present myself above them, but I wanted Aertes out before them first.

Loxos had been instructed to assume the role of Master of Ceremonies and, after a suitable time, when it seemed everyone who had decided to attend had arrived, he hopped up onto the raised platform in the centre of the yard. Everyone turned towards him expectantly, and the tiresome old goat spent several minutes in jocular repartee with them, before he must have sensed my critical scrutiny and sobered himself enough to make a dignified yet flowery introduction of Aertes.

At that point, I flung off my cloak and made haste to the room which led to the balcony. I hid among the drapes before venturing outside and watched Aertes emerge from a doorway opposite. He looked magnificent; his hair plaited with glossy ropes of ivy, his robe of snowy white, edged with a discreet yet stylish border design of heavy gold thread. One shoulder was bare and, in the torchlight, his skin glowed tawny, fitting his bones with svelte and supple tension. I half expected his retinue to come after him, licking the ground where his feet had trod. It gratified me to notice he flicked a quick, nervous glance at the balcony and seemed a trifle surprised to find it empty.

As he alighted upon the platform, many in the crowd – already familiar with his work because of his recent local performances – began to cheer and clap their hands together over their heads. Aertes puffed up with arrogant vanity like a sail full of wind and bowed to them, holding out his arms, his hair falling forward like ropes of dark gold. Someone besotted with the man might have regarded him as an incarnation of Apollo. I, thankfully free of such fancies, saw only the monstrous love Aertes reserved for himself. He glowed with it, and the feeling was merely intensified by the adoration of his audience.

Sensing the moment right, I glided through the drapes and stood against the balcony. Picking up a spray of blossom, I tossed it down to land at Aertes' feet, thankful that, as a child, my propensity for injuring servants' brats with hurled stones had bequeathed me such an accurate aim.

Aertes, seemingly already engrossed in performance, picked up the blossom with a misty eye and held it to his nose, gazing at me in apparent veneration. The crowd all made nauseating cooing noises, so that I had to gesture abruptly for Aertes to begin his recital.

I have to admit, he was really rather accomplished. To prepare himself, he walked with bowed head up and down the platform, while a few of his followers strummed on lyres to invoke the correct atmosphere. One of the boys began to sing sweetly and, as one, the crowd was transported to some distant field, where asphodels bloomed beneath the moon, and shadowy, rustling trees moved restlessly at the corners of vision.

As the voice died down to a whisper and the lyres

merely insinuated a plaintive threnody into the night, Aertes began to speak. His voice rang out into the scented darkness, his body swayed like that of a rearing serpent. He leaned towards the crowd, arms extended, his fingers clawing their hearts to his. He spoke of love among the asphodels, the forbidden love of a young priestess for a wild hunter. His voice invoked the trembling nuances of timid obsession, the heavy scent of the flowers, the still, humid presence of the night. The words effortlessly conjured up those precious, sacred feelings of a young girl's first love, when all is a terrible yet fascinating secret. A woman could not have composed the piece with more accuracy. In my heart, a wistful poignancy reanimated forgotten feelings; the breathless expectancy of youth. I closed my eyes and lay back among the fleeces, listening to this intoxicating syrup of words that Morpheus himself could not have drooled more convincingly.

The relationship he narrated was doomed of course, and as Aertes' voice rolled ever louder over the crowd, he invoked the agony of grief, anxiety and guilt. I felt the angry, confused frustration of the nubile priestess, as her older guardians discovered the illicit affair. I clenched my fists and raged with her as she argued with their passionless resolve. I wept with her as the order was given for soldiers to be sent out to hunt down the importunate hunter and slay him. I could have lived it all, lying there among my fleeces. I could have let Aertes finish his performance and leapt to my feet as the crowd applauded. I could have showered him with blossoms, my adulation, my respect.

But, Dark Hecate was in my soul.

As I gasped upon my couch, she prodded me from within with a stiff and icy finger. 'What is this girlish fluttering of the heart?' she demanded. 'Wake up, Circe, and go about your business, or I'll see to it you're punished sorely! Let another man into your soul and you risk the true destruction. Wake up! Get on with it!'

I felt as if someone had doused me with a pitcherful of cold water and all at once I emerged, almost spluttering, from my delirium. Below, Aertes continued to exhort the crowd, and they, hypnotised by his story, stood around with mouths agape. The performance was reaching its climax, that of agonising grief, lost love, blood and death. All was silent, but for Aertes' hypnotic voice, which was descending in timbre, unravelling the black threads of his tale. And I, reclining, extended my long legs to rest my feet upon the balcony. With one sandaled foot, I furiously scratched at the other, until the thin, soft leather gave way. The sandal fell over the edge of the balcony and, because of the hush, made quite a satisfying slap as it hit the ground. Aertes' eyes jerked briefly upwards and, using the moment wisely, for I knew it would be brief, I leaned forward and rubbed my feet as if they pained me. Aertes caught my eye. I smiled, and steepled my fingers beneath my lips. 'I hope you do not recall this conversation...'

He could not help it. My gesture reminded him of what I'd said, and his voice faltered. I rested my elbows on the balcony, and directed the full force of Hecate's malignancy in his direction. *Do not continue*, I urged him. *Lose the thread. Forget the words.* The expression he sent back to me was one of anguish, even of disappointment and regret. I knew that a host of images were tumbling through his mind; images of aching feet, unwashed dishes, animals and faithless boys. His mouth worked on silence. He could not speak. The crowd began to murmur.

Fortunately for Aertes, one of his catamites had the wit to strike up a doleful song, and after a few moments, the poet recomposed himself and ended the recitation. But the magic had bled from it, and the applause, though loud, lacked the real emotion I knew Aertes expected as his fee. I had seen enough. Standing up, I arranged my robes, and went back into the palace. If Aertes glanced at the balcony again, he would find it empty.

At midnight, he came to my chamber. I was waiting for him. The incense was lit, the room full of the scent of the cypress. He flung open the door and stood facing me at the threshold. 'I saw you,' he said, in a low, hoarse voice, pointing at me like some vengeful spirit. 'I saw you crouched there on your balcony like a serpent drenched in blood!'

I laughed in a low, musical tone. 'Blood? I think not. Tears, maybe.'

Aertes made an ugly snorting sound and gestured stiffly with his hands. 'I know your kind! She-dogs! The first requisite of your nighted breed is a complete lack of any natural feeling! You are scarcely human! Like a ghoul feasting on the flesh of the dead, you suck the very substance from men's souls, seeking to bloat yourself with those finer attributes which you lack. You mock life! I despise you!'

'An impassioned speech, Lord Aertes, perhaps more so than the conclusion of your recital tonight!'

He pressed his fingers against his brow. 'I curse my foolishness! To think I felt sympathy for your circumstances!' He lowered his hands and stared at me steadily. His eyes were almost golden in the dim light. 'I realise I have been an unwitting component in some malignant scheme of yours,' he said. 'I hope it gave you pleasure, Lady Circe.'

'It did,' I said, quite simply.

I had ruined him, taken from him the soul of his art. I knew he would never perform again, not without fear. And yet, his arrogance demanded he should seek to retain some dignity.

'I pity you,' he said pompously. 'You lead a desolate

life. You have suffered at the hands of men, perhaps, and I had hoped we could be friends. When I saw you step out from your balcony curtains tonight, I had resolved to take you away from this island, take you with me when I leave.'

'Pah!' I spat. 'You dare to imagine I would concede to such a plan? I do not need rescuing, poet, and certainly not by you! What conceit!'

Aertes continued to stare and I was uncomfortably reminded of black Ishti's eyes as he meditated upon the secret arcana to which all cats are privy. Then, he shook his head. 'I was wrong about you. I believed you to be an intelligent yet restricted soul, someone whose only sourness was lonely pain. I know now this is not so. As you sought to trivialise my performance tonight, I realise your whole existence consists of petty spite and paltry malevolence. You are like an evil little girl, pulling the tails of her pets to hear them yelp with pain, to see how they wriggle. How ignorant you are! Don't you realise I am beyond the touch of your sick iniquities?'

'So beyond them, you felt moved to come and scream upon my threshold!' I smiled calmly, although my heart had begun to race unaccountably. There was a disturbing tremble in my limbs. I needed a weapon, oh how sorely I needed a weapon, and yet my sharpest darts, my words, all seemed to have fallen from my tongue, leaving me as an empty quiver filled only with the vanished prospect of injury.

Aertes drew in his breath, folding his arms. His skin had the soft velvet bloom of fur.

I sniffed and turned away. 'Aertes, you are misguided. Stripping a woman of her magic, whatever her character, is no charitable or friendly act.'

There was a brief silence, then his voice came, merely a whisper. 'I cannot forgive you,' he said. 'I live for my art. It is my soul.'

'Then the feeling is mutual. Yours is not the only art! You are a smug braggart!' Did he also think he was the only one capable of hurling insult?

Sadly, just as I seemed to be given a new quiver full of darts, he deprived me of continuing the assault.

'We will be leaving with the tide,' he said. 'I thank you, my lady. You have given me much material for the major epic I am composing, although the manner in which I acquired it brings me sorrow.'

'Good speed, then. May your journey be... safe,' I said, refusing to look at him, although I felt him hovering at the door. He did not want to leave, I am sure. 'Please, do not linger, Aertes. After all, you must be wanted elsewhere...'

'Of that, you can be sure!' he said. 'I realise I was wrong to dismiss the gorgons of legend as being entirely fictional, Lady Circe. You have taught me that much, because they live, at least, in you. Long may your royal father keep you chained to this rock. You deserve no other accommodation!'

With that, the door slammed. He left me.

And now I stand beside the waves, Helen pressed against me, and together we throw the vial of blood into the water. Aertes sailed away last night, but even so, I know his spirit, his grovelling dog-like spirit, haunts the curtains of my chambers. He will linger there for eternity, whining and snuffling. His vain words did not fool me; I know he lied. He'll never perform again. He won't! He can't! My magic is too potent. He is a dog now, craven and whipped into submission. Didn't he say himself I turned men into beasts?

Let him think that distance weakens my influence if he likes. Time will prove I'm right. One evening, in the exotic city of a distant land, beneath the light of a softer moon, among the summer, moth-dusted blooms of flowering trees, he will attempt to perform for an audience again. I can see him now: his proud beauty, his gleaming skin, his hair... At the climax of his recital, my face will come to him, and his pretty words will blow right away from his mouth like scented petals on the wind. Like a dog, he will court praise he no longer deserves; tail wagging sheepishly, dog-eyes blinking in a humiliating search for love and adoration. My face will come him. He will remember.

Men are all fools. I have proved them so. I have power here on my island.

Such a Nice Girl

The residents of Willowdale Farm estate were united in the opinion that Emma Tizard was *such* a nice girl. Nothing bad could possibly have happened to her: she was so *sensible*. She never walked out at night alone, never invited strangers beyond her security chain and would never, ever *dream* of stopping her smart new car on a deserted stretch of road at night. The residents decided her mysterious disappearance could only be due to some straightforward, rational explanation.

A family emergency perhaps? She had never spoken of family to her neighbours but she must have some relations knocking about somewhere. She certainly didn't give off the air of someone who was alone in the world. Emma Tizard was always smiling and polite, elegantly dressed and immaculately groomed. People supposed none of them could really claim to know her because of a natural, sweet reticence on her part. She was shy. On weekends, she liked to work in solitude. Not even the sourest female voice on the estate gave tongue to the detriment of Emma Tizard. That alone was strangely unnatural.

The first time any of them got to know that Emma was actually missing was when her employer, Michael Homey, knocked on Cynthia Peeling's door that Tuesday morning. Mrs. Peeling lived in the bungalow next to Emma's. She and her husband Rodney thought of themselves as well-to-do (he was sales manager for a successful firm), and had an eighteen-year-old son away at university. Cynthia belonged to that breed of women whose hair becomes blonder as they grow older, whose clothes became more youthful, and who gets away with it because of sheer panache. Michael

Homey automatically straightened his jacket when she opened her door to him. Apparently, Emma hadn't turned up for work the day before, hadn't telephoned to give an explanation – which she always did if she was ill – and was still absent today.

'It really isn't like her,' Michael Homey said apologetically. 'That's why I felt I ought to come round. I know she lives alone and wondered, well, if she'd had an accident. There doesn't seem to be anyone at home...'

Although Cynthia could hardly claim to know Emma Tizard well, she knew the girl sometimes disappeared for days at a time. Usually, she popped over to ask Cynthia to keep an eye on the bungalow for her, never giving any explanation for her absence, other than a bright remark such as: 'Time for a change of scenery! Going to recharge my batteries!' This made Cynthia think of open spaces, sporty pursuits. Emma always looked so healthy. Ms Tizard also gave the impression she was a person who could look after herself more than adequately. Therefore, Cynthia was not that perturbed by Michael Homey's worrying. She invited him in for coffee and Viennese fingers, in the hope of calming his fears. It was unlike Emma to take off without informing her employers, Cynthia felt, but perhaps the extent of Homey's concern gave an indication as to why she'd felt the need to disappear for a while. Emma was Michael Homey's secretary. From his distressed bewilderment, Cynthia guessed Emma must be indispensable to him in more ways than one. He refused to be convinced by Cynthia's gentle arguments.

'We should check she isn't lying unconscious in the house,' he said. 'I would never forgive myself if something had happened to her, and I'd done nothing to help.'

Cynthia grudgingly conceded Homey was right. 'Thank God there are no stairs in the bungalow!' she exclaimed with a laugh. Michael Homey bared his teeth without humour.

Peering through the spotless windows of Wren's Nest, they were joined by the elderly Mr. and Mrs. Godleigh from no. 10 and young Mrs. Treen with her toddler, Danny, from *Blossoms*, no. 15. Everyone tried the windows, which were, of course, all sensibly locked from inside. The bungalow looked immaculate, not a cushion out of place, not a single item of crockery left on the kitchen drainer. In the bedroom, the pale grey duvet was undented and there were no clothes lying around. Admittedly, they couldn't see into the bathroom, and curtains were drawn over one of the frosted windows. Through the garage door, the red gleam of Emma's car could be seen.

'Do you think we should break in?' Lily Treen suggested.

'That's against the law,' Mr Godleigh said. 'Perhaps we should call the police.'

'Oh, I don't think that's necessary,' Cynthia responded hurriedly, visualising Emma's alarm should she turn up again. She really didn't feel that Emma was inside but didn't want to say so, not having any proper foundation for her feelings. 'There's bound to be a good reason why she's not here. She might have caught a train to visit relatives, got a cab to the station. Do you know any of her family, Mr. Homey?'

Michael Homey shook his head. 'Perhaps Mr. Godleigh is right,' he said. 'It's better to be safe than sorry.'

'I think we should wait until tomorrow,' Cynthia insisted, and her tone of voice brooked no argument. 'Emma is a respectable young woman. I don't think it's seemly to have policemen breaking her windows just yet.'

At five past six that evening, a long ring on the doorbell disturbed the Peelings from their salad and quiche. Cynthia opened the door to a rather sinister-looking couple, who turned out to be detectives. They asked if the Peelings had a spare key to Wren's Nest, as Emma Tizard's parents thought they might.

Taken aback, Cynthia shook her head. Was anything wrong? Her guts, ahead of the subsequent information, began to churn. She could see two police cars parked at the kerb: uniformed officers were looking in through the windows of the bungalow next door.

Emma Tizard was dead, the detectives explained. Her body had been discovered by children playing truant from school. It appeared she'd been brutally murdered, horribly mutilated as if with mindless fury.

If the police found any evidence in Wren's Nest, they presumably removed it from the property. As the last panda car pulled away, the two plain-clothed detectives came back to interview the Peelings. Cynthia was feeling utterly sick, guilty for not having suspected something was wrong after all, and confused as to why her instincts hadn't alerted her. She'd felt so sure Emma had been all right.

'Did Miss Tizard tell you what she was planning to do over the weekend?'

Cynthia shook her head. 'No. She never told me things like that. We weren't that close.'

The male detective made a swift note on his pad.

The body had been found still clutching a handbag. The authorities had had no difficulty discovering who Emma was.

'And you never met any of her friends?'

Cynthia uttered a brittle laugh. She was still deeply shocked. 'No, no. It seems quite odd now when I think about it, but none of us in Cherrytree Lane know much about Emma at all.'

'So you don't know what kind of interests she had?'

The female detective seemed to conceal an unpleasant implication in the words.

'Art,' Cynthia said, 'History too. She borrowed books from me once, well, from my son. Ancient history.'

'She never mentioned anything a little more... *unusual?*'

'What kind of *unusual?*' Cynthia didn't like the tone of the question.

The female detective shrugged. 'Well, anything to do with the occult.'

Cynthia had to laugh. 'What? Emma? Certainly not. She was a very down-to-earth person. What are you trying to say?'

The male detective cleared his throat. 'Certain items in the house suggest she had an interest in that sort of thing. Books and so on...'

'She must have used them for her art,' Cynthia said lamely. She could think of no other explanation. Emma had been such a nice, ordinary girl.

The detectives wanted to know when Emma had last been seen. Cynthia couldn't clearly remember, but thought it was before the weekend. 'She used to paint and draw a lot. Sometimes we'd never see her at weekends. That was quite normal. She used to work then, you see. She worked very hard.' Cynthia felt tears come to her eyes, remembering the watercolour that hung above her bed, a haunting scene, painted by Emma, depicting *La Belle Dame Sans Merci*. Soft Emma, gentle Emma, a quiet, artistic soul.

'And there was never any mention of the time she lived in the city?' The female detective's voice had taken on a softer note, as she registered Cynthia's distress.

Cynthia shook her head. 'No.'

'It may just be a coincidence,' the male detective said, carefully re-capping his pen, 'but the young lady Miss

Tizard used to share a flat with in London disappeared under strange circumstances too. Unfortunately no trace of her was ever found. Are you completely sure Miss Tizard never mentioned this to you?'

'Quite, quite sure.' Cynthia collected herself, straightened her spine. 'How dreadful. Do you suppose the same person...?' She shuddered eloquently, pressing a handkerchief to her lips.

The female detective shrugged. 'It was several years ago. Perhaps, as my colleague said, a coincidence.'

Numbed and troubled by this ghastly and previously inexperienced unpleasantness in their lives, the inhabitants of Cherrytree Lane were sleeping badly. Those who were not shy of confessing it spoke of disturbing dreams in which the figure of Emma Tizard, unfamiliar in its disarray and horrible mien, took centre stage.

'It's only natural that it should affect us like this after what the police said to me about Emma having peculiar interests,' Cynthia Peeling said to a particularly distraught Lily Treen on Thursday morning. 'It's just our imaginations running a bit wild.'

Lily nodded, although her face was still troubled. 'But Cynthia, in the dream, Emma swore at me! Not just little words, but real swearing. It was revolting. She was half naked, her hair all hanging round her face in rags and swearing. She called me names and laughed.'

Cynthia Peeling put a comforting hand on Lily's shoulder, mouthing platitudes, while neglecting to mention the dream she'd experienced herself, in which she had witnessed a coarse and brazen Emma Tizard violently making love with Mr. Peeling. To make it worse, Cynthia had enjoyed the dream. Her waking self found sex rather ridiculous and unnecessarily messy. Rodney Peeling had been puzzled by the peculiar looks his wife had given him over breakfast on Thursday morning.

The police could not solve the mystery of Emma's death. During the next week, television reconstructions of Emma's supposed last movements, and flashes of telephone numbers which people could contact to give information only served to remind Cynthia of the grotesque horror of her neighbour's murder. She hardly dared turned the television on. The tabloid press found out about the occult angle, and lurid headlines suggested the dead girl's involvement in Satanism, inferring she had been the victim of a ritual killing. Cynthia's heart felt tight with pain; she sympathised with Emma's parents. How dreadful for them to read such rubbish. She herself knew it to be untrue, and considered writing to the press about it, but Rodney advised her against it. You never know what might result from such action. The Peelings could be cited as devil-worshippers, too. Reluctantly, Cynthia agreed with her husband, and the letters in Emma's defence remained unwritten. Everyone on the estate who had known Emma agreed that the occult stories were rubbish. Cynthia took as much comfort as she could from that.

'She was arty,' said Lily Treen over coffee one morning. 'She might have had a few odd things in the house. Arty people are like that. My sister-in-law has crystals and funny little statues around the place. She's an arty type too.'

'But Emma wasn't a peculiar sort of person, she was *normal*, Cynthia said. 'She just liked to paint and draw in her spare time.'

Lily nodded vigorously. 'Oh, I know, I know, but artists sometimes think peculiar things are, well, *artistic*.'

The day of the funeral dawned unexpectedly dull and overcast, after a week of sunshine. A sizeable group of

Willowdale Farm residents gathered in cars around Wren's Nest to escort the funeral cortege to the crematorium.

Emma's mother and father, who introduced themselves as Ruby and Steven, had arrived the night before. Ruby Tizard was a frumpy sparrow of a creature who wore grandmotherly hats and who, Cynthia suspected, was probably younger than herself. The Peelings had kindly offered them accommodation for the night, because Mrs. Tizard was obviously too upset to spend it in her dead daughter's bed, the only one available in Wren's Nest. The Tizards were strangely reluctant to enter the bungalow at all. Cynthia supposed that was because of their grief, and was sorry she couldn't offer them more comfort. She'd had to admit she and Rodney hadn't really known Emma very well, although they'd both liked her very much, and found her a pleasant, polite person. Michael Homey had probably known Emma better than they had. Cynthia wondered whether she should comment on the newspaper stories, and make it clear how wrong they were, but decided it was too soon to broach such an intimate subject. Perhaps later.

To make things worse, the funeral, which should have been a dignified occasion, was fraught with minor mishaps and irritations. The minister whom the Tizards had especially wanted to lead the service at the crematorium, being a close friend of the family, telephoned at the last minute to tell them a train had been de-railed on the route south, holding up his own indefinitely. It was too late to reach them any other way. A quick replacement from the local church proved unsatisfactory, since the man knew nothing of Emma, save what he'd read in the papers, which didn't give him much scope for a moving, personal sermon. As he swayed before the congregation, singing the praises of a girl he'd never met, the lights in the chapel flickered, threatening a total failure that never quite happened, while the public address system, which should have carried his voice to the farthest ear, spluttered and buzzed, reducing the earnest tones to a wobbling fart.

Halfway through the service, Lily Treen's young son began to scream inexplicably. When Lily took him into the hall outside, he threw up with gusto onto the marble tiles. Everybody must have heard. Mrs. Tizard began to cry. Afterwards, when questioned and consequently disbelieved, the child gabbled incoherently about a nasty lady who had put out her tongue at him. From what the adults could gather, the tongue had been black.

Back at Cherrytree Lane, the Peelings hosted a wake for Emma. Lily Treen stood sipping white wine with her back to the lounge window, her subdued son clinging morosely to her skirt. Every now and then, she felt compelled to turn round and look out. Wren's Nest regarded her silently, emptily, almost with scorn. She remembered her dreams and shuddered.

Mrs. Tizard, who hadn't eaten properly for days, drank far too much and became inconsolable. So much so that Cynthia Peeling felt obliged to call out her family doctor to give the poor woman a sedative.

'But she hadn't finished, hadn't finished!' Mrs. Tizard raved deliriously to anyone who would listen as she was led to the guest-room.

In fact, Rodney Peeling considered, as he surveyed his guests, everybody seemed to be drinking too much. Faces were flushed, voices raucous. One or two petty arguments seemed to be in progress. Perhaps he should tactfully try to start nudging people home. He could hear Michael Homey telling the Godleighs how he had secretly been in love with Emma since she had come to work for him two years ago and that her salary had been disproportionately high because of this. 'Not many secretaries could afford a house like that,' he said, miserably, flapping an arm in the direction of Wren's Nest.

The following morning, Cynthia Peeling offered to accompany the Tizards over to Wren's Nest to look over Emma's belongings, so they could decide what they wanted to keep once the police had finished with everything.

Cynthia thought this was the most forlorn and depressing of post mortem tasks. Mrs. Tizard was still not quite with it, and the Peelings had already whispered to each other about how things were likely to go from bad to worse with her. They did not envy Mr. Tizard. Not surprisingly, his wife had taken his daughter's death very hard and Cynthia thought Ruby Tizard a more than commonly weak woman.

The police hadn't come up with anything yet either. Nobody appeared to have seen Emma since she had left work on the Friday evening before her death. She must have come home because her car was in the garage, but after that...? A couple of Willowdale Farm people thought they had seen lights on in the bungalow during the evening, but no one could be sure. As for a motive for murder, none could be found at all. Emma did not appear to have close friends, but she certainly had no enemies either – at least none that her acquaintances knew about. 'Some maniac must have done it,' the estate residents decided and waited perversely for news of more killings in the media.

Mr. Tizard opened the front door of Wren's Nest and the three of them shuffled inside. Cynthia Peeling thought of how this was only the third time she had ever set foot in the place. True, Emma had often popped over to share a quick coffee with her neighbour, especially in the summer, but reciprocal invitations had been non-existent. It certainly couldn't be because Emma was ashamed of her home. The walls were papered in the most modern, expensive prints that money could buy and the furnishings bore the stamp of a top interior design house. *Always a loner*, Cynthia Peeling thought. *Perhaps a sad girl, really.*

'What a peculiar smell!' Mr. Tizard exclaimed as he went into the lounge.

Cynthia Peeling followed him and sniffed.

'What is it?' queried Emma's mother querulously from the hall

'Nothing alarming!' Cynthia was conscious of her voice being too loud and jolly. 'Some kind of perfume. A bit stale, that's all. The windows have been closed.'

The smell was strange. It caught at the back of the throat, half pleasant, half noxious. Cynthia thought that, in abundance, it would probably cause a headache. Had Emma Tizard been burning incense of some kind? There was an oriental muskiness to the smell. Cynthia firmly dismissed a rising sense of unease.

'She was such a tidy girl,' Mrs. Tizard said, standing pathetically in the doorway, holding her handbag in front of her. The place didn't look lived in. No ornaments, no books, no magazines, no sense at all of occupation.

It looks like a show home, Cynthia thought. She examined the gleaming hi-fi system and television. It appeared they had never been used.

'I don't think she lived in this room much,' Cynthia said. The place could be sold as it stood. What items were there could hardly be termed personal effects. Neither was there any evidence of eccentric interests. Moving close together, the three of them advanced into the dining room. Here, the same clinical tidiness prevailed. In a drawer, Mr. Tizard discovered a stainless steel cutlery set still wrapped in plastic.

'Emma didn't entertain much, it seems,' he said.

'No, she never brought friends home, not that we saw,' Cynthia Peeling said. 'I understood she liked to work at her painting the whole time she was off work.' She eased herself past the Tizards and quickly passed through the dove grey and pale lemon kitchen that bristled with factory-new appliances. 'Perhaps we'll find more sense of her in her workroom.'

All the doors in the bungalow were featureless and modern, except for the door to Emma Tizard's workroom. It was made of heavy wood, panelled, and had a huge brass handle. 'Perhaps she was changing the style of the place,' Cynthia said. She opened the door. All three of them had to gasp. Not because of anything unpleasant exactly, but just because of the contrast between the workroom and the rest of Emma's home.

The heavy door had acted like a seal. Inside there was a choking stench of stale cigarette smoke and stale alcohol, mixed with heavy incense. The curtains, thick blue velvet, were drawn across the window. Cynthia quickly went to open it, craving fresh air. She threw back the curtains. Beyond them, the window was frosted. All this time, having only viewed it from the outside, Cynthia had been under the impression that Emma used the small dressing room next to her bedroom to work in and that this was part of the bathroom.

It was not a big room, perhaps partitioned off from the bathroom itself. There was barely space for the large, ancient desk under the window and the huge cupboard against the far wall. Bookshelves lined the walls from floor to ceiling, apart from a place opposite the door where a huge, gilt-framed mirror hung. Papers were strewn everywhere; ashtrays overflowed onto elderly coffee-mug rings; an easel stood folded in a corner draped with rags. Empty gaps in the clutter suggested items which had been taken away by the police.

'Yes well, I certainly think we have a sense of Emma here,' Mr. Tizard said dryly.

'You think so?' Cynthia Peeling was not so sure. What

they had found here had little link with the girl she'd thought Emma to be. It was so sloppy, almost aggressively so. Books leaned everywhere on the shelves. Cynthia was compelled to start straightening them. The subject matter was wide, but again didn't seem the sort of things Emma would have been interested in. Here were the 'unusual' belongings, to which the police had alluded and the tabloids had made such a meal of. There were books on mysticism, erotica, occultism and a pile of cheap, tawdry novels. Cynthia shook her head. She picked up a small volume that had been lying open on the desk. A chapter entitled 'Higher Levels of Awareness' had been heavily underlined in places. 'Polarity disposition,' Cynthia read, 'Ritual dissimulation and embodiment.' It made no sense to her but still disturbed her, made her skin prickle. Unpleasant thoughts were starting to form and, superstitiously, Cynthia had no wish to think ill of the dead.

Mrs. Tizard was collecting up a selection of gin bottles from the floor. Her mouth had become a thin, disapproving line. Cynthia had no wish to speak to her.

'Well,' Cynthia said to Mr. Tizard, hating the brightness in her voice, 'it would appear Emma lived mostly in this room. I told you she worked very hard. It's not really surprising that she allowed the place to get a bit messy.'

Mr. Tizard didn't respond. He had picked up a sheaf of sketches and was impatiently leafing through them. 'Do you know this man?' he said and thrust a sketch into Cynthia's hands.

'Er… no. I don't think so,' she replied, feeling heat suffuse her face. The subject of the drawing was naked, sporting an undisguised erection. She dropped the paper quickly onto the desk. The drawing seemed to leer at her.

Mr. Tizard had slumped heavily into the swivel chair in front of the desk. Cynthia empathised with what he must be feeling. She started to tidy the scattered papers into one pile. Apart from reams of illegible notes written in a careless scrawl, there must have been hundreds of sketches and watercolours, many of them depicting the same naked man. Some of his poses were so explicit, Cynthia had to keep averting her eyes while tidying them. She was also distressed to find his face becoming more and more familiar to her. Could it be Michael Homey? No, of course not, and yet she'd seen no other man with whom Emma had had any connection.

Apart from these disturbingly erotic sketches, there were also many watercolours similar to the one Emma had given to Cynthia; strange, unearthly landscapes in flowing, muted colours; ethereal beings floating in clouds that looked like palaces. Holding them up one by one, Cynthia was tempted to keep some of these for herself. Emma Tizard had been unbelievably talented. Some of the pictures had the quality of photography, so detailed was their content. Where had Emma got the ideas for these paintings? Then she came upon a series of violent, horrifying scenes, where grinning demonic shapes inflicted torture on bodies that spouted blood, and in some cases, entrails.

Cynthia winced. No one had spoken in the room for several minutes. Books on art, shells, native cultures were heaped on the floor. Cynthia arranged them on an empty shelf. Perhaps if the room looked tidier...? Mrs. Tizard had opened the cupboard. She uttered a dismal squeak and Cynthia turned round.

'What is it?'

'I... I don't know. Not really.' The door swung back and forth. A grinning human skull was the first thing to catch Cynthia's eye. Everything else in the cupboard looked as if it belonged to a medieval apothecary. There were jars of roots and powders, an ornate, spired incense burner (that explained the smell), curly-handled knives, an abundance of other strange paraphernalia. A bizarre diagram, surrounded by what appeared to be foreign words, was scrawled in chalk on the back of the cupboard. 'Why?' Mrs. Tizard said, weakly. 'Why?'

Cynthia Peeling steeled herself. She gestured for Mr. Tizard to follow her into the kitchen. Sunlight was struggling through the cloudy sky outside, filling the room with a comforting glow. The fridge clicked on and hummed. Cynthia spoke in a forced whisper. 'Steven, I hate to have to say this, but I must. Do you suppose what we've found in there *did* have anything to do with Emma's death?'

Mr. Tizard didn't appear to take offence. 'Well the police wondered the same thing. There're some funny types interested in this sort of business.' He looked very tired. 'It's an explanation, but not one that I'd like to be true. You never saw anyone odd with Emma, did you?'

Cynthia shook her head. 'No. I never even saw her have a visitor.' She sighed. 'It's all so strange. Emma seemed so ordinary.' She was now at a loss for words.

'Seemed to be, yes,' Mr. Tizard agreed, 'but we can't deny what we've seen in that room. As you know, she spent a lot of time alone. Perhaps too much so. If Emma *was* messing around with something, or someone, peculiar, it's too late to do anything about it now.'

'I can't believe it!' Cynthia announced firmly.

Mr Tizard sighed. 'You didn't know Emma that well,' he said. 'I don't think any of us did.'

Cynthia was appalled to hear a parent say such a thing of their child. She found herself thinking of her own son. Did he get up to terrible things when he was away from home? She couldn't bear to think about it.

Mrs. Tizard came out of the workroom and announced that as soon as the police had finished with her daughter's belongings, she wanted the lot burned. There was nothing of Emma there that she wished to keep. To lose a daughter under such awful circumstances was bad enough, but to discover she had some kind of weird alter ego was even worse. Even their memory of her couldn't survive intact. Cynthia was now convinced that somehow, unknown to anyone, sweet, innocent Emma had become unwittingly involved with unsavoury characters, who had been instrumental in her death. An ingrained sense of decency, along with her superstitious dread, made her feel that no one but the three of them should ever know exactly what had been found in Wren's Nest. Let it be burned and forgotten. Nobody could do anything about it now.

Some weeks later, after the inquest had taken place, and press interest had died down, Mr Tizard came down alone to see to the disposal of Emma's belongings. The police had come up with no further leads concerning the murder, and it seemed it would remain a mystery forever. The Tizards had put the house on the market. Probably, they would have preferred to burn it down. Obeying, or agreeing with, his wife's desires, Mr Tizard packed everything, including Emma's smart, expensive clothes into plastic bin liners.

Cynthia Peeling drove him in her estate car up to the borough dump and disposed of the lot. It was late afternoon by the time the job was finished. Cynthia was in two minds about what they were doing. She couldn't help feeling it was wrong that all Emma's beautiful clothes and the more expensive of her books had been destroyed, yet she must respect the parents' wishes, and part of her could understand why they felt the need to dispose of everything so finally. However, what really went against the grain was throwing all Emma's drawings and paintings into a skip along with other paper rubbish. Whatever the Tizards might think of the subject matter, Emma had been a superb artist. Wasn't it the worst insult anyone could give, to destroy an artist's work after their death? Didn't artists want their work to be immortal? She told herself that it was for this reason she rolled up a sizeable number of Emma's paintings and stowed them in her bedroom while Mr Tizard was occupied elsewhere. Why she also pocketed the book that had been lying open on Emma's desk, she didn't consciously examine.

Cynthia was relieved when Mr. Tizard told her he was going home that evening. She quickly agreed to keep the keys for Wren's Nest and to show prospective buyers round it. For some reason, Mrs. Tizard hadn't wanted to leave them with an estate agent. As she drove him to the station, Cynthia took the opportunity to direct a few more questions at Mr Tizard. They had been forming in her mind all day. She didn't like to pry in other people's affairs normally, but felt she just couldn't exist if her questions weren't answered.

'What was Emma like?' she asked. 'When she was a child, what was she really like?'

'You've lived next door to her for two years,' Mr. Tizard answered. 'You've probably seen more of her than we have. She left home at eighteen, went away to college. We only got about two visits a year out of her after that. Sometimes she asked for money, but it was always paid back.'

'But as a child...?'

'She was a very private girl,' Mr. Tizard answered. 'Quiet, well-behaved'. There was a few moments' silence. 'I don't think we ever knew her.'

'What about boyfriends? She was such an attractive girl. She must have had boyfriends.'

'Not that we knew of. Did you ever see her with a man?'

Cynthia shook her head, quickly passing to the next subject, thinking of the drawings they'd seen. 'And the girl she lived with in London, the one who disappeared, did you know about that?'

'Emma came home for a couple of days after that. I think she was quite upset. She slept most of the time. Never spoke much about it though.' Mr. Tizard suddenly looked at Cynthia very keenly. 'I can't help you,' he said. 'The police have already asked all these questions, and if they can't work out what happened, I don't suppose we can. Perhaps you should forget about Emma Tizard and hope that a nice young family buy Wren's Nest now.'

Cynthia had her suspicions, from a couple of veiled remarks that Mr. Tizard had let drop earlier while they were clearing the work-room, that he knew more than he was telling of his daughter's strangeness, but she was wise enough to recognise 'keep off' signals and let the matter rest.

That night, she lay awake in bed next to her snoring husband. *Emma Tizard, who were you?* her mind chanted. The house, so unused; the strange room with its uncharacteristic disarray. Cynthia had never seen Emma smoke and Emma had always politely refused any alcoholic drinks at the Peelings. Gin bottles and overflowing ashtrays? Had it really been Emma who'd lived in that room?

Cynthia tried to sleep. Dream fragments swooped around her, all of Emma. Emma laughing, her long red hair blowing in an angry wind. Emma hunched over her worktable, frowning in concentration, one hand plunged into her hair, the other lovingly shading in an outline of male genitalia. And there was Emma, naked, arms raised to the sky, dancing herself to a frenzy beneath a full, pale moon. Now, she and Emma were walking arm in arm through a park, Emma chatting girlishly, no longer shy or withdrawn. 'Of course, it takes so long and there are always errors,' she was saying, 'but it doesn't matter, the result is always the same.'

'I don't understand you,' Cynthia said.

'Of course you don't, you're so fucking normal! Frigid bitch!' And Emma was laughing at her.

Cynthia woke up, panting. She felt that a noise must have awoken her but could hear nothing. There was a movement in the corner of the room, in the shadows, where Cynthia's plump, decorative armchair stood; the chair behind which she had stowed Emma's paintings. Cynthia blinked. Was someone sitting there?

A movement, a shift of moonlight. Someone rose, snake-like, from the chair and came towards the bed. It was Emma Tizard herself! The witch Emma, the secret Emma, and undeniably, a possibly vengeful Emma.

Cynthia could make no sound. She couldn't see Emma's face, but the hair was unmistakable, not bound, not plaited, but loose and glorious red in the half-light. The figure moved to the dressing table and picked up the photograph of Cynthia's son, Richard. Cynthia saw the pale flesh, the long fingers, the perfect unvarnished nails.

Emma looked at the photograph and chuckled. She turned to Cynthia. 'What a white little worm. Bet he's a lousy fuck,' she said.

Cynthia Peeling could not scream, but her muffled, petrified squeaks woke her husband. He turned on the bedside light. 'Cyn, what's the matter, love?' He shook her. 'Wake up! Cyn!'

She opened her eyes, puffing and gasping as if she'd been drowning. The bottom sheet had come untucked and had wrapped itself around her hot legs.

'She!' Cynthia said emphatically.

'What she?'

Cynthia felt she shouldn't say the name. 'The dead girl. Her from next door. My God, Rod, she was here!'

Rodney put a comforting hand on his wife's shoulder. 'Come on, love, bad dream, that's all.' He made soothing noises and arranged the pillows beneath her head. 'Get back to sleep. You'll soon forget.'

Cynthia felt her breathing slow down. She closed her eyes. No one could ever have called her an imaginative person. She did not believe in ghosts and thought witchcraft was an excuse for bizarre sexual practices, but if her husband had known what was going through her head at that moment, he would have thought her a stranger.

Emma Tizard will haunt me now, Cynthia Peeling thought. *Because of what I've seen, she will haunt me.*

Next morning, once Rodney had gone to work, Cynthia had to go into the lounge and draw the curtains on the window that overlooked Wren's Nest. She considered calling up Lily Treen to see if she'd suffered any more nightmares about Emma, but refrained from doing so for fear of looking foolish. She thought with dread of the rolled up paintings behind her chair in the bedroom, and the little book in her dressing-table drawer. However, by lunchtime, being a strong-minded creature, she'd managed to pull herself together and examine rationally the way she was feeling. She drank a glass of milk and made herself a salad sandwich.

It's over now, she thought. *We will never know what happened to Emma Tizard or find out any of her secrets, but it doesn't matter. I don't want to know. It's been horrifying but the funeral's past, the sorting out has passed and soon someone else will live in Wren's Nest and it will be alive again.*

Having comforted herself, she went to wash her glass, plate and knife at the sink. Leaves had begun to fall from the apple trees in the garden. The season was changing and the sun looked low in the sky. Cynthia put the radio on to listen to the afternoon play and went to open the curtains in the lounge. *No more of this!* she thought, briskly pulling the drapes apart.

There was a light burning in Wren's Nest.

Cynthia's first thought was that the estate agents were showing someone round the place, but that was impossible because she had the only keys. Almost automatically, she slung a jacket round her shoulders and was running out of the house and over the lawn towards Wren's Nest, before she realised what she was doing. In her heart, she knew that someone was there to whom Emma had already given a key. There was a warning that it might be dangerous to confront whoever it might be, but Cynthia couldn't stop herself. She sensed answers. Despite her attempts to convince herself otherwise, she still wanted to know the truth.

Breathless, she rang the doorbell. Nobody came to answer it, but she felt the presence of someone pausing inside, looking up from what they were doing, waiting. She rang again. Nothing. She thought of the keys hanging up in her kitchen, the keys that had come from Emma's handbag with the plastic tag advertising Michael Homey's firm. Should she fetch them? Should she go back and call the police? She took a step backwards, hesitating.

The front door to Wren's Nest opened. A tall, pale girl stood there, long blond hair falling over her face. She wore a dark coat, hanging open. She and Cynthia stared at each other for a moment. Cynthia was unsure of what to say. 'I'm Emma's neighbour,' she said at last, gesturing back towards her house.

The girl frowned. 'Where are her things?' she demanded. 'What have you done with Emma's things?' Her voice showed she was a person used to being obeyed, someone at home with authority.

Cynthia felt small. 'Well, her parents came...' she

began lamely.

'They had no right!'

'Well, no one else came!' Cynthia said indignantly. 'It's been so long! Was there something of yours Emma had?' She was wondering whether she ought to invite this strange person over for coffee, a natural instinct for hospitality. 'You missed the funeral? I'm sorry. A friend of Emma's were you?'

The girl smiled grimly. 'There's nothing left here,' she said. 'I didn't mean to be so late. I thought I'd be in time.'

'Well...' Cynthia shrugged awkwardly. 'Would you like a hot drink? It must be cold in there and... the... electricity's... turned... off.' She tried to peer past the girl to see if the lights were on. Perhaps a candle? The girl considered for a moment, then held out her hand.

'I'm Felicia Browning. Yes please, I would like a drink.'

The name seemed to familiar to Cynthia. Where had she heard it before?

The girl looked out of place in Cynthia's kitchen, too large somehow, too awkward, yet she was graceful and slim. As Cynthia plugged in the kettle, Felicia Browning said, 'Can you help me get Emma's things?'

Cynthia dared not look at her, fiddling with the on/off switch needlessly. Never a person to lie, she now had the strongest reluctance to confess she'd virtually stolen some of the paintings and the little book. 'Well, I'm afraid that's impossible. You see, Emma's parents took her effects to the dump.' It sounded sordid now, a foul and spiteful act.

'The stupid bastards!' Felicia Browning exclaimed vehemently. 'That was years of work! Years of it!'

'I'm sorry. I'm inclined to agree with you,' Cynthia said, 'But unfortunately Mrs. Tizard was adamant. She found some things that quite upset her, you see.'

The girl nodded. 'Yes, Em was careless. She should

have cleared things away. She should have told me earlier. Now, it's all gone!'

'What do you mean exactly? Was Emma planning on leaving anyway?'

Felicia looked at Cynthia with a certain unattractive furtiveness, then shrugged. 'She was making preparations but the timing didn't quite work out.'

'It certainly didn't!' Cynthia said cynically. She poured hot water into the coffee mugs. 'Have you known Emma long?'

'I suppose so. We used to live together in London.'

Cynthia looked up sharply. Of course, the name! She must have read it in the papers, or had the police mentioned it? Emma's erstwhile, disappearing flat-mate.

Felicia took her mug and sipped, speaking to Cynthia over the rim, confirming her hostess's suspicions without further prompting. 'I can see you've heard about me. I've been away for a while.'

'Away!'

'Don't worry about it!' Felicia said, laughing.

Cynthia felt herself flush. 'It's just that... people had assumed...' She gestured helplessly with one hand.

Felicia narrowed her eyes, ignoring Cynthia's lame comments. 'Emma was going to join me, fucked everything up, which is why I'm here now. Totally disorganised she is, totally! I'm not sure what I'm even supposed to be looking for here. There's a communication problem at present.'

Cynthia was beginning to wish this person would go. There was something eerie about her, disturbing. She had spoken of Emma in the present tense.

As if reading her mind, the girl stood up. 'I'll be off now. Thanks for the coffee.'

'Would you like to leave an address? If anything should turn up, I could contact you...' Cynthia offered vaguely.

Felicia laughed. 'That's not likely!' She strode out of

the house, leaving the door open.

Cynthia had to sit down and compose herself again. Whatever Emma had been mixed up in, Felicia Browning had been part of it, and she had sat in Cynthia's kitchen and drunk her coffee! Cynthia quickly picked up the half empty mug and dropped it into the sink, running hot water over it for several minutes. She worried about Felicia having another set of keys to the bungalow. Later, she had better phone the Tizards and tell them. It was their problem, not hers. Felicia Browning, registered missing for two years, turning up here; an unhealthy girl, unnatural. *Thank God I was nice to her*, Cynthia thought, wondering why she should think that.

Rodney rang to say he would be late home and not to hold dinner. Cynthia ate early, making herself a mixed grill, and drank two glasses of wine. After eating, she went into the bedroom and fetched Emma's paintings and Emma's book. Using ashtrays, mugs and ornaments as weights to stop them rolling up again, she laid the paintings out on the floor and sprawled on the sofa to study them, drinking another glass of wine.

She had only taken one study of the naked man, one of the less erotic sketches. Now, it seemed to stand out from all the rest, commanding her attention. His eyes stared up at her, knowing somehow, and mocking. It was not unpleasant to look at him though. He was quite beautiful, almost effeminate, slim but with a hint of strength within the litheness. The face was disturbingly familiar. Who? Who?

Of course! Cynthia realised, wishing she'd thought of it before, the drawing was reminiscent of Emma herself. Did the Tizards have a son? Cynthia shuddered. Good God, was incest, or at the least the thought of it, another of Emma's dark secrets? No brother had been mentioned though and surely he would have come to the funeral... *if he were alive.*

Still glancing at the drawing, she opened the little book and tried to read some of it. A hopeless task really. It was not a work written for the uninitiated and she could barely understand a quarter of it. The feeling she got from it, however, was that of power, the lust for power, the desire to transcend the fragile husk of human form. Was this research for Emma's unearthly paintings, or something darker, more personal? Sighing, Cynthia put the book down. It would not give up its knowledge to her.

A phrase repeated itself endlessly in her head: *There's a communication problem at present.* Virtually without her realising it, Cynthia Peeling chanted herself into a mild trance.

The light had faded completely from the sky outside and she sat in darkness, drinking and staring through the window at Wren's Nest. Her eyes were narrow, her gaze strangely vacant. Her breathing had become shallow and misted on the air. Something nagged inside her head; a voice almost heard, but not quite. She felt she knew the answer, had all the pieces to reveal the picture, yet was too close to see it as a whole.

I must go back. It's there. Felicia missed it. I must go back.

The compulsion could not be ignored. It was six o'clock

Cynthia raised herself jerkily from the sofa, and padded into the kitchen. She put on her shoes, her coat and lifted down the keys to Emma's bungalow. From the back of her pantry she took a flashlight down off its hook and marched out of her home, with purpose, to the house next door.

Nothing happened when she tried the light switch in Emma's hallway. For a moment, Cynthia was afraid of the dark, but the fear had to be ignored. Feeling her way along the wall, she went into the lounge. Here, she turned on the flashlight, illuminating the ghostly clouds of her breath. The incense smell had gone. The Tizards had left all the furniture in the house; most of it was brand-new. Cynthia felt it would be useless – mildewed and rotten – by the time someone else bought the place. She herself would not want to sit or sleep in the furniture of the dead.

In the kitchen, all the cupboard doors were open. Felicia Browning must have made a thorough search, but all were empty. Cynthia closed them, took a deep breath, and went out into the hall again, pausing before the workroom door.

It looked much larger now that all Emma's papers and paintings and rubbish had gone. The desk had been polished, the floor cleaned. Cynthia went inside. There was nothing there. What had she been expecting? Her body gave an involuntary jump, as if responding to a sharp, unheard sound.

What the hell am I doing here? An empty house, there's nothing here. Too much wine? Am I obsessed? Get home, you stupid creature, get out of here! Go home, draw the curtains, put on the lights, watch TV.

But the thoughts were separate from her. She realised she hadn't the will, nor even the desire to move from the room. Was she afraid? It was hard to tell. She felt electrified, poised, apprehensive, somehow out of control. None of these feelings were familiar to Cynthia Peeling.

Opposite her, the ornate mirror on the wall had misted over with condensation. Cynthia pulled herself together with rational, organising thoughts. Perhaps she should arrange to have the heating turned on. New residents wouldn't want to cope with problems caused by damp. The mere invocation of these mundane ideas seemed to change the atmosphere in the room. Cynthia swept the light beam around her, still strangely reluctant to leave. She went to the mirror and wiped it. Her reflection looked ghastly, surprised, in the stark light.

'You've gone, Emma, haven't you?' she said softly.

Her breath fogged the glass again and, mistily, it seemed to Cynthia that her reflection wavered and convulsed, twisting her dimly-seen reflection into something different; more strange yet more familiar. Could that be? It seemed she stood against a background of rock and cloud.

Cynthia uttered an alarmed mewing sound and abruptly wiped the glass. Relieved, she found her own, familiar image looking back at her. *An illusion. I've had enough of this place, enough of Emma.* Sniffing, Cynthia turned around. This time she meant to leave.

A tall figure stood in the doorway, caught in the beam of Cynthia's flashlight. She cried out in alarm. It was a young man, vaguely familiar, arms above his head, resting his hands on the doorframe. There was a certain proprietorial air about the pose.

The silence lasted only seconds but in that time, Cynthia saw and realised who he was. She recognised the beautiful face, the red hair, the long, white hands. This man had Emma's face, Emma's hair, Emma's eyes, Emma's cruel smile of the nightmares. She had seen his image in a hundred of Emma's sketches and paintings. She had seen him naked. Now, she was faced with more than an erotic image; he existed before her.

The man came into the room, leisurely closed the door and, folding his arms, leaned back against it. He said nothing, although he didn't seem surprised to find Cynthia there. Had he watched her enter the house?

Cynthia tried to take a step backwards and found she couldn't. Her shoulders were against the mirror. 'What the hell are you doing here?' she demanded, aware of the tremor in her voice. She realised she was trapped. Fear paralysed her.

'I might ask the same of you,' said the man.

'My husband and I look after the place. He'll be over here soon...'

The man laughed. It was a melodious, musical sound. 'You're a good woman, Cynthia,' he said. 'I'm glad you liked my paintings. I'm glad you saved them. You've been a good friend to Emma.'

Cynthia's mouth had turned to glue. Her jaw ached and she was conscious of a numbness creeping through her limbs, as if presaging a faint. Images of her own comfortable, safe living room flashed before her eyes. A mockery; she was neither comfortable or safe and further away from home than she'd ever been. An image of violence and murder superimposed itself over the fading memory of her familiar setting. '*Who are you?*'

'A friend,' he answered. 'Don't be afraid.' He unfolded his arms, rubbed his hands together. 'I've been waiting to speak with you. I want you to help me.'

This apparently reasonable request slightly reassured Cynthia. Perhaps everything would be all right. 'You had better come over to the house. My husband...'

'Who is still at work...' The man laughed again. 'I want you to help me *here*, Cynthia. It won't take a moment.'

Panic slipped back into Cynthia's mind. He knew her name. Her voice was a squeak. 'What do you want?'

'It's quite simple. I want you to turn around, very slowly, and take down the mirror from the wall.'

'Why?'

'Please do as I say.'

Cynthia's mind quickly juggled the thoughts of whether it would be wiser to comply or refuse. She would be helpless with her back turned. Why did he want *her* to move the mirror? But even as she was still trying to come to a decision, she could feel her body moving by itself, turning round. Her neck felt wrenched; she did not want to take her eyes from the intruder. An urge to scream built up within her, a scream she knew would never escape the constriction in her chest.

'That's right,' said the man. 'Gently now.'

A weird sound, that of strangled sobbing, whined from Cynthia's throat as her neck cricked round to face the wall. She watched as if from a distance as her arms moved automatically to ease the glass from its hanging. Its damp surface pressed against her cheek and she staggered under its weight.

The man didn't move to help her. 'I still need it, you see,' he said. 'Just for a while, until I know what I'm doing. You can help me, Cynthia, because I don't think the new residents of this place would want to, do you?'

Cynthia was draped over the mirror, mouth hanging open, fighting for breath. 'Who *are* you?' she managed to whisper and then the fatal question, the one she didn't want to ask but couldn't stop. 'Did you kill Emma?'

The man smiled. 'I suppose I did, in a way, but not in any manner you could imagine or comprehend.' The smile faded from his lips. 'I'm disappointed you haven't worked it out, really. I thought you would. You picked up the right clues.

He moved quickly towards Cynthia and put his hands on her face, ignoring her cry of horror. 'Cynthia, please know me! Please! I need your help!'

Cynthia's flesh chilled. She wanted to pull away from the warm, slim hands, for she knew their touch. 'No!' she said, but it was a weak sound.

'Yes! Yes!' There was fire in the man's eyes, a dancing light. 'Cynthia, I had to do this. I can't explain why to you, because you wouldn't understand. It's something that's been with me for a long time. I created the image, and put it into the mirror. With my eyes, with my sex.'

'Emma,' Cynthia said.

'I had to undress myself from the flesh, for the new flesh to *become*.'

The man moved away from Cynthia's tense, crippled stasis. He glanced around the room. 'Everything's destroyed. It's as it should be, but you...' He turned to her again,. 'You kept some of it back. You are my gateway, Cynthia. Felicia is my guide, but I've missed her somehow...'

'She's been here,' Cynthia said. Was it possible to converse outside reality? It seemed absurd.

The man nodded. 'I know. She's waiting for me, somewhere. Once the image was fuelled, it could act, it *became*. I know this all sounds bizarre to you, but there are wondrous things in the world, things you can be, and do, if you only admit the possibility. I'm here now, Cynthia. This is me as I want to be.'

'You killed yourself,' Cynthia said. Her instincts hadn't lied to her the day Michael Homey had turned up. Emma had been fine, more than fine. Cynthia wanted to sit down; her skull felt as if it was about to crack with the weight of the unbearable knowledge it now contained.

The man smiled at her gently. 'Do I look dead? You have touched me, haven't you?'

'What is the mirror for?' Cynthia asked.

'I'm not fully out of it,' replied the man. 'Not yet.' He shivered. 'It's yours now, Cynthia. You must put it on your bedroom wall.'

'No,' Cynthia said, uselessly.

'Come on, it's cold in here. Let's go home.'

Back in her own house, the mirror propped up against the wall, Cynthia curled up in an armchair, and drank a large tumbler of Scotch. She was alone. The back door had been left open and all the rooms were in darkness. She hugged herself tightly, cold. Cars passed the house, lights from the other houses glowed into the dark. Behind other doors, husbands talked about their day to wives, and children splashed in steaming, bedtime baths. Dreams would settle, and when the new residents of Wren's Nest moved in, memories would fade. Life would go on.

Cynthia, sitting somewhat apart from this world of cosy domesticity, gazed into the mirror and drank her Scotch. The moment when the unseen becomes seen changes life forever. There is a sense of loss, when ignorance dies. Emma Tizard seemed such a nice girl.

The Oracle Lips

Sheila met the woman she should have been in the ladies wash-room at Euston station. It was very early in the morning, two o'clock; a time of day when memories of Old London seem very near to this reality, perhaps seeping up from the drains. People like Sheila were like bright flames to these fleeting ghosts. She didn't want to be there; the empty, echoing chamber, with its weirdly dull strip lights, felt like an abattoir or an operating theatre. Sheila saw blood on the tiles in some places. Ghost blood.

She had seen ghosts all her life; one of her many unusual talents. She read cards for her mother's friends; that sort of thing. Sheila felt it was only her abilities that made her interesting to other people. Nobody would want to know her otherwise. She was like a ghost herself.

She wasn't used to being out so late; the night often unnerved her. It was when the whispers were loudest and it was hard to shut them out. She had washed her hands and gone to the mirror to comb her hair, which was so wispy, it needed to be brushed every half hour; an inconvenient task that Sheila rarely had time to attend to.

Shadows wanted to manifest, but she fought them. She was exhausted, having been awake for nearly twenty hours. Perhaps she should have stayed overnight in London with her sister. Her mother would have approved. But Tess gave Sheila a head-ache - too energetic, too noisy. The trip had been meant to be a treat - Mother had paid - but to Sheila, outwardly grateful, it had been nothing but a trial. Her craving for the solace of her bed-room, which had begun virtually the moment she'd stepped off the train that

323

morning, had become more painful as the day progressed. In the end, she had fled, mumbling about an appointment she had in the morning. Dentist. A good excuse. Tess would not have believed anything more exciting.

Hard to retain control now. Too weary. At the corner of her vision, a tired shadow woman mopped the floor in endless silence. What kind of life had she led only to end up haunting this joyless place? But the shadows weren't only of the dead. Flickering images of other, busy lives hovered round, buzzing from cubicles to hand basins to mirror. Their energy made Sheila dizzy.

Then, behind her, she heard a lavatory flush and, in the mirror, saw a tall figure march out of one of the cubicles. A real woman, not a shadow or a memory of a thought. Flesh and blood. At once, the shadows disappeared and Sheila felt a weight lift from her body. She and this singular other were alone.

The woman wore a beautiful long dress of soft moss-coloured fabric, quite severe in cut, which described eloquently the perfect lines of her body. Over her arm, a mass of black velvet coat hung. Ignoring Sheila, this vision stalked up to the mirror and placed a large shoulder bag on the shelf before her. For a moment, her hands lay long upon the leather, and she flared her nostrils at her reflection. Then, with business-like economy of movement, she opened the bag and withdrew a lipstick. Thoughtfully, almost reverently, she removed its cap.

Sheila's comb was stilled in her hair. Her heart, unaccountably, ached. If only her hands understood the tools of beauty magic. If only her hair hung lush and dark and foaming around straight shoulders. Such eyebrows - a statement of command and control. No fear. None. This woman was not plagued by shadows, for her life was full and absorbing. She was more than whole, at home in her skin, pausing here to preen, before whirling back into adventure and experience. Her movements were concise yet graceful. She was not pretty, but had strong, striking features and the proud stance of a woman who was comfortable with her body.

Sheila was not disposed to envying other women. She liked to look neat, but otherwise never fussed over her appearance. There seemed no point. Where nature had given some women poise and arresting faces and bodies, it had spent little time crafting Sheila's mortal form. Plain but homely: her mother's description; meant to be a palliative, she supposed. She was not fat, but not shapely either. Straight up. Straight down. A sort of solid chunk.

The woman caught Sheila's eye in the mirror. Her hand froze half-way to her face, her fingers curled around the bullet of brilliant red lip-stick. Tightly, she smiled. Pity. A moment of it. Sheila withered in its beam. Then, the woman focused in upon herself and pressed the waxy colour against her mouth. The movement was sensual, almost choreographed. Sheila's lips were thin, but this woman's were autumn ripe, the lower lip fuller than the upper. Their cushiony flesh sank beneath the invading stick of pigment. Round and round. Twice. Colour so thick it must surely dry to a hard, gloss finish.

Sheila became aware of staring, and coloured up. She stuffed her comb back into her own small purse and leaned forward to rub at her nose. It was shiny.

Beside her, the woman took a tissue from her bag and pressed it to her mouth. She dropped the kissed paper onto the floor, didn't even look at it. For a moment, she pouted at herself, then frowned and applied another layer of colour.

It seemed purposeful.

The woman gazed haughtily at her reflection, smiled to herself, and leaned forward to press her mouth against the mirror. A guileless act of self-love. It seemed as if another woman behind the glass leaned forward to accept the kiss. Then, she dropped her lipstick carelessly back into her bag, slung it over her shoulder, patted her luxuriant hair and walked regally out.

Sheila stared at the ghost of the lips on the mirror. Shockingly red. The woman was still here. She had left a part of herself behind.

Outside, the tannoy announced the imminent departure of a train, Sheila's train. Hurriedly, she zipped up her purse and scraped her hair behind her ears. But she could not walk past the lips on the mirror. They glared out at her, summoning.

Almost without thinking, Sheila found herself standing on tip-toe to place her own mouth against the print. The glass was cold and unyielding. She could not feel the thick colour.

Suddenly self-conscious, she jumped backwards. Her reflection showed a startled pale face, its mouth daubed with a gash of raw red that engulfed her own narrow lips. She rubbed anxiously at this invasion and bent down to pick up the tissue the woman had discarded. This, she shoved into her rain-coat pocket, then scurried out to the concourse. Her face was flaming, she could feel the heat. Platform 15. Hurry. Hurry.

Defences down, shadows assailed her from all sides. She felt as if she was pressing through a throng, although the station was unusually empty, just a few clots of people staring up at the board announcing arrivals and departures. All the shops were shut, fenced off by metal grilles. Sheila ran down the ramp to the platform, where the train panted softly. There was hardly anyone on it. She leapt awkwardly through the nearest door and found a seat quickly. Her face was still burning. She could see herself reflected in the window. A wounded mouth. Remembering, and wanting to scrub her lips, she took the tissue from her pocket. It was white as a towel, the blot like a flower of blood upon it. Sheila stared at it in her hand. The ghost mouth was an oracle, it might speak. She laid the tissue out on the table in front of her, smoothing carefully around the print. Someone sat down opposite her, but they were not really there, so she ignored them. The lipstick had sunk into the fibres of the tissue, revealing every line of the lips they had touched. It was perfect, like a painting. Red on white. The lines, Sheila thought, are so personal, like those on a palm. A woman's life might be encrypted in the print of her lips, or her future.

The train shuddered, creaked. A guard stamped past the window, blowing a whistle. Doors slammed. And they were moving, away from London, out into the darkness of the sleeping land.

Sheila could not sleep. She stared at the red lips on the table, and when she closed her eyes, the pouting shape burned behind her lids, neon green. She wanted to know the woman who belonged to their shape.

Sheila's mother let her sleep without interruption until one o'clock the following afternoon. Sheila had arrived home at four thirty in the morning, creeping into the house as quietly as possible, although her mother, whose hearing seemed as acute as a bat's, called her name as she tip-toed up the creaking stairs.

'Sheila!'

'Yes, Mum.'

Silence.

In her bedroom, Sheila had laid out the tissue carefully on the dressing table where her tortoiseshell brush and comb set lay on a lace mat. The lines in the lip print were more defined now, as if the colour between them was bleeding away. Hyper-sensitive with exhaustion, Sheila's eyes had blurred as she stared at the shape. The lines were widely spaced, most of them without fork, which to her spoke of an open personality, but at the corners of the mouth, a series of links hinted at secrecy and deceit.

Sheila's mother breezed into her room without knocking, bearing a large mug of weak tea. Sheila loathed weak tea. 'Morning, love,' said Sheila's mother, whipping open the curtains. Sheila blinked in the light and accepted the warm mug. It had clearly been standing on the kitchen table for some time. Full-cream milk fat made oily puddles on the surface of the liquid. Sheila looked up at her mother's face. She wore thick lip-stick too - some of it had smeared onto her front teeth - but the effect was not the same.

'Good trip? Why did you come back at that godawful hour? Why didn't you stay with Tess?'

Sheila began to reply, formulating excuses, but her mother breezed on,

'Oh, Sheila love, Marj is round, with her sister. I told her you'd do the cards for them in a bit. You won't be long, will you?'

Sheila sighed. 'No.'

Sheila's mother paused, frowned at her daughter. 'What's that on your face? Lipstick?' She laughed. 'Don't tell me Tess gave you a make-over!'

Sheila felt her face grow hot. She mumbled incoherently.

'Right,' said her mother. 'I'll pop down and put some toast on for you.'

Left alone, Sheila stared glumly into her tea. Why must her mother make her feel like a freak show? Her gift was special; it was wasted on divining the narrow lives of her mother's friends. This was not the first time Sheila had thought it, but now there was anger behind the thought rather than simply numb acceptance.

Sheila dressed herself and went to her mirror to brush her hair. She was taken aback by the red stain, which still covered her lips. Rubbing it, she found it would not come off. Soap and water, then. She glanced down at the lip-stick print on the tissue, which seemed to smile up at her provocatively. Those lips had not felt soap and water for years, not since their owner had been a child. Only the best, silky cleansers and toners had stroked them clean, only the richest of moisturisers had nourished their soft folds. Sheila lifted the tissue and sniffed at the print. A faint aroma of fading perfume, cinnamon or ginger. And something else. Tobacco smoke, wine, the bloody smell of rare meat; the tinkle of silver against china; the glint of candlelight reflected from diamonds and eyes. Sheila closed her eyes and inhaled. A glimpse of that life, the sureness of it.

Among Sheila's many prognosticative talents, psychometry and palmistry ranked high. She knew that the lipstick print was a gift. It would give her a story, a life to invade and explore. What was she doing now, that woman who had kissed herself in the mirror?

I need a name, Sheila thought, and willed it to come to her, but then her mother was calling, 'Are you coming down, Shee? Marj has only got an hour.'

The impressions fled; back into the print, back into the past. Sheila sighed again, more heavily, and carefully placed the tissue in the top drawer of her dressing-table, so that her mother wouldn't inadvertently throw it away.

Downstairs, Sheila came across Marj and her sister, Joyce, who were sitting with her mother at the kitchen table. On the stove, greens boiled for later consumption by her timid father when he returned home from work.

'Oooh, Sheila!' Marj exclaimed. 'Bit of a cold sore there, is it?'

Sheila rubbed her lips, went red. She had washed her face thoroughly, but the scarlet stain still haunted the corners of her mouth. Her mother swept over to investigate, and gripped Sheila's jaw in a fierce squeeze. 'Dearie me,' she said, squinting. 'Does seem inflamed, you know.'

'It's nothing,' Sheila snapped, pulling away. 'Lip-stick.'

Sheila's mother nodded to her friends. 'Tess has really fancy make-up. Expensive, you know.' She shook her head. 'Not really your thing, is it, Shee!'

'Oh, I don't know,' Marj rejoined. 'She is looking a bit perky. Must've done you good, girl, a nice day out.'

Sheila had to admit she did feel more energetic than usual. She associated it with the anger she'd experienced after her mother had left her bed-room. She felt more alive than she had done for months.

Breakfast eaten, she spread her old tarot cards on the kitchen table. What could she tell Marj and Joyce? Nothing. Because nothing much happened in their lives, other than petty squabbles with friends and families, along with the occasional unexpected pregnancy from younger and wilder relatives. 'You will be feeling reckless,' Sheila said, 'but there could be disappointment.' An extra round on the lottery perhaps - to no avail.

As the women stared down at the cards, Sheila couldn't help but examine their lips. Could they possibly reflect what lay in the readings? Joyce, silent and with a perpetual worry line between her eyes, had flaking lips; dry and bitten. They didn't seem to have lines, as if she'd nibbled away all her personality. Marj's upper lip was virtually non-existent, while her lower lip stuck out petulantly and always appeared slightly wet. Marj was hungry - for gossip and control. Sheila smiled to herself. Over the years, she had trained herself in many disciplines of divination. Now, she had something new to work on.

The lipstick woman's name was Francesca. It came to Sheila as she went back upstairs after giving Marj and Joyce their reading. She wasn't entirely sure whether she'd simply dreamed up the name because it seemed so appropriate, or whether it really belonged to the woman whose mouth print lay hidden in the dressing table drawer. Francesca. She could not be called anything else.

Looking at the print once more, Sheila strained her psychic sight to acquire more details of Francesca's life. She was a woman who lived on the edge, who was often disliked, especially by other women. Sheila saw an indolent selfishness in the lines of Francesca's mouth, perhaps even a streak of cruelty. But she also had humour and hedonistic desires. Sheila glanced at herself in the mirror and was surprised by the expression she saw on her face; a watchful sneer. Do I want to be like her? Sheila wondered. Francesca was glamorous and beautiful, but had few female friends. Sometimes she felt lonely although she never admitted it. Sheila realised that she herself never felt lonely, despite her own lack of close friends and the gulf between her and her family. She liked her own company and was not totally dissatisfied with herself. Her part-time job at the local news-agent fulfilled her modest financial needs and gave her more than enough contact with the world. Why then this growing obsession with an alien creature, this woman of secrets and dangerous passions?

Sheila put the tissue back into her drawer. She shivered involuntarily, suddenly craving a walk in fresh air.

Sheila strolled across the common, where people walked their dogs and children played in the cold, winter sunlight. The trees were stark against the sky and crows rasped from the naked branches. The town beyond the expanse of grass looked squat and grey. There was so little colour in the hibernating world. Sheila thought of red lips and heard a peal of free laughter in her head. A ghost of giant lips kissed the grainy sky and Sheila knew that somewhere Francesca was sitting in a wine bar with a group of men, her eyes restlessly scanning the room, searching for someone. She despised her lecherous, overweight companions, but she had information now; information to sell. Sheila could feel Francesca's impatience and also a shred of uncertainty. It was a seed of fear, hidden in darkness. Perhaps Francesca could not sense it herself.

Sheila closed her eyes to blink away a band of pain that gripped her temples, her eyes. Her glimpse into

Francesca's life scared her, but she was still curious, still wanted to know more.

On the High Street, Sheila ambled along gazing in shop windows. It was one of her favourite pastimes. She passed an array of satiny continental chocolates, then the winter coats of the ladies' dress shop, on to the garish jumble of children's toys and the sleek, sinister pyramids of electrical goods. The shoe shop, Sole Partners, lay at the end of the street, where what had once been a market square had been turfed over, flower-bedded and stuck with benches, bearing the names of dead town councillors on small, metal plaques. Sheila decided to go and sit there for a few minutes, watch the clouds of scavenging pigeons lift and fall, before making her way home via the coffee shop in Church Street. She looked into the shoe shop window as she passed, and her attention was caught by a pair of shoes in the display before her. Shiny black patent leather with high, high heels. A strong impression assailed her: they were power shoes, designed for treading on human flesh; figuratively if not literally.

Sheila wanted the shoes immediately and with a hunger she had never experienced before. The lust to acquire flooded her system. Her heart beat fast.

The shop assistant looked at her strangely when she stammered her request and pointed at the window. Sheila knew she did not look like the kind of woman who would buy shiny, spiky shoes. As the assistant flounced out from behind her counter, she glanced down, taking in the worn-down, flat-heeled pumps that currently encased Sheila's feet in scuffed, tan leather. The black shoes were removed from the window display and presented with reverence for the customer to inspect. Sheila looked at them nervously and the assistant suggested she try them on. For a moment, Sheila considered saying that they were for someone else - a gift - but then she was told the size of the shoes, which was hers, and it seemed too much of a coincidence. 'All right,' she said, and sat down on a plush-covered seat and bared her stockinged feet.

The stiff patent leather slid over her right foot, crushing her toes. 'They're too small,' she said, with some relief, but the assistant frowned and lifted Sheila's foot, declaring that no, they were a good fit.

'You're just not used to wearing shoes like this,' the assistant said. 'Slip the other one on. Stand up, walk around.'

Of course, Sheila could not walk in them and suffered the humiliation of staggering up and down in front of the mirror, while the assistant chewed the inside of her mouth in a clear attempt to stem her laughter.

'Yes, I'll take them,' Sheila said.

What am I doing? she thought as she numbly made out a cheque for what was to her an extortionate amount. The assistant packed the shoes into a box amid a froth of black tissue paper.

Out in the street, the maroon and gold carrier bag weighed heavily in Sheila's hand. She could no longer face sitting among the empty flower beds of the square and made her way directly home. She would never wear these shoes. Why had she bought them?

The answer was obvious. These were Francesca shoes, worn with sheer black stockings, the toenails hidden within lacquered to a red gloss.

Back home, Sheila scuttled into her bedroom and sat panting on the bed, the carrier bag lolling between her feet on the floor. After some minutes, while her ears strained to detect the approach of her mother, she took the shoe box from the bag. She could hear her mother's voice downstairs; a monologue to her father, who was silent. Sheila lifted the shoes from the box, held them in one hand. She felt guilty, ashamed, as if she was about to examine a pornographic magazine.

Her feet seemed to slip into the shoes more easily

now. She looked down at her feet, the toes pointing inwards. Her ankles looked slimmer, although her beige tights spoiled the effect somewhat. Sheila stood up in front of the mirror and was surprised at how tall she appeared. She took a few tentative steps. Away from the deriding eyes of the shop assistant, she could take her time, and realised she could learn to walk in these torturous contraptions, if she wanted to. But still, the feeling of shame persisted. Sheila knew that in some way she was stealing something, from a woman who was unaware of the theft. Like a magpie, she had snatched up the glittering fragment of Francesca's life and taken it back to her nest to gloat over. She could never truly appreciate the glittering thing, because she was not a creature who could make use of it properly. She could only admire its lustre.

Sheila paused before her mirror and straightened her spine. She lifted her hair in both hands and held it on top of her head. With the extra height of the shoes, she did not appear so chunky, and her face, free of its customary veil of drab hair, looked stronger somehow. Sheila was suddenly filled with fear. She sat on the bed and kicked off the shoes. Do I want this? She asked herself. Do I really? The shoes lay on their sides before her, provocative and gleaming. Waiting.

Sheila took to walking in the shoes at night. She would leave the house at seven o'clock, her clandestine purchase hidden in a large shoulder-bag that Tess had left in the cupboard under the stairs. Once she had sauntered a couple of blocks away from home, she would change her shoes. They hurt her at first. She would walk with her hands deep in her pockets, the collar up around her ears. She liked the sharp tap of her heels against the damp sidewalks, although the new leather, stiff with cold, ate into the soft flesh of her feet. She carried the lip-stick print in her coat pocket, her fingers barely touching it. As she walked, impressions of Francesca's life would flood her mind: impromptu parties, city lights, music, laughter. And Francesca's shadowed profession; the secrets of the enchantress had been revealed.

Sheila was now sure that Francesca was involved in dangerous business. She had visualised Francesca seducing men of power, stealing information from them with soft words and deft hands, then selling what she had learned to other men, who paid her highly: politicians, industrialists, high priests from the inner cabals of mega-corporations. Francesca was cold and greedy, wrapped in a veil of ice, yet she slunk with movie star gloss through the adventures that Sheila applied to her. The evening walks were spiced with endless day-dreams of Francesca's exploits, yet even as she fleshed this fantasy out, Sheila couldn't help feeling impatient about Francesca's failings. The woman had so much, yet abused her privileges. She was the kind of person Sheila normally despised - spoiled, selfish and avaricious - yet their lives had inexplicably become entwined. It could be no coincidence. They were linked by more than a chance meeting at Euston.

About a week after buying the shoes, Sheila went into a cosmetic store on the way to work and bought the brightest red lipstick on sale. She did not attempt to use it, but removed it from its paper bag several times during the afternoon and twisted the colour up out of its casing. Later that evening, during her walk, Sheila went to rest her aching feet in a cheap café. A couple of down and outs mumbled at one another in the dim light, and the only other occupants were a group of teenagers who were clearly on their way to somewhere more interesting. Sheila ordered coffee and spread out the tissue on the Formica table top. The fibres were fragmenting badly now and would soon would be nothing more than wisps of fluff in the bottom of her pocket. The lipstick print had faded to a mere filigree of lines and looked aged. When the tissue had fallen apart completely, would she lose this strange half-life she had begun to enjoy? No, Sheila thought, determined. I took some of her into me. I kissed the mirror. The print has sunk into me. These thoughts made her heart beat faster, shortened her breath.

She stared at the lip print without blinking, until her eyes watered. *Tell me, tell me...* She had exciting images of Francesca's life, but she wanted more: the future. Some of the lines were broken, perhaps because of natural decay. Perhaps they had always been broken, but the details were only now becoming clear. The print itself, while fading, had spread outwards, almost as if the lips were bloated.

Strangled lips. Breath squeezed out. The heat. The darkness. Gasping, struggling.

Sheila shuddered, and nausea churned through her body. She almost cried out, but managed to control herself and stuff the tissue back into her pocket. Her heart was pounding now and specks of light boiled before her eyes. She mustn't faint - not here.

She lurched from her seat and felt her way between the tables to the rest room at the back of the café. Here, she pushed open a door and virtually fell into the cramped cell beyond. She leaned over the stained sink, taking deep breaths. A bare electric light-bulb hummed over her head, echoing the buzzing in her mind. She splashed some cold water on her face. *Mustn't think about what happened. It's fantasy. I dreamed it up.* Her hand dipped into her coat pocket, seeking the tissue in reassurance. She found instead the smooth plastic case of the lipstick she had bought. Sheila couldn't remember having put it into her pocket. Her fingers were steady as she took it out. She removed its case and with one twist exposed the rod of colour. Almost involuntarily, she applied a layer of it to her lips. The colour glowed like neon in the dim electric light. It made her look startled. Shoes and lips. Top and bottom. But what about the expanse in between? Was it still hers? She shuddered and remembered she'd left her bag outside at the table. She must go back: someone might steal it.

By the time she returned to her seat, Sheila had managed to compose herself, and was relieved to find her bag where she'd left it under the table. She forced herself to examine the lipstick print again. Red waves of danger and darkness seethed up to her, yet she could fix on no definite image. The fading image of Francesca's mouth looked misshapen, bloated. Sheila took a sip of coffee to calm herself and an unusual craving crashed through her. She wanted a cigarette, badly, but she had never smoked.

Numbly, she found herself outside, tapping down the sidewalk to a convenience store, where she knew exactly which brand to ask for. The implications of what was happening disorientated her, yet at the same time she felt calm and focused. Sheila lit a cigarette, took the smoke into her lungs. Her body coughed and spluttered, yet her inner self revelled in satisfaction. Leaning against the shop wall, Sheila closed her eyes to the night and forced herself to examine what had happened in the café. *She can't be dead, can't be...* Yet how could she doubt her talent? It had never failed her before. What she'd experienced in the cafe must have been an intimation of the future. Sheila opened her eyes. She had no choice now but to find Francesca, seek out her home, make sure the dreadful prophecy never came true. Although she did not wholly like the woman, Sheila realised she looked upon her as a wayward sister. She could not judge Francesca for her actions; she could only love her - unconditionally. Sheila glanced at her watch. Was it too late to start looking now? There was a train to London in fifteen minutes. She could make it; if she hurried, if she ran.

On the train, breathless and hot in her raincoat, Sheila removed the tissue from her pocket once more. She needed to direct all her energy and intention into the print now. She needed hard information. Her vision blurred as she stared unblinking at the red stain, and an image of a cat filled her mind; an animal wholly suggestive of Francesca's nature. *No, no, concentrate!* Sheila saw a hill, a spire and superimposed over it, a cat's face. Cat, church, hill. Perhaps the cat was relevant then; part of a road name. She would have to buy a street guide as soon as she got into town.

Sheila sat in the smoking carriage, lighting cigarette after cigarette. Her body protested, but her mind ignored the physical pleas, some distant part of her mind.

The station shops were just closing as she charged up the ramp from the platform into the concourse at Euston. She marched into a Menzies shop and snatched an A-Z street guide off a shelf, setting her face in a determined expression. The bored assistant behind the till clearly wasn't going to argue the shop was closed.

Sheila made her way down to the tube station. It was only ten o'clock; there was plenty of time to search. She could look all night if necessary. Her body bubbled with energy. If by any chance tiredness overcame her, she could go to Tess' place. Some explanation would be needed, but - it just didn't seem important now.

As she glided down an escalator, Sheila scanned the index of the book. It was almost too easy. There it was. Catchurch Hill. Virtually tearing the pages, Sheila found it in the map section: a tiny curl of a road on the fringe of the West End.

The last time she had been in London, the tubes had terrified her, with their crowds and labyrinthine lines. Now, she marched directly to the escalator for the Northern Line, ignoring the people who pushed past her in needless hurry. Some part of her seemed to know already exactly where she was heading.

The streets were empty around Catchurch Hill. No raucous crowds, no brightly lit bars. It was a quiet little corner of London, a place where it was easy to forget you were in the heart of a sleepless city. It was a cul-de-sac, used mainly by vehicles belonging to the residents. At the end of the street, beyond some black and gold painted iron bollards, the bulk of a gas-works rose ghost-like in the non-dark of the city night. Naked lime trees reared before it, promising that in warmer seasons, the power plant would not seem so imposing. The street did have a slight rise to it, but could hardly be termed a hill. Its lights were ornamental, and the four storey houses, which ran down the right side of the road, had an almost continental appearance: wrought iron balconies girdled it on every floor and it was plastered a pale pink. Ivy seethed up the walls, gripping the curlicues of the balconies, where lanterns burned softly. On the other side of the street, bare magnolia trees in bud murmured of spring. Sheila thought of summer evenings, and what it would be like to own one of these apartments, to sit outside in the warm air among sighing trees, sipping icy wine, with music drifting out into the perfumed dusk. She could almost see herself in that situation, as if she'd already experienced, or would.

All of the residences were apartments, but which one was Francesca's? Sheila became aware of her throbbing feet, and also the fact that she hadn't felt or seen any spirit presences since she'd boarded the train back home. Her vision had been wholly focused on the search, eclipsing all other thoughts and impressions. She stared up at the curtained windows. Too close now. Hard to tell. She dug into her coat pocket and took out the tissue and with one hand, flung it up into the air. It seemed the scrap of crumpled paper would fall immediately back to earth, but then a breeze took hold of it, and it was swinging up and up, spread out like a white leaf, until it came to rest among the dead twigs of an ornamental shrub that stood in a pot, decorated with dragons, on a balcony of the third floor.

There must be security locks, Sheila thought, and sure enough a dimly-lit intercom system was placed next to each front door. She went to examine the list of residents of the building she was interested in. Most were listed only by their surnames, without even an initial to give a clue. Green, Chevalier, Elstone, Buckingham. None of them seemed to fit Francesca. But she could be wrong? A disorientating moment of panic spun through her. What if she was in the wrong place entirely? The list of names blurred before her, and then she saw it. Flat 7. On the third floor. Sancha. That was it. She just knew it.

Sheila reached out and touched the plastic covering the name, then pressed her finger against the buzzer button. When Francesca answered, what would she say? Now, her adventure was real. She would have to explain herself.

There was no response at first. Perhaps Francesca wasn't at home. She pressed the button again. After a few seconds, she heard the intercom click into life, but there was no voice at the other end, just the rushing of empty wires. 'Hello,' Sheila said. 'Ms Sancha?'

There was still no response. Sheila leaned forward and pressed her cheek against the intercom, willing her intention into the mechanism. *Answer me, answer me...* There was nothing but the hiss, and a sense of waiting, of observation. Then, the front door clicked too, and Sheila realised its lock was open.

Quickly, she went through it, afraid she was being offered only a fragment of time during which to enter the building. She found herself in a plain hallway of dark grey stone. Two black doors clearly led to ground floor flats. Against one of the walls, a large dead yucca plant listed in an earthenware pot, but otherwise the hall-way was unadorned, disappointing. The steps leading up to the next floors were concrete with a functional metal hand-rail.. Sheila began her climb. Her heels clicked dryly against the stone.

On the third floor landing, the ceiling lights were set into the plaster and covered with metal grilles. A corridor yawned before her, disappearing into darkness, because a couple of the bulbs had blown. Sheila did not like the atmosphere. It seemed polluted somehow, or perhaps essentially unclean. There was an emptiness to it; loneliness too. She couldn't hear a single sound of human habitation. Shivering, she made her way to the door of flat 7. The tap of her heels seemed dull against the bare floor. The building seemed like a representation of Francesca herself: decorative on the outside but bare and cold within.

There was a small spy-hole in the centre of the door. Sheila approached it cautiously. Was Francesca looking out at her now? She placed her hand against the door, then knocked. She could hear nothing, aware only of an air of desolation. She knocked again, and again, then tried the handle. It was unlocked. Sheila froze, afraid of opening the door. What might she find beyond? Someone was in there, because someone had activated the intercom and the door mechanism downstairs. That someone might not be Francesca. Francesca might be...

Sheila opened the door and flung it wide. It took a moment for her senses to register what she saw. The door opened directly onto a large living room. The windows must be open, for it seemed to be full of a whirling wind, that had sucked up tatters of paper and scraps of cloth, creating a tornado of debris. But the room was derelict. Sheila could see that through the maelstrom. The plaster had fallen from the walls in places, revealing a skeleton of wooden slats. There was no furniture, just bare brown drabness. No-one lived here. No-one had lived here for a long time.

She felt compelled to step over the threshold. What did this mean? Was she seeing reality now, or something else? She had lived with strange phenomena all her life. This was no different. She just had to interpret it. The wind snatched at her hair and flapped the skirt of her coat. The air smelled acrid, and it was very cold.

How dark the room was. Shadows swirled and spun

amid the litter circling in the wind. As Sheila observed, the shadows coagulated to form a figure in the centre of the room. At once the scene before her became flooded with brightness, bleaching out like an over-exposed photograph. The figure was its dark core. Francesca. Her body was erect and rigid; the eye of the storm. Her hair was a writhing halo around her head and she was wrapped in a black cloak or sheet. One white hand was visible where she clutched the cloth at her throat and her face was startlingly pale. The red gash of her mouth seemed painted onto the black and white image. Her eyes were black holes, open wide.

Sheila stared at this vision, involuntarily holding her breath. Francesca's full lips opened up. It looked as if she was screaming, but there was no sound. There could be no doubt now. This was not the image of a living woman. As the red mouth worked noiselessly, the lips became engorged, their colour bleeding from red to blue. A series of bright flares dazzled Sheila's eyes, like the acidic splash of a camera flash. She glimpsed broken images, in black of white, what she assumed were freeze frames of the past. A hotel room. A man. Francesca's wide eyes. Furniture falling. A struggle. But when? In the past? Recently? Soon?

Sheila felt as if the images were crowding in upon her, until she would be crushed beneath their weight. She had to take a step backwards into the hallway, and the door slammed shut immediately in her face. She was held in a caul of silence; there was no hint of the chaos beyond the door. For a few moments, she stood motionless in shock, then began to back slowly away down the corridor. She heard a sound of a woman's voice, speaking low and quickly. It came through the walls of the flat opposite Francesca's. A domestic dispute or a heated debate. She passed the door to flat 8, which hung open. It too was derelict. There was no-one there.

Sheila fled the building, out into the night. The stars wheeled crazily over-head and the gas-works pumped like a bellows. Spirits fled in scraps of mist through the branches of the trees, wailing in torment. Litter pursued her out of Catchurch Hill into the main street beyond. Traffic flashed past too fast; she could see only the coloured blurs of their tail and head lights. She knew where she had to go, what she must do.

As she marched back to the nearest tube station, her feet were bleeding in their high, spiky heels. Her mouth was bleeding red lipstick. All she could see in her mind was the wide expanse of mirror in the ladies' rest room of Euston Station. She was compelled to return there, hoping that by going back to the beginning, she would somehow acquire more information, answers.

By the time she reached Euston, Sheila was surprised at how late it was. Perhaps she had stood, transfixed, in the strange apartment for longer than she'd thought. Had that really been Francesca's home? The experience was blurred in her mind now. It didn't seem real.

Two women came out of the rest room as she pushed her way through the turn-stile. Inside, she was relieved to find it empty. This time, there were no shadows to distract her.

Before she turned to face the mirror, Sheila experienced a moment of pure fear. She could turn back now, abandon this ridiculous obsession. Her life waited for her - grey, temperate and safe - at the end of a line. If she followed this through, there would be no going back.

Sheila turned round. The room in the mirror looked larger than reality, an endless tiled corridor, a clinical representation of Hell. The first thing she saw in her reflection was the red of her lips, then she realised the face was not hers, and that it was Francesca looking back at her. Her eyes were steady, full of knowledge, yet hooded. The mirror was a veil between the worlds of the dead and the living, and the realm of the dead lay beyond the glass.

With business-like economy of movement, Sheila

delved into her pocket and removed the lipstick. Thoughtfully, almost reverently, she removed its cap.

It was then she became aware that someone else had come out of a cubicle behind her. Another woman stood next to her, dragging a brush through her drab hair. The woman caught Sheila's eye in the mirror. Sheila's hand froze half-way to her face, her fingers curled around the bullet of brilliant red lip-stick. Tightly, she smiled. Pity. A moment of it. The other woman withered in its beam. Then, Sheila focused in upon herself and pressed the waxy colour against her mouth. When she had finished, she took the old tissue from her pocket, and pressed it to her mouth, then she dropped the kissed paper onto the floor, didn't even look at it. For a moment, she pouted at herself, then frowned and applied another layer of colour.

Francesca smiled back at her from the mirror. Sheila leaned forward to press her mouth against the glass and it seemed as if Francesca dipped towards her to accept the kiss. When Sheila drew away, she saw only her own reflection looking back at her, the mark of her lips and also the surprised expression of the woman beside her. I was her, once, Sheila thought.

Perhaps the other woman might have lingered, waited to pick up the tissue, kiss the glass, but she hurriedly stuffed her hair-brush into a shoulder bag and almost ran from the room. Sheila smiled to herself. She saw, in the mirror, a woman of medium height, with soft, fair hair, whose square face was not pretty, but strong and striking. She looked as if she'd escaped from a 'Thirties film with her raincoat collar up around her ears.

Sheila now had all of Francesca's knowledge. It no longer mattered whether she had lived in the past or very recently, or whether she had lived at all.

The woman in the mirror. She is a ghost of life, like clothes hanging in a wardrobe, devoid of feeling or essence. The body, the feelings, the depth, stand before her in the world of the living. Now they are one. She is on her way somewhere, urgently. She might not come back.

Sheila had business to finish. She put her lipstick back into her pocket and walked out of the station to an assignation. Her feet would lead her there, in their high, spiky shoes. The future in the lip-stick print had been hers, but now she had kissed another future over it, and the outcome would be different. Her hands were strong and steady deep in her raincoat pockets.

Other Selected Storm Constantine

Titles from Immanion Press

Student of Kyme
A Wraeththu Mythos Novella
Storm Constantine
9781904853411 £9.99 trade paperback
IP0016 A sequel to The Hienama. The young Wraeththu har, Gesaril, has been shamed and cast out of Jesith, after an inappropriate affair with his hienama, Ysobi. Taken in by Huriel Har Kyme, a codexia of the famed Alba Sulh academy, Gesaril vows to begin his life anew in the Wraeththu city of learning. But sometimes the past will not lie quietly in its grave, and Gesaril soon learns he must confront the restless ghosts and fight them. This is a powerful story of obsession, betrayal and doomed love, sure to be a hit with Wraeththu fans and followers of the dark and Gothic alike.

The Wraeththu Chronicles
Omnibus edition of The Enchantments of Flesh and Spirit; The Bewitchments of Love and Hate and The Fulfilments of Fate and Desire
Storm Constantine
1904853293 £16.99 trade paperback
IP0012 The expanded versions of Storm Constantine's ground-breaking trilogy. Wraeththu have inherited the world from the dying race of humanity. Androgynous, exotic and psychically powerful, they struggle to avoid the mistakes that led to humanity's downfall. The trilogy follows the story of the human boy Pellaz who is led to become Wraeththu by the charismatic and enigmatic Cal. Pellaz eventually becomes a figurehead of his people, whereas the doomed Cal trails destruction wherever he wanders. The story of their tragic and fated love has enthralled readers for over twenty years and continues to do so.

The Grigori Trilogy

The Grigori are an ancient race; powerful people who possess abilities and powers humans do not. They gave rise to the legends of the fallen angels, and their descendents live on among us, hidden within human society, moving wheels within wheels, making changes unseen across the world.

Stalking Tender Prey

IP0014
9781904853336
£14.99

The twins Owen and Lily Winter always have always known they are different to everyone else who lives in the quiet village of Little Moor. Their mother is dead and they never discovered who their father was. When the mysterious stranger, Peverel Othman, arrives in Little Moor, their lives are destined to be changed for ever, and ancient secrets are unearthed in the High Place in the forest and the haunted towers of the shuttered and deserted mansion, Long Eden.

Among the upper echelons of Grigori society, the search begins for an Anakim – a rogue Grigori whose existence threatens the security of his race and the lives of those who cross his path. Aninka Prussoe, whose own life has been shattered by contact with the Anakim, is among those who are led towards Little Moor and the final climax to a story that never ended and which has haunted both humanity and Grigori alike for millennia.

Scenting Hallowed Blood

IP0017
9781904853206
£14.99

High Crag on Cornwall's desolate storm-lashed coast is a mysterious place with dark secrets. On these bleak shores, the rebel offspring of the angelic race landed many millennia ago. Their memory was never forgotten and across the centuries, seers, mystics and witches basked in the occult power of this prehistoric landscape, awaiting the rebirth of the Fallen Ones. Yet their modern day descendents, the Grigori, are already among humanity, hidden yet preparing for world dominance as the new millennium approaches.

One rogue Grigori, the fallen angel Shemyaza, once reborn as the mysterious figure, Peverel Othman, is ready to spoil the careful plans of human and Grigori alike. Having escaped from the destruction he wreaked in the sleepy village of Little Moor, Shemyaza walks the earth as his giant forefathers did long before him. Accompanied by the hybrid twins, Owen and Lily Winter, and the seer, Daniel, he is drawn to High Crag. Here, he must journey into a domain deep beneath the serpentine cliffs, where an ancient power sleeps and the secrets of the past wait to be rediscovered.

Stealing Sacred Fire

IP0018
9781904853244
£14.99

Through the ancient magic of the Grigori, the rogue Anakim, Peverel Othman, is once again Shemyaza, king of the fallen angels, benefactor of humankind, who was once doomed to an eternity of torment and imprisonment. Now his soul is free and incarnate in the world, and as the millennium draws to a close, Shemyaza calls his followers to him for the final battle to decide who controls the fate of humanity.

Along with his brother Salamiel and his human vizier Daniel, Shemyaza journeys to seek the place of his creation; Kharsag, the Garden in Eden. Along the way they fall in with the Yarasadi freedom fighters, who are inspired by a dynamic new leader whose identity is an enigma. In the mountains of these eastern lands, Daniel discovers a forgotten part of himself and begins to learn the secrets buried long ago by the forebears of the Anannage, the original angel race.